THE DEVIL'S BACKBONE

KIRSTEN BOHLING

First published in the United States of America 2024
by Lake Country Press & Reviews.

This edition published 2026 by Kirsten Bohling.

Author: www.kirstenbohling.com

Edited by Tara Sexton
Interior design by Andrea Quigley (@bazaroffisbinding)
Cover illustration and design by Lilith B. (@lilitherie, pg)
Author Photography by Alicia McCoy (@mccoy.film.photos)

This book has been typset using Aguante by Germano H.R.

Library of Congress Cataloging-in-Publication Data is available.

ISBN 979-8-9940263-0-4
ISBN 979-8-9940263-1-1 (ebook)

For Trever—I'm your Huckleberry.

"Courage is being scared to death and saddling up anyway."

— John Wayne

THE DEVIL'S BACKBONE

Before

I N HER IMAGINATION, THEY WERE THE LORDS AND LADIES of their tiny desert kingdom, something beautiful tucked between the mundane. Cassidy's perch was perfect for watching; cowboys strolled back into town after a long drive, offering a tip of their hat as ladies whirled past with a swish of petticoats and demure smiles from beneath a bonnet.

There may have been better vantage points to witness the promenade, but the window of the Callaghan General Store was her favorite for seeing Faraday Creek come to life in the early morning. Daylight was only beginning to climb to its peak, beating down on dusty streets as a filly strolled by with its rider. Wisps of soil whorled into the dry air with each step, clinging to delicate beams slicing between colorful but worn clapboard.

Cassidy pictured them all as something else, characters in the cavalcade of her own making. Ginghams became shining silks, leather dusters embroidered waistcoats— magical details stacked atop the other. A world that went beyond the ordinary of a humble life.

A rider exploded down the street, scattering townspeople

like a flock of birds; her daydream shattered instantly. He pulled hard on the reins of his gray gelding, halting in the shadow of the church at the heart of town.

Cassidy couldn't look away, skin prickling as he marched to the Callaghan family shop. Even at nine years old, barely up to her Da's shoulder, she knew something was horribly, terribly wrong.

The door burst open, nearly sending a little brass bell off its mount. Dirt clouded from his duster, attention flickering to Cassidy momentarily before snapping to the couple bolting in from the back room.

"Thomas." Da stepped closer. Her mother hovered behind him, a gentle touch of her fingers grazing over his sleeve. "What did ye find out? Do we still have time?"

Thomas's face was grim as he shook his head. Cassidy's stomach sank. His wasn't a look of hope but of dread. "The best thing for you to do now is hide. Hide the girl, at least. The less he knows, the better. Else, he'll take her. Some kind of sick prize."

"Never," her mother choked, voice strained with panic as she soundlessly called Cassidy with a stretch of her fingers. She hopped from her stool, placing a trembling hand into her mother's palm. Aisling's green eyes glittered, searching Cassidy's. She sucked in a shaky breath. "How long do we have?"

"Moments, if we're lucky." He contemplated the girl, a furrow to his brow before nodding. "I'll do what I can to hold them off. Maybe I can buy you more time."

Aisling's attention slid to her husband as Thomas fled to the street. "It won't help, Ian. There *isn't* any time. Not anymore. *Cassidy*—" she breathed, squeezing her hand, staring at the sudden cacophony beyond the shop's window.

"The cellar. *Now.*" Da reached for Cassidy, hoisting her in his arms. Before the girl understood what was happening, she was face-to-face with their grief-stricken expressions.

"Whatever happens, love—" Aisling cupped the curve of her cheek, forcing a brittle, motherly smile. She meant it to be comforting, but even Cassidy saw through it, witnessed her pain, her regret. "No matter what you hear. No matter what you see. *Stay hidden.*"

"I don't understand." Cassidy sniffled, tears falling unbidden. Her stomach was an iron brick, sinking lower and lower with each passing second.

"Don't make a sound, *a stórín.* Not one, ye'hear? *No matter what.*" Da lifted a hidden panel into the cellar running the length of the store, lowering her amongst stores of potatoes in the darkness.

"Da, I don't want to go in here. Don't leave me alone in the dark," Cassidy cried out, reaching for him as he moved to close her in. "Will you come back for me? Promise you'll come back!"

Ian didn't answer, blue eyes soft behind dark eyelashes. "We love you, sweet thing. Just remember every'ting I taught ye, and it'll be fine. *Remember,* Cassidy."

The world went black when the wooden planks settled, and her Da slid a rug over the seams to conceal the door. Cassidy spun in the dank darkness, seeking the strands of light seeping through the floorboards.

Above her, there were whispers from her parents. Tender reminders of love and other things she didn't understand when, all at once, everything went deadly silent.

Cassidy heard him first, watching wide-eyed through cracks in the floorboards as her parents clung to each other. Ian pressed a desperate, lingering kiss to Aisling's lips, only to tear himself away in a flash when the door burst open.

The couple scrambled back. Screams erupted on the street, accented by the slow thump of bootsteps with the distinct chime of spurs on wood.

More cold came when a shadow filled the doorway.

He was tall. Taller than any man Cassidy ever saw. Clothed in all black, the sunlight not blocked out by square shoulders glinted in sharp shards on the silver points of his boots.

That wasn't what set a shiver slithering down her spine.

With a gloved hand on the crown of a black hat, he pulled it away to reveal a sloping brow and dark eyes. Most of his face was hidden by a blue handkerchief. He pulled it down a long nose, displaying a chilling smile.

Ian curled an arm around Aisling's narrow waist, moving her behind him as the stranger strode into the shop.

Unruffled by the gesture, he hooked his hat on one of a dozen jewel-colored bottles lining the windowsill, turning a gleaming gaze toward them.

"*Jack,*" her mother breathed, coiled like a spooked mare as he paced around the quaint shop.

"You've built quite the life here, haven't you, Aisling?" he murmured with a slip of a leather-clad finger along a shelf.

"It's too late, Ransom. Yeh lost," Ian spat.

Beneath the floorboards, Cassidy kept as quiet as a mouse—quieter, even—like her Da instructed her to do. *No matter what.*

"A lot has happened in the decade since I've seen you last. I thought, at first, I could let you go. It looks like we both knew better, didn't we, darling?" Ransom glowered, wearing the same curl of his lips. "You know, I could have given you the world, don't you? Anything you could've dreamed, I would have laid it at your feet."

"Everything I've ever dreamed of is right here," she whispered, shoulders square as she twined her fingers with Ian's. "Everything I need."

"*Really?*" Ransom preened, peeling the gloves from his hands, finger by finger. He folded them into his breast pocket with a tut of his tongue. "Here I was, thinking I might convince you to leave this dreg behind and come home. Pity." He faced the window, surveying the street where the sound of chaos reigned. "I suppose violence will have to do."

Ransom withdrew a blade—a dirk with a jeweled hilt—from his belt at an achingly slow pace. The chime of metal against firm leather rang through the tension in the air. He lifted it, cutting it through a shard of sunlight streaming through the window. He twisted it to and fro, almost in a daze, as the light bent and moved in the unearthly glow of his eyes.

In a single breath, Ransom's gaze snapped to Ian and Aisling. A flurry of activity erupted—punctuated by a piercing scream.

Cassidy smothered a cry when Ian landed hard on the floor above her, mouth slack as he blinked in slow motion. Her chin trembled, heart hammering so loudly, she swore the man in black was bound to discover her.

Ian's breath came in sharp, wet gasps. Cassidy stumbled into the darkness, holding her own when he gave her the smallest of imperceptible nods.

One last gesture to tell her he loved her.

Aisling fell to her knees, cradling Ian's head in her hands with a keen. Her slight shoulders shook. Cassidy couldn't look away.

A growing wetness speckled her cheeks. Cassidy wondered in a daze if she'd been crying, too. Maybe she hadn't realized. Maybe she'd never stop.

She swept the tears away. Her stomach lurched, and she thought she might be sick if it hadn't been for her promise to stay silent. She couldn't break it, couldn't be discovered. Even when a horrified sob lodged itself in her throat, begging to be free as she smeared her father's blood from her face.

Even then, she couldn't break. Not even when the cold grip of fear clawed its way out in a silent scream.

Ransom turned his attention to her mother, wiping the blade clean with his coat.

Aisling's sobs quieted as she lifted her tear-strewn face from Ian's bloodied body.

"H-h-h-ow could you?" she stammered between sobs, a river of tears streaming down her cheeks. "He was like a *brother* to you."

"*Brothers* don't steal from one another," Ransom answered with a shrug, fitting the jeweled dirk into his belt. He crouched and lifted her hand, thumbing a thin, gold wedding band. "Where is it?"

"I don't have it." She shook her head, swallowing thickly. "I left everything behind."

He laughed, dark and low. It split Cassidy to the bone.

"Oh, Aisling, that's not true." Ransom curled his fingers around her jaw. She resisted at first, pulling back with bared teeth, but he held firm. "You're a sentimental little dove, aren't you? There was no blade of grass on that pathetic little island you didn't want to press between the pages. No moment you didn't want to write down. We both know some of you wanted to hold onto some of me."

Aisling was wordless, with nary an argument as she stared back. He held her gaze, bending over the murdered man between them to brush the ghost of a kiss on her lips and whisper—

"Come with me, darling. Let's go home. We can start over. Paint the world anew and leave all this nasty business behind us."

He gently stroked his fingers against her cheek, tucking a red curl behind her ear.

Familiar. Loving, even.

"Jack." Aisling's face softened beneath his touch. A moment stretched between them.

Cassidy was left on bated breath while waiting for her mother to speak, to argue, to say anything at all.

Aisling's eyes shifted from fear and grief to something else entirely. Green burned brightly, her lovely face darkened, and Cassidy thought she might set the whole world ablaze in a single look. She sucked in a deep breath, brows pleated as she spoke a series of words that'd change their lives forever.

"I would rather die than go *anywhere* with you."

Ransom's face fell, jaw tight. He let Aisling slip from his grasp as he sighed, standing and placing his gloves back over long fingers. His face remained eerily passive. Even though the floorboards obscured her vision, Cassidy saw how his mind fixed on a dark thought.

"Well," Ransom tutted, tugging on leather at his wrist. His attention fell to Aisling. "That can be arranged."

With a snarl, he fisted the copper curls atop her head.

Aisling screamed, clawing at his hand as he dragged her out the door and into the street.

Cassidy lunged from her hiding place, crawling over the

dirt floor of the dank cellar to wooden doors in the corner leading out to the deceptive sunshine.

The hustle and bustle she watched earlier was gone, a hushed, brittle quiet in its place. Doors of shops lining Main Street waved on their hinges, their creaks as loud as a bullwhip in the fresh, fraught silence.

In a matter of moments, Faraday Creek became a ghost town.

Nestled in the eerie calm, a human drumbeat lifted on the wind. Fists on faded shiplap sounded from the church at the end of the street. Cassidy shivered. All the people, every cowboy, every lovely lady—all of them barred inside.

Between the deadly cadence sang the cries of her mother, the melody of a tragic symphony.

Ransom came back into view, dragging her through the dirt, undeterred by Aisling's fight to be freed from his iron hold.

The trail from her body grew longer in the soil, leading to the stretching shadow of the church's steeple on dried land.

Through her sobs, Aisling was unrelenting, mangling the fine leather of his sleeve with her fingernails until they might bleed. Even when he threw her down, she didn't give in.

She pressed her palms to the ground, lifting her shaking body to her knees. Her chest rose and fell with each labored breath, looking up with a scorching fury to stare daggers at her would-be executioner. She defiantly lifted her chin as Ransom pulled a revolver from his belt and raised it to her skull.

Cassidy wanted to scream. She wanted to cry, to beg him to leave them alone. But she could only watch in horror as Ransom coldly implored Aisling one final time.

"Even now, I am willing to forgive you, my darling. Just say the word, and we'll leave all this behind."

Aisling sucked in a trembling breath. Her attention darted to where Cassidy hid in the shadows.

She met her mother's gaze. How Aisling saw her, she couldn't say. But Cassidy knew in her heart her mother was telling her something.

Run.

A smile curled across her lovely face when she looked back to Ransom and whispered, "Never."

"So be it," Ransom answered.

The gunshot rang out like a crack of thunder on a quiet winter's night. It buzzed in her ears as silent tears streamed hot tracks through the dried blood on her face.

A pair of thugs flanked Ransom, looking to him for instructions on what came next.

With a nod, he barked a curt, "Fire the church. We're leaving."

Cassidy sat transfixed, caught in a web of dread as, with the flick of a torch upon a gabled roof, the chapel started to burn. Helpless, trapped in the cellar of the general store until she was sure it was safe to emerge, she could only stare as flames ripped through the wood.

In the dry Nevada desert, the building was a tinderbox, feeding the ferocity of the fire as spectral cries of the people inside branded upon her soul.

Time slipped away with each charred board. The roof crumbled, taking the steeple with it on a gravity-propelled ride to the heart of the church, silencing everything beyond the vicious crackle of the flames.

When the world was silent again, Cassidy emerged into the fading daylight. With a single glance behind her at home, she did as she was told.

She ran.

[1]

S HE WISHED HE WAS WORTH MORE DEAD THAN ALIVE. Three days of bellyaching at a slow trudge through the desert made any level-headed bounty hunter want to put a piece of lead between a man's eyes. But Cassidy Callaghan wasn't one to waste a shot—even on someone as crooked as Moody Duncan.

Every bullet had a consequence, good or bad. Besides, there was only a half-mile of dust between her, a glass of whiskey, and fifty dollars. That was enough motivation to keep her from dragging a corpse through the streets of Gallow Gorge.

They'd been at it all day. The afternoon sun stretched high in an endless expanse of bright blue. A shimmer bloomed on the horizon, the hazy heat blurring the lines of worn clapboard buildings sprouting up against a rocky hillside.

Sounds of life sprouted: raucous voices and the rattle of a wagon wheel. In the distance, floating on the wind like far-off rumbles of thunder, were periodic reminders of silver in their hills.

The town went about its day like any other, save for the magnetic tension when Cassidy drew their eyes as she stepped within city limits. Maybe the striking sable stallion she rode halted the steady rhythm of the farrier's hammer. Perhaps the lanky man stumbling over his boots—sunburnt, covered in red-tinged dirt, and towed by a rope around the wrists—slowed the barber's sharpened blade from a twenty-cent shave.

Cassidy was used to the looks. She knew they were for her. Not the lazy gait of her horse nor the commanding ease of her grip on the reins. Nothing an acrimonious stare from pale green eyes couldn't drive away.

She wasn't regarded as the friendliest visitor in those parts, not by a long shot. Not like she gave them a chance to see her any other way. Besides, what was one more whisper?

The way the townspeople of Gallow Gorge skittered away like a flock of birds when she lifted the brim of her hat was something she couldn't help but enjoy.

She liked it that way. Wrapped up in a metaphorical suit of armor, she was a knight delivering justice on a steed as black as a nightmare. Cassidy *was* the nightmare, made of shadow, a ghost amongst men. She hid in darkened corners, lying in wait—an unexpected benefactor of the law. Never faltering, no matter how tough the bounty. Aim so sharp, she could hit a jackrabbit in the dark.

Cass tugged on the reins with a press of her heel into the horse's flank, pulling their odd little trio alongside a railing in the shadow of the saloon and hotel, The Copper Queen.

Swinging herself to the dirt, she carried a gentle swirl of dust with every step to secure her bounty. She pulled a canteen from a leather saddlebag, dropping it in Moody Duncan's lap as he sank to the dirt.

"Drink," she barked. He barely wheezed a reply.

Dramatic. Cassidy rolled her eyes, flipping his rope over wood, tugging at it to ensure the knot wouldn't come loose.

The ghost of a smile curled at the edges of her mouth, the secret kind reserved for the Mustang nibbling the end of her braid.

"Stay here," Cass said, rubbing the star on his forehead before stepping onto the arcade that ran the length of the buildings along Main Street.

"Who, me? Or your pony?" the bounty drawled with a delirious roll of his head against the wooden pegs behind him.

Cass stopped, a smirk stretching across a freckled face as she twisted towards him.

"My *pony?* That's Solo. He's a stallion, one who used to be wild. I've seen him kill a man, so I'd be careful if I were you. You're worth the same dead or alive, so it wouldn't matter much to me what 'ole Solo wanted to do with you should you insult either of us again."

Solo nickered long and low, swinging his great big head around to blast the man's hat from his head with a snort.

Satisfied her bounty wasn't bound to run off, Cass kept her gaze ahead as she walked along the arcade. She focused on the steady *thunk* of her boots, ignoring the eyes that watched her every step. Men, mostly. They always found ways of making her life more difficult, especially the bounties. *Especially* when they found out a woman came knocking to bring them in.

Her latest catch proved extra challenging, like hauling a herd of cattle on a long drive. Moody Duncan yowled and bellowed until his voice was sore, then brayed some more. She was half-tempted to smother him in his sleep the first night at camp and wanted to shoot him when he started to sing on the second day. But being annoyed wasn't a good enough reason to do him in.

The drive was arduous. She was thirsty, and by God, she earned herself a fucking drink.

Cass followed the tinny jangle of a player piano and a chorus of men at play from within The Copper Queen, sucking in a deep breath as she pushed in the swinging doors.

Nearly every eye in the darkened room turned her way. A collection of faces lit by daylight seeping in around her, painting a vivid picture of the world Cass tried so hard to fit into, yet keep at arm's reach.

A group of dour-looking men paused their round of Faro. A second casually sipped at their glass as another player used the distraction to their advantage, placing a card from their sleeve into a shitty hand.

The players' attention returned to their games, ignoring her, as usual—just how she liked it. But one man's attention dawdled long after all the others fell away.

"Whiskey." Cass lifted the black hat from her head, placing the gambler on the bar. She fished into her vest pocket, slapping down a worn quarter. "Just leave the bottle and gimme a glass, would you?"

The barkeep's mustache twinged, maybe with the slightest hint of a grin. Not at her, but at the shadow that arose in her periphery.

Cass didn't need eyes to know who it was. The youngest deputy of Gallow Gorge took up all the space at the bar. In the entire room, really. The whole town. It may have been the obvious size of him, tall and broad, at least a head over the average man in town. Maybe it was everything else about him. The easy way he won people over with conversation, where Cassidy pushed them away. Or how he never seemed to shy away from her like everyone else—even when she tried to push him away, too.

The women whispered over the width of his shoulders, the curl of his sandy hair, and a hidden dimple that'd appear when he offered a passing smile. Not whispers, no. They never quieted, and their words followed Cassidy day in and day out. Because whenever she was in town, there was no more determined a shadow than one, Deputy James Moone.

"Here, have mine," his low voice rumbled at her back, undeterred by her blatant disregard.

Cass sighed, curling her fingers around the ball glass that appeared beside her, refusing to meet his gaze as she poured two fingers. There'd be no getting rid of him, but a sip might soften the edge of her annoyance.

She brought the glass to her lips, ignoring Moone as he leaned within her line of sight, gulping it down. It was easy to see he was waiting for her to give in and speak first, but Cass was well-practiced in their particular game. So, instead of acknowledging his existence, she poured herself another.

He let out a deep huff of laughter as she tipped back the second glass, and let the sharp, smokey tang of the whiskey warm her from the inside out. Out of the corner of her eye, Cassidy couldn't help but notice the stub of a cigar perched between plush lips. Or how he brought the tip to a bright, golden ember with a single pull. A slow swirl of smoke spilled from his mouth, washing over her as she tossed back a third.

Not that she was paying attention to his mouth, of all things. Cassidy just paid attention to everything all the time. It had nothing to do with Moone, just the heat of his stare, the prickle of it down her neck, and the little voice in the back of her mind telling her to give in.

If she wanted to keep sweating, she would've stayed outside.

Cass gripped the neck of the bottle, sliding it lazily from the bar as she put on her hat. She stepped away with a gracious nod at the bartender and flipped her braid over her shoulder—smacking Moone square in the nose.

"Thanks, Jesse," she said. He answered with his own and the slightest hint of a smile as the man who'd given her a glass pushed off the edge and chased her outside.

"You're gonna have to talk to me sometime, Callaghan," he called after her, heavy footfalls trailing close behind.

Cass tugged on her bounty's rope, giving the now-dozing man a sharp kick to send him scrambling to his feet.

"Can't. Got a package to deliver," she drawled, towing the man across the dusty street. She paused for a passing stagecoach, waving away the dust before pushing through blinding sunlight to the arcade on the opposite side of the street.

Cass shoved her bounty through the door of the Sheriff's station, casting her eyes on the deputy snoring with his boots up on a desk by the front window. She cleared her throat, loudly knocking her knuckles on the glass.

He scrambled awake, reaching for his hat as Cass propped a hand on her hip.

"W-what can I do you for, sugar?" He offered a drunken smile and a burp once he took her in, swaying as if a gentle breeze might blow him over. "You seen this pretty thing before, Moone?"

A quiet tut sang from the shadow haunting the doorway. "Best be careful."

Cass cast a venomous look over her shoulder at Moone.

She hated how casually he lingered, flipping a gold pocket watch from his vest as if he timed how long it'd take before she lost her temper. She'd dealt with Lucas Smith and a hundred other men like him. She'd keep it together this time… probably.

Tucking the bottle of whiskey beneath her arm, Cassidy pulled a yellowed piece of parchment from her pocket.

"You know full fucking well who I am, Lucas, but *fine*. If you wanna be difficult, we'll be difficult." She slapped down the warrant. "I am Cass Callaghan, duly sworn warrant officer of the State of Nevada. I am here with a charge, wanted dead or alive for murder. One man named Moody Duncan, otherwise known by his alias—Knuckle Duncan— for the reward of fifty dollars."

Lucas, an older man—round and filthy like a beer barrel rolled through a barren field—spent too much time in the brothel and couldn't handle his liquor. He looked at Cass with a greasy smile. Ripping the warrant from her grip, he took his sweet time looking over the crude sketch.

"Hm." He sniffed, noisily smacking his lips. His beady eyes went up and down the bounty behind her, who'd started to sag. "That looks like Moody Duncan, alright, but I ain't convinced you'll be gettin' any reward."

Cass bristled, eyes flashing. "And why the hell not?"

Lucas rolled his shoulders. "Well, *see*, I'm thinkin' this here document you say you've got that says you're a duty sworn—"

"*Duly* sworn."

"Right." He burped again, punctuating the end of the word with disgusting crispness. "That's what I said. Ain't no way they legally gave a girl that kind of power. Must've lied on the paperwork or somethin'. Ain't no place for dishonesty

of that sort in our righteous society here in Gallow Gorge." Lucas tilted his head smugly, showing off a collection of rotted teeth. "So, I ain't payin' you shit."

Cass's skin prickled, buzzing with rage. "Lucas Smith, your knife's so dull, it couldn't cut hot butter," she seethed, squeezing her fingers around the bottle of whiskey. She wanted to take a swig right then and there to wash away the bitter taste in her mouth, but she resisted. "You better take that back."

"Why? 'Cause you're a lady?" he chortled. "Hell, Callaghan, I can find twice the woman you are for a fraction the price just around the corner. Can't imagine you'd get paid any better there when you ain't got no meat on them bones."

Cassidy saw red. To hell with keeping her temper.

With a yell and the biting shrill of shattering glass, Cass swung the bottle in a wide circle—and connected it to the side of Lucas's head.

She was barely afforded a moment to enjoy the trickle of blood from the tiny cuts marring his ruddy cheeks or the way his face contorted from the sting of whiskey running through them.

Long fingers clamped around her arms, yanking her hands behind her back.

"Now, why'd you have to go and do a thing like that, Freckles?" Moone said with a spellbinding grumble. "Do you know the mess you just made for me to clean up?"

"You know I couldn't let him talk to me like that. Wouldn't be right." Cass huffed a laugh, fluttering bits of copper hair that fell into her face when her hat went askew in the scuffle. "Can't a girl have a bit of fun before she leaves for her next job?"

He drove her against the wall, breath tickling her ear as he pushed apart her feet with the toe of his boot and slapped a pair of shackles on her wrists. "Afraid not."

"Spoilsport," she complained, still laughing when he pulled her towards a cell at the back of the Sheriff's station.

Lucas glared at her, wiping bloodstained whiskey from his eyes. "Fuckin' Callaghan! Lock her up. She's a goddamn menace, so fuckin' mean, she'd steal a coin from a dead man's eyes."

"Only if it was your eyes, Lucas Smith. Besides, it all spends the same." Her giggles died off when the Deputy Sheriff gave her a pointed look and shut the iron door with a *clang*.

He stayed silent, blue eyes sparkling as he swirled a finger and told her to turn.

"Wait." Cass rubbed her wrists, freed from the shackles but locked in the cell. "You can't keep me in here forever. You're supposed to give me another bounty."

The deputy flipped the cuffs into his broad palm with a smirk. "Well, see here, Freckles, it's my sworn duty to uphold the peace 'round these parts." He leaned closer, lifting a brow. "And you just assaulted an officer of the law."

Cass rolled her eyes. "Lucas Smith doesn't deserve that badge."

He shrugged, letting out a boyish chuckle as he strode away. "That's above my pay grade."

"Then talk to the Sheriff. Tell 'im that one of his deputies is a two-timing fink."

"You don't know a damned thing, Callaghan. Lucas may be a drunk, but he's not dirty." Moone made a face. "Besides, the Sheriff is on an extended hiatus. And I got an errand to run."

She gave the bars a noisy shake, teeth bared. "Moone, you better let me outta here right quick, or I'll be assaulting another one. Come on, come back. I swear I'll behave."

He paused in the doorway, so tall and broad, he filled out every inch. Only the barest threads of daylight seeped around him. He smirked again, lifting a hat to his head, blue eyes twinkling. "Nah. I think you'll keep 'til tomorrow."

Cass rattled the bars again, swearing loudly. "Dammit, James Moone! Get back here, or I swear I'll not bring in any more bounties for you. I'm not playin' around."

"We'll see about that." Moone gave her a wry grin, turning to Lucas. "Get Duncan here in the next cell. Don't cause any more trouble with Ms. Callaghan while I'm gone. Her aim is deadly—you're lucky you got a bottle instead of a piece of lead."

"Nobody better try and walk off with my horse, or they'll be sorry," she hollered after Moone, open-mouthed when he stepped back and out the door. At the last glimpse of the bothersome deputy, Cass swore he was still wearing a smile.

She paced in her cell, resigning herself to her temporary fate—a predicament she'd found herself in more than once, thanks to him. Each time, even though it meant she lost whatever nameless game they were playing, Moone wouldn't let her rot in a cell for long, especially because she was the best damn bounty hunter within fifty miles.

He needed her.

Her buzz from the whiskey fuzzed the edges of her vision most deliciously—a feeling she wished she could use up in a warm bed with a beautiful woman. The more she thought about it, the slower the minutes ticked by. With each one, Cass grew increasingly frustrated at one, James Moone, who kept her from it.

Daylight dimmed, oil lamps were lit, and Lucas Smith returned to snoring at his desk.

The room felt a little smaller in the muted light, her body looser, sending a surge of prickly heat over her skin. Cass shrugged the leather duster from her shoulders and made the brim of her hat double as a fan until a wash of sleepiness took over where drink began.

Maybe Moone was serious about letting her keep until morning. Either that, or he got lost between somebody's thighs, never to return until the daylight did.

Her stomach twisted at the thought. Cass blamed the whiskey.

She plopped onto a bench at the back of the cell, ducking her duster beneath her head, and balanced a boot over the other to get comfortable.

Blinking up at an odd collection of knife hashes and bullet holes riddling the wooden planks, Cass wondered how much trouble she'd be in with the good deputy if she shot her way out. She eventually lost count with each heavy blink until the shores of an always fitful sleep claimed her.

Before

"Right. If you're goin' to hit the target, ye can't be holdin' yer breath, *a stórín.* Now—breathe—and keep ye eyes sharp as a tack. I want you to be tinkin' 'bout each time ye aim 'tis weapon—what'll change if ye do? Every bullet has a consequence—good or bad. That's what ye need to decide. Do you understand, lass?"

A gentle hand curved around her shoulders, ensuring they were straight before adjusting her grip. She was focused; she'd always be focused. Too focused.

"Cassidy Kathleen Callaghan, I need ye to answer if we're goin' to keep on wit' dese lessons." He nudged her heel with the toe of his boot.

They stood out past the pasture of their modest cabin; waist-high grasses bent and moved with each sigh of the wind. There was no place more beautiful than their home.

"Yes, Da. I understand. Choose wisely," she murmured, wrinkling her freckled nose as she adjusted her aim.

"Dat's a good girl," Ian Callaghan answered, playfully twirling one of her copper curls around his finger. "Right, let's decide about 'dese cans behfare yer Ma calls us in for supper. What do ye think?"

"I think"—Cassidy stuck out her tongue, brows furrowed—"I think those bastards need to go." She giggled like mad when her Da shushed her as if Aisling could hear from a hundred yards away.

"C'mere, lass. Give it yer best shot." He stood back, arms crossed over a narrow chest, combing his fingers through a russet beard.

Cass centered her attention on a dented can perched on a fence post fifty paces away, sucking in a slow breath as her Da told her to do. The breeze carried her dress around her ankles in soft waves of blue gingham, but nothing could distract her. With bright, pale green eyes trained on the can and the tip of her tongue stuck out, Cass squeezed the trigger.

The scrap of metal flew high with a zing of lead against tin and a triumphant squeal of delight from the little girl.

"Dat's me girl," Ian hummed with a squeeze of her shoulder. "You'll always remember what I've taught ye?"

Cassidy lifted her chin, offering her favorite person on God's green Earth a brilliant smile. She leaned into his touch as he tenderly held the curve of her chin with his thumb.

"Forever, Da. There's no way I could ever forget."

[2]

Moone

James Moone wasn't someone who forgot things. He was a grudge-holder if ever there was one. He lugged his experiences around daily like a weight chained to his heart. Towing them along was something he needed. He had to do things differently, to be better than the man he was before—to remember the people who impacted his life. And for that reason, he'd never forget the moment he clapped eyes on Cassidy Callaghan.

He'd only just arrived in town, and the badge on his chest was as shiny as could be. The first time he glanced up and saw the tiny little thing on a big, black stallion, James wondered if she was a mirage coming off the plain. He'd dragged his palm down the scruff on his jaw, helpless but to follow behind them in the shadow of the arcade to see if she was real.

Wild, like the desert raised her, Cass was mostly a thatch of unruly hair and freckles. Maybe not quite seventeen, by his guess. Not like he was much older back then, just shy of twenty-one, but James Moone had been a man for longer than he could remember.

The world made sure of that.

He'd lost his way for a time, raised by thieves. Riding alongside them with a pistol in his hand, Jimmy Moone received an education. One that required him to grow up right then and there—or pay the same price as their victims.

Eventually, he turned his eye toward bigger, brighter things. More responsibility. A future, too, if he was lucky. Not long after, he found himself in the dusty streets of Gallow Gorge, following a fair, freckled lass down the bridleway like a shadow.

He'd been foolish to think Cass didn't already know he was tracking her. When her attention latched on him as her boots met the dirt, it was too late to run and pretend he hadn't. Her eyes flashed when he offered a friendly smile, but she knew better.

Just like that, he bought her already easily earned mistrust. He'd have to work harder to earn it back than better men with riches or glory. It'd be worth it, too.

She was a puzzle he wanted to solve. The first clue was easy enough—she avoided the people of Gallow Gorge like a cold she couldn't afford to catch. Being a woman seemed to be a nuisance to her. James earned himself a scolding as soon as he acted like she was one.

He vowed right then and there to treat Cass like everyone else—woman or not. After all, why shouldn't he? Especially when so many other men didn't.

When her edges softened the minute he treated her like an equal, it warmed a part of him that he thought was long dead. It made him hungry for more of the feeling. Of being good enough to earn anything someone like Cassidy Callaghan was willing to give.

It was a promise easily kept on his part at first.

Keeping his genuine affection from showing was next to impossible. Favoritism didn't suit his position or convince anyone he was as fair and just as a deputy ought to be. But he was powerless, spurred on by the blazing green of her eyes when she was angry with him. He might've fallen in love with her a little, star-struck with admiration when she returned to town and hauled a man twice her size into the Sheriff's office by his rope-bound wrists.

James couldn't help it. There was no one like his wild girl.

Years went by, and one thing remained clearer than anything else: Cass Callaghan was strong—an understatement if ever there was one—and stubborn to a fucking fault. There was no bounty too tricky for her to bring in. No law she wouldn't skirt around just to annoy him.

She only got bolder as their friendship grew. As her trust in him grew, too.

Sometimes, James swore she'd test the limits of his patience. It was her favorite game, seeing how long it'd take before he'd toss her in a cell for a well-earned timeout.

James never tired of it, that was for sure. Not even when she crashed a bottle of whiskey upside Lucas's head right in front of him. At least the drunk saved him the hassle of *literally* dragging her kicking and screaming from the saloon.

Every damn time, he'd haul her over his shoulder until she relented, unable to wiggle from his grasp around the back of her thighs.

Her tenacity and drive grew stronger the older and more experienced she got. She'd excitedly take a bounty from Moone's hands. He'd watch her read over the page, freckled face falling into a scowl by the time she got to the bottom. Every time, she'd hope it was the one.

It never was.

He wished he believed in something the way Cassidy did. He wondered what it'd feel like to have that unshakable focus, the unimaginable grit of giving blood and sweat, her very bones, if she had to. Just to taste a whisper of the justice she sought.

Not like he hadn't fought his own battles, but it wasn't the same. Cassidy was an arrow flying free and true to the target's center, whereas Moone was the sharp end of a knife wielded by another hand.

James knew she was waiting for something. Her impatience manifested in sullen moods, stealing away from the lightness between them he came to depend on.

Cass told him about it once. Only the barest of details—a single day in her life, the entire reason for living the way she did.

They leaned against the bar on a Tuesday afternoon, slowly swirling a finger or two of whiskey in the bottom of a scuffed glass when she murmured a name.

"Jack Ransom."

Dread bloomed in the pit of his stomach as it left her mouth—frozen in the shadow of the Scourge of the West. He wouldn't budge an inch, couldn't say a thing until she unmasked more of her past into a tobacco cloud.

"He's the one who did it, the reason for all this. Each time you give me a fresh bounty, I hope it's some sort of clue. But the longer I'm at this, the further away I feel, the more he feels like a figment of my imagination. Some monster I dreamed up in my head to blame for them dying."

Ransom's reputation stretched for hundreds of miles, whispered between the dregs of society. All while he simultaneously fooled the upper crust. Cass wasn't wrong about his existence, but she was wrong in her pursuit of him. James knew their lives would change the second she stepped in front of him.

So be it if he had to help keep her from everything Ransom was and what he believed in. No matter what it'd cost him.

James kept her busy and well-paid. He let her have any bounty she wanted. All of them, except one.

His blood went cold when the warrant came in for Lawrence Ball. There were others before then he shuffled to the bottom of the stack, and even considered tossing in the fire. But Ball was a different breed of heinous than any of them.

He instantly knew the face despite the sketch's mediocre quality. The artist captured the most important attributes about him, from the sharp cheekbones, the sunken eyes, and the telltale faded blue bandana each of Ransom's lackeys wore. The knotted scar twisted down Ball's cheek was one James had memorized as long ago as he could remember. When he closed his eyes, he heard Ball's voice and the smell of whiskey on his breath.

One look was all it took for James to snatch the warrant from the stack, haphazardly fold it up, and stuff it into his vest before Cass could see.

For weeks, he kept it there, and it haunted him. He wanted to feel guilty about hiding it, but he had his reasons, whether Cassidy would like them or not.

It burned a hole in his pocket as he looked over her sleeping so soundly in the back of the cell he'd put her in. He might've locked her in there (for being a menace), but she lingered everywhere beyond the bars.

Her bounty, Moody Duncan, snored noisily in the cell

next door, and the station still smelled faintly of liquor and blood.

He was sure she was sorry she wasted the bottle on Lucas Smith, the damned lunk. The first deputy deserved the whoopin' Cassidy gave him, but Moone hadn't lied. Of all the crooked people in their town, he wasn't one of them.

James thought of Duncan, a dangerous man in his own right. He was a killer through and through. Lesser men would've struggled to apprehend him, but Cassidy extricated him from wherever he'd dug in like a tick. And she'd done it faster than any of them anticipated.

If she could do that, if she could handle someone as rotten as Knuckle Duncan, maybe he underestimated how she'd deal with Doc Ball.

The warrant said dead or alive.

Perhaps Cassidy would rid the world of his scum—and Moone of the dread of facing him again. And if it all came crashing down upon her as he feared, James would hold it up and beat it back with a hammer.

Maybe then, he would finally be free.

A whinny echoed down the street. Moone huffed, chuckling when Cassidy's devil horse demanded he release her from her time-out. He couldn't watch her sleep all night, no matter how tempting. Even when her lips curled into the slightest smile, summoned by whatever she dreamed of. Perhaps it was a fond memory. Maybe it was of him.

His stomach twinged at the welcome thought, but guilt swallowed it whole. He didn't deserve it, not yet. Maybe not ever.

He didn't want for affection, per se. There was enough to go around at Ridley's, and James was better looking than most. He wasn't prideful; that's just how it was. A fair share of young, eligible ladies fawned over him as they passed the station. No matter the day nor the season, it happened without fail. He heard their heated whispers when he offered a friendly nod in return.

As pretty as some of them were, as flattering as it was, he had other aspirations—and another woman—on his mind.

He struck a match against the steel bars of her cell, taking his eyes from her for a moment to bring the fledgling flame to the end of a cigar. The tip flared when he gave the finely rolled tobacco a slow pull, waving it out with a lazy flick of his wrist. The station was dark, faintly lit by a lone oil lamp at the desk where Lucas slept the day away.

He leaned a shoulder against the cell bars, idly looking over the fold of elegant hands beneath the swell of her chest. Her hair, in a thick braid slung over her shoulder, was shinier than he remembered. And her freckles, *God*, her freckles. Plentifully painted like stars on a winter's night, they framed every inch of her face—from the bud of her lips, over dark eyelashes, to the slender line of her jaw.

He couldn't. He *shouldn't*. Considering Cassidy as a friend complicated things enough. Now this. It raised the swell of his guilt to unfathomable levels. He wouldn't dream of hurting her, couldn't imagine her finding the drawer full of unanswered letters he kept hidden away. Ones he wanted nothing more than to be free from.

All from the hand that wielded him, the absent Sheriff of Gallow Gorge.

[3]

CASS WOKE WITH A YELL WHEN A BANG RANG OUT against the iron bars of her cell. Dreams clung to her consciousness like molasses. But she couldn't wash them away as easily, and they weren't sweet, either.

What started as nostalgic wonder, a vision of home, shifted into something awful. If she closed her eyes, Cassidy saw her Da's death mask. And the rain. Rain poured down in thick, hot rivulets until she drowned in his blood. Until she woke and remembered he was long gone, and she wasn't a little girl in the cellar anymore.

Every night, it was a different version of that horrific day. Every day, her nightmares reminded her why she needed to see her mission through. Maybe then, Ian would finally rest. Perhaps she'd finally be able to rest, too.

She sat up in a flash, glaring up at the smug smile of James Moone swinging open the door.

"Your horse is getting impatient, Callaghan. I won't try to get him in a stable by myself." He lifted his hand. "I value my fingers too much."

"Like he'd let you," Cass grumbled, standing. She strode

to the door, sliding her arms through the sleeves of her duster. With her hat held firmly in her fingers, Cass stopped in the doorframe already occupied by the deputy sheriff.

Cass was fearless regarding men, giving no shits when it came to their feelings or opinions of her. There was something different about him. Perhaps it was the rumors of a rocky past or the twinkle in his eye when they'd frustrate each other to the point it was almost *fun*—but Moone never made her feel small.

Even then, practically looming like a mountain as he took up every spare inch of the space, so tall Cass looked up at him like stars in the sky; she was only ever his equal.

He regarded her, smelling of whiskey, leather, and tobacco smoke, wearing a playful smile. One that tempted her to linger, to think of him another way.

"You got another job for me?" Cass pressed, rolling the brim through her fingers.

He tucked the stub of a cigar between his teeth. "You go on ahead, Callaghan. You're not leavin' until tomorrow as it is. So go. *Rest.* Eat. Do whatever else you do to keep yourself busy at night. Stock up on supplies, and for God's sake, do something with your horse before he kicks someone out of spite."

"Who, Solo?" Cass laughed, sidestepping her way from the doorframe. "Why, he'd never hurt a fly. How *dare* you suggest such a thing?"

Moone shoved his hands in his pockets, blue eyes drifting over her as she placed her hat over unruly copper hair. She wondered what he was thinking and what thoughts he kept hidden away. Was the twitch of his mouth, the bend of his brow about the past he never spoke of? Were they about her?

He dipped his chin. "You and that horse are a match made in heaven… maybe hell. You know that?"

"Why?" Cass smirked with a lift of her brow as she backed toward the street. "Because we're both impossibly charming, and everyone loves us?"

"Or somethin'," Moone murmured, leaning against the Sheriff's office door behind her with a lazy drag on his cigar. "Until tomorrow, Cassidy."

Her stroll across the bridleway was unhurried, even with Moone's eyes tracking her the entire way. There wasn't any rush to get to tomorrow, not with a warm bed a few minutes away and free entertainment within view.

Cassidy laughed at the wide berth folks gave the sable stallion—making a run for it when he'd whinny at anyone who came too close.

Once she bribed Solo with a sugar cube or two, Cass wandered a few doors down to Ridley's.

The sweet, smoky air was a balm to a weary heart. Rose perfume lingered in the haze, kissing Cass's skin as she planted a coin in Madame Ridley's palm before meandering up the stairs.

Hours later, as the first flicker of morning light crept over steep plateaus on the horizon, Cass pulled on her boots while a warm breeze fluttered freshly cleaned curls around her face.

A hot bath, that warm bed, and a little company were a relief.

Cass smiled over her shoulder at the dozing blonde beauty. Sometimes, she spent weeks in the wilderness seeking a bounty. There weren't many friendly faces on the road. Upon a return to Gallow Gorge, she was more than happy to spend an evening with Katie Mays.

Sweet kisses, fervent touches, and long nights helped her feel human again.

She warily peered at her reflection in the washbasin and sighed. Lucas Smith wasn't wrong. She *was* skinny. Skinny but strong. Strong enough to hold her own in a fight and win.

Still, through the years, as she grew older, Cass noticed her face caught people off guard. Maybe it was because of her sex or the way the pale green glimmered behind dark eyelashes.

Cass knew who she was in her heart, but all she saw looking back in the mirror were pieces of her mother—the kind of face belonging to a great lady who once danced at parties and drank champagne. The type of woman she imagined gave it all up for the love of her life, for their daughter, and home far away from the island of her birth.

While alive, Aisling Callaghan lived in Cass's mind like a storybook character. She still did. She was always far away like one, too, trapped in the tallest tower of her mind— still on that island. The most beautiful of women, nearly dreamlike in her loveliness. Fair skin, jewel-like eyes, petal pink lips, and a smile that could catch the attention of a blind man.

Beyond reading lessons at the table and stories by *sean-nós* at night, Cassidy could never reach her. There were fewer pieces of a mother held in her memory than her Da. Fewer given, no matter how badly she wanted it. She sought it out as often as possible, begging for stories and rifling through hidden treasures in the bottom of a trunk. Details of a story she didn't understand, one Cassidy would unravel if she had the chance.

Cass felt undeserving of Aisling's face. She lived a life

far, far away from the one a mother might've ever hoped for her.

In that other life, Cassidy Kathleen Callaghan might've been beautiful.

"It's no use, sugar," a voice sweet as honey whispered behind her, drawing a spill of copper curls over Cassidy's shoulder. Katie Mays and her doe eyes met Cass's in the looking glass. "No matter what you do, you can't hide it."

Cass huffed a laugh. "Hide what?"

Katie nosed her ear, following it with a kiss as light as a feather. "How pretty you are."

"*Pretty.*" She wrinkled her nose.

The blonde nodded, slipping her fingers through Cass's curls, folding together braids more intricate than she ever managed on her own. "More than pretty."

"*Pretty* never helped me a day in my life."

"What about these?" Katie tied off the braid, rising on her knees. She pressed in, sending a river of flaxen hair over Cass's shoulder, trailing a finger over the thick sheet of freckles on Cass's nose. "They're *pretty.*"

Cass leaned closer. "Proof I spend too much time in the sun." She chuckled. "Or that I need a bigger hat."

The blonde pulled a copper ribbon between her fingers. "And this *pretty* hair?"

"Makes it easier to spot me in a crowd." Cass sighed, lips parting when Katie brushed her own against them.

"...and this *pretty* mouth?"

Groaning, Cass twisted, palming the golden, bare skin of Katie's back, taking a kiss for herself. She pulled away too soon, wanting to linger but eager to get on the road. "It never helped me rope in a bounty."

The chatter of voices filtered through the open window.

Gallow Gorge was waking up, and Cass was wasting daylight—officially.

Katie leaned away, chewing her lip. "Stay. Just one more day."

"Can't." Cass thumbed her cheek, kissing her once more as she rose. "I've got shit to do. You know I don't do well sitting in one place too long."

"Who says we'd be sittin' down?" The blonde smirked, stretching like a lazy cat in sunshine. Her smile fell as Cass wrapped her gun belts over her hips with a whisper of leather on brass. "I know—another day, another bad man to catch." She rose to her knees, looping her arms around the redhead's shoulders. "Maybe today will be *the* one."

Cass snorted. "Katie, I've been doing this since I was sixteen. That's eight years since I started bounty hunting, chasing everything that smelled like a lead. Always coming up empty."

"First time for everything." Katie wrapped herself in a shawl, giving Cass a hopeful smile. "A girl can hope you might stick around more than a night one of these days."

"The people of this town don't want me here forever," she drawled. Between the looks and how Cass kept them at arm's reach, they probably hoped she'd take a bounty and never return. It'd save them the trouble of making fake niceties.

"That's not true," Katie argued, unhooking Cass's black hat from the bedpost.

"Maybe one day. First time for everything, right?" Cass slipped it from her fingers, placing it on her head before kissing Katie one last time, long and slow. A whinny around the corner drew her attention—a bellyaching Solo, raring to get a move on. "I'll see you in a few days."

The halls of Ridley's were quiet in the early morning hour, save for a softly purring cat curled at the foot of the stairs. Even Madame Ridley went to bed hours before, with all her girls occupied and well-paid for a night's service.

Met by the crisp desert morning on her way to the stable, Solo squealed when she stepped inside, stamping his hooves with an impatient snort.

Once Solo was saddled, he pushed Cass out of the stall, ready to seize the day. His nose at her back urged her to fill his saddlebags with a heavy load—one to last a long time out in the thick of it. Out where they'd be wonderfully and delightfully alone, with only an endless sea of sagebrush and stars between them and the horizon.

Cass stepped into Booker's General Goods, awash with memories of herself tucked in every corner, but no more than the little girl with plaited hair sitting at the counter in her crisp pinafore.

"Hi, Miss Callaghan." She gave her a crooked grin, half her teeth missing.

"Hey there, Miss Daisy." Cassidy gave her a friendly nod, lifting her hat. Her heart always did the strangest things when she visited the General Store. It was a reminder of the past, but different from what her dreams offered. Here, she remembered all the *good*. Like everything might never have happened. It didn't bring them back or erase the past. But she'd take this, just the smallest slice of joy. "Did you get the thing I asked for?"

"Sure did," Daisy exclaimed in a hushed whisper, hopping from her stool. She rummaged behind a cluster of jars on tiptoe, pulling a dusty book from behind them. Slapping at the cover, Daisy dropped it in the crown of Cass's hat just in time for her father to step from the back room.

"Pleasure seein' you in town again, Ms. Callaghan," he grumbled. "I suspect you'll be headin' out again soon?"

She forced a smile, one so unnatural that it wavered. "I like to keep busy, Mister Booker."

He bristled, nose wrinkled. Just another unfriendly gesture in a list long enough to last a lifetime. "So, I've seen. The usual, then?"

Mr. Booker lifted a brow, waiting for Cass's approval before giving little Daisy a twitch of his head and a playful wink.

Unfriendly. That's what Cassidy always told herself they were. Were they all really so bad? Perhaps it was just Booker's nature, especially with so sweet a daughter as Daisy.

Maybe she ought to let up; she didn't have to be as prickly as a cactus. Not with as often as she frequented Gallow Gorge. Of all the places she'd been, this might've been her favorite. It might even feel like home, someplace to stay a while, like Katie hoped.

Cass slapped down a couple of dollars, watching in nostalgic wonder when Daisy burst into action, gathering supplies from every corner around the shop. She bounded from one side of the store to the other, building a parcel of tobacco, canned beans, cured meat, and a box of .45.

The thought of home pried its way into her focus. Even as she safely packed her goods away, it lingered. It tapped all the louder when she turned her attention to the Sheriff's station.

She eyed the worn wooden sign, giving Solo a fond pat on the rump before stepping into the shade of the arcade.

Inside, Cassidy was amused to find Lucas Smith long gone. In his place was a soundly sleeping James Moone.

Clothed from head to toe in black—from silver-tipped

boots to a worn vest stretched across a broad chest—he always looked ready to attend a funeral. Leaned back in a chair with long legs draped over the desk and a hat over his eyes, there was just a glimpse of his lips and the three days of scruff that framed them.

Just enough of a peek to have her thinking about the damned thing, *that mouth*, all over again. The softest movement of them with each rise and fall of his chest, or how his cupid's bow was the valley between the perfect peaks of his upper lip.

Part of her wondered if she ought to let him rest and return when the town's clock rang seven o'clock, but Cass wasn't that nice regarding the good Deputy Sheriff—no matter how distracted she was by watching him. He had something she needed, and daylight was already slipping away.

With a sly grin, she leaned forward and shoved Moone's big, black boots from the desk.

He woke with a yell, jolting to his feet, blue eyes wild, with a quick hand on his revolver.

Cassidy wondered if he was haunted in his sleep, just as she was. Maybe it was muscle memory of that rumored past life. One of a younger man involved with the less savory sort.

Maybe he was the sort of man she'd chase across the desert.

Cass laughed to herself. If he were, James Moone—the man who slept at his post—would be the easiest bounty she ever brought in. As interesting as the gossip could be, she couldn't see him as anything but what he was: a constant sentinel for the town of Gallow Gorge, keeping a watchful eye while she did all the work.

Maybe, sometimes, they were a team. But Cass would rather be caught dead than say it to his face.

"Mornin' Sleeping Beauty." She crossed her arms, wearing a smug smile. She shouldn't find so much amusement in his sleepy haze or how he searched for his bearings. As if they'd be lying on the desk where he left them. "You said come back in the morning. Well, it's morning, Moone, so here I am. It's not my fault your definition of holding down the fort is sleeping on it."

"Morning. Right." He worked his jaw, smoothing a thatch of chin-length, tawny waves.

"The warrant?" Cass planted her hands on her hips impatiently. "And you owe me fifty dollars."

Moone sucked in a deep breath, slipping a worn flier from an inside pocket. His brow creased as he unfolded it and looked it over. Cass wondered for a moment, *just* a moment; if he wasn't such a thorn in her side, he might've been handsome.

He ran his tongue along the seam of his mouth. "I've had this for a while. I still don't know if I ought to give it to you."

"Why?" she snapped, pushing in with her shoulder to try and get a look. He was stalling. To hell if she'd let him.

Moone's expression darkened. He held it away, jaw ticking. "At the very least, you shouldn't go alone. Maybe I could go with you. Stay a day or two. We'll come up with a plan together. It's not the safest of marks."

"*Safe?*" Cass barked a laugh. "James Moone, since when do you care so much about—" She tore the paper from his grip and read the name. Then again. And again. Once more, to make sure she wasn't seeing things. The sound rushed from her ears, heart roaring like a freight train's whistle. "—

my safety."

Moone hovered over her shoulder. She was frozen to the spot.

There it was, right in the palm of her hand. The invisible lead she chased for years, always hoping the next warrant on the stack would point her in the right direction. The moment she'd worked her entire life for, her reason for living. All of it led to a scrap of paper—something so infinitesimal and unimportant in the grand scheme of things.

To her, it held the weight of the world.

Moone cleared his throat, scrubbing a palm over his jaw. "Lawrence 'Doc' Ball is a well-known accomplice of—"

"Jack Ransom," Cass whispered, sliding her gaze to meet his as shivers clawed down her arms. She was so close, closer than ever before. "The man who murdered my parents."

Nerves lit like a live wire, her body and brain set to charge—ready and waiting to combust.

"Last seen on a bank job in Cold Creek. Rumor says he's hiding out in Lonely Bellow, but you know how reliable those are." Moone shifted on his heels, moving to lay a comforting hand on her shoulder, but thought better of it.

"That's only a few days' ride." Cass snapped to attention, folding the parchment and stuffing it in her vest. "There isn't any time to waste."

Cass spun, flipping her braid over her shoulder as she marched out the door. She made quick work of Solo's knotted reins. Thinking wasn't required; her hands just knew what to do.

The stallion reared up in anticipation, black eyes wide and nose flared, kicking up dust with each stomp of his hooves.

She vaulted herself into the saddle. With a push of her

heel into Solo's flank, he pivoted toward the street, ready to take off and leave Gallow Gorge in the dust.

Moone seized the bridle. Solo whinnied and stomped some more.

"Get out of my way, Moone," Cass ground out. "You know full well I'm not afraid of bowling you over.

"Be careful." His blue eyes flashed. "If you bring Ball in, it'll put a target on your back."

"Good," she spat, teeth bared. "Let the bastard come to me and get what he deserves."

"No," the deputy cautioned. "You have no idea what he's capable of. What kind of shit he'll bring down upon you if you go against him. This isn't going to go the way you think."

"Like hell it isn't," Cass hissed, giving the reins a sharp tug and a quick *heyaw*.

Solo answered her command with a fearsome squeal, rearing back on his hind legs. Moone had no choice but to release him and avoid a pummeling.

The pair of them, the sable stallion and his human sister, took off at a ferocious gallop. By the time the dust cleared, they were only a speck on the horizon, chasing the promise of long-sought vengeance.

[4]

CASSIDY

THE BLAZING NEVADA SUN BEAT DOWN UPON HER BACK as Solo cantered through an endless sea of sagebrush. Reins loose in her grip, Cass balanced her body forward in the stirrups, making her and the stallion of one mind and body as the miles fell away.

Not a soul stood between them and their destination. Nothing except a vast blanket of gleaming cerulean stretched over a deep ochre of scorched earth.

Solo's hooves pounded the dirt like a drum, punctuated by hard blows from his nose. His mane whipped and swirled with every bob of his noble head. Every few seconds, his ears flicked back, tuned to Cass's voice as she urged him on, praising his hard work with a smile as the wind whipped through her hair and whistled in her ears. Their dance was her favorite.

With nothing in their way, Solo practically grew wings—he *flew*. With him, Cass felt free. Free from her past, free from the expectations of who society thought she should be—free from who *she* thought she ought to be. There was no mystery of her mother, no duty to her father. No

Ransom. Just she and Solo, quick and nimble as the wind.

When they'd surely put more than a few miles behind them, Cass leaned back in the saddle to get him to—reluctantly—ease up. He wanted to run; he was born to do it, but Solo would run himself ragged for her. Cass wasn't willing to risk it—risk him.

He was her companion, her friend, her *family*. Protecting him was more important than he realized.

Eventually, they carried on so long that the sun had since surpassed its peak. As the sky burned with blazing orange and deep turquoise, Cass pressed her heels into Solo's flank. They needed to take shelter for the night.

Solo grumbled an unamused snort, whipping his tail in distaste as she lifted the saddlebags from his back.

"You hush. We *cannot* run all day, you big lug. No matter how much you want to." Cass chuckled, setting to work on a fire to keep her warm and dissuade coyotes from getting too close.

She built a fledgling flame with help from a flint and steel, one coaxed to grow with the softest breath. She smiled when it crackled into something sustainable, just enough to warm a can of beans.

She stretched out over her bedroll, slipping the boots from her feet, making a mental note to shake them out in the morning. Solo wandered over with a low nicker, blowing at her hair—a request.

"C'mon, I'll make some room for you, ya big baby." Cass laughed when Solo sank to his knees behind her and flattened out with a dramatic groan. She shifted, laying her head on the thick curve of his neck, brushing her fingers across his cheek. "There. Now, you won't be sleeping alone."

Solo blinked, answering with another warm, throaty

nicker.

The sound stirred Cass's heart. "I love you, too, sweet thing."

They had something special, something Cass didn't give to anyone else. Not like she'd be capable of it, anyhow.

Solo was different. He didn't come with expectations, didn't ask questions or make judgments. It was easier that way.

Not like Cass was ever left wanting when finding a warm bed or some company for the night. A little conversation if she was in the mood. Katie Mays came to mind, bringing a smile to her face. They had something special, too. Something Cass might call friendship if she ever stuck around long enough to find out.

There was some kind of magic brewing when Cass met Solo. A few days after the massacre at Faraday Creek, Cassidy was broken inside and out. She'd run from home, surviving in the desert alone with nothing but the clothes on her back and a knife in her hand.

Solo was practically still a yearling, bright-eyed and beautiful. As a competing male, his herd likely abandoned him, but she knew better; he was waiting for her.

There was no reason for a wild mustang to take to a human, let alone a little girl. Cut from the same cloth, birds of a feather, a bittersweet kismet—two orphans meant to find each other right when one needed the other.

Meant to be.

Cass yawned, pulling out the worn copy of *Pride and Prejudice* Daisy Booker found for her. She cracked the pages, inhaling the sweet, musty scent of old parchment and ink before turning to the first chapter.

"It is a truth universally acknowledged that a single man in

possession of a good fortune must be in want of a wife," Cass read aloud, eager to keep her mind firmly planted in the affairs of the Bennet sisters—far, far away from thoughts of Doc Ball and Jack Ransom.

The Callaghans fostered a love of reading from before she could remember. Through bedtime stories sung by *sean-nós*, and wild tales of emerald moors spun few and far between by her Da, Cassidy hungered for far-off places and romance—especially once they were gone.

As soon as she earned enough, Cass only went to fetch a bounty with a book in her sack.

While Solo was good company, reading helped keep her connected without having to connect herself.

There, amongst the quiet flicker of flames against the red desert bluffs, she lived in a different world as the nocturnal chorus of cicadas chipped the steady trills of their nighttime melody. The lonely owl whispered a hoot, the coyotes sang a mournful song, lifted on a breath of wind winding its way through a bend in the earth. Cassidy was in Longbourn with the Bennets.

It was how Cass liked it: quiet, but not really—just her and her horse.

She already had a family once. Cass didn't think the idea of a different one suited her much. While some people had their uses, and the occasional bout of company was nice, Cass didn't want or *need* anyone else.

It was too complicated, otherwise.

With a breeze at her feet, a fire by her side, and Solo at her back, Cass dozed like she'd done a thousand times before—with her father's voice in her ear.

Just remember every'ting I taught ye, and it will be fine.

In the morning, Cass woke to a slow, warm, *wet* lashing

from Solo. He worked better than a rooster's crow, drawing her from her fitful sleep to tell her the sun was awake—and so should they.

"Solo, get *off*," she grumbled, shoving him away by the muzzle. It wasn't as pleasant a *good morning* as Katie the night before, but Cassidy was grateful to have him to ease the ache from unpleasant dreams.

The early morning sun barely crested the horizon—golden strands stretching toward an inky expanse of deep blue. She was sure they might've afforded another few minutes of sleep, but Solo was right. Daylight was already ticking by, and they didn't have a precious second to waste.

[5]

CASSIDY

B Y THE SECOND DAY OF A HARD RIDE, CASS SPOTTED THE
seedy town of Lonely Bellow. It rose on the horizon
quicker than other settlements. Unlike bigger cities like
Chicago or Sacramento, Gallow Gorge wasn't particularly
glamorous. Lonely Bellow was in between and especially
grimy—the perfect place for someone like Doc Ball to hide
in plain sight.

The desert wind cut through dusty streets as she and
Solo ambled up a curved bridleway. Her attention darted
from door to door, keenly peering from beneath her brim
across the weary faces of its residents. With the sun's setting,
shopkeepers shuttered their shops in preparation for the
nightly storm.

Born like other settlements, a collection of clapboard
buildings sprung up when some lucky soul discovered gold
downriver.

Lonely Bellow did well enough, building a community
around the gold boom. Along came everything from a
bakery, laundry, and a trio of competing hotels. Even a
casino at the center of it all.

Like so many other places, the gold eventually ran dry. Those who searched for it flocked to other, more plentiful hills with newer, bigger cities to build.

Lonely Bellow bore the brunt of their abandonment.

In the process, they sunk to something more disreputable, inviting the depraved to its streets with the promise of soiled doves and *filles de joie* in every corner and plenty of bloody money to win at the casino.

A wretched hive of scum and villainy.

Cass led Solo down the dusty road, slipping from the saddle in the blooming lamplight of the local livery. She pulled a pair of quarters from her pocket, depositing them in the palm of the stableboy. She tapped a finger on the side of her nose, a silent message to keep her presence there quiet, hoping her bribe would buy enough time to get a good look around.

Solo let out a low whinny when Cass led him into a stall, keeping his tack on. He didn't want to be far from her; she knew that much. Still, the search might take longer than she expected. Cass couldn't leave him roped up outside. He'd draw too many eyes with his bellyaching.

She was so close to Ransom that she could taste it. She wasn't about to let Doc Ball slip from her grasp because she was hasty.

"I'll be back before you know it." Cass splayed her fingers against his cheek. "Be patient but stay ready. We might have to leave in a hurry."

He gave her a push with his muzzle, displeasure abundantly clear when he let out a loud, disapproving neigh as she moved toward the door. Maybe he was telling her to be careful, worried like Moone seemed to be.

Cass stopped by the stable boy, lifting her hat.

"Have you seen this man?" she murmured, crouching to his level. Cass tugged the warrant from her vest, pointing to the sketch. "There's another quarter in it if you know something."

Bribery was a good tool for her line of work, and Cass was ready to use *any* tactic to catch this particular bounty. There was too much at stake for her not to.

The boy's brow furrowed—a flicker of recognition. "Yeah, I'd seen that feller before, ma'am. He's been keepin' his horse in that stall right there." He nodded behind her. "I've been seein' him hang around the casino at the Grand Hotel at night. It's just two doors down."

Cass ruffled his dark hair with a grin. "I'll make it two whole dollars if you make his bridle disappear."

Anything to slow him down.

She pulled a few more coins from her pocket, leaving them on a stool by the door as the boy dashed to the back of the stable with the promise of so large a prize.

The casino made for an exciting challenge. Not like she wasn't already used to setbacks of every sort because of her sex. Women were likely unallowed to play and, therefore, gamble away their husband's money. Not when they were property, themselves.

Should she need to step up and interact with men deep in a game of Faro, Cass would have to get creative.

She twisted her thick braid around a gloved hand, tucking it into the crown of her hat. It was a man's world; Cass would melt into the crowd as best she could. She shifted her gait, changing the cadence of her steps with a quick pass over the gun belts slung around her hips.

Cass counted how many extra rounds she stored there, thinking of her Da when her fingers curled around the pearl grip of one of her pistols.

Every bullet had a consequence.

She'd taken a life before without a second thought, but she'd always been *sure* when she pulled the trigger, just like Ian Callaghan taught her. This time, she'd save her lead.

There wasn't any question about it—Cass needed Ball alive and talking. Dragging in his corpse for a bounty wouldn't do her any good, not if she wanted to find Jack Ransom.

The twang of a piano filtered out onto the street as night fell, carrying the low din of voices inside, punctuated by the occasional clink of glasses at the bar. She hoped the men inside wouldn't look past their whiskey-soaked haze and see her for what she was.

Cass asked the barkeep for a drink. This time, it was just for show. She liked keeping a clear head about her when she worked; the glass of whiskey was another tool in her belt.

Lifting it to her lips, she surveyed the room. To the untrained eye, nothing remarkable was afoot at the Grand Hotel. Cass saw beneath all the *normal*, listing every eye twitch and sneer.

On her left was an ongoing game of Faro teetering on the edge like a powder keg rigged to blow. She looked from eye to eye at the men gathered around the table, sure one was cheating. He was bound to pay the price at the end of a barrel in the street later that night.

Keep an eye on that one. She hoped it wouldn't hinder her plans or scare away Ball.

Whiskey coated her lips, motivation as she squinted through the fog of smoke curling toward the ceiling—eyes drawn to the table having the most luck. It was easy to spot by the girls perched on the arms of the players with the

largest pile of winnings.

Cass would have an easier time blending in if she embraced the gifts she inherited from her mother: the pretty face and the smile men would go to war for, like Helen of Troy. But, getting tied up in a corset to hang on some man's arm wasn't something Cass Callaghan was willing to do unless she was truly desperate.

A smile curled at the edges of her freckle-framed mouth concealed behind the glass of whiskey. There, with the biggest pile of them all, was the face splashed on the warrant burning a hole in her pocket. There was no mistaking him.

A long, crooked nose, prominent brow, cheekbones that could cut glass, and a jagged scar down his left cheek— Lawrence *'Doc'* Ball.

Moone said he was dangerous. That, as a member of Ransom's inner circle, he was protected by the law. She'd suffer the retaliation of the entire gang should she interfere. But Cass was as stubborn as they came. When she looked at Ball and the pretty blue hanky tied around his neck, she didn't fear a damned thing. All she saw was Jack Ransom— and the burning bellows in his eyes as he put a bullet through her Ma's skull.

Then, Aisling Callaghan told Cassidy to run. Ian told her to remember everything he taught her. James Moone told her to leave well enough alone.

But when Ball lifted his glass with a celebratory smile as he won another round, Cass decided there was no turning back.

She'd nab him, hogtie him, and drag him across the desert if she had to—as long as it led to Cass putting a bullet of her own through *Ransom's* skull. She was willing to go to Hell and back to do it.

She fished out a ten-dollar bill—a large enough buy-in to catch their attention. Usually, she'd be the picture of calm. In her element as she faked her way through a poker game while analyzing her mark. Now, her hands shook with nervous anticipation, on the edge of everything she'd worked toward for years. She prayed they wouldn't take notice.

"Count me in, fellas." Cass attempted her best James Moone growl, swinging her leg over an empty chair. A few seconds crawled by while they eyed the money she slapped down. She hoped they were too drunk to notice the feminine lean to her voice, the slenderness of her shoulders.

Thankfully, they kept their attention on the girls cooing in their ears, senses too clouded by a thick layer of perfume to notice anything unusual about her.

The dealer doled out a fresh round. The players' faces shifted when they looked over their hands, trying as they may—in her eyes, at least—to keep their expressions passive as they glowered at their cards.

Cass's attention was fixed on Ball.

Up close, she learned details a crude sketch couldn't capture. How the scar tissue wound around a distinct, bullet-shaped divot in his flesh, or the droop of his left eye as a result. His skin was tan, leathered from years spent in the sun, but his clothes spoke of money—brown damask and a fair blue pinstriped cotton sleeve. He was a piece of shit but a well-paid right hand.

Around the table, they went, betting and raising. Each player took their sweet time, taking a long drink here, a drag on their cigar there. Cass wondered how they saw their hands through the smoke.

The man beside her held out a cigarillo, grunting to offer one but careful not to show his cards. Cass took one with a

gloved hand—taking great care to conceal the most ladylike thing about her. She placed it between her teeth, striking a match on the heel of her boot.

Lifting the flickering flame to the tip, Cass lit the end of tightly rolled tobacco, gently pulling smoke into her mouth until the end burned red. She was thankful to have something to serve to deter suspicion from the fact the whiskey in her glass hadn't gone down, even though she brought it to her lips half a dozen times.

Cass took a deep drag, using it to her advantage, letting the smoke fall from her lips and over the table. All eyes expectantly turned to her—it was her turn to reveal her hand, and she'd won.

Three of a kind over a flush and two pair.

All of them groaned—except Ball. They threw down their cards as she swept the pot to her corner. It was a few dollars, which was all well and good. But she planned to stay at the table as long as she could. And keep her mark there until it was time to strike.

Apparently, Ball was the quiet type. But, behind his dangerously calm facade was a look of the purest fury, barely contained in the whites of his knuckles as he spun a fifty-cent piece on the tabletop.

You're getting to him. Good. Cass hid a wry smile behind her glass as she feigned another sip.

One round, then another, and another.

Ball checked a silver pocket watch no fewer than four times as the pot grew larger with each hand. He finally snapped when he folded, and Cass won on a bad hand.

"You've got a lot of nerve comin' in here, spoilin' my winnin' streak." He thumbed the same silver coin, barking at the dealer, "Another."

Cass wondered how much abuse the employees of The Grand Hotel put up with in a town like Lonely Bellow. It might've been prosperous once upon a time, but as the promise of gold slipped away, the quality of the patronage slipped, too. The local law enforcement was likely bought by Ransom's gang. She imagined they all feared what he would do should anyone go against his bidding.

After the first round of betting, two of the five folded, leaving Cass, Ball, and one other. The dealer burned another card before flipping a King of Spades skyward.

Cass sighed, taking another drag from her cigarillo. Patience. Hers would pay off.

Ball was relentless, but so was she, unyielding and stubborn to a fault. There was no way in hell she'd crack first.

Cass's jaw clenched. She tossed a pair of quarter-eagles—worth two and a half dollars each—into the pot. Her mark stiffened, and she held back a smile when his eyes flickered to the river of cards and back to his hand.

She'd spent ages studying the body language of people around her, learning—even as a little girl—the silent ticks and behaviors etched into their faces and twitches of their fingers. Without meaning to, Ball was giving her *everything*.

With each tic of his angular face, Ball rolled the risks over in his mind as he fiddled with his winnings. *Plink-plink-pliiiiink* went the stack of dollar coins as they flipped through his fingers until he relented with a gruff, "Raise."

Shit. The fool wanted to keep going, hoping she'd give up and fold. Back and forth, Cass would raise instead of calling, and Ball's face got redder and redder.

Elbows on the table, brim tilted down to hide a self-assured smile, Cass was pleased when Ball called, and the round moved forward. Their third long since abandoned the game, his winnings whittled to almost nothing.

Cass was glad that the game came down to her and him, teetering on the edge of getting exactly what she wanted.

The dealer burned another card and laid one final face at the center of the table. They'd attracted the eyes of everyone in the casino as the stakes grew higher and higher, the smokey air around them brittle with tension.

A wrong move, maybe even the strike of a match, would set the air ablaze. One final round of betting was between her and getting Ball alone. As the seconds ticked by, she started to enjoy the chase a little too much.

Round and round, they went again until Cass pushed her entire stack of winnings into the pot.

That's when Ball finally snapped as spectacularly as she hoped.

Cass lifted the still-full glass to her lips, feigning a sip when Ball sent it careening to the floor with the flash of his fist. Shattered glass punctuated sharply against the twang of the piano in the corner, bringing the low hum of the casino to an abrupt halt.

Ball shoved his chair back.

"What in the goddamned hell do you think yer playin' at?" he bellowed, drawing more attention to the bout of trouble brewing in their corner.

Cass's gaze slid to the shattered glass strewn over weathered wood, mourning the loss of the golden elixir.

"I was drinking that," she griped, lifting her hat to reveal her braid.

If his face wasn't red enough already, Ball went truly scarlet when he looked upon the woman who'd been besting him for the better part of the evening.

He sputtered, reaching for the pistol hanging from the back of his chair.

Cass's hand flew to her side, pulling back her black duster to brush her fingertips over the pearl grip of one of her twins.

She shook her head, tutting. "Sit your ass back down. We've got a game to finish." Her fingers hovered over her weapon. Ian's words echoed in her mind while she hesitated to put a bullet in him right then and there.

Cass jerked her head toward the table. Ball clenched his jaw, shooting wordless daggers with his eyes as he sank into his seat.

Her smile grew when he heeded her words, weary of nimble fingers on her pistol.

Perhaps he'd heard whispers on the wind of a bounty hunter with hair like fire and hands as quick as lightning— one not to be trifled with.

Satisfied he'd stay put, Cass pulled the worn warrant from her vest, making a show of it as she unfolded it crease by crease.

"I'm looking for a man." She glanced at the parchment before looking at him with a simpering smile. "He kinda looks like you. Wanted on four counts of murder, six counts of attempted murder and is directly connected to Jack Ransom—Lawrence Ball. Goes by Doc. Ever heard of him?"

Cass laid the sketch over the pot, noting every twitch in his face when he looked it over and back at her with a flash of fear in his eyes.

"I h-haven't the faintest—"

"I'm not so sure about that." Cass's smirk lifted. "See, I've been watching you this whole time, looking at that pretty blue hanky you've got. I'm starting to think I've got my man." She leaned in, inches away, balancing on her elbow as she pointed at the jagged scar down his cheek. "Rumor has it that 'ole Doc Ball pulled a piece of lead out of his own face, and that's how he earned his name. I don't know about you, but the evidence is starting to stack up, *Lawrence*."

"There ain't *shit* stackin' up, missy." Ball pressed in, the stink of whiskey and scurvy twisted in his breath. He jabbed a finger at the blanket of freckles on her nose. "You come in here, steal my winnings, and now you expect me to, what? Tell you I'm this Doc Ball or something? The game's not even over!"

Cass shook her head. "Mm, no, Lawrence. I'm afraid you're wrong again." She stood, flipping her cards atop his scarred face on the warrant, revealing a damn lucky hand—a royal flush. "This game's been over since I stepped foot in this town, and I *won*."

[6]

Moone

J AMES KNEW HIS GIRL. SHE WAS ANGRY WITH HIM, AND it'd be a good long while until forgiveness came his way. Especially if Ball ended up slipping through her fingers.

Then it'd be his fault for keeping the warrant from her for so long.

In those initial moments, once she plucked it from his grip with breathless anticipation, Moone regretted not trying harder to warn her, to talk some sense into her before she galloped away from Gallow Gorge like a bat out of hell. But he knew there was no stopping her, not ever. Even if he lit the sketch aflame, Cassidy would've found a way to combine the pieces from bits of ash.

Her want for revenge was limitless, infinite to the point that, no matter how he tried to reach her, it'd only light a furious fire that sent her racing toward the horizon.

For days, he waited. He'd offer a "good morning" to the regular passerby as he stood at his usual post, leaning a broad shoulder against a wooden column while he cast a shrewd eye on the horizon. They were none the wiser to the anxiousness of his heart; each thunderous beat threaded

with the hope she wouldn't find any trouble with Ball. Unspoken prayers she wouldn't find him at all.

By mid-afternoon on the second, a quiet shadow appeared beside him.

Katie Mays looked different away from the rosy, diffused lamplight at Ridley's. In the sunshine, her hair was a bright golden wheat, her eyes the sweetest caramels at Booker's General Goods. He hadn't realized until then how tall she was, a hand over Cassidy, and one below him. There hadn't been any reason to notice before. Not when there were so many other delicious distractions—other comforts to be had.

James wasn't a stranger to the company of a borrowed bed, of love for sale. After all, his first time had been with a girl whose company was bought for him. With her, over numerous nights, he'd learned things he couldn't have ever come up with all his own. He—and any lover he'd taken after—was more than grateful.

It was different with Katie.

He'd been lucky to find her. Badge brand-new, lonelier than he'd ever felt, Moone drunkenly tumbled into Ridley's and found a refuge he didn't expect. His age, with no better an upbringing, Katie tucked his sorry ass into bed. In the morning, over a strong cup of chicory coffee, James *talked*. He talked to her more than he had anyone ever before. Eventually, they dabbled in something more than conversation.

Together, they shared more than the barest hint of a past, long nights well-spent and lessons boldly taught. Katie Mays and James Moone were the same. Kindred spirits who understood the heart of the very same thing—Cassidy Callaghan.

Admittedly, once Katie became the same kind of sanctuary for Cass she'd been for him—once he wanted to be a haven for Cassidy, too—Moone never made it back upstairs at Ridley's. Not for Katie or anyone else.

While the nature of things changed, the fondness never faded. The kind illustrated in bright smiles across the arcade, a box of sweets that'd materialize on Ridley's stoop, or a fine bolt of fabric. Even as they got older, wiser, and wary about a certain bounty hunter, there was an ease to standing beside her.

But it wasn't enough to shake free the worry, the torment of waiting for Cassidy to return.

Katie's shoulders heaved with a sigh. Moone understood without asking.

"Is this the one?" she said into the breeze.

"Yeah," he answered, gooseflesh lifting into fine pinpricks, the weight of all his secrets catching the wind like a kite. "It'll lead straight to who she's been looking for."

Moone didn't dare meet her eye, for risk of Katie reading them all over his face. Not even when she slid her hand into his palm, seeking comfort he wasn't sure he could give.

"I need you to do something for me." A squeeze.

"Anything." Lord knew if it was for Cassidy, he'd go to hell and back.

"I need you to find a way to finish this. End it, or she'll never be still."

His heart caught in a vice that wound tighter and tighter the longer he thought of it. Could he kill Jack Ransom for Cassidy? Was there a way to weasel his way in and put a bullet in him? Not without a sound plan, not without so much fucking risk.

It could ruin everything he tried to build. Everything he

wanted to. Everything good.

But it could help them instead. It might let Cassidy finally live.

"She wouldn't understand." Moone focused on the feeling of Katie's slight hand dwarfed by his, on the plea written in her trembling fingers. What might Cassidy's feel like? He'd never know, not really. Not if he stole what she hungered for out from under her. "She'd never forgive me."

Katie's golden-hued gaze slipped from the horizon, meeting his. There was something Moone understood, a wish—a worry—knitted in the wrinkle between her brows and the glimmer of tears brimming on her eyelashes.

"James, *please*." No one called him by his first name. Not even Cassidy. "I'm not asking you to make any promises, not yet. Just give it some thought, is all. She might not understand, not at first, but she would eventually. Better to earn her forgiveness and get the chance to build a life together than her to not have one at all."

Moone freed his hand, palming his jaw. "A life? *Katie*"— he huffed, a poorly faked chuckle he choked on—"Cass and I are barely even friends."

Sure, he'd had the odd sort of daydream of what things could look like in a perfect world. But their world *wasn't* perfect, and neither was he.

"I see the two of you. How you look at her when you don't think anyone's watchin'... how she tries *so hard* not to smile whenever you're around. She doesn't smile like that for anyone. Not Solo. Not even me." Katie forced one of her own, stepping away to leave Moone to brood at the horizon alone and beg it for Cassidy's return. "The only people in this town that don't realize what's between the two of you... is the two of you."

Moone couldn't stop thinking about Katie's request; how tempting it was to force that chapter closed. Maybe he could claim something for himself, too.

All this time, he'd been worried about protecting Cass, but how much protection did she really need? Of course, he wanted to keep her safe. He didn't want to send her on a fool's errand that'd only get her killed, but Katie was right; if Cass never stopped, if she never found Ransom at the end of her barrel, she'd never truly rest.

She'd never really live.

He thought about sending her in a different direction, throwing her off Ball's scent. But Cass was smart enough to see past that in a heartbeat, past the deception. Besides, he was a shit liar unless he had the proper, selfish motivation to spin the truth the way he needed.

James tried to live his life as an honest man but lies were like a knife in your boot—hidden away until the right time to use them to your advantage.

There was no advantage in keeping Ball's warrant a secret from Cass, though there were still others James would rather die than have her find out.

Time went agonizingly slow by the third day. Each time he saw a figure on the horizon of the sleepy town, his heart would fervently skip a beat. He hoped it was her—alone, angry, and empty-handed, without a trail to follow Jack Ransom. It was better that way. Eventually, Cass would realize that.

Maybe she had.

Dusk already fell over Gallow Gorge. The saloon was lively, and the shops boarded up for the night when a loud whinny flew on the wind.

At first, James brushed it off. Surely, it only came from

the livery in town.

Then he heard it again. Loud enough, the sound drew his eyes to the faint glimmer of light on the horizon—and the sable stallion *without a rider*.

James knew that horse like he remembered a bad dream.

He jumped into action—unsure whose horse he took—cantering toward the black dot, chasing the sound of Solo as he called out over and over again. Once his black eyes landed on Moone, he reared, letting out a fearsome squeal before wheeling around and taking off in the opposite direction.

James dared not question it, blindly following where Solo led him. His stomach twisted and churned as they left a cloud of dust behind them, only knotting all the tighter when he spotted a flash of copper between the sagebrush.

He threw himself from the saddle, stumbling to his knees beside her and gently rolling her to her back.

Cass groaned, brows creased, mouth forming words James couldn't make out. He didn't care what she said. All that mattered was that she was *alive*.

"I've got you, Cass. I'm here. It's gonna be alright."

"M'fine." She shoved his hands away, grunting as she stubbornly pushed to her knees. Her eyes blazed in the fading light, their brilliance only added to by the waxy pallor of her skin and the sheen of fever on her brow. She limped, boots dragging through fine silt as she trained her gaze ahead. "That rat bastard. He stabbed me right in the gut. Should've shot him right then."

"Who did?" James hovered, hesitating as he reached to steady her.

Cass didn't answer, not with words, but with a grit of her teeth when a fresh wave of pain crashed over her, staggering her to a halt. Pride flared in his chest at her unstoppable tenacity, even as a fever coursed through her veins.

She pushed forward, holding her side as she connected a hard kick to what James thought might've been the shadow of a boulder tucked between the brush. But, when the stone whimpered, he froze.

"You got him."

"Damn straight, I got the bastard," Cass spat before her lovely face contorted, and the light flickered in her eyes. Her balance shifted, cheeks paling seconds before she crashed to the dirt.

James darted to her side, wrapping his arms around her. Cass's consciousness wavered. She sluggishly shoved at his hands as he tried to peer at her wound.

"Ge'off," she mumbled, wincing when stubbornness to keep him away sent another bolt of pain flittering across her face.

A hot huff of air and a rough push at his back sent James's hat flying to the ground. He turned his gaze and met the muzzle of her horse.

The stallion tried to communicate with him, showing worry for his human sister in any way he could. Solo pawed at the dirt with a black hoof, nickering as he mouthed the loose curls around her face.

"I'm tryin', pal," he answered, brushing his fingers against the softness of the horse's cheek, surprised when Solo accepted the touch with another blow against James's shoulder. "She's gotta let me, though."

The heat of Cass's fever burned through the fabric of her clothing. James's stomach twisted when her hands stilled, and he could finally lift the blood-soaked cotton to peek at what lay beneath.

The puncture wound in her side was small, almost

nothing to write home about, but the flesh around it was angry and hot to the touch—infected, feeding her fever as it overtook her body from something so small as a blade from a dirty boot.

Solo's loyalty knew no bounds. Attuned to Cass's every need, he sank to his knees beside James without being asked. The good deputy slipped his grip around her lithe frame, careful not to touch the seeping injury, laying her over the saddle. He kept his hand balanced on the curve of her back as the horse drew to his feet, confident he could get her to the town surgeon before the fever progressed too far.

With Cass secured, James turned his attention to the other figure. Expertly tied at the wrists behind his back by the bounty hunter, he writhed and twisted in the dirt as the Deputy stepped closer.

James's hand twitched, reaching for the gun in his belt. He could kill him right there and then. He *should*. No one would be the wiser.

'Round the wooden grip his fingers curled, stopping only when Solo grumbled at his back.

James blinked past his fury at what Ball did to Cass, pulling himself away from the sea of his memories and the temptation to silence it all right there and then. He shifted his focus back to the task at hand—his duty as a deputy of Gallow Gorge.

The wind ruffled his hair. He looked at the dots of blinking lights in town and sighed. Time was wasting. Cass needed him.

Everything else could wait.

[7]

A FIRE BURNED INSIDE HER. NOT THE FEVER OF VENGEANCE she was used to. One that spurred her every movement and thought, pushing her toward a goal with nothing to distract her from what mattered.

No. This was a fever of a different sort, one that fogged her senses, wracking her body with a painful ache that surged and sent her spiraling. Cass had been sick before, but never like this.

Voices were everywhere—rushed, worried. Arms wrapped around her; firm, gentle, *safe*. Even as each drum of boots on wood were a hammer to her flesh.

"It's going to be okay, Cass. I've got you. Just hold on."

She wanted to argue. She wanted to push him away. Cass Callaghan was independent. Capable of any undertaking. She certainly didn't need *help*. Her lips parted; she tried to speak and lift her hands, but they were tied down by invisible, leaden ropes. All she managed was a wiggle of her fingers.

Let me down, and I'll walk.

"I need your help, Doc. Found her just outside of town. She's hurt pretty good."

"Lay her down right here, Deputy. Lemme take a look at her."

A cold, solid surface met her back. Cass shivered, trying in vain to stubbornly push the hands away as the layers of her duster and vest were peeled back. She was exposed, practically naked, when Lord knew who was looking.

Hands brushed her shoulder, a thumb's soft caress as a face hovered over her.

Cass blinked through the haze, meeting worried blue eyes, but only momentarily before he looked away.

Da?

"Think you'll be able to help her?"

That voice. Like smoke and honey.

Not Da. *Moone.*

"The infection is advanced, but you got her here in the nick of time, Moone. If we're successful, this girl will owe you her life."

"Better not tell her that."

Cass knew the cadence of it, the lyrical baritone of her favorite good deputy. His voice was so warm, sometimes—when she was in a good mood—it made her feel like butter melting on a bit of warm toast.

Not like she'd ever admit it to his face.

"M-Moone?" Cass croaked, lifting the deadweight of her arms with all the might she could muster, clamping her fingers around his wrist on her shoulder. "What... *happened?*"

His eyes snapped to her, mouth quivering with a quiet rush of relief. "You're real thick. Do you know that? I told you not to go."

"M'stubborn."

"Damn right you are, Cassidy," he murmured, pressing a hurried kiss to her feverish forehead.

"If you two are about done," Murray, the town surgeon, grumbled. "I've got to suture this wound. It will hurt, and I'd prefer to let her sleep through it."

"No!" Cass dug her fingertips into Moone's skin, pleading through the fevered haze. "I can take it."

"You don't have to." His warm waves hung low over his forehead, jaw clenched as he worked through things in his mind. He *knew* her. He knew she was strong. Giving her a nod, he looked to the doctor and answered, "I'll hold her steady."

He gripped her shoulders so firmly it almost hurt, attention woven with hers as they waited for the doctor to deliver on his promise. And, *oh*, he did.

The moment a dull needle pierced her fevered flesh, a white-hot bolt of pain cleaved through her, swelling the dull ache to something more frightening.

Cass's body canted. She held her breath, teeth clenched through the blinding pain. Another pierce of flesh ripped a mangled scream from her throat and bowed her back from the table as Moone tried to hold her still.

"*Don't leave*," she panted, changing her tune. She didn't want him. She *needed* him. She grasped at his sleeves, searching for purchase. As if his hands could contain multitudes and smother the pain.

His head sank closer, holding her gaze with a soft brush of his thumbs against her cheeks.

"Shh, hush now. It'll all be over soon. I've got you. You're not alone."

Another flash of pain sent tears streaming down her face and another sharp cry from her lips. Cass tried to center herself in Moone's eyes, but the agony of the poisonous infection only served to make each action by the doctor all

the more excruciating.

Cass hated it—despised that Moone saw her cry. She wasn't weak. She'd made a four-day ride in three with a man on her back and an oozing wound in her side. As a little girl, she fearlessly marched forward when she left Faraday Creek and the Callaghan Ranch behind and never looked back.

Cassidy Callaghan couldn't afford to be so feeble as a fever and a few stitches.

No, her quest demanded she be more resilient than the last trickle of a creek during a drought. Then, her parents would finally be at peace.

"*James!*" Cass cried through each lance of pain tearing through her frame, fisting her fingers in the fabric of his shirt and detesting the words as soon as they fell from her lips. "I can't do this. I'm not s-strong enough."

"You *can*. You've never given up on a damned thing your entire fucking life. Now, *breathe*."

Cass saw the way he looked at her, the way he worried about her. If she wasn't in blinding pain, part of her wanted to tease Moone that he might actually like her, but as soon as the thought crossed her mind, she was crying out and writhing again.

"She's moving too much, they'll tear." Murray's voice split the haze. "Take this."

All Cass had to go by was the look on Moone's face, the fleeting, conflicted bend of his brows before a whisper.

"I'm sorry."

The white rag covered her nose and mouth before she had a chance to argue, hands slapping at Moone's collar a moment before Cass found herself overwhelmed by the sickly-sweet scent of ether.

Her eyes drooped, hands falling as her vision faded to

black that pulled her deeper with each passing second until the pain fogged and memories swam through her mind.

SOMETHING WAS PULLING HER, TUGGING HER FORWARD BY her soul.

Hope.

Just the slightest flicker of it in her heart. Potent enough, she ached with the feeble wish that the listless body lying where the shadow of the church's steeple used to be, was merely sleeping.

"Mama." Her voice cracked as she tried to whisper her name. It was the first time she'd spoken in hours, having not uttered a word since her Da lowered her into the cellar.

She honored her promise to stay quiet and avoid being discovered. No matter what, Da said. She held his words in her mind, silently repeating them over and over like a prayer.

Even when his body landed on the boards above her, his blood freckling her face, Cassidy listened, not making a single peep until she called out for her mother. Even before all this, she was constantly calling for her.

She landed in the dirt with a huff, reaching out for Aisling with a trembling hand. Her fingers pulled on faded blue pinstriped cotton, rolling the woman into her lap. Cassidy choked out a sob. She didn't dare breathe as she brushed the curtain of dust-tinged copper curls from her mother's lovely face, assuming the worst when she met cold skin.

It couldn't be real. None of it. Aisling was sleeping. They were all sleeping.

Nightmares felt real before, curling around her like the wind of a midnight storm—over just as quickly. Cassidy brushed the back of her hand over freckles scattered across her Ma's cheek as Aisling did for her morning and night. Maybe, just maybe, Cassidy could wake her. Maybe she could slip away into the same sleep. Maybe they'd all be together again.

She closed her eyes, chin trembling. Her tears came free, and her mother's rarest lullaby fell from her mouth in a whisper. One of Erin's Isle—their home.

Cassidy imagined those rolling hills, wishing they'd never left. Maybe then, they'd still be together. Maybe then, they'd still be alive.

When she closed her eyes and sang the words, she saw herself there, hand in hand with her Ma as they wandered over emerald grasses. The wind whipped through their hair and tugged the hems of their dresses as her mother murmured stories of faeries that built houses in the stone crags—just how she always wished she would.

To her, it was a magical place where fairytales were real. One where her mother was a beautiful princess, swept off her feet by a handsome stable boy who defeated the jealous prince to whom the princess had been betrothed. Maybe that's where they were now, living happily ever after on the knoll as the wind kissed their skin.

She couldn't stay there forever; she knew that much. As sunlight slipped away behind the brightly painted clapboard

of the buildings that lined the Faraday Creek thoroughfare, Cassidy looked upon her mother's face for the last time.

Not until she was a woman, herself, and looked upon her in the mirror.

[8]

Moone

James needed something to do, an occupation of his mind. Else, he might go insane.

Something to stamp out the feeling of Cassidy limp in his arms on Doctor Murray's table. When he discovered her in the dirt, she was still well enough to argue with him. After he doused her pain with the taste of ether, she went leaden like the dead. Nothing stirred her. Not the surgeon's needle. Not even the sound of Lucas making himself useful battling against Lawrence Ball while he wrestled him into a cell across the street.

Moone thought he'd feel better once she woke, expecting the drug to wear away in less than an hour. He hovered at the end of the surgeon's bench, counting her freckles and eyelashes, waiting for her to wake and show him he hadn't sent his girl to an early grave by letting her chase this damned vendetta.

Wake up. Wake up. Wake up.

But an hour passed, then two. By the third, Doctor Murray insisted they'd have to wait for the infection to pass. She might not wake until then, if at all.

Days, he said. It could take *days* until James was sure she'd be alright.

Until then, he'd stand watch as he was duty-bound by his badge; as he was duty-bound to his bleeding heart.

He thought for sure he'd rid himself of it a long time ago, but there it was, beating, lurching, *aching* when he insisted on carrying her listless frame up the stairs of The Copper Queen.

It'd been out of necessity that he'd done away with it, but Cassidy Callaghan had gone and made it grow back three sizes bigger than it'd been before. She made him want things he never considered; things he knew he couldn't have. At least, not now, not with her so tethered to her need for vengeance or him beholden to a master of his own.

The news of what happened to Cassidy spread like wildfire through Gallow Gorge, even at the late hour.

Katie Mays appeared in the hotel room within moments of their arrival. Her brown eyes welled up at the sight of Cassidy, broken, bruised, and bloody. She snapped to attention, rolling up her sleeves as she demanded he find her hot water and soap.

He was thankful for another task, even if her reason for it banished him from the room as she tended to Cassidy in a way he wouldn't dare witness. Not yet, not until something changed for them, too.

That's not to say he wasn't willing to strip away her layers and reverently draw away earth and blood. It was all he could think about as he returned his borrowed gelding and bribed Solo with a handful of sugar cubes to let him remove his tack.

He even got as far as currying the stallion until his ebony coat gleamed in the lamplight, telling him all the while that his human sister would be fine after a few days' rest.

But she wasn't fine.

Nothing, no one, would scrub away the sight of her looking so sick, *so small*, in that bed. There wasn't a drink that'd ease the smell of her blood when Doctor Murray filled a ceramic basin with it over and over until Moone thought he might be sick himself.

He insisted it was to remove whatever caused her fever from within. But as days passed, and Cassidy still hadn't awakened, an infection of a different kind took root within James.

Anger churned like a bellow-fed furnace—a slow, steady rage tingling in his fingertips.

Fury that Ball did something so dirty when Cass was more than capable of bringing him in—even *if* he'd been a handful. Irritation she was so stupid, so reckless to let Ball get the jump on her.

All of it, her injury, the fever, the fucking *worry*, James had no room for it—and it was only the start. It wasn't too late, though. He could stop things before they got too far out of hand.

Another part of him knocked at the door in the back of his mind. It *pounded*. The darkness of his past licked at the edges of his vision; the ghost of that other life awakened by the evening's events. It beat like a drum, blaring louder and louder as he watched the surgeon bleed Cassidy dry.

He couldn't stand to carry another man's sins any longer. He wouldn't be the blade another hand wielded. Not if this was the cost. Not if he had to give another piece of himself away.

As it turned out, James liked having a heart. He loved how it did the strangest things when Cassidy strolled into

town. Damn it all if he was ever forced to throw it away again. To hell if it'd break with the loss of her because of this rotten bastard.

Moone would kill the fucker if he had to.

He smiled, humming. What a marvelous thought that was.

James struck a match along the wall as he strode through the muted light of the lonely oil lamp in the Sheriff's office, lighting the tip of his cigar as he stared at the back of a cell.

Lucas Smith eyed him warily, more sober than Moone had ever seen him. "Callaghan alive?"

"For now," he answered, taking a deep drag as he glowered at the man-shaped shadow. "No thanks to him."

"Good." Lucas's mouth thinned. "I'm glad."

Moone's brows rose. "Don't go all maudlin on us, now. Cassidy won't know what to think if she comes to."

His stomach took a sour twist. *When*. When she woke up. She was too stubborn not to. And Moone didn't know what he'd do if he didn't have her to anchor his heart to any longer.

"This one's been among the willows for a bit too long. Heard all the things. Never seen his face until now. She did us all a favor findin' him. Say what you will about ladies dabbling in the law, but she still don't deserve to die for it." He motioned at the scabbed-over cuts on his ruddy cheeks. "Not like I probably deserved this. Or the rope this fella is bound to get by the end of the week."

James took another drag before motioning at Ball, hoping the smoke would cloud his surprise at Lucas's admission. "You have a bone to pick with Doc, here?"

"I'm not. I don't," he argued, unable to meet his eye. "It just don't sit right with me what he did to her, is all."

"Well." Moone held the cigar between his teeth and tugged open the desk drawer where Lucas sat. "I can assure you, Deputy Smith"—twirling a set of keys 'round his finger, he met the man's gaze in the cell—"Lawrence Ball will get *exactly* what he deserves."

He had the bastard's attention, then.

Ball glared. "What are you two on about?"

"What's your plan?" Lucas Smith eyed him warily. "Do you want me to take a stroll?"

Moone teetered on the edge between wanting to follow the law to the letter and making Ball disappear, to start where he wished he'd left him—in the desert to die. But that'd only bring chaos, just as he worried it would.

James didn't want the wrath of Jack Ransom to burn everything down, not when he could do the same and take efficacious payment for what'd been done. Maybe he'd use it to wash his hands of all he'd done before. Maybe he could start over and finally be the good man Cassidy seemed convinced he was.

A good deputy, she called him.

If only that was the case.

"Stick around, Lucas." He jangled the key in the lock and swung open the door. "I need a witness."

"A witness?" Ball chuffed, laughter sticking in his throat when a flicker of recognition flittered over his angular features. "You won't kill me."

Moone reached out, noting how his prisoner was paralyzed in his shadow. *Good.* James was barely a man when he saw Doc last. There was no guarantee Ball would remember who he'd been, the weapon he'd become all those years ago.

But he did. Lawrence recalled how James scorched his

soul until it was blacker than the night sky. Until there wasn't a single star left.

Not until she appeared on the horizon, gleaming as brightly as Venus in dusk's dusty glow.

"Oh, I won't have to kill you." His mouth lifted, a grim smile stretching when he stole the faded blue bandana from Ball's neck. He twisted it around his knuckles. There was no sense in breaking a hand, even if he decided to beat him to hell. And if Ransom's fucking mark was so important a symbol, James would paint it red. "But—I do want to know why."

"Why I stabbed the bitch?" Ball leaned away, brow furrowing, eyes darting to Moone's fist.

"No," he answered, glancing over his shoulder at Lucas. "You were always the slipperiest. The biggest wretch. Why you'd bring a dirty blade from your boot to a gunfight isn't a mystery. A fight you knew she'd win unless you didn't play fair. But that's the other thing… of all I know Jack Ransom to be, even as the Scourge of the West, he's an honor-bound man. Is that why he sent you to Lonely Bellow to hide out? Did he find out what a lying sack of shit you are and finally send his favorite away?"

"You and I both know I've never been the favorite." Ball swallowed hard. "I was looking for shit about Dusty Fulton before heading back to Sacramento after Cold Creek. I got to playing the tables and lost track of time. Until—"

"—she came and dug you out."

A shiver crawled down Moone's spine. He didn't expect Ball to give him a name, let alone one he recognized. One look told him Lucas heard it, too; witness for this, for now. For the unexpected details before he delivered a beating his fists ached to carry out from the moment he found Cassidy in the dirt.

From the second Ball hammered *him* into the dirt a decade before.

Moone sucked in a steadying breath, staring at the blue bandana around his hand.

"The Sheriff sends his regards." He slowly lifted his gaze to meet Ball's, noting how his shrewd eyes widened a breath before James's fist collided with the sharp edges of his face.

He landed in a heap, wheezing on battered wooden planks.

Moone stared down at Ball's heaving lump. "You tell *him* I'm coming."

Hell would come with him—a vengeance of his own.

Moone would burn it all down and finally be rid of the bloody legacy he never chose to have.

[9]

IT FELT LIKE A DREAM. HEAVEN, MAYBE. HAD SHE FINALLY died? It wasn't what she daydreamed it'd be, far away from those white cliffs and emerald moors. Softer, warmer, more musical, maybe.

The muted twang of a piano and the muffled echo of voices blew in through an open window, ruffling the curtains hanging from the pane, casting the swirl of tobacco smoke into a spin that followed the breeze.

Cassidy rubbed her eyes, sure what she saw was some sort of desert apparition because—sitting in a chair by the window with his hat slung low over his forehead—was James Moone.

She pushed herself to sit, hissing when a piercing pain in her side reminded her of her last waking memory.

The sound woke the good deputy, whose blue eyes grew wide as he gave her a boyish smile. "Hey there, Freckles. I was wondering when you would finally wake up."

She sat up further, squinting in the bright light. Her head pulsed like she'd been a bottle deep the night before. "What happened?"

"You didn't listen to me. That's what happened," he answered, drawing himself to stand with a slow stretch of his broad shoulders before perching on the bed beside her. "I warned you it would be dangerous, didn't I? Lucky for you, that damned horse of yours wouldn't give up until we got you some help." Moone paused. A shadow passed over his eyes. His mouth quivered, but only briefly before he met her gaze again. "You gave us a right scare."

"Us?" Cass quipped with a half-smile.

"Me. You gave *me* a good scare." Moone loosed a stuttering sigh, attention combing over her from head to toe like he couldn't decide which part of her he wanted to take in first. The sound of it stirred something strange in the pit of her stomach. She'd never let herself feel anything like it, especially for someone as much of a pain in the ass as James Moone. But when Cass remembered how he held her steady on the surgeon's table, she allowed herself a little. Just once.

"I'm sorry." She stared at her hands, twisting the blanket with a bite of her lip. Anger festered in the back of her mind—a bitterness that she'd let her guard down long enough for Ball to get in close. "I had the bastard. I really did."

Moone shook his head, skeptical, a look painted in *I told you so*. "He got the jump on you, though."

"Yeah, but not until the first night of the ride back. That cheatin' son of a bitch." She grimaced as she brushed a curtain of freshly cleaned copper curls away from her waist and skimmed the ghost of her touch over where Ball stabbed her. "He had a knife hidden in his boot."

"You shoulda checked him." Moone's answer was curt, plush lips bent into a scowl.

"I was cocky, I'll admit it. I didn't think he'd try anything

after the whoopin' I gave him in Lonely Bellow or the one I'm gonna give when I question him with you." Cass's anger simmered in her fingertips as she ran them over the ghost of a bruise across her knuckles.

She wasn't a stranger to a fight or the marks she'd carry with her the day that followed. Only, the evidence left behind wasn't the mottled purple of something fresh. No, they bore the yellowish hue of something nearly healed. But it took days for that to happen. There was no way she'd been asleep that long.

"How long have I been out?"

He scrubbed the back of his neck, working his jaw.

"Your fever was bad. I put you here because Doc Murray said you'd need the care. He bloodlet you so many times those first couple days to get rid of the infection; I was afraid he would drain the red straight outta your hair. So, I stayed here and stood watch. I didn't want you to be alone."

Cass swallowed the sudden lump in her throat. "You've been here?"

He nodded. "Yeah."

"Who's been down at the station watching Ball?" Cass sat forward and cast a waterfall of auburn curls over her freckled face, heart pounding when Moone stared at his boots. "Where is Lawrence Ball, Moone?"

The good deputy rose, striding back to his perch by the window, like he needed some space to break the bad news. It was always bad news.

"I'm sorry, Cass. Ball escaped two days ago."

[10]

# CASSIDY

"WHAT DO YOU MEAN, *ESCAPED?*" CASSIDY LUNGED from the bed. Her clothes were nowhere to be found. Someone dressed her in a thin shift that fell just past her knees and wouldn't stay put over her shoulder. Had it always been so fucking cold in here, or did her fever stick to her skin with this sudden chill?

She pushed past the feeling, snatching a shawl draped at the end of the bed. It'd keep her warm enough for now, for what she needed to do. She twisted it around her shoulders, eyes darting around the room as Moone drawled out an answer.

"Gone, Cass. Long gone. Sometime in the night."

"And you were here with me, huh?" Cass ground out. "Some man of the law you are. Who knew *I* was the real prisoner in this situation? You realize *he* had the bounty on his head, right? Which, by the way, you owe me fifty fucking dollars when I get back."

Moone rose to his feet, eyes dark. "What do you mean *when you get back?*"

"You're a daft fool if you think I'm staying here another

second. Ball is gone, and I've wasted too much time sleeping." Cass spun, gaze snapping from corner to corner of the room. "Where in the hell are my gun belts?"

"Cassidy, quit it." Moone gripped her shoulders, crowding her with his warmth. Such wonderful warmth. "Get back in the fucking bed. You need to rest."

Her skin prickled at the contact, but she wouldn't give in to the distraction. There was too much to do, too much at stake.

"The hell I do." She shrugged him off, shoving against his chest as hard as she could muster.

Moone stared down at her, as tall and immovable as a mighty oak. He crossed his arms, frowning. She was a petulant child he was patiently waiting to tire.

He jerked his chin over her shoulder, wearing a cocky smirk. "If you need 'em so bad, they're in the wardrobe behind you. But I'm telling you, Cass. You won't make it far out of town before I have to come collect you."

"Collect me? What are you, my father?" Cass bit, wrenching open the doors, wearing a momentary victorious smile when she found the gold-flecked pearl handles of her pistols. She promptly wound them over her hips, never mind that she was not *at all* dressed to set off into the desert.

Maybe it was the fever. Perhaps her desperation of being so close to Ransom kept her from caring how she looked. All that mattered was that she leave—quickly.

"I have news for you, James Moone. My Da's dead. I'm not exactly looking for a replacement family at the present." She jabbed a finger in his chest. "I am *fine* on my own. It's been that way for years, and I don't need anyone else. 'Specially you. Got it?"

Moone held up his palms in mock surrender, but his

smirk remained as she tugged the shawl tighter and went out the door. "Yeah, I got it."

The Copper Queen's afternoon crowd grew louder once she broke the door's seal. She cast a quick glance back at Moone, who oh-so-casually leaned against the bedpost.

Did he have to be so fucking patient, kind enough to let her have her moment without interfering? Did he have to act like he cared?

Too many eyes tracked her from the saloon below, but she'd have to grit her teeth and deal with the unwanted attention. Cass hissed, holding her side as she staggered against the maroon-papered wall down the staircase.

Chairs screeched. Four different men leaped to their feet, rushing to help. But before a single one laid a finger on her, Cass yanked a pistol from its holster.

"Take another step, and I'll blow a hole in your boot," she snapped, swaying when a wave of dizziness and pain took an iron hold of her senses.

"Miss Callaghan, we're just trying to help." A brave soul tiptoed closer. He was handsome, with dark eyes, black hair, and tanned skin—not much older than her. She'd seen him time and again, one of those faces whose looks lingered longer than the others. Cass wondered then, what if it'd been friendliness, not disdain?

That didn't do much to sway her. Even as her barrel trembled with the effort it took to hold it aloft, Cass held firm to her stubbornness.

"I don't need anyone's help," she wheezed through gritted teeth, staggering one foot after the other towards the door. Another pair of men hovered between her and the sunshine outside. She swung her pistol at them. Her grip started to waver.

"It seems like you might," another murmured.

The bastards were belittling her. They had to be. Handling her with kid gloves because she was a girl. Usually, they were smarter than that, deterred by a glare from beneath her brim. Cass knew she looked like hell, barefoot with her hair cascading down her back and little clothing to keep her looking modest—a weak *Miss Callaghan* was all they saw.

"Let her go," Moone's baritone called from the balcony above.

Everyone turned toward the Deputy, even Cass. Their eyes met, and for a moment, she was grateful. Especially when the men barricading her escape route backed away, keeping a respectful distance.

Cass put the pistol in its holster, lifting her free hand to block out the light when she stepped onto the arcade. It took a moment to gather her bearings as the whole of Gallow Gorge looked on with pity and disgust. Normally, she'd relish the thought that she sent the rhythm of the farrier's hammer off-kilter, but this was different. Different and awful. She couldn't be weak. She *wasn't* weak.

She paid them little mind, planting one bare foot after the other into the street, sighing when hot, dusty earth shifted between her toes.

In the livery one street over, Cass swore Solo knew she was coming for him. She smiled through her pain-fueled fog when a loud whinny rang over the din. It was a rope, towing her inch by inch. Her heart ached for her brother, her truest friend. Sometimes, family was who you chose. Solo chose *her*, and she didn't need or want anyone else.

While her heart and spirit wanted to run for the hills and chase Ball down, her body betrayed her before she made it halfway to the next street. The faintest bit of strength she mustered to get out of bed began to fade. She walked her hands along the weathered clapboard between two buildings, blinking through the pain and haze.

She was hardheaded, she knew it—a fact James Moone never missed an opportunity to point out. But she was too close to the stables to give up, turn back, and admit to his face he'd been right about her needing to rest.

The anxious stallion grew louder with each labored breath Cass took. The sound shifted to the throaty nickers of a happy horse as she murmured a breathless, *I'm comin'* and stepped through the livery door.

"Hey, sweet thing," she croaked, brushing her fingertips against the star on Solo's forehead. Relief flooded her, head swimming as he pushed into her. "I'm so sorry for leaving you."

The sable stallion gave another nudge with a quiet nicker, just enough pressure to send Cass swaying on her feet, consumed by the exhaustion she'd been battling.

She staggered, vision hazy, breaths shallow, pressing her back to the wall as she sank to the floor of Solo's stall.

"M'fine," she mumbled, closing her eyes when he rubbed his muzzle against her cheek. Cass smiled when Solo spoke to her in his way, communicating his version of the harrowing tale—most of which were complaints of being stuck in the livery.

"You did good getting help. Was he the one who put you in here?"

Solo answered with a low vocalization.

"Well now." Cass sighed, letting out a low huff of laughter when the Mustang sank to his knees and laid his head in her lap. She rubbed his neck and relaxed against the wood at her back. "I suppose Deputy Moone has treated us

real nice the last few days, hasn't he?"

Cass's vision started to clear. Maybe in more ways than one.

Moone warned her. Cass berated him, pushing him away every chance she got. Between the two of them, she was the bigger pain in the ass.

And yet—*and yet*—Moone was the kindest friend to her without four legs.

True, she'd ended up in a cell at his hands more times than she could count, but it was never for anything she didn't deserve. Moone was probably more lenient because of their friendship.

Yes, friends. They were at least that much.

Cass carded the ribbons of Solo's mane through her fingers, thinking how Moone had watched over her when she had arrived back in Gallow Gorge. Never before, not since her parents, had anyone given a damn the way he did.

Maybe he had a point. Maybe he had her best interest at heart. Maybe she ought to listen.

Still, her need for justice for her family and the people of Faraday Creek was more potent than any other feeling. No matter how willing she was to listen to Moone and stay put, to rest and heal, Cass knew that she'd be taking up chase as soon as she was well enough.

"Gee, if I'd known that getting the two of you in one place would finally make you sit still, I woulda brought Solo straight upstairs at The Copper Queen," a deep voice drawled from the doorway.

Cass rolled her eyes as best she could, but they so badly wanted to close and drape her in another profound sleep. Still, she couldn't prevent her smile from blooming when James Moone stepped into the stall and slid down the wall beside her. She sighed when his shoulder brushed against hers. She didn't mean to, but the touch was so welcoming and warm. It only made her want to go straight back to bed.

"Careful now. Last I checked, you and Solo weren't on the friendliest terms. You told me you value your fingers too much." Cass meant it as a joke, but it came tumbling out in half a choked whisper. One so unlike her when Moone leaned in and brushed his hand over the top of hers to rub the stallion's star.

"Nah, me and Solo are old pals, aren't we?"

Solo answered with a nicker and a swish of his tail that made them laugh. But the momentary, effervescent energy settled as the gravity of what happened swooped back in.

"*Cassidy*." Moone's voice was low, tinged with the same worry when his face hovered over hers on the surgeon's table. His hand settled on her knee's freckled curve, a touch that simultaneously anchored her and sent her floating. But that was probably the fever.

"I know." Cass lifted her gaze to meet his with as much sincerity as someone like her could muster. Her heart fluttered when the pad of his thumb skimmed across the constellations on her skin, but she banished the thought as quickly as it arrived. Try as she might, no matter how she tried to chase them away, the damned thing skipped a beat again and again. That was probably the fever, too.

From his touch on her knee to the warmth of his body molded to hers, Cass was sure that if she hadn't been bloodletted to high heaven over the last couple of days, there would surely be an unbecoming rosy flush in her cheeks.

"I know I need to stay." Cass stared at the straw-strewn floor. "But you know I'm going after him as soon as possible, right?"

Moone nodded, squeezing. "I do."

"Did he, *did you*… did you get a chance to talk to him before he slipped out? Did he say anything?"

Moone stiffened. He was quiet, crease bent between his brows, lips thin. "He did."

Cass pitched forward, jostling his palm from her knee. "And?"

"Tell you what, Cassidy. You let me take you to bed, and I'll consider telling you. There's no way I'm giving you any details with you this close to your horse. Can't risk you riding off again. Look what happened already."

Cass put on her sweetest smile, attempting her best eyelash flutter. "Aw, come on. It wasn't that bad, Moone."

He chuckled, but the worried valley between his brows didn't go away. "Sure, it could've been worse, but forgive me for saying that this isn't exactly what I had in mind when having a roll in the hay with you, Cassidy."

"Fine," she groaned, patting Solo on the cheek.

Cass rose from the floor with the stallion's help, twining her fingers in his mane. As soon as she was on her own two feet again, her head felt a little lighter, her vision a little hazier, and her legs like nothing at all.

Cass's eyes fluttered shut.

"*Shit.*" Moone snapped to attention, slipping a hand around her waist when her legs buckled.

Her head lolled against his broad shoulder, breath catching when her fingers skimmed the barest threads of chest hair through an open button of his shirt.

Cass found his face with a sleepy grin, letting her touch linger as he lowered her to the floor. "What do they feed you back home, Moone?"

"Oh, you know"—Moone tucked a ribbon of hair

behind her ear—"mostly whiskey. It's a wonder you're as skinny as you are when we've been raised on the same diet."

They shared a laugh, but it fell flat when Moone's face sobered.

"You're not gonna make it back to The Copper Queen like this… and you can't stay in the livery." Days of worry etched deep into his skin. All of it, his care and the insistence to keep doing it, stirred that same foreign feeling in her.

"Why not?" Cass argued, noting the sunlight seeping through the window. How dust danced along the beam, or how it all lit the gentle wave of Moone's hair. She'd always considered it closer to the color of trough water. But like this, the way it caught the light made it burn like raw, unpolished gold.

"I'm afraid they only allow pain-in-the-ass horses, Cassidy. No pain-in-the-ass people." He gave her one of those not-smiles, where the corner of his mouth tugged upward by an invisible thread.

She answered with a playful, pretend nicker. "Their loss. I'm a right treasure."

"To me, you are." Moone sighed, rising to his feet, shrugging the worn jacket from his shoulders. "And, because of that, I'm going to save your damn pride by carrying you out instead of letting you faint in the street and carrying you then. Got it?"

"I suppose," Cass conceded, nodding toward his jacket. "What's that for?"

Moone's gaze darkened, sliding down her body. "You're nearly naked, Cassidy. I'm not about to let all of Gallow Gorge get another look at you if I can help it."

"You think I care about a little thing like that?" she teased, swaying like a tree in the wind as he draped warmed

leather around her slender shoulders.

"Yeah." His face was grave, strong brows hovering low over cornflower with a purse of his lips. "I think you care a whole lot about this town respecting you, Cassidy. You've always worked damn hard for everyone to see you a certain way. This quest of yours with Ball has made you stupider than usual." Moone gave her a look when she started to argue. "I'm not trying to be mean, but you plowing out into the middle of the street in nothing but a shift and your gun belts wasn't exactly your most fearsome moment, Freckles."

Cass bristled. "I'm sure those hens are already clucking, spreading lies about me, about what happened."

"Give them more credit. They understand what happened more than you think." Moone stood and extended a hand. "But, no. Seeing their feared, *respected* bounty hunter gone a little crazier than normal isn't what they expect to see when you ought to be holed up in bed. So—you're going to shut up. You're going to listen to me for once in your goddamn life, and you're going to let me carry you straight back to bed, where you will *stay* until you're feeling more yourself. You got that?"

Cass looked from Moone's stern gaze to his proffered hand, sighing as she rolled over his words. Maybe what she did wasn't the wisest choice. What did she think she would accomplish barefoot with nothing on her back but thin cotton and no idea where to start looking for her escaped bounty?

With Ball four days long gone and a robust eastward wind, it was wishful thinking to imagine there'd be much of a trail to follow—even if Cass was well enough for a long-ass ride.

Moone was right. She was in no state to travel.

Her fingers slipped beneath the weight of his coat, brushing against the tender flesh of her injury. She hissed when her fingernail caught the edge of a suture, reminded again of the ordeal when Moone brought her back into town.

She'd never forget his hands holding her steady or his repeated whispers that she wasn't alone. The more she thought about it, the less sure she was that she could do it alone if it happened again.

What an odd feeling to realize Cass might *need* him, someone other than herself. She prided herself on her independence—a lone wolf, part of no pack except the one she and Solo made. Families could be taken away in the blink of an eye, and Cass had no use for the longing ache those sorts of attachments—and losing them—would bring her.

Until James Moone.

ℬEFORE

THERE WERE TINY TREASURES IN EVERY CORNER OF THE Callaghan's cabin. Precious memories stolen away from a different life.

Silver salt and pepper shakers, a bottle of perfume that still held a drop or two. A green silk ribbon and a white taffeta gown Aisling wore for her wedding. There were others, priceless in a way the diamond ring on that ribbon could never compare to.

From the gingham curtains Aisling proudly stitched together to the homely table where Cassidy used to scratch out C-a-s-s-i-d-y K-a-t-h-l-e-e-n on parchment with a bit of graphite as Ma hummed over the fire. Even the pasture just outside held more value.

Merely a patch of earth where she shot tin cans off a post, the memory of her Da's hand on her shoulder was irreplaceable. Those lessons he'd whisper in her ear— promises anchored in her soul. The songs that had her burning with curiosity to know more. All of it. Her. Them. Home.

Now, it would never feel like home again.

Still, it was safe enough, and Cassidy barely made it inside as coyotes sang at her back. She didn't mean to; she just followed her feet away from the slaughter in Faraday Creek—and found herself there. Under a patchwork quilt, she collapsed from the relief and the warmth.

She imagined those treasures of Aisling's, of *sean-nós* the two of them would sing together. Maybe there were secrets she didn't understand. Some she'd never find out now they were gone. There, Cassidy slept with her mother's smell woven into cotton on her nose, the stories in her mind, and their song in her heart.

But danger wasn't far away.

Voices drew her from a fitful sleep with a start. She dared not move a muscle, listening for them again in case they were only in her head.

Met with silence, she wondered if it had all been a bad dream. A figment of a little girl's imagination—the same one who imagined lords and ladies strolling down Faraday Creek's bridleway. As if at any moment, Aisling and her lovely smile would stride through the door with a warm, 'Good mornin'.

But it wasn't a dream. Her nightmares from the day before were real, and the voices were too.

"One of yous get in there and check the place. Ain't gon get paid 'til Ransom knows there's nowhere left to look."

"Make him do it, I gotta take a piss."

"Dammit Smitty. You make evry'thing difficult." A pause. "Well, go on. Ya heard 'im."

Footsteps sent Cassidy bolting from the bed. She slid beneath it as the front door creaked open. They slowly tread through the kitchen, followed by the slow clink of dishes set to dry the morning before.

Cassidy held her breath, her Da's last words to her ironclad in her mind. She pressed trembling palms to dusty floorboards. Panic rose within her when the boots came into sight. They moved across the room, pausing to rifle in a trunk beneath the window. She saw a flash of her mother's green ribbon and the glimmer of her secret ring as it was stuffed in a pocket.

She wanted to argue, to say it was a sin to steal, but when they twisted in her direction, she feared her death wasn't far away. She hadn't even made a sound.

Closer and closer they came, each footfall slower than the last until they were close enough that Cassidy could reach out and mark a clean stripe in the dust with the tip of her finger. She wanted to cry out, to scream for help when the stranger sank to their knees. To Cassidy's surprise, she looked back at the face of a boy not much older than she, blue eyes shadowed with pity.

"Ay, boyo! Rattle yer hocks, we been here too long! Did ya find it?" A voice called from the front door. Close. Too close. The boy's attention snapped away, then slid right back to her.

He held a finger to his lips, nodding before calling over his shoulder. "It's not here."

Cassidy held her breath, clamping both hands over her mouth as he stood up and out of sight. His boots turned away, back to whoever called him before they ventured inside and discovered her. The chorus of voices—maybe three or four—continued, punctuated with sharp snorts from their horses and the jangle of rusty spurs.

"You better have been real thorough, Jimbo."

"I told you not to call me that."

"As long as the boss is makin' me babysit ya, I'll call you

what I wants to. Like I said, you better have combed the place real good."

"What'd he expect us to find, I reckon'?"

"Some ring, but does it matter? The boss said to check, so we check."

"Should we burn it?"

"Nah. We're bound to pass this way again on our way back to Ballarat. We'll bring a wagon for the rest. Might make use of them taters in the cellar. Boss'll wanna comb through the town and take anythin' we might be able to use before we head up to Sacramento."

"Lord knows he's already headed that way, leavin' all the work for us."

"Watch yer mouth, Ball. Don't fer'get what he's done for us—more than enough to pay for your loyalty. I ain't gon' hear ya say another peep 'bout it, or it might make it to the wrong ears, ya understand?"

Cassidy heard the huff of horses and a snap of the reins. Hooves beat the earth, growing farther and farther away until she was sure it was safe to finally emerge.

She couldn't stay. They'd be back, and she'd been lucky they hadn't fired the house and barn right then. Nothing would stop them from doing it once they returned.

With a bag and few possessions on her back, Cassidy went west. She followed her feet as the sun climbed high, casting a shadow on her old life, her old home. The memory of what was and never would be again.

She'd follow her Da's advice. She'd remember everything he taught her. She'd survive, and maybe one day, she'd return as the woman she was bound to become.

[11]

EVEN AFTER A WEEK, THE ACHE IN CASS'S SIDE LINGERED. She tried to appear like the hard-hearted bounty hunter, her regular frown firmly in place. Especially since all of Gallow Gorge watched her stumble from the Copper Queen a few days earlier in nothing but a shift, her gun belts, and wild hair. But it was a lie.

Something in her shifted when she was on that table and asleep in a bed with James Moone watching.

Tucked in the shadow of the arcade, Cass slipped her fingers beneath her shirt and brushed against the puckered pink flesh. Doctor Murray removed the stitches the day before.

She shuddered, reminded of the jagged sting of Doc Ball's dirty blade. The fever overtook her quicker than she expected, and if it weren't for James Moone (and Solo, too), she'd probably be dead.

Cass was nearly giddy when Murray declared her healed enough to ride but shrank like a scolded child when he followed his statement with a stern warning not to push too hard.

She wanted to argue, to insist she could head off on her quest, come what may. But she was silenced by Moone, who'd agreed with the doctor and promptly promised to keep her in line.

A southern wind flicked loose copper curls around her shoulders as she fiddled with her hat. Cass kept a keen eye on the good deputy—*too good*, in her opinion—as he stepped around the corner from the farrier, leading a freshly shoed Solo and brown filly. After everything, she still didn't understand.

At first, Cass couldn't put her finger on why Moone lingered so close when she'd returned from Lonely Bellow. They were friends, sure, but the way he hung around and watched her every move was different than their typical brand of tomfoolery. It felt like—

No. Cassidy knew precisely what it was, the things he was thinking when he looked at her lately. She wouldn't let herself consider it. She wouldn't even let herself entertain the idea. It was a preposterous and unnecessary thing. An attachment Cass didn't have time to want. There was a job to do, and she was determined to see it through—*without* distractions.

Moone was bound to be one. He insisted upon tagging along to Sacramento. Naturally, it wasn't without protest from her. How could a deputy freely leave their post?

"The sheriff gave his blessing," he'd said.

Cass would just have to take his word for it.

The ride would take a few days as they headed north, and he'd taken it upon himself to prepare for their journey. Cass lingered in the periphery, sure he knew she watched him, illustrated by how he squared his shoulders and the tiniest quirk of his mouth.

Smug bastard.

With the wind at her back, she stepped onto the dirt, placing her hat on the crown of her head. Sidestepping a horse and buggy as it rattled by in front of her, she fell into step beside Solo, brushing her hand over his silky coat before grabbing the reins from Moone's grip.

"Can we get outta here yet?" Cass quipped with a perturbed pout.

He rolled his eyes. "Patience isn't your strong suit, is it?"

"You'd be surprised." She followed him to tie off the horses before Booker General Goods. "Been waiting this long for your ass to pack everything, haven't I?"

But Cass *was* patient, waiting her entire life for this journey, for the chance to bring her family to justice. Now, she was unbearably close, and that patience was starting to waver.

Moone paused in the doorway, a cheeky smile on his face as he perched a cigar between his teeth. "Don't worry, Freckles. I won't be long."

Solo pushed her shoulder with an affectionate nicker. She palmed his muzzle, laughing when he blasted the hat off her head with a huff of hot air.

"Don't tell me you're fond of him." Cass shook her head, kissing his nose, when a small voice stirred her attention.

"Miss Callaghan?"

The redhead spun on the heel of her boot and found a pigtailed Daisy Booker, fresh from the schoolhouse with a crisp white pinafore and Cass's gambler in her hand.

"Hey there, Miss Daisy." Cass motioned toward it. "Thanks for snaggin' this for me."

"You're welcome." The little girl gave her a toothy grin, holding it aloft.

Cass knelt, dipping with a broad smile as the little girl placed the black hat back on the crown of her head.

"Well done." She nodded, pulling on the brim with a smile.

She didn't know what to call the strange thump of her heart, the fondness of it that bloomed whenever she saw her. Maybe it was the image of herself, the memory of what was. Or maybe what might've been if things were different and she'd ever had a sister.

If she'd ever have a daughter, too.

Daisy's eyes fell to her black boots. She drew a stripe in the dirt with her toe as she reached into her pinafore pocket. "I got somethin' new for ya, but don't tell my Pa."

"Cross my heart and hope to die." Cass traced an X on her chest and crouched to the girl's level. She breathed a shaky sigh when Daisy placed a copy of the well-sought-after book *Jane Eyre* in her palm. Her eyes stung at the sweet gesture, despite trying to hold it in.

Cass tucked it to her heart, voice thin. "I surely don't know what I did to deserve this, Miss Daisy. Where'd you get it?"

"It don't matter much, Miss Callaghan."

"*Doesn't.*" Cass flipped one of the little girl's braids. "And call me Cassidy. That's what my friends would do if I had any."

"*Doesn't.* Right." Daisy nodded, smile melting away, brown eyes growing wide as she whispered, "I hope you find that bad man, Cassidy."

Cass cocked her head, puzzled. "How'd you know about that?"

Daisy shrugged. "Heard it somewhere. They said you were gettin' close, and that man who hurt 'cha was your ticket to findin' that bad man. I'm sorry he got away."

Every part of her tingled, a sudden swell of cold that hit straight to her core. How could Daisy Booker, of all people, know what Cass was after? It wasn't like she blabbed about it to everyone wandering through town. She'd only ever told Moone and Katie the barest of details.

No one on earth knew what truly happened except Jack Ransom and her.

Cass shoved the feeling down, banishing the flush of her surprise. Her trauma wasn't something she should've carried as a little girl. She certainly wouldn't let it weigh on someone so sweet as Daisy.

"Don't you worry about that." Cass fondly knocked her chin with her knuckle. "I'm real good at finding people who don't wanna be found, and it's his turn. Soon, it'll all be over, and you and I can open a library once it is."

"I'd like that." Daisy beamed, bouncing on the balls of her feet like a jack rabbit about to leap away, especially when her father's booming voice echoed out onto the street from the General Store. "Good luck in Sacramento!"

The little girl darted away in a flash of freckles and pigtails, skipping by Moone on her way through the door.

He ambled by, wearing an amused grin as Cass watched the little girl perch on a stool by the window.

"What is it?" he asked, hoisting a canvas bag of supplies into a saddlebag.

"She reminds me of someone," Cass breathed, blinking away rose-colored memories to take away Moone's haul before he could make a mess of things. He chuffed when she pried a can of beans from his hand, carefully loading it inside. There'd be no wasted space, no wasted moment on her watch.

Her mind returned to Daisy's worries for her, no matter how she tried to keep it away. She secured the leather flap, attention sliding to Moone. "She knew where we were going. *And* why."

Moone lifted a brow. "Was it some big secret?"

"Not really," Cass conceded, frowning. Not a secret, no, but she'd done her best to keep the people of Gallow Gorge at arm's length. Knowing her goal like she'd published some manifesto felt too close. Too much like a family waiting in the wings, wishing her luck, hoping she'd succeed. She didn't have any use for it. She didn't want it. None of it. "I hate that they talk about me like they know me. Nobody knows me, not really."

"But I do, Cassidy." He squeezed her shoulder. "You've done a lot for the people 'round these parts. People talk. They put two and two together. They aren't as dumb as you think they are. Except me, right?"

"Right," she grumbled, sighing as she looked down the street, moving from face to face of the townspeople from whom she kept her distance, convinced they didn't give two shits about her. Cass was good at keeping to her different corners, less than friendly when someone got too close.

Moone knocked his shoulder against hers. "Like it or not, Freckles, the people of this town care about you."

"Sure they do," she argued, biting the inside of her cheek when she met a passing young man's smile, cheeks heating when he flirtatiously dipped the brim of his hat.

"Come on, Cass, don't tell me you're so daft you haven't been paying attention."

Her breath fell away when Moone stepped behind her and settled his chin on her shoulder. Turning his head, he pointed her gaze down the street.

"See her? Her cousin worked at the bank in Cheshire County you brought the Hardy brothers in for robbing." His hand curled around her waist, turning her with the slightest press of his fingers, breath kissing the curve of her ear. "And him… Whip Dillon killed his Ma, and you brought him in when you were practically still a kid."

Cass frowned, swallowing the lump in her throat when Moone pointed out more and more of them she'd somehow touched in one way or the other, bringing them the justice she craved.

"What's your point?"

"My point, *Cassidy*," he growled, holding her firmly and leaning so close, Cass found herself nearly overwhelmed by the blend of sweet tobacco and spiced whiskey. "Whether you like it or not, no matter how hard you try, you stubborn piece of work, these people might give a shit about you."

She turned, lifting her chin to meet his eyes. "Why do you keep calling me that?"

Moone gave her a cocky smile, placing his hat back on his head. "That's your name, isn't it?"

"Yeah," she breathed, licking her lips when his eyes flickered to her mouth. For a moment, only a moment, Cass considered the possibility of what her life might look like if things were different. If Ransom never existed. If she lived a normal life and somehow ended up in the same place. Would Moone have noticed her, or would she have noticed him if she wasn't who she'd made herself to be?

Solo whinnied, impatiently stamping his feet, blessedly pulling her from the odd little trance Cass got caught in. She cleared her throat, flipping her braid as she spun around and promptly placed her boot in the stirrup.

She let out a strangled cough when the warmth of

Moone's touch pressed against her ass, sending her flying, nearly out of the saddle as she boosted herself into finely worn leather. Torn between wanting to kick him and demanding more of the feeling, she glared down at his grin.

"What in the hell do you think you're doing?" she snapped, fisting the reins with a frown.

Shoulders trembling with barely contained laughter, Moone hoisted himself onto the brown filly. "Looked like you could use a hand, being freshly injured and all."

The heat in her cheeks flared, damn him. "James Moone, the only time you get to help me into a saddle is if I'm wearing a ballgown, we clear?" She gave Solo a nudge, sending him into motion, tugging the reins with a twist of her shoulders.

Moone's smile widened. He clamped his mouth shut when she glared back, swallowing another laugh. "You can count on it, Cassidy."

"You shouldn't," she barked, following it with a quick *heyaw* and a snap of the reins. Solo jolted forward, eager to run. Cass was, too, with insufficient daylight left and too far to go.

With the wind in her hair and rushing through her ears, Cass felt at home. The black stallion hurtled through the sagebrush, leaving Gallow Gorge in the dust—and James Moone, too.

[18]

HAVING A COMPANION ON THE ROAD WASN'T SOMETHING Cass was used to. Sure, from time to time, she might have a talkative bounty who'd run their mouth for the first few miles. They always gave up once their legs started to tire.

A partner was something else.

James Moone was a talker. She'd always pegged him as the strong, silent type, but with each mile they went, the more he had to say.

Solo was in on the damn plan, refusing the press of her heels to encourage him to put some distance between them and Moone's filly—like he wanted her to give in and answer the man's questions.

Being out in the wilderness *alone* with Solo was sacred to Cass, something she looked forward to. She wasn't one for attachments or sentimentality; there was a peace she found under a blanket of stars she never found anywhere else.

Things finally quieted when daylight dimmed, and Moone declared they should make camp.

Cass took off into the wind, eager to be the first to find a safe place for them to shelter. Her boots hit the dirt in the shadow of a stone bluff before Solo trotted to a stop. She didn't look back at him when he arrived just after, mumbling under her breath about needing firewood.

When she returned, Moone smiled and offered to build a fire, leaving her to read in peace as he heated a couple of cans of beans for dinner. They ate in blissful silence, crouched around the flames as the night's chill crept across the plain.

More than a few times—every time she'd stupidly look over the fire and meet his gaze—Cass saw how Moone's need for conversation burned. With every twitch of his jaw and sharp intake of breath suggesting he was about to speak, Cass shot him down with a glare.

On the second day, Moone's patience started to dwindle.

Cass kept her distance, far enough he couldn't start a conversation she'd rather avoid. It wasn't that she hated talking to him. James Moone was one of the few people she actually *liked*. But without all of Gallow Gorge as a buffer, Cass worried he'd back her into a corner, pinning her down with a subject she couldn't run away from. She couldn't just sass him and walk away.

When they stopped to make camp the second day, Moone was sullen. He hopped down from his filly with a huff, grumbling under *his* breath about needing firewood as he disappeared down a hill.

Cassidy nearly burst with laughter when he came back with half a tree—making a show of it as he tossed the armful down with a clatter. The slightest squeak, barely a chuckle, tore its way free. She couldn't help it. It deepened his frown, so she returned to keeping to herself. It was better that way.

After dinner, as the moonlight grew brighter, Cass settled in against a stone and cracked open the pages of her book.

As she tried to lose herself between the lines, her attention threaded with a skitter of pebbles. Over. And over. And *over* again.

Tink. Thunk. Thwack.

Every so often, Cass heard a grumble or groan, punctuated between soft blows and the gentle *swish* from the horses who stood shoulder to shoulder a few paces away. She'd glance up from her book and take in the scowl of the good deputy—thick arms crossed for a second or two until he reached down, plucked a stone from the earth, and chucked it into the flames.

Cass snapped *Jane Eyre* shut the fourth time he interrupted the narrator in her mind. "What is it?"

Moone's jaw ticked, blue eyes glued to the fire between them. "Nothin.'"

"James Moone, you're a terrible liar."

He pursed his lips, gaze snapping to her with a sniff. "Yeah, maybe I am. And you're shit company. You know that?"

She made a face. "*Shit company?*"

Moone plucked another pebble and pitched it into the fire, mouth curling into a grimace. "Was your plan to ignore me this whole drove, or—"

Frowning and wordless, Cass clambered to her feet and strode to the saddlebags. She rifled inside, digging to the bottom until she tugged out a brown bottle. She went back to the fire and shoved it to his chest.

Moone sat straighter, brow furrowing. "What's this?"

"I don't normally do this," Cass said, boots slipping as she sank beside him. She tugged the cork from the mouth with a *pop*. "I've kept this bottle around, just in case."

She couldn't help the amused giggle when Moone lifted

the bottle to his nose and recoiled with a cough.

"What in the hell?"

"Moonshine, idiot." Cass snatched the bottle from his grip, holding his awestruck look while she took a healthy swig. She hissed through her teeth, wiping her mouth and grimacing as the burn overtook her. But then it gave way to the most pleasant, unfurling warmth in her chest. She smiled. "I'll have you know, Madame Ridley is good for much more than her girls. Got a good little setup in her back room. Don't tell the Deputy. Here."

Moone chuffed, shaking his head as he took the proffered bottle. He brought it to his nose for another tentative sniff before he thought better of it and put it to his lips. When he burst into a coughing fit, Cass's shoulders shook with laughter. She stole the bottle before he spilled a precious drop.

"Why?" Moone coughed, rubbing his nose with his knuckles.

"Gotta make a dollar somehow, dummy." Cass tipped the bottle back again, slowly breathing through the delightful burn.

"No." He shook his head. "Why don't you drink on the job?"

She shrugged. "I like to keep a clear head. Otherwise, someone will try to take advantage. As a lady, *as a woman*, I have to be better, more aware of everything. Or there are consequences. Ones I'm not willing to risk."

"Aren't you afraid I'll take advantage of you?" he teased. His mouth twitched, and he licked a drop of moonshine from his lips after taking another drink.

Cass found it impossible not to look.

"No." Cass shook her head, face somber. "I trust you. I

feel *safe* with you."

"Oh." Moone studied the flames, working his jaw. "I'm glad."

Cass took the bottle again, already a bit overwhelmed by how the hooch heated her blood and how it spurred on the conversation she'd been so intent on *not* having.

"Can I ask you something?" She lifted her gaze, eyes darting over every sun-worn line in his face. To hell with it; if they were finally going to have an honest-to-god conversation without the distraction of Gallow Gorge, Cass might as well go all-in.

"Anything."

Cass swore he leaned in. Maybe it was a trick of the light—orange and gold flickers dancing together with shadows on stone. Maybe it was the moonshine making her fuzz around the edges. Maybe he actually did.

"I've heard some things." Cass didn't mean to whisper it, too focused on picking at a smudge on the side of the bottle.

"About me?" Moone took it from her, brushing his calloused fingers against hers. She hated that she noticed.

She followed his hands, how they curled around the darkened glass and made it look so small. She hated that she noticed that, too.

He took another swig, sucking in a breath through his teeth with a wrinkle of his nose.

"I know you haven't been a Deputy in Gallow Gorge long before I came along. And… I listen." Cass met his eye. "A few folks think you got involved in some more questionable things before you came to town. You were part of a gang, and now you're some kind of outlaw turned lawman."

A wry smile curled over his handsome face, though it didn't reach his eyes. Shadows stayed there, ones Cass recognized. A history he never talked about.

"Well, hell. I suppose I should've stayed in longer. Then maybe this girl I heard of could've been the one to bring me in. I might've been a handful, though I'm sure she could make out just fine."

Cass coughed on a mouthful of moonshine. "Moone, you would've been the easiest bounty I ever caught."

His face grew grave, but the glimmer in his eye was back. "You've never had a bounty like me, Cass. If I were, it'd be one hell of a chase. And believe me, if you finally captured me, I'd go willingly."

"I'll hold you to that, Mister Moone." She lifted the bottle and took an extra-long drink before returning it. "How, though? Of all the men I bring in, I never understood how someone gets mixed up in all that."

He shrugged. "Repayment of a bad debt. Desperation. Loneliness. The need for a family, even a shit one. Lots of reasons. I never had a choice, not at first."

"What happened?" Cass drew a knee to her chest. She needed something to hold onto to keep from reaching out for his hand, to anchor her away from the want to feel his fingers between hers.

Moone glanced down the mouth of the bottle, seemingly lost in the fragrant liquid for a few moments before answering—

"I've met him. Ransom."

Cass swallowed an unwelcome lump in her throat at the mention of his name. "Oh?"

Moone nodded. "After my Ma died, my Daddy fell down into the bottom of a bottle. He owed Ransom's gang money, so much that—when I was still a kid—they came and beat him within an inch of his life and left him for dead." He

took another drink of moonshine. "And took me as their pound of flesh to pay off his debt."

Cass was quiet, lost in the rapid beat of her heart and the crackle of the flames. She didn't know what to say. Why didn't she ever consider someone might've suffered like her, that someone else would've lost something because of Ransom?

She leaned closer, pressing her shoulder against his. "I'm sorry."

Moone nodded, giving her a gentle nudge back. "Don't be. I learned a lot of valuable lessons. I grew up. Did some things I regret, like most folks. Now I'm here, doing what I'm supposed to."

"I'm sure you probably made more money the other way," she joked, sure there had to be deeper pockets the dirtier you got.

He shrugged again. "Some things are more important than money, I suppose. I do alright, but mostly, I want to do something I feel good about. You helped me see that."

Cass teetered on the edge, filled with more questions, amazed she got him to open up so much. Was this friendship? Was this what it meant to finally let someone in?

Elbows balanced on her knees, she flicked at a pebble with a sigh. "So, if being a deputy in Gallow Gorge is so important to you, why come with me?"

She expected another lull. She expected him to never answer and the two of them to drown themselves in the bottle of Madame Ridley's moonshine. But, like so many times before, James Moone surprised her.

"I had to."

Cass made a face, turning toward him, but was instantly caught off guard when she found him so much closer than before. He smelled of spices and sweet tobacco, tawny curls hanging loose over his forehead. The smallest voice told her she ought to tuck them back into place, but she resisted.

"Why, though?" she argued. "Why would I matter so much that you'd leave your post?"

Moone's face was impossibly solemn, steely blue eyes darting over her freckles. Maybe it was the moonshine that made him look at her that way. Perhaps it was the moonshine that made her not pull away.

Who was she kidding? It was *definitely* the moonshine, and when he leaned closer still, brushing his thumb against her cheek, Cass let him.

"Because I like you, Cassidy. I—" His eyes fell to her mouth. He wet his lips. Her heart stumbled. It didn't take an idiot to figure out what he was thinking. What they were both thinking.

"You shouldn't." Cass tried to laugh him off, laugh it all off.

Moone leaned closer. "Too late for that."

Bad. He was a bad idea, a distraction waiting to happen. They were friends, maybe, but certainly nothing other than that. Cass couldn't afford it. She didn't *want* it.

[13]

CASSIDY

THANK GOD FOR SOLO. CASSIDY MIGHT'VE DONE something miraculously stupid without him and his muzzle coming between her, Moone, and a bottle of moonshine.

He tugged on her braid, declaring it time for bed with a swish of his tail in Moone's face.

Cass took it as a sign, promptly shifting far, *far* away from the good deputy. She warmed her back by the fire, letting the thrum of the moonshine carry her the rest of the way to sleep.

She saddled up at the first sliver of daylight while Moone still dozed. She didn't exactly go about it quietly. Cass wondered if she should wake him when he hadn't stirred as she tightened her bedroll.

She never thought she'd think of Moone as handsome, but with the curls hanging over his face while he lay half-folded up with his boots still on, Cass couldn't help it. Not when his lips parted with every slow breath—black eyelashes and dark brows framing his sun-lined face.

A week ago, she might've kicked him awake. It worked

better than a rooster's crow. But after the last few days, his kindness gave her pause. He accompanied her on her journey because he made the sad mistake of *liking* her. Cass thought—just this once—she'd be a little nicer.

"Moone," she whispered, crouching beside him. She made to jab him in the chest, hesitating with a curl of her fingers until she decided a gentler touch might be okay. Cass brushed against worn leather, splaying her fingers over the beating of his heart. She gave him a shake and another whisper. "James, wake up."

The sound of his name tasted odd on her tongue. Strange, but not unwelcome.

His brow scrunched. "Cassidy?"

When a sliver of blue peered from behind those black lashes, Cass jerked away, not wanting to give the impression she *wanted* to linger. No matter how true it might've been.

"We gotta go. We're wasting daylight. Camp's mostly packed, just waitin' on you and your bedroll," she said, gruffer than she meant. So much for a gentle approach. She softened a little, offering the smallest of smiles. "There's a little coffee, too."

"Thanks, Freckles," he groaned, climbing to his feet.

Cass tried not to watch him as he sleepily stumbled around the scorched earth of their fire, drinking down the tin cup of hot bean water—mostly dregs—with a grimace. There was something that amused her and stirred a warmth in the dark recesses of her black heart. A fondness, perhaps. Maybe she liked him, too.

Moone quickly packed, and before long, they set off at a steady northbound trot. The hours bled away—ones where Cass didn't shy away from talking. He didn't press about subjects she was sure to keep locked away, opting instead

for the books she loved to read and her favorite kind of whiskey.

"The wet kind," she joked between bites of jerky when they stopped to let the horses rest midday.

"That's every kind." Moone snorted, smiling softly at the hills in the distance. "It's been a long time since I picked up a book."

"How long?"

He shook his head. "*Long*. Didn't really ever read for fun."

"No?" Cass couldn't imagine picking up a book for any other reason.

"Nope. I studied."

She laughed. "Don't tell me they had a schoolhouse you attended between thieving runs."

"Nah, not a schoolhouse. I had a tutor." He paused, working his jaw. "He wanted me to be more than what my Daddy was, more than they planned for me to be. I wanted that, too. So, I learned everything I could. Philosophy. Latin. Law. I can even fence a little."

"*Fence?* You mean like—" Cass wiggled a bit of jerky, sinking into an awful lunge, imagining she was a pirate fighting for a bit of booty.

Moone's cheeks reddened. "Yes, exactly like that. Except—"

He plucked the last bit of jerky from her fingertips and popped it in his mouth.

Cass made a noise to object but fell silent the second he stepped behind her and palmed her torso.

"What are you—"

"Hush," he said in her ear. "I'm teaching. Hold here, keep your back straight." His hands shifted, sliding down her leg. Her breath hitched; she prayed he didn't hear it. "Stretch further. *Deeper.*"

"Like this?" Cass's ankles protested, wavering as she precariously shifted her weight forward. It felt strange. Nice, even. Especially with Moone's fingertips anchored around her hips.

"*Good*," he murmured, patting her thigh. "An extra inch on your lunge can make the difference between victory and loss. And"—his hands journeyed up, again, over her shoulders to beneath her hair and around her jaw—"Keep your head up, eyes straight ahead. Always on target."

"Now that's something I understand," she whispered, thankful she had her back to him, grateful he couldn't see how her cheeks burned. His touch brought a sheet of goosebumps in their wake, making her hair stand on pinpricks. Cass blamed the fresh air, or maybe leftover moonshine churning in their blood that heated it so.

Cass cleared her throat, rising from the lunge, shaking her limbs as she looked anywhere but at Moone. "We'd better get going."

"We stopping in town tonight?"

"That depends. Rose Reach is close enough, but we wouldn't get there until after dark."

"But?" Moone's brows rose. He knew there was a caveat, something else on her mind. Cass smiled a little that he knew her well enough to know she still had something to say.

"Cody isn't far off." She surveyed the horizon, squinting in the bright afternoon light. "We might be able to call it an early night, get some apple pie at Marion's, and find a bed to sleep in."

"I like the sound of that," Moone answered, nodding.

They didn't waste another second, climbing back into

the saddle to set off toward Cody. The slightest flicker of joy bloomed in her chest the closer they came. Only a little town, it wasn't much to write home about, but it reminded her so of Faraday Creek, a place filled with friendly faces, ones Cass stopped to see as often as she could.

But her joyful anticipation twisted into something more sinister, the cold grip of a memory she wanted to bury.

On a sliver of a breeze, Cass spied a slow, curling plume of black smoke rising from the horizon—above Cody.

Without a second thought, she snapped her reins. Solo responded in kind, rearing with a squeal, lunging forward to answer the call of his human sister. Cass's heart raced with each thunderous gallop of hooves against earth, breaking free from the easy gait she and Moone traveled.

The stallion was fast but not fast enough to chase away the gnarled twist of fear and fury in her gut as they drew closer.

The town drew up on the horizon. A collection of pale clapboard faded by years in the California sunshine. Cass passed through more times than she could count.

It was so, so much like home.

Cass leaped from the saddle before Solo took more than a few steps onto the main thoroughfare.

A layer of smoke settled onto the ground, shifting around her boots as she chased the haunting ring of a school bell splitting the eerie silence.

Her chin trembled, green eyes darting every way as she counted the bodies littering the once-lively town. Blood stained the soil, buzzing at the edges of her vision. Cass squeezed them shut, staggering, wiping her fists against her cheeks, smearing away the blood from her memory.

Moone's voice was there, hovering in the back of her

mind, hidden beneath echoes of the past and the heartbeat drumming in her ears. She paid him no mind, too lost in the horrific display.

Cass shifted, rolling away a hand on her shoulder as she pressed on. She stepped over a twisted corpse, around two, then three more. She couldn't look away from the scorched skeleton of a schoolhouse on the corner.

Flames curled around the tower, where a brass bell hung precariously from its hinges, ringing a final farewell as everything burned around it.

Cass drew her gaze down the arcade, silently begging for someone, anyone, to have been left alive—if only for her to find and bring to justice the monsters who massacred all of Cody in cold blood.

She burst through door after door, finding only death inside each one.

Blood spattered across calico at the dressmaker's shop. Even the horses at the farrier were still.

Her stomach twisted with each stolen soul she stumbled upon, unwilling and unable to hear Moone at her back. Cass's anguish threatened to drown her. Curling at the edges of her vision, it oozed down her skin like poison, covering her until Ian and Aisling's little girl was gone, and only the bitter bounty hunter remained.

She kicked in another door, swinging it on its hinges with a *bang*. The sight inside was achingly familiar to her. From the colorful glass bottles lining the shelves to the grain bags along a back wall.

The bottles had been broken, and the bags pierced with a sharp blade, spilling the precious contents inside over the floor. All of it was stained by a pool of blood.

Cass staggered, met by a warm, firm wall of man at her

back.

He reached for her, tried to *reach* her with questions, pleading for answers. But when she looked upon the body at her feet, and the crimson pooled around her toes, seeping through cracks in the floor, all she saw was her father.

Bile rose in her throat. She tried to swallow it and send it to the depths where she kept her feelings. There wasn't any time to dwell, no time to think about anything else but the goal. Still, up it came. No matter how she pressed her knuckles to her lips, there wasn't any stopping the poison that begged to come out.

Cass lurched, stumbling over the slick beneath her boots, reaching for the door. Her fingers gripped worn wood while her body trembled, coughing out every last bit of her breakfast as Moone pulled back her braid and rubbed slow circles on her back.

She rolled his hand from her shoulder with a sniff. "M'fine."

"You aren't." Moone warily took stock of her freckles as she straightened.

She smeared the back of her hand over her lips, chewing on her words when he stepped closer.

Cass saw how he analyzed her, how he thought he knew the thoughts and memories, the nightmares churning in her mind. As if he knew exactly what'd happened in Faraday Creek when she'd only told him a name.

Moone wasn't without his own trials and suffering because of Ransom. If she told him everything, would he understand? Part of her wanted it, wanted to let out that piece of herself, to let James understand her the way he always tried to.

Still, the past clouded her vision, blooming into rage

when the titter of voices echoed down Main Street.

Cass shouldered past Moone in the doorway, fingertips twitching when she spotted rowdy bandits spilling out from the saloon on the corner.

"Quit your bellyaching. They was warm enough."

"I prefer my women to have a bit more life in 'em, is all."

"Yeah, but then they'd say no t'ya, Felix."

"Can't help but like it when they's a bit of a challenge."

Her blood simmered. The twisted crooks paid her no mind as they zigged and zagged through the dirt, whiskey-soaked and disgustingly satiated from soiling dead doves against the bar. Four, she counted. Only a handful to cause so much destruction and pain. And for what? To dip their wicks in lukewarm, spoiled wax?

One by one, their eyes all flicked her way. A snicker fell through the group like a ripple in water. Each one of them cast the other a sickly, lewd look before they all came back to her.

A man at the center spoke first, still buckling his britches.

"Well, well. Looks like we missed one, fellas."

Cass dragged her gaze from one shoulder to the other, tilting her head with a curl of her lip. "Was this you?"

They all shared another look before another spoke up.

"What of it, missy?"

The heat of her wrath coiled and wreathed, twisting into something else as she took another sure-footed step closer.

"You slaughtered them all like animals." Cass sucked in a stuttering breath, blinking away the image of her mother's deathly still face. "Why?"

The same one who'd spoken first—a tall man, thin like a string bean with greasy tendrils of dark hair falling to a shallow chin beneath his hat—swiped a match on his belt,

lighting a stub of a cigar perched in his mouth.

"They all bleed the same, and I got a pocket full of fresh tobacco because of it. What's it matter to you?"

Cass barked out an incredulous huff of laughter. Moone hovered in her periphery, attention keenly trained on the gun belts growing heavier by the minute.

Eyes falling to her boots, a smile twisted across her face. When Cassidy lifted them back to the group, she welcomed the cold sense of clarity that came to her on a ruffle of wind through her hair.

"*All bleed the same*," she echoed, fingers curling into her palm until they ached. "So, some supplies and a fuck are worth the lives of all these people?"

Another man stepped forward—shorter, broader, fatter than the other. A scraggly beard brushed his collar, still dripping with pillaged whiskey.

"What are you going to do about it, girlie?"

Cass's attention snapped to him in a heartbeat. "Nothing you'll like, I promise."

The same man elbowed the one beside him with a guffaw. "Looks like we got yer type, Felix. You said you like a challenge. This one looks like she's got some fight in'er." His yellowed grin settled on her, growing wider by the second. "But I wonder how warm you'll be once yer dead and Felix is done with you. Though, I reckon' ya bleed the same as the rest of these folks."

At her side, Moone charged forward, but Cass threw out a hand to halt him. She could take care of herself.

Cass lifted her chin, shifting in the silt with a twist of her heel.

"I'm willing to bet you do."

The cold zing of lead split the air, ringing out before

anyone could blink or even breathe. Smoke coiled from the end of Cass's barrel, pearl grip tucked firmly in the palm of her right hand.

She couldn't ignore the cold curl of delight wrapping around her, spurred on by blood spilling from the fresh bullet hole in the center of the speaker's forehead.

His face wore a rotted smile. One that faded as he staggered, plummeting to the dirt one knee at a time.

One of the men reached for his gun—Felix, the one who liked a challenge.

Cass didn't think. She didn't have to. The pistol on her left flew into her hand, putting him down as quickly as the first. She practically buzzed from the thrill of it.

A hand around her wrist yanked her back to the present.

Moone's face hovered close to hers, ruffling a spray of red curls around her face. "Cassidy, stop. Leave it up to the law."

She tore away from his grasp, flipping the Colt revolver in her left palm back into the holster. "These people deserve justice."

Moone shook his head. "Killing these men isn't justice, Cass. You're better than this."

Her eyes blazed, the blackness of her heart growing deeper, darker by the second. "Am I?"

Cass rolled his touch away, marching through the dirt, pistol raised.

One of the bandits tore his gun loose, but not fast enough.

Her shot sliced through the quiet, dropping him to the ground before the sound ricocheted to the end of the street.

One. Two. Three.

Cass counted each one of the bodies she'd added to

the collection of corpses lying still in the dirt. Three shots fired. Three bodies laid in a row… but one of the group was missing. He'd likely run off when Moone distracted her. But no matter, she'd find him. She always did.

Her keen green eyes darted every which way, scanning the shadows until, with a catlike smile, she found her final mark.

Cass pulled back the hammer on her pistol, sucking in a deep breath as she raised the barrel. There, tucked in the shadow of the arcade in front of the undertaker's workshop, he hid in plain sight.

The bullet spat from the end of the revolver, cutting through the lingering smoke in the air until, with the blistering of split wood, it struck inside a coffin leaning against the arcade's railing. She heard a satisfying *thunk* of a heavy body inside, striding forward as she patiently waited for the next eventuality.

As she expected, within moments of settling the still-warm barrel of her gun back in her belt, the splintered lid of the coffin fell open, and with it, the man inside.

He landed face-down in the dirt with a puff of fine dust clouding around him. Beneath him, seeped a slow trickle of blood, winding its way through the earth like a river coursing a path through the desert.

Cass shoved the toe of her boot beneath him, flipping him to his back with a kick. She crouched, pressing her weight on his chest with her knee. When his face contorted, an odd sense of bliss buzzed in the back of her mind. It fed the fever in her heart, the one calling out for more blood to fuel the coldest part of her.

It seeped from his gut in bursts, gushing a crimson stream with every slow beat of his pulse.

His lips parted to speak, struggling to draw enough breath to utter a syllable. "I… don't deserve to die like this. I swear. I'm… not a bad man."

Cass barked out a laugh, peering over her shoulder at the corpses scattered through the once-lively town of Cody.

"You mean you don't deserve to die like an animal like your lot did to them?" She pushed her knee harder against his chest. The monster inside practically preened with glee when his face twisted in pain.

"I never… I didn't… this wasn't my plan. We needed the money."

"*Oh*, I'm not a priest. I don't get any satisfaction from your confession. Forgiveness is between you and God," Cass tutted, copper braid falling over her shoulder upon sticky leather, wet with blood she'd spilled.

Swathed in the icy thrill of her fury, Cass squeezed her fingers into the warmth of the bullet hole in his chest. Agony gripped him, arms flailing while she held the rest of him still.

She held them to the light, smearing the bright scarlet between them. "Looks like I was right. You *do* bleed the same."

The bandit weakly lifted a hand and motioned toward the inside pocket of his vest. "*Please.*"

Cass pulled the worn, yellowed corner of a photograph from inside with her soiled hand. The faces sent her reeling, falling back to the dirt with a strangled gasp.

Two young boys stared back at her, wide-eyed and stoic, as they held still for the shutter.

"M'boys," he groaned beneath her, wheezing with each labored breath. "Their Ma's sick."

Cass staggered to her feet, chin trembling as the horror

of her actions rushed to the forefront of her mind, splitting her rage into something darker and harder to shake.

Her father's face washed into her mind, carrying the promise she'd made.

Cassidy Kathleen Callaghan, I want you to be tinkin' 'bout each time ye aim 'tis weapon—what'll change if ye do? Every bullet has a consequence—good or bad. That's what ye need to decide.

With every thunderous beat of her heart, Cass wished her shame would swallow her whole. She failed him. She allowed herself to be drawn into her anger, the importance of her mission, and why she believed so heartily in justice being served. In the process, she'd robbed those boys of their father.

Now, she'd be their Jack Ransom.

The thought made her stomach twist.

Cass skimmed her tongue over her bottom lip, flicking the photo down onto his body.

"I'm sure they deserved better," she muttered, drawing a pistol from her hip, putting him out of his misery with a shot between the eyes.

Turning on her heel, Cass stared straight ahead, shirking Moone's touch with a roll of her shoulder. She vaulted herself into the saddle in a single, fluid motion, taking off through the center of town as quick as a lightning bolt through the night sky.

With Cody left in her dust, Cass barreled ahead, thankful

for Solo's ever-vigilant call to aid and watch out for her. He galloped so quickly, the wind stung her eyes, thundering over the sagebrush until the black curl of smoke was merely a dark spot on the horizon behind her.

They'd gone a mile, maybe more, when the sable stallion finally slowed to a trot, sniffing out a bend in the river that'd twisted their way as he cantered over the vast California desert.

Cass fell from her saddle, staggering while Solo gently dipped his muzzle into the cold, mountain-fed water. She paced back and forth through the rocky soil, gasping for breath with each fevered twist of her boot in the dirt.

She knew it was in the past. She *knew* Cody wasn't Faraday Creek. It hadn't been her father on the floor at her feet, and Jack Ransom wasn't anywhere to be found. Yet, she let her fury get the best of her like all those things were true, twisting her up in blinding rage. So much so, she neglected her promise to Ian Callaghan in the moments before his murder.

She didn't mean to forget.

In the moment, faced with the ugliness of the men who'd destroyed the town in cold blood, Cass only felt her anger. The kind that built her, the kind that made her construct a life so far away from the girl he and Aisling raised her to be. She wondered how ashamed they'd be if they knew what she'd become.

The boys in the photograph haunted her, flashing with every blink of her blurred vision. She pulled the back of her hand over her cheeks, hoping to clear the haze. When her knuckles came away wet, Cass turned her palms over in the fading daylight and let out a strangled cry.

Blood coated her hands. In a matter of moments, she

was that little girl hidden in a cellar with a baptism of Ian's on her face.

Cassidy smeared her cheeks again. Had she been crying? Or were her nightmares personified as punishment for the atrocity she'd committed against her word?

She lurched forward, sloshing into the stream before her knees gave way and sent her wading. Not even the frigid water splintered the haze of her bloodlust or washed away the bitter taste of her guilt.

Her hands shook while she held them beneath the glassy surface. Blood bloomed in crimson clouds. She frantically scrubbed them together, but no matter how firmly she did it—again and again and again—the stain remained.

Cass shifted through the river rock, digging until her fingers ached, and she came up with a rough-edged stone. She scrubbed at her flesh, tearing away at his blood until her own surfaced to join it.

"M'sorry," she gasped through her sobs, heart rattling away like a runaway train. Her feet tingled, and her hands trembled, but not from the water. Blood pounded so fiercely in her ears, they rang, drowning out every sound and thought until her guilt was all that remained.

It pulsed in her palm, painting the crystal-clear water a milky red. Cass thought she might drown in it; she deserved it after what she'd done. She closed her eyes to the sight, choking on the image of her father's death mask.

No, it was bile rising in her throat to silence her whispered apologies to a dead man.

"Cassidy."

They called to her. She batted the thought away, swinging at the air before delving into deeper water. It was just another ghost. Another heartache. Another crime.

"Cassidy, stop," it said, firmer this time.

Warmth on her face. Hands, not tears. Not his blood.

Cass blinked. Her vision cleared enough to see blue eyes filled with alarm. His mouth moved, calloused hands wiping away her tears as tawny waves hung over the crease in his brow. Closer, he came. Words, too. One after the other, though she couldn't hear it over her rattled heartbeat.

"M'sorry," she gasped with a strangled sob, collapsing into him under the weight of what she'd done. "*So sorry,* Da."

Moone wound his arms around her, lifting her from the water as if she weighed nothing. "I've got you."

A comforting hand braced against her back, pressing her to his chest as she listlessly wrapped her arms around his shoulders. The feeling was foreign, one of comfort, but Cass recalled flickers of his face above her on the surgeon's table—the same anxious look in his eye.

Had he been worried?

She allowed herself to sink into his warmth, burying her face into his collar, praying the steady *rum-tum-tum* of his heart would banish her dark passenger for a little while.

[14]

MOONE

OONE KNEW HER. HE KNEW SHE WAS HARD-HEADED. He knew she had a reputation for a hundred miles of being the kind of bounty hunter you didn't want coming after you. He knew she had an unbreakable focus on justice and a fast draw quicker than any gunslinger he'd ever seen. Cassidy never missed.

He knew her, but he'd never seen the cold, calculating woman he witnessed in Cody.

Before, in the moments leading up to their discovery of the massacre, Moone saw another part of her, someone far away from the sour-face teenager he first met on the streets of Gallow Gorge. Back when she was mostly freckles and a thatch of wild copper curls.

In the light of a campfire's glow, he saw the woman beneath what she let everyone else see. He saw something special. He saw *her*. Someone so different from the woman who killed in cold blood.

One after the other, she put down the thugs responsible for Cody. With a flash in her eyes and at the end of her barrel, James watched her change—a metamorphosis from a stubborn woman hellbent on revenge to the Devil's daughter, hungry for the taste of blood and the sight of a man's life fading from his eyes.

He tried to hold her back, to remind her of the girl she was. As soon as he feared she slipped too far away, something else stepped in. Like the flip of a switch, the cold, vehement vision of her went right back to the lost, scared little girl she'd told him about. She left Cody and all the blood in her dust before Moone had the chance to utter a single word.

He *knew* her. The ghost he found wading in a blood-clouded mountain creek was far from Cass Callaghan; Moone worried what'd happen if he tried to force her from it. But he didn't have much choice. Not when she rubbed her skin raw and sent a river of her own to join the blood she'd spilled.

He pulled her from the river and hoisted her onto Solo's back, who noisily nickered until James joined her. Snug in the saddle, they rode for miles, chasing the last threads of daylight.

If it'd been different, if the glimmer hadn't vanished from her green eyes, James would've relished the feeling of being so close. He might've delighted in his hand tucked firmly around her waist and thighs pressed against hers.

But, as she whispered, *M'sorry*, over and over again, his only concern was getting her out of the wilderness. One night free from it would do her good.

Rose Reach appeared on the horizon like a beacon, bright and beautiful as they charged north through the California desert. He'd wandered through a few times in his youth, riding the coattails of an enviable, formidable gentleman. The whiskey well ran deep; the pockets, too—a stream of wealth fed from Sacramento just upriver.

That only meant one thing—they were getting closer to Ransom.

The thought twisted his gut, but it was a worry for another day. What he would do, if there'd be some kind of plan he'd pull from his back pocket.

He wanted to deliver on his word to Katie; he *needed* to sort out his business, but there was so much more at risk than he had ever considered. Secrets he planned to take to the grave and never tell Cassidy. But now, there was no escaping the day she'd discover the depth of his depravity.

Tomorrow, probably. Never, he hoped. But at least now he had a good reason to stall her, to have a little more time— just them.

It could be what James needed, what *they* needed. Something to go to shit, something to be imperfect for them to feel something. That's just the way it was for people like them. James never learned to accept anything else, not until her—not until she stirred something inside he never thought he'd feel.

Kicking in the door of The Palace Hotel may not have been the brightest idea, especially with a half-unconscious Cassidy slung over his shoulder.

"The brothel is three blocks over, sir," a man at the counter sneered. "Perhaps you'll find a room there to suit your taste"—his withered gaze traveled up and down their dirtied clothes—"and budget."

Moone frowned, thinking quickly of a lie to explain their appearance, something that'd buy them enough time for Cassidy to be well again.

"Uh, *well.*" Moone's eyes shifted over the lavish lobby, summoning the kind of honeyed tone he was taught, the kind that could get him anywhere he wanted. "Our carriage lost a wheel out past Cody. I'm afraid my wife and I took a bit of a tumble. We'd greatly appreciate it if we might get a room for the night. Your best, if you please."

He dug in his pocket and slapped down a stack of money that'd put any high roller in his place. The kind of cash he kept buried far beyond the boundaries of Gallow Gorge— literally. Not when he meant to live on a Deputy's meager salary.

The mustachioed man's haughty smile melted away, and he took no time in sliding over a key with a look that made James confident he wouldn't ask any further questions about his appearance or the blood on his sleeve.

Besides, they were still far enough away from true "civilization" that some questions were better left unsaid.

Moone trudged up the stairs and down the hall to their room with a listless Cassidy tucked in his arms.

It was a grander scene than he'd seen since finding his way to Gallow Gorge. The Copper Queen was all fine and good, luxurious for their dusty old town. But this—this was something else.

A four-poster bed with crimson velvet curtains sat amongst carved wing-backed chairs on a Persian rug. A copper tub sat before a blazing fire, freshly filled by his request.

James didn't know what he planned to do or where he'd sleep. It didn't matter, anyway. Not when she was still so far away from herself.

His heart stuttered when her hands gripped his sleeve after setting her on the edge of the bed.

She lifted her sallow, blood-stained face to his. Still wordless, but her eyes said plenty.

"I've got you, alright?" James took her cheeks in his

hands, sinking to his knees. "Don't worry, I won't peek."

Cass nodded, closing her eyes as he peeled away her clothes. First, her boots. Then, the buttons on her worn leather vest, one by one, until he pushed it over her shoulders, shivering when her shallow breathing kissed the hair on his neck.

James rose, holding her fingers like a fine lady, pulling the sleeve of her cotton shirt down her arm until a meadow of freckles lit up in the firelight. He'd seen them before, when he watched her sleep at The Copper Queen, long enough to construct a vivid fantasy of the next time he'd be lucky enough to catch a glimpse of them.

It was a moment steeped in fiction, much like the books her nose was always stuck in. One closer to a dream than he'd ever be lucky enough to get in real life. Someplace where she'd let him pepper each one with kisses, where they explored the meaning of something more—something beyond the contentious friendship they'd built over the years.

No, it wasn't how he imagined it, the undressing of Cassidy Callaghan—shirking the hardened armor of her bounty hunter persona until only the woman remained. His heart ached, his mouth dry as he handled her with the gentlest touches, cradling her limbs while he worked.

When she was finally bare, Moone scooped her up, careful not to look—just as he promised. He held her close, gingerly lowering her into the copper basin's fragrant liquid.

Cass brought her knees to her chest, burying her face into them as James sank to the floor beside her. He rested his chin along the edge, chewing his lip as the quiet ticking of a clock counted the seconds she stayed trapped in memories he couldn't see, couldn't fathom.

He scooped his hand beneath the surface, letting it slip

from his fingers in rivulets down her back. He rubbed soft circles with murmured words, telling her she wasn't alone, that she was safe—anything to pull her free.

Little by little, in their room's quiet and the fire's warmth, the light returned to her eyes.

"You don't have to do this," she whispered, voice stumbling as a silvery tear slipped down a blanket of freckles.

James leaned over the edge, catching the next with his thumb. "I'm not going anywhere."

"Alright." Cass nodded, drawing closer.

Things shifted. Moone's skin buzzed, caught in the magnetic pull of her gaze and gratitude, unable to ignore the twinge in his heart when she looked at him like *that*.

He brushed the damp curls from her forehead, close enough to—*no*. Not like this. Not with her so broken. Oh, he was tempted, but she finished the thought before he let it firmly take root—slipping her wet fingers in his hair to press a chaste kiss to his lips.

Moone's eyes closed, collecting the taste of it, of her, with a swipe of his tongue. It was over so quickly he couldn't be sure it actually happened. When he opened them again, Cassidy was just as close, knuckles pressed to her mouth.

"What was that for?" He cleared his throat, silently willing his heart to quiet and his hand to quit aching to reach out and take another.

"To say thank you," she whispered. The corner of her mouth quivered, even through the guise of her frown. A tell. A beautiful little tell. "I'm sorry."

James frowned. "You keep saying that."

"I'll never stop." Her eyes fell. "I don't deserve any of this from you."

"Sure, you do." He lingered on the edge, resuming his

quiet reverie of washing away her worries with each quiet eddy of bathwater. "Why are you talking like that?"

Her chin trembled. Their eyes met, but only for a moment before she sucked in a deep breath and slipped beneath the surface.

Moone lurched, holding the copper with a white-knuckle grip. She hovered there, like staying under the water would act as a sort of baptism—a way to wash away the sins she thought she committed.

He counted the seconds, holding his breath beside her until his chest ached.

Enough was enough.

Moone sloshed into the water, gripped her elbows, and forced her to the surface. "If you don't want to talk to me, just say so. Don't try to fucking drown yourself. I'm trying to *help* you, Cassidy."

She coughed, leaning into him as he drew water droplets from her chin.

He waited for her to say something, to answer his question. Hell, she could've told him to fuck off, and it would've been enough. He would be satisfied.

Moone was ready to give up and leave her side when Cassidy finally spoke and rooted him to the spot like a hundred-year-old sequoia.

"My Da taught me everything I know. *Everything.*" Her lovely face lifted into a wistful smile that broke his heart. "It's like he *knew* I'd be alone and need to know it all. And… because of him, I survived. Before he died, I made him a promise. I've honored it as best I could. Today, I broke it."

Moone didn't dare speak or even breathe, not at the risk of breaking the spell. Cassidy was opening up to him and *finally* talking—something rarer than her smile.

She traced her knuckles over her lips, closing her eyes with a lift of her chin, like it carried her to another place and time.

"Tin cans," she murmured, far from their room at The Palace Hotel. "He'd stack them on the fence in the pasture, poke at my boots, and whisper in my ear—*I want you to be tinken' about each time you aim 'tis weapon. What'll change if you do? Ev'ry bullet has a consequence—good or bad—dat's what ye need to decide*, he said. I promised him I would never forget what he taught me, but I lost sight of it today. I-I can't let it happen again. *I can't*, or I'm just as bad as Ransom and his gang."

Moone's stomach twisted. He swallowed a sudden lump in his throat. "You could never be like them."

Her eyes shone, and she bit back a sob. "How do you know?"

He wanted to tell her how wrong she was, that she'd never be as bad as the rest of them. He'd bring hell down if it could make her see and pay the Devil twice as much to keep her soul from delving deeper into this darkness.

"Trust me, I know." He hooked a knuckle beneath her chin, tempted to kiss away her tears, but resisted. "Besides, if you think you're as bad as him, what the hell does that make me?"

"That makes you…" Cassidy's green eyes darted 'round his face. She slipped a knee from where she'd firmly held it against her chest. Water sloshed over the basin's edge, and red curls sprang up around her face. The only thing Moone could focus on was the soft upturn of her mouth.

It was different than before. So different.

Their breaths intertwined. Cass blinked at him, and Moone was left achingly aware of how close she was, her flesh burning against his knuckles on the tub's edge. Her heart hammered away, though he wasn't entirely convinced it wasn't his own. Not when he snuck a peek at her beneath the water for the first time that evening. A glance that only served to fuel the slow ache in his body that grew firmer by the second.

"That makes me what?" he growled, not daring to move a muscle for fear of spoiling the illusion. Fuck, he wanted her. He always wanted her, but it was a bad idea. Dangerous, even.

The water couldn't be muddled between them. Not yet, not like this. Especially when he was trying so hard to be a better man. But would it be so bad to be wanted by her in return? To taste her, even if just for the night?

Moone brushed his nose against hers. Cass gasped at the contact. It only urged him on, to cross the line that always stood between them. He wanted to demolish it, tear it to pieces until there was nothing left but the two of them. It was a slippery slope, and the catalyst was in his hands.

"Solo," Cassidy breathed, pressing her palms to his face. Rivulets of warm, perfumed water cascaded down his neck and disappeared beneath his shirt, only increasing his need to rip it away and join her in the bath.

He slipped his eyes shut, leaning into her touch with an unappeasable need to taste her lips again—when the name registered in his mind.

Moone blinked, cleared his throat, and leaned back, frowning. "I've been called a horse of a man before, Cassidy, but I'm *not* that goddamned Mustang you call a brother. Are... are you saying I'm like your *brother?*"

She bit back a giggle, barely holding more back with her fingertips. "You think real highly of yourself, don't you?"

Moone's heart felt a little lighter seeing her smile, green

eyes glittering. The water seemed warmer, the lamplight brighter. Hell, the fire's radiance burned hotter in the brilliance of it.

"Answer the question, Freckles."

Cassidy's laughter evaporated. Her gaze softened. "I've never considered you a brother, James Moone." She shook her head, drawing her fingertips over the freckled seam of her mouth. "I don't think I ever will."

Moone saw the unspoken words on the tip of her tongue, how she hesitated to say something else.

"But?" he pressed.

She gathered her knees to her chest, resting her chin as she examined the room. "Where's my horse?"

He chuckled. "Did you expect me to bring him up here? I already told a lie to get them to rent me the room in a hurry, so something tells me they might've objected to a stallion in the lobby. He's hitched to a post out front."

"You *left* him?"

"Cassidy, he's fine. Besides"—Moone pawed a hand through his hair—"I was in a hurry to get my incapacitated wife upstairs before people started asking more questions."

Her eyes widened. "Your *what?*"

Moone leaned away, palms raised, but couldn't help but grin at the fire in her eyes. "Apologies, Missus Moone. I did what needed done."

"You ought to do what needs done *now.*" Cass rose, sloshing water over the side of the copper basin.

Moone didn't know where to look, not at first, not with her every freckle glistening and gleaming in the firelight. He knew what he wanted—his body told him so—but his mind shouted what he needed to do when she teetered.

"*Shit,*" he choked, jolting to his feet when Cassidy

tumbled. There was a yell, another swear, perhaps—then charged silence; the hushed quiet of their breathing and every unspoken desire he feared she'd notice without effort.

Before, she'd been easier to resist. Now, with her body pressed against his chest and his fingers pressing divots into soft skin, every part of James ached to fulfill his wildest daydreams. The ones that snuck up on him more often the closer she allowed him. The ones that flickered through his mind like the reel on a player piano when he least expected it. One that wound the melody of her face, her kiss, her body—her anything at all.

"James," she whispered. Then again, more firmly than before. "*Moone.*"

She held his face between her palms. He closed his eyes, soaking up the warmth, letting her light bleed into him, snuffing out the darkness planted there by another man. The end was coming, and the idea of them was dangerous. One he ought to put a stop to.

—one Cassidy put a stop to first.

"Hand me that robe? *Please.*"

He righted her, averting his eyes as he snatched a bundle of fabric from the bed and thrust it into her arms.

"Thank you." Her voice was gentle. Like she saw every dastardly thought and despicable secret rattling around in his head. Cassidy said she didn't deserve his kindness, but Moone knew the truth.

If anyone wasn't worthy, it was him. Once she figured that out, there'd be no telling what she'd do. She'd most certainly never allow him so close as tonight. This was all Moone would be given, and he couldn't justify any of it.

His spurs chimed with every anxious tear across the Persian rug. If he wasn't careful, he'd wear a hole in it before he figured out what to say.

"M'sorry." Moone dragged a palm across a week's stubble. "I should've let you be."

"I know what you want." Cassidy pursed her lips, collecting a droplet of bathwater with the tip of her tongue. She wrapped the robe around her narrow shoulders. Gathering it close to her chest, she gripped it with the authority of a cowboy with a steer on the end of his lasso—always in control. "I want it, *want you*, too. But it's a bad idea. You see that, don't you? It'll cost us in the end, and we'll both be sorry."

Moone sniffed. She was right. He knew it. Still, the disappointment of hearing her say it out loud was unbearable, confirming what he thought—that she wanted him just as badly, but not enough to give in and forget everything else. "Can't say I would be."

"Would be what?"

"Sorry. Can't say that I'd be sorry." Moone met her gaze and nearly left every apprehension behind. Their regrets would keep until tomorrow.

A thousand thoughts flittered over her lovely face, ones she tried to hide behind the softness of a towel, gathering water droplets clinging to her eyelashes.

But Moone *knew* her. He saw his desire reflected in her eyes and the nearly imperceptible shadow of a dimple. The same rare, secret smile he'd come to love and collect.

"Never say never." Cassidy pulled her metaphorical armor down, hiding away the broken little girl who stumbled free in Cody's aftermath. "But you will be if you don't put Solo up in the livery. Give him extra oats, or he'll be a stubborn ass all day tomorrow."

"More than usual, you mean?"

She laughed, musical and light-hearted—something Moone could bottle and drink on a cold desert night and let warm him like the richest whiskey.

He reached for the door, but she spoke as he made to step into the corridor.

"Do me a favor?"

His heart stuttered at the sweetness of her voice. "Anything."

James didn't mean for his voice to tremble.

"Take a bath. You smell rotten."

Moone smiled, taking one last glimpse of his wild girl looking wholly at home in a velvet, gold-fringed robe beside the four-poster bed. She was a queen, and he was her servant; whatever she'd ask, he'd deliver.

He was good at that.

"As you wish, Freckles."

ℬEFORE

THE LETTER BURNED A HOLE IN HIS POCKET. HE'D BEEN gone too long and done too little to serve the family. He had everything to go back to. A life, a home of sorts, a purpose—even if it was one he didn't believe in. Apparently, two years was enough before that home came calling, luring him back.

Gallow Gorge was more than good enough. The people were welcoming when he first arrived, forged papers in his pocket that'd buy him into any Sheriff's station he wanted.

So long as he fulfilled his end of the bargain, James would be allowed the space he asked for.

There was a peace in their streets he hadn't expected; a hollowness inside him filled by the quiet simplicity of it.

But most especially when it was interrupted by one particular person.

Dealing with Cass Callaghan was a chore, one he never minded much.

James flipped a gold pocket watch into his palm, tossing the nub of his cigar to the dirt as a ruckus erupted from inside The Copper Queen right on cue.

Shouts poured from its doors, followed by a spill of light when the door burst open, and a man tumbled out.

He landed in a heap, swearing as he gathered himself up from the dirt.

"You fuckin' bitch," he spat, weaving as he glared at the saloon's doorway.

"At least I'm not the type who screams like one," a voice answered.

Moone saw her shadow first, one that bent and moved as gracefully as a reed in the wind. At nineteen to his twenty-three, Cassidy Callaghan was barely thicker than one, while he grew broader like a mountain with each passing year. He didn't know where she put all the whiskey she drank that night—or how she was still standing, let alone tossing a man out on the street with her bare hands.

"You didn't have to hit me," the man ground out, reaching for his pistol. "No one makes me bleed."

An audience began to gather, voices hushed as the evening's entertainment played out in the middle of town.

Moone closed the space at a saunter, keeping his distance—just enough to see what she'd decide to do. Admittedly, while his task was to uphold the law and keep the peace, the chaos she brought stirred something in him—a fondness for her fight, the wildness woven into her, and the righteousness she carried on such slight shoulders. He wouldn't let her kill a man, but he would at least let her deliver enough punishment on her own that maybe he'd think twice before acting so unseemly again.

"That's all you'll do," she crooned, stepping into the muted glow of the darkening street. It lit the fire of her hair in a way Moone couldn't help but notice, to take note of the shine and the bend of the curl at the end of her braid.

Or the curve of her lips when she continued, "Didn't your mother tell you not to touch someone else's things without permission? I ought to teach you a lesson for what you've done."

The man burst out laughing. "You're too drunk to hit a goddamned thing."

"Oh, sure I could." She grinned, palming the pearl grip of the pistol in her belt. "I've got two of these beauties. One for each of you."

She flipped one free faster than anyone could blink, firing a shot square between his boots.

The man cried out, reaching for his own.

Moone decided it was time to intervene. There was no sense in spilling blood in their streets for a squabble so small.

"All right, that's enough," he said, stepping between them.

Cassidy's attention slid to him, face souring when he flipped a pair of handcuffs into his palm. "You've gotta be kidding me."

He shook his head. The man chuckled at his back; Moone wished he hadn't. She'd be harder to catch if he pissed her off further—like shaking a box with a rattlesnake inside. It'd be Moone she bit, maybe literally. "You and I both know I'm not much of a joker, Freckles."

"No." She shook her head, stepping backward down the arcade. "You can't arrest me again. I didn't do anything he didn't deserve."

"Deserve? Who gives a shit if I touch the whore?" the man groused from behind them, wiping blood from his mouth. "Just takin' a sample of the product. S'not against the law."

Cassidy blasted forward with a pointed finger, teeth

bared. "Talk that way about Katie again, and I'll make you bleed someplace worse than your face."

When she moved for her pistol again, Moone lunged, hooking an arm around her waist.

"I said that's enough," he murmured, so only she could hear.

Cassidy twisted and shoved him square in the chest. She stumbled when he didn't budge an inch, and all her effort bounced right back.

"Well," she bit, staring at him with such venom, James felt the prickle of it down the back of his neck. "Arrest me, then."

One step, the scuff of her toe along the arcade, and Moone knew what was coming.

"If you run,"—he took a steady step forward—"You know I'll chase you."

A smirk, one as wild and beautiful as a desert sunrise, split the sea of freckles on her face. "I'm counting on it, Deputy. Betcha won't catch me, though."

It wasn't the first time they'd played this game, a kind of cat and mouse. She'd poke and prod, testing his patience. James was sure it was to annoy him, but he couldn't be bothered. Not when that same wildness in her called to some part of him. One that flared brightly when she darted around the corner, offering a girlish grin before disappearing into the alleyway.

The men who raised him were never this free. They sought to feed a hunger, to fan the flames of corruption, greed, and more devilish things Moone didn't dare think of. Lest he stir a beast he'd long-since put to bed. Those men never tasted this. Something that might've resembled fun.

He couldn't help but give in every chance she baited him,

challenging him to play. It was those days he looked forward to most. To see the flash of her eye from beneath her brim when she'd meander back into town.

James wondered what drew her to their streets over and over again. She hadn't any family, not from the barest whispers he heard. Cass had never spoken to him more than a few words at a time over two years. Some knew a little more—especially the girl she'd been defending tonight.

Katie offered what she could—something about a lifetime-long vendetta against a man who'd done Cass wrong.

He recognized something in her—another sad, lonely orphan like him. Maybe that's what brought her back. Perhaps part of him wished it was. Maybe she found a kind of home in Gallow Gorge, in him, the way he did in her and the game they played.

It only took a moment before he caught up to her. She was fast, but he had nearly three hands over her in height— long legs that made it easy to close the distance, nab her by the wrist, and pin her against the wall.

"Caught you," he breathed in her ear, grip firm as she tried to wiggle free. "You know I gotta take you in, right? Set a good example."

"Somebody had to do something," she bit, huffing a spray of copper curls from her forehead. "I couldn't let him do that to Katie."

"I know," he said, gently looping the shackles around her wrists. He almost felt sorry this time. Had he been there, Moone might've done the same. "But there's no law against it, as much as there should be. And I can't have you fighting in the streets. We're better than some of those other towns."

Cassidy shoved backward, momentarily molding their bodies together in a way he couldn't help but notice. He was sure the thought would linger hours later, but not so much as how her voice threaded.

"Aren't you the one who's supposed to protect them?"

"Why do you care so much?" James argued, dropping her wrists. "I don't see your badge, there's no duty to uphold, and you make an awful big show about not giving a shit about anyone here. So, why?"

With just a few words, it didn't feel like a game anymore. Her head hung as she turned. Goosebumps crawled down his arms. Cassidy was about to give him a gift—a piece of herself. He ought to pay attention and keep every syllable in some place sacred.

Her shoulders slumped as she turned and drooped against the wall. "There's this darkness in me, Moone. This noisy thing that won't let me be. I refuse to be silent, to shut my eyes to wrongdoing like that. I did; I have. I watched, voiceless, as a man took whatever he wanted. There wasn't anybody to help me then. Now I've got the strength to try. I don't have any other choice but to help—to be good. I might be a bitch who doesn't give a shit, but there's some goodness in most everyone—even in me. Maybe I can keep someone else from that shadow."

"You might be right, Freckles." James chewed his words, staring down at her as the nighttime ruckus continued one street over. He dared reach out, hooking the tip of his finger under her chin. The touch sent his synapses spinning, especially when the pain in the ass disappeared, and a woman looked back. One whose lips parted, face slack the longer they lingered. Especially when he whispered, "Will you show me how?"

Her brows shot up. "To be good?"

James nodded. He used to know, once. A long time ago.

Too long. A lifetime, another person—the man who'd never be, but still could.

"It can be hard, doing the right thing. It doesn't have to be. You just have to have the balls to do it."

He decided right then that he believed in her more than any creed or persuasion taught to him by other, more important men. To be good for the sake of being good, to help those who couldn't help themselves. Maybe eventually, Cass would let him help her, too.

Then he might bury that other man for good.

"I'll give it my best shot, Cassidy." James smiled at the taste of her name, how good the weight of it felt on his tongue. He'd never called her anything but Callaghan before. Now, he'd find any excuse not to.

The creases around her eyes grew. "Now what, good deputy?"

He bent to her level, brow quirked. "Since I chased you all the way over here, I can't come back empty-handed. I got a reputation to uphold. So, if you're a good girl and make a real show of it, I'll undo those when we get to the station and pour you a glass of whiskey as a thank you."

Her answering smile was one James could let the world burn for. Maybe he would.

But he'd start with a letter. He'd light it up, ignore it, and never return.

Not when he could be good, instead.

[15]

Moone

SACRAMENTO WAS A CITY BURSTING AT THE SEAMS—A MAZE and a mystery he knew Cassidy wanted to unravel. But beneath the brand-new electric light, boisterous streets, and luxuries bought by new money, it was haunted.

The ghost of James Moone traipsed those alleyways, his hands bloody, soul tarnished beyond any hope of recovery. He prowled the shadows, that blade wielded by another hand, delivering *justice*. At least, he thought so at the time.

Now he knew better.

The final leg of their journey got an early start from Rose Reach. Moone was tempted to stay another night or two. Forever, even.

Logic said he needed the time to consider a plan, a way to stall her, to send her back home. She'd already spilled enough blood; he could do this for her. For them. Not just because Katie asked him to.

His body—his heart—couldn't bear to leave the sacred space they built in the quiet of the firelight.

They made good time, making it to the outer threads of the burgeoning metropolis with daylight to spare. Cassidy was a woman on a mission, pointing out the busiest casino, insisting they'd gather plenty of information with all the tongues wagging inside.

She wasn't wrong.

Moone could hardly hear the piano's twang in the corner over the patrons' coarse din. He was thankful for it; each man was too busy with their cards to look up and pay him any mind.

Things had changed since he last stepped foot in the city, and so had he. Altered to his core by the memory of her body against his, the unrelenting insistence in the tips of his fingers to feel it again.

"You sit. I'll get us a drink and speak to the barkeep," Moone rumbled in her ear, giving into the temptation at the small of her back. Just the slightest push toward a table in an empty corner.

Cassidy shivered—another in a growing list of infinitesimal moments and touches he couldn't ignore. He saw how she battled with it, blinking away the fragile intake of breath, slamming down the armor she wore.

"Find out all you can. Where he's at. How many might be there."

"Cass, I know." He lingered longer than he needed, chewing on the beginnings of a smile. Especially when she tried *so* hard to hold onto her usual scowl. "Want some whiskey?"

She gave him a look. It warmed him from the inside out. *There she is.*

"Don't be an idiot, Moone. Bring the bottle."

That lovely, floating feeling sputtered out, dampened by the cloud of guilt. That haunted part of him.

"Too late for that, Cassidy." James tried to laugh, but it

died quickly, taking his smile, too. "Already am an idiot."

For lying. For keeping any secrets from her and never telling who he'd been before—why he needed to keep looking over his shoulder.

Moone felt her gaze as he strode to the bar. It wasn't unwelcome, having the opposite effect from a moment before.

He drummed his fingers on worn wood, thoughts shuffling through every second the night before. Every minute that morning when they woke—moment after moment with Cassidy Callaghan that had them feeling far, far away from *friends*. Something he'd only just let himself accept.

The bed in Rose Reach was too big. Cassidy couldn't hope to fill it, even if she stretched her arms and legs to the furthest corners. In it, she looked so small, so lonely. A void begging to be filled by him.

The thought wouldn't leave him alone as he fulfilled her wish. The water was freezing, but he didn't dare utter a sound to suggest it. Not at the risk of waking her, of altering the sweet song of her steady breathing.

He smiled at the memory, hoping she'd been pleased he'd taken her advice. There'd be no erasing it, the glances across the room at her shoulders' subtle rise and fall as he scrubbed away days on the road in the perfumed water. He wished he could wash away his past as easily.

Maybe it'd have to be baptism by fire and blood.

Moone finally captured the attention of the barkeep. He kept him for a moment or two, speaking of things like the weather, the slightest hint of gossip come downriver. He didn't bother prying for more.

All the while, he felt distracted, anchored by the thought

of her, the feeling of her watching him.

James skimmed his attention across the saloon and met her gaze, inexplicably caught on how her cheeks burned like he'd seen her without her britches.

Except, he had. *More than once.*

She dipped her chin, quick as lightning, hiding the enchanting rose petal hue of her cheeks beneath her brim.

Moone wondered if she was thinking the same thing he was, recalling when he took a fool's chance—fulfilling that insatiable need to fill that chasm of a bed, to have her believe she wasn't alone. She never would be.

Not if he could help it.

He tried not to stir her, holding his breath when he pressed a knee to the mattress. It bent beneath his weight, but there was no turning back. Not then, nor when he laid beside her, pressed his fingertips to the supple softness of her stomach, and dragged her to his chest.

Moone expected his heart to run away like a spooked horse. He expected her to shove him away, boot him to the floor, and demand he sleep in the livery. But when he pressed his nose to her hair, breathed her in, and whispered, "Goodnight, Cassidy," she melted, molding their bodies together.

James couldn't deny how good it felt. Not the weight of her in his arms nor the shiver that poured down him when she caught his hand in her own, brought it to her mouth and promptly fell asleep.

At that moment, Cassidy's presence comforted him like the fire's glow in the bitter cold. One James couldn't shirk if he wanted to.

He thanked the barkeep, returning the bottle and glasses to their table.

She jumped at the squeal of wood against slate, blinking away whatever cloud of thought she'd been caught in.

"What'd you hear?"

Moone slid into the seat across her, plunking the whiskey between them. She promptly pulled it toward her, pouring three fingers into each tumbler.

He drank down the glass in a single gulp, slamming it to the table with a lick of his lips. He hoped it would coat every forthcoming lie in a layer of believability. It was for her own good.

"It's not good news, Freckles."

"I don't care what it is. I've weaseled my way into tough situations before. Out with it."

Determination ground in the tick of her jaw. Whatever it was, good or bad, the steady bounce of a nod told her she thought she could handle it. She'd come too far for James to lead her completely astray, so they'd have to come up with a plan, some way for Moone to get in and do what he promised.

"Beatrice." The truth.

Cass made a face. "What, is that his wife?"

Moone perched a cigarillo in his mouth, striking a match on his heel. He took his time, shuffling the words into the right order. "The city. Just outside of it, anyway. Not far, but it's practically a fortress overlooking the Sacramento River. The only ones going in or out are his men and live-in ladies he cycles out once he tires of them."

"So?" She shrugged, leaning over the table to snatch the freshly lit tobacco from his grip.

God, he was so easily distracted by her mouth now he'd had the barest taste. He'd been focused a second ago, but now all he had was the shape of her lips as she took a long drag. The next, his attention was caught on how smoke spilled over them and flooded their empty glasses with sweet, Cassidy-flavored smoke.

"Sounds like any other job," she muttered. "They hide in their houses and their saloons. I lure them out, or sneak in, and pry them out kicking and screaming."

A plan. They needed a fucking plan. One that'd cost the least time and kept her far away from Jack Ransom.

Wild restlessness twisted in his gut, an urgency to leave her for the afternoon and get it over with. A pistol, maybe a knife; Moone didn't care. He knew it wouldn't be that easy. Cassidy would never let him go without harnessing herself to him first.

"Have any of your other jobs owned the Sheriff's department from here to Guadalajara?" Another truth, much to his dismay and utter shame.

Cass swallowed, gaze falling to the bottle, defeat written in the bend between her brows. "No."

Moone lifted it and sloshed another finger into each glass. Something to do with his hands. "He pays into the Union and has all of Sacramento society in his pocket." Another. "Plus, he controls every ounce of opium that crosses state lines. He owns them all."

"So, he's a rich bastard."

If only she knew just how deep those pockets went and who he kept within them.

"They're all fooled. Everyone in here." He leaned back, attention wafting over gaming tables and soiled doves perched over the players' arms. "You wouldn't think someone like him would settle so well here—a *gentleman*." The word turned bitter on his tongue. "But he's really made himself a home here. They love him; he's manufactured it that way, and they don't know any better."

Cassidy rested her elbows on the table, drumming her fingertips on her mouth, that delectable fucking mouth. She followed the journey his eyes traversed over the barroom. "I assume we can't just knock on the front door and ask *real nice* to see Ransom."

Moone chuckled—he couldn't help it. "Nah, Cass. Don't think that'll go the way you want it to."

"Damn." She sighed, staring thoughtfully at a beautiful woman perched on the arm of a chair. He wondered what detail she took in first: the ironed curl over a powdered bosom or the tremble of a wilted rose in a loose chignon. Then she started to wander, green eyes glazing over with an idea.

"I see that mind of yours working, Cassidy. What is it?"

Her gaze flicked to him like the crack of a whip. She jolted forward, sending the half-empty bottle of whiskey skittering across scuffed wood.

She caught it without blinking, pointing it at herself. "I'm pretty, aren't I?"

Moone coughed, snorting into his glass. "You? Um… *Cassidy.*"

How could she expect him to answer such an inquiry with a single yes or no?

"Sorry. Dumb question." She slouched, chewing on her lip, clearly disappointed in a way James wouldn't stand for. He couldn't have her going another moment thinking she was anything but what he saw.

"You're not pretty." Moone's voice, the earnestness of it, caught him off guard. Her, too, luring her attention from the bottom of the bottle. He took in her features, unsure which part of her he wanted to talk about first.

Perhaps the bend of a copper curl over her shoulder, the memory of them against his nose branded into his brain. Maybe the bright hue of her eyes, like polished sea glass, or how the dusty blackness of her lashes made them stand out in a way he could never describe.

"You—" He swallowed, wishing he was a writer, pen and paper in hand. Then he'd be equipped with a better word than *pretty* to define her. "You're the most beautiful thing I've ever seen."

Her mouth hung open. An argument sat on the tip of her tongue before a barking laugh cut through the lovely feeling flittering about in his chest.

"Katie Mays is pretty. My mother,"—her breath stumbled on a broken sigh—"Aisling was beautiful. I'm not… I'm not like them. I've always laughed off those kinds of things, shit like *pretty*, and left it to more capable women."

"Who says you're not?" Moone countered.

Cass hugged the bottle to her chest. "You've clearly had enough of this. It's making you hallucinate."

"I'm not seeing things—except you blushing." And what a sight it was to see Cassidy Callaghan, someone who lived and breathed control, so affected by *him*. He smirked, cocking his head. Maybe he could do it again. "Did I get to you? Who knew a compliment would do the trick."

It worked.

Cassidy lunged, swinging the bottle, but Moone was faster than her.

He snapped his fingers around her wrist, grinning wider as he twisted it from her grip.

"I don't blush," she hissed.

"If you say so, Freckles." He leaned in, holding the whiskey out of her reach. "Why bother asking if you didn't want the answer?"

God, he was so tempted to kiss her right then and there, but then she stole the thought with just a few words.

She shook her head. "It's not that I didn't like it."

"But?"

Cassidy licked her lips, glancing back at the women across the hall—an idea, plain as day.

"What if we *could* walk in the front door?"

[16]

MOONE CROSSED HIS ARMS, WARILY EYEING THE CRIMSON glow from behind curtains fluttering through open windows.

"I don't like this," he grumbled. "What are we doing here?"

Cass dusted her palms over a still-soiled vest. "We're seeing an old friend."

His brows disappeared, hiking up beneath tawny waves. "You have an old friend at a brothel in Sacramento?"

"Oh, be quiet. Don't act like you haven't paid good money to disappear between a beautiful woman's thighs." She winked, smirking when the tips of his ears pinked. "Besides, Madame Aurélia Dubuisson is the richest woman in Sacramento and a well-respected businesswoman. As old friends go, she's a good one to have. Although, it stings knowing I was this close to Ransom for so long."

"Yeah, I reckon it does. What"—Moone scrubbed the back of his neck, ears reddening further—"What did you do here?"

Cass punched him in the arm. "Don't let your mind run

away with you. I cleaned, cooked, and went to school. Same as you."

"School?"

She nodded. "Madame Dubuisson took me in when I was a little bag of bones—a feral little thing. Barely eleven years old, with nothin' but my horse and a pair of pistols I stole off my first kill."

Cass fiddled with the hammer of one of the pearl-gripped revolvers, heart twisting when she thought of that nightmarish day. By some miracle, she survived months in the desert.

No, not a miracle. Cassidy was armed with the skills her Da taught her. With them and a scavenged set of clothes, plus Solo on her side, she lived longer than any little girl ought to.

They wandered from riverbed to wind-swept bluffs. Somehow, maybe with fate's cruel guiding hand, Cassidy found herself back in the ghostly remains of Faraday Creek.

At first, she cried, begging Solo to take her away. But when he refused to give into the way she tugged and pulled at his mane, then took up residence in a barn outside of town, Cass decided to make good on the resources laid out before them.

Cassidy avoided the Callaghan General Store like a bad dream. Aisling's corpse had long since been dragged away by coyotes; Ian's body had to be long gone, too. Still, she couldn't risk seeing the stains left behind.

She gathered her fill from household cupboards, filling a scavenged set of saddlebags to the brim. There was even a fine leather saddle in the tack that fit Solo just right.

To that day, Cass didn't know how she got it on him or why his wild heart let her fit a bridle over his ears. Maybe that was fate, too, giving where she took away, offering a brother where a mother and father used to be.

Solo never left her alone long, insisting with loud whinnies to sleep beside him in the barn. Cassidy didn't mind it. It was warmer there. Safer, too. It was always safer by his side.

That much was made clear when a pair of thugs wandered into town—twins, like their pistols. They came looking for trouble with a Ransom-blue hanky. Trouble they found at the bottom of Solo's black hooves the minute they threatened her. Trouble they got when Cassidy pulled a pearl-gripped revolver from the belt of a dead man just in time to silence the remaining brother.

Cass didn't have to keep the pistols, but she couldn't bear to leave them behind when they set off the next day. It wasn't like she needed them to survive; she'd proved otherwise. Part of her wondered if they might've been a trophy of her first. Maybe they were an excuse to practice the art of her quickdraw the way she did with Ian. More than anything, perhaps they were a reminder of the promise she'd made to him, to question every bullet, every kill.

"I owe her a lot," Cass breathed. "She educated me, took care of me, and taught me all the other ways to take care of myself my Da didn't... *couldn't*. I stayed until I saved enough money and was strong enough to make it alone."

Moone nodded in quiet understanding, another orphan who did his best in the shadow of a tragic beginning. His eyes slipped to the red, blue, and white striped flag in the window.

"So, she's French?"

"No, not in the slightest." Cass laughed, ringing the bell. Her hands battled the wild curls from beneath her hat,

slicking them down with a lick of her fingers. "But Willie Grover isn't the… *hell*… kind of name you think of… *damn curls*… when you hear about a prestigious madame in Sacramento, is it?"

Moone frowned, puzzled. "What in the hell are you doing?"

"Nothing. Well… *ugh*." She straightened her coat, fiddled with her brim, and promptly decided to forego the hat entirely. "I was always taught you oughta look your best when seeing your mother for the first time in ages."

He bent, gripping her shoulders, fluttering the curls around her face. "Cassidy, quit. It's gonna be fine."

The door swung open, and the pair were promptly greeted by half a dozen women crowding the frame, whose eyes wasted no time in sizing up her companion. Whispers fluttered through them. Ones that made Cass's insides churn in a way she hated.

"Move aside, girls. *Allez! En avant!* Let me pass." The crowd of girls split like a river around a stone, revealing a small woman. Madame Dubuisson never let that deter her, making up for her stature in fierceness. Her features hadn't changed much with age. The fine lines and spots only accentuated a sharp jaw, high cheekbones, and a long, aquiline nose. Her deep-set, hazel eyes shimmered when she laid eyes on Cassidy, but she didn't crack a smile. "Cassidy Kathleen. *Years.* Years it's been since you've been to see me. You could write to your poor *maman* more often. Then she worries less."

"Hello." Cass smiled. "You're right. I'm sorry."

Madame Dubuisson turned, waving them in, scattering the girls throughout the house with a single, withering stare. "Well, come on. I assume you need something—*desperately*."

They ventured into a wood-lined foyer featuring a prominent staircase curling up the side wall. Perfume clung to thick wafts of smoke, sticking to velvet curtains and brass sconces.

The old woman led Cassidy up the stairs, slapping down her cane when Moone made to follow behind her. She glared down at him from the third stair through a pair of *pince-nez* she whipped from a breast pocket. "Are you paying?"

Moone's attention snapped to Cass, silently pleading for her help, then back to the madame. "No. No ma'am. I wasn't planning on being a proprietor of this fine establishment this evening."

Her hazel eyes narrowed, deconstructing him piece by piece, straight down to the bone. Then she smiled with a knowing nod. "Because Cassidy is the one you want, no?"

"I… um." He stuffed his hands in his pockets, flushed beneath his whiskers. "No, ma'am."

Her grin grew. "Can't fool an old lady like me. I know men. I've seen them all. I've seen *everything*. This,"—she poked him in the chest with her cane—"is a love-sick fool. *Pauvre mec*. Be careful of him, *mon chéri*. They and their hearts get in the way of business. They cause trouble."

"I'm not here to create any problems, ma'am." Moone held up his hands, an attempt at a peace offering. He stepped closer, but she pushed back.

Cass's stomach twisted when his blue eyes met hers again. Softer and more earnest than she'd seen them, steeped with the things that happened the night before—and all the things that never would.

She shook her head, banishing any thought entertaining the idea of *love*. There wasn't any time for that nonsense, even if there was room in her black heart for such a thing.

Cass turned up the stairs, leaving her mentor to question Moone at her leisure, unwilling to waste another second on the mere idea of someone loving her, let alone someone as good as James Moone.

She wandered down a corridor lined with half a dozen closed doors. Behind each was a beautiful woman, her wares, and the highest quality of love for sale. At the end was Madame Dubuisson's private sitting room. One reserved for only the closest friends of the house.

Cass shut herself in the quiet, breathing in the sweet scent of cassia and cinnamon as she traced her touch over jade birds and a carved pipe lying on a table. Different treasures, other memories, were hidden in the corners of this house than that of Faraday Creek.

A home-cooked meal—the first in years. Warm water in a porcelain basin. The lace-trimmed cloth that drew the grime away and revealed the hidden hue of her hair. The tender touch of a mother's embrace when nightmares of a crimson-eyed man locked her in a burning church. One that never shirked away, never looked the other way when Cassidy was filled with questions.

Cass received an education at the hands of Willie Grover. A love she needed—as unconventional as it may be. Math lessons came in the form of balancing a ledger, cooking with an army of sisters, adding spices in a cloud, and writing by copying down words from books borrowed from bedside tables.

As wonderful as it may have been, and even if Willie planned to give her everything one day, Cassidy couldn't sit still. They both knew she wouldn't stay once she was able to leave.

The call to arms was too strong to ignore. The hunger

for the hunt.

"That boy is bound to get his heart broken." The madam's familiar, tobacco-stained timbre made Cassidy smile. With the door sealed shut, leaving only the two of them, Willie Grover let the persona of Aurélia Dubuisson fall away. Silver threaded the black hair artfully gathered on the crown of her head, hair that cascaded over her shoulder in loose ringlets. No curl was out of place, even when she shook her head and tutted in motherly displeasure. "I know what you're up to. Why you're here."

"I know what you're going to say." Part of Cass deflated under her sharpened gaze, but she couldn't give in and quit. Not when she was this close. "I know you'll tell me not to go."

"Don't claim to know my thoughts, girl." The old woman was quiet, drumming her fingers on the head of her cane. "Though, I have half a mind to tell you to stay a while, maybe wait a week or two. Perhaps unravel whatever knot you've got yourself tied up in with that tall drink of water downstairs."

Cassidy stared at her boots, chewing her lip. "It's tempting."

So tempting, so inviting to feel at home, to have another quiet moment with James. A hundred of them, maybe. But she knew her mind; it'd never be silent, never be still with Ransom so close and the deed undone.

"But?"

"I've waited too long already. Counting the days until something fell into my lap." Cassidy wrung her hands. None of the words made her feel lighter, like she imagined confessing things to your mother ought to feel. All she had was the unbearable gravity of what was within her reach, but still so far away.

"I know." Willie's weathered but still beautiful hand found her shoulder. "But you know you're always welcome here, don't you?"

"Yes." Cassidy nodded, smile weak. "I do."

"Lord knows I could use your help with some troublemakers around here, but they'll keep. My girls are safe enough for now." Willie tapped the head of her cane with a ring-laden hand. "Time's wasting, girl. Tell me what you need, and I'll tell you what you need to know."

Cass wanted to pry, but her *maman* tugged her to her feet.

"I need to hide in plain sight as one of your girls. I need to convince him I'm worth keeping. Long enough to catch him unawares." She motioned at her worn leather vest, everything that branded her as a bounty hunter. "I'm not exactly *high quality* like this."

The madam sniffed, eyes sliding to a trunk tucked away in a corner. "I have a few things I've been saving for you. Just in case you changed your mind about the trousers." Her beautiful, weathered face cracked into a smile. She stepped forward, spinning Cassidy to face a floor-length mirror. Her knuckle fondly paved a trail down her freckled jaw. "But you've always been worth keeping, *mon chéri*. Even like this."

"Thank you," Cassidy breathed, the barest slice of relief oozing down her arms.

The madam stepped between her and the trunk—a barrier. "You realize what he'll expect of you, don't you?"

She nodded, shivering. "I do. I know."

"You'll have to be one hell of an actress not to let him see that fire in you." A worrying crease split her brows. "You've had murder in your eyes since you were a tiny little thing. But"—she paused thoughtfully—"He's always had a taste for redheads. Perhaps that'll serve as a welcoming distraction. Something you can use to your advantage."

Cassidy's stomach churned, thoughts zinging through everything she might have to do. She'd only been with a man one regrettable time. But, for months, she'd thought about *things* with one in particular. Years, maybe, much to her dismay. He waited for her, tempted her, just downstairs.

Sometimes, Cass might even fancy herself a bit of a flirt, especially where Katie and Madame Ridley's girls were concerned. Maybe, *somehow*, she might scrounge up a character to play.

Piece by piece, Cassidy's armor came away. It was different than the night before when James reverently obliterated every haunting thought with each layer. No, this time, each threadbare, sun-stained bit of fabric was replaced by protection of a different kind.

One made of a thick cotton chemise and a bone-lined corset that changed her shape, transforming her like a chameleon into someone with curves. The freckles on her arms were covered with stacks of emerald silk, her wild copper curls tamed, ironed, and pinned until her neck ached from their weight.

Hours later, after she was primped and prodded, a stranger looked back at her in the mirror, rosy and bright-eyed—more like Aisling Callaghan than Cassidy ever thought she'd look.

She didn't know anything about fashion, never around women who cared about it long enough to see them in anything more than a chemise and stockings. Even then, it'd find its way to the floor with little thought to what something was called.

Still, even though she couldn't recall the name for the ruffles at her elbows or the bump over her ass, Cassidy thought the dress was *beautiful.* Expensive to the touch, the deep green fabric shimmered in the fading afternoon light. Each tuck and fold created curves where Cass had none. Pink satin roses were gathered at her hips and at the end of a weighted bustle—at least, that's what Willie called it—and buttons hid along her waist. A modest, fashionable trick to shift her gown from day to night.

Cassidy saw her freckles as dusty reminders of how much time she'd spent in the sun, an unattractive quality in a woman. Madame Dubuisson worked some kind of magic and made those beautiful, too. She glowed from within, only an echo of the woman she was when she and Moone rode away from Gallow Gorge.

It was wrong, the stranger looking back at her. So unlike herself, but precisely what they needed to let Cass slip between the cracks at Ransom's estate—enough to get noticed.

"Here." Willie rustled in a box on her desk, wearing a wicked look. She twisted something to and fro—a silver hairpin with a looping knot at the end. "Some of my girls wear these as an extra precaution. I thought you might find it of use."

"A decoration will help me?" Cass was unconvinced how a bauble would help her kill Jack Ransom.

The madam nodded knowingly, flicking a hidden blade free. "Stick this between the fourth and fifth ribs, and even a man like Lord Ransom will die."

Something strange flared within her, the barest hint of hope. With Willie's help, she might actually pull this scheme off.

"Now, I've only met him a time or two. All of Sacramento society speaks highly of him. He's always been a bachelor. A rich one, which is good for me and great for my girls. He's not unkind to them, but the others—be wary of his men. They haven't the same manners as he," the madam said, brushing out a wrinkle, a distraction for them both as details spilled forth Cassidy could barely believe. How could the monster she witnessed be the generous benefactor she spoke about?

"I could tell you a thing or two about his *manner* when he came to Faraday Creek," Cassidy bit.

"I know," Willie answered with a soothing hand down her arm. "Don't think I don't worry about what lies beneath his mask. That I won't worry about you while you're there, for however long. Be careful."

"I'm always careful," Cass argued.

The madam wrinkled her nose. "Tell that to the bullet holes in my carriage house."

The pair burst into effervescent laughter, Cassidy's cheeks warm with the memory of a simpler time—before the burden of her task settled on her shoulders.

It did then, quieting their momentary joy.

Willie leaned on her cane, giving her an appraising look.

"It's a few years out of date, but it'll do. You look expensive. Jack Ransom won't be able to say no." She picked at a stray thread on her sleeve. "The housekeeper greets all my girls upon their arrival. Through the back door to the kitchen, the guards won't let you in the front. That's for guests of the house only. She'll put you up with the other girls. I haven't one there at the moment. I can't say who the other houses send. There are a lot of men in the house and plenty of money going around. Be patient but persistent.

It'll take heaps of luck for you to see him that first day. Once he does, I have no doubt you'll be the apple of his eye, my love."

Cassidy swallowed, cheeks flushing the longer she stared at her reflection. Her stomach twisted at what awaited her at day's end. Could a lifetime's obsession really be just within reach? "I hope so."

She wondered what it'd look like, how it'd feel being beside him when the floorboards acted as a barrier before.

Perhaps luck would be on her side; maybe she'd catch his eye that first day. He'd be as enchanted by her as she was of her own reflection—the lovely lady she'd daydreamed about as a child. *Jack*, she'd call him, sweet as a siren's song. Honeyed and saccharine, enough to tempt him to bed where she'd strangle him with her bare hands. Perhaps she'd poison him or slit his throat as he slept. There were too many options to choose from. Any of them would be good enough—so long as he'd be dead and buried by her hand.

Maybe then, she could finally be still.

Cassidy gave herself a final once-over, gathered her gun belts, and left her dusty clothes behind. As she wandered back down the corridor, echoes of lovemaking made her insides churn. Her face heated at the thought of how close she and Moone came the night before and the taste of him she wore on her lips.

It was for the best they didn't give in to the feeling. Moone was a distraction. Cassidy couldn't be led astray because a man looked at her a certain way. No matter how much she liked that Moone saw her for who she was beyond the bounty hunter. No matter how much she loved how his blue eyes lit up when she turned down the stairs.

[17]

MOONE

MOONE WONDERED WHAT WAS IN THE WHISKEY THEY drank earlier that afternoon. What other reason would there be for the disequilibrium of his limbs, the sharp, unsettling churn of his stomach? Of all things he should be, James was flustered to high heaven when Madame Dubuisson picked him apart with a single look.

Cassidy disappeared up the stairs, but the old woman didn't follow. To his eye, she was on a mission to decode him, separate the threads of his soul, and see him straight down to his bones.

She jabbed him in the chest with her cane again.

"Ouch. Stop it!" He stumbled back, jerking further when she made to prod him again. He didn't want to go somewhere else; he wanted to be with Cassidy. Always. Especially now, with the Devil so close.

"*Chut! Vas-y, vas-y,*" she bit, herding him into a room down the hall. Beautiful faces sprouted in the doorways, eyes wide and curious, hungry smiles displayed as their mistress dressed him down.

Their whispers followed within the four walls of a small

parlor, but Moone couldn't pay them any mind. Not with Aurelia Dubuisson glaring daggers up at him. Until then, he'd never felt so small.

Her rings clacked on the head of her cane, followed by a deep, frustrated sigh. *"Quelles sont tes intentions avec ma fille?"*

"J'sais pas. Rien du tout." He whirled away from her, answering without thinking how it ought to come out. In a single sentence, he didn't sound at all like the humble Deputy Sheriff of Gallow Gorge.

Her brows lifted with the detail about himself Moone didn't intend to give away. His lie was written in the twitch of her eye and impatient tilt of her mouth.

"Do not tell me there's nothing between you. *Cervelle de petit pois.* Do you think me to be imbecilic?"

He stood straighter, shaking his head. "No, ma'am." Of all the things Madame Dubuisson—Willie Grover—might be, an idiot wasn't one of them.

"Does Cassidy know you speak so well?" She sniffed, staring out the window—as if all his secrets rattled by in one of those fine carriages. "You have a Parisian accent."

"Do I?" He tried to deflect, to shrug away the memory of the year he'd spent there with a weapons master in a marbled salon by day. By night, Moone was a *flâneur*, aloofly observing glimmering nighttime boulevards and visiting Le Chabanais. Not to mention winter on Tenerife; he, a ghost in the shadows of a great house in La Orotava as deals were struck with the tip of a pen or the end of a knife. Or the year he lived in England. The summer spent in London, dancing with wallflowers on the ton, always at the beck and call of the man who raised him.

He hadn't lied when he told Cassidy he had a tutor. The tutor and master were one and the same.

His master had a lot to teach and to pass on. Moone wanted to learn it and was happy with the life he got to live—until it became too much.

James Moone lived a dozen different lifetimes in seven years. He was a dutiful student, eager to learn and do as he was told.

But not anymore.

"Hm." The madam regarded him warily, running a tired old finger along the edge of her *pins-nez*. "I don't like secrets, but I understand them. Whatever reason you have for the lie, can I assume your affection for Cassidy is not a deception?"

"No," he answered as earnestly as he could. "It isn't."

"Good," she said, focus far, far away again—the spitting image of a worried mother. Moone had one of those once. He wondered who he'd be if he still did. "I need you to do something for me."

"Ma'am—"

She silenced him with a hand from her cane. "There's no stopping her, no chance of changing her mind once it's set. You and I both know this."

"I do," Moone said gravely. If her marching out into the street in naught but her gun belts were any indication, being stubborn might be what Cassidy was best at. She'd see things through, even if it came at the cost of her own life. "You want me to stay with her."

"No"—she stepped forward, hazel eyes boring into him, mining through every minute and hour of his past, seeing what he was capable of—"If you see an opening," she said, French accent bleeding away to her true self, to Willie Grover. Too desperate to hide behind the facade any longer. "End this. End him. End it all before it takes her, too."

While Madam Dubuisson fussed with Cassidy upstairs, Moone underwent a transformation of his own, stripped of any ounce of Gallow Gorge's Deputy Sheriff. Gone were his vest and dusty boots. A stack of finely made clothes awaited him on a table, delivered with a porcelain basin filled with warm water, a mirror, and everything he needed for a shave.

Moone wasn't a stranger to the barber in Gallow Gorge, but among their humble people and grimy streets, he found it easy to go a week—sometimes a month—between shaves. He didn't mind the whiskers much, but where they were headed, who he needed to be, required a more drastic alteration.

At the washbasin, shirt discarded, James scrubbed through his face and hair, shuddering when a bead of cooled water trickled down his back. More heated whispers seeped through the barest crack in the door, maybe the keyhole.

Back home, that kind of thing always amused him, but not now. Not as he cleaved away at the man he'd become, who he wanted to be. With each careful slash of the razor's blade, with every band of shave soap, James uncovered who lay beneath. Someone he never thought Cassidy would see. There was no avoiding it now.

He considered Katie's plea. Willie's, too; a mother's invocation, an insatiable need to see her daughter safe.

There was no escaping thoughts of his own mother. How she tried so hard to do the same. Jolene Moone acted as a shield. While she wore the stain of a fist or belt meant for him, she held fast to the belief that, somehow, someway, James could be good like her. He could be a protector, a stalwart bastion even the fiercest waves could crash against, and he wouldn't waver.

Moone tried, and he still would. He wouldn't lose sight

of that good deputy, even if that other man looked back at him in the mirror.

It was odd how welcome and familiar a stiff, starched collar could be. An uneasy feeling built within him, not because of buttoning a fine damask vest or the weight of the navy tailcoat. No, Moone figured his discomfort had everything to do with how *comfortable* he felt in that other man's skin. Like coming home after too many years away.

He wouldn't let it—let him—take over. He'd never give back his soul now he'd finally taken possession of it.

The sight of her would make it easy to keep it at bay; the peculiar tremor in his belly when she crested the top of the stairs would be the blade with which he'd beat it back.

Moone swallowed the sudden lump in his throat. He was used to Cassidy a certain way, freckled face half-obscured by a brim—just enough, he memorized the curve of an almost smile.

But now, framed by emerald, James saw all of her. Unlike the overwrought silence of their suite in Rose Reach, it wasn't her body that caught him off-guard. No, that had been molded into a different shape, the rest of her hidden behind voluminous skirts.

Her face, though. All of it was on display, accentuated by a rosy flush in her cheeks. While so much of her had been changed, Cassidy was still herself. Pieces of her were illustrated in her tongue stuck out in concentration as she descended, and a curse under her breath when she wobbled on brand-new carriage boots.

There was no thinking, no second-guessing his actions when he bounded up to meet her.

"Here, let me," he said, extending his hand. Familiar, all of it painfully, so.

A frustrated divot rolled between her brows.

"Well, aren't you the gentleman," she groused, taking his hand anyway.

Moone kept firm, a stable platform for her to balance against. He relished the feeling of it, the memory of those fingers in his hair the night before.

He stretched his own when she, regrettably, released her hold. Maybe it was to rid himself of how his skin tingled from her touch, to regain his focus. The rest of him might've buzzed, too. He couldn't help it, the way his chest warmed or the beginnings of a smile the longer he looked at her.

"You look—" he started.

She *glowered* up at him. "Don't get any ideas, Moone. I'm wearing this for one reason and one reason only."

James swallowed the lovely feeling. He tore away the wannabe grin with a lick of his lips, stuffing his hands in his pockets to avoid touching her again. "Right."

He regarded her carefully, taking in every brittle second as she stared down the nest of leather and steel; a quick glance over her shoulder at her *maman*. The old woman shook her head—ladies didn't wear revolvers over their dresses, and he didn't think she could fit them beneath her petticoats.

Moone was still as a statue when she unwound the weighted leather and held her gun belt out.

"Will—" Her voice trembled. Other men would say it was silly to have an attachment to a weapon, but Moone understood. They'd been with her since the beginning. Parting with them, even for a day or two, would be like saying goodbye to a friend.

His hand covered hers. "Yes, Cassidy. I will."

His heart flipped, stuttering the longer she stared at the scars carved into his knuckles.

Cass lifted her gaze. Never mind Madame Dubuisson watching a few steps away or the echoes of well-paid women coming from upstairs. Maybe it was the smoke-stained perfume. Perhaps it was the curls of it dancing on golden-hued light streaming through heavy velvet curtains. Perhaps it was the fragility of her trust, so freely given to someone who didn't deserve it. Maybe it was the remnants of her gratitude for what he'd done for her that made him want to wind his arms around her waist and finish what they started.

He swallowed that feeling, too. That, and the thundering beat of his heart when she slid the edges of her lead-leaden belt beneath the seams of his tailcoat, fastening the pistols around his hips with a whisper.

"Keep them safe, please."

"As I intend to do with you, Cassidy," Moone answered truthfully, barely a whisper. He looped his hands around hers, squeezing. "Unless." He gulped down a breath, working his jaw. "Unless you changed your mind and want to go home? It isn't too late."

Cassidy stiffened, leaning away.

He was a fool for asking, for thinking there was anything left for them in Gallow Gorge without seeing this through.

"No. I didn't come all this way for nothing." She lifted her chin, side-stepping him toward the door. "We're leaving. It's time to end this once and for all."

Finish this, Katie pleaded. *End this, end him*, Madame Dubuisson commanded.

They wanted him to do it for her, but Moone wanted it for himself, for her as well.

For them.

Only then, they might finally have the chance to be free from his grip—to finally *live*.

[18]

Moone

THEY BID FAREWELL TO MADAME DUBUISSON AS afternoon light gave way to lustrous luminance along the horizon. It was so beautiful—and so was she. James wanted to linger in the sight of backlit buildings down the Sacramento boulevards. But there were too many miles to cover before nightfall. Too little time to make their way to Ransom.

Still, Moone wasn't ready to let go—to break the ease of just being *them*. He wasn't prepared to face what violating her trust would look like, or how hard he'd have to work to gain it again.

There'd be no going back once she knew the truth.

So, he centered himself in it, basking in the warmth of their friendship, the remarkable familiarity of it all.

"Are you sure you can ride in that?" Moone rolled a cigarillo between his teeth, eyeing Cassidy from stem to stern.

Solo shifted impatiently, chomping on his bit. Apparently, one night and an afternoon holed up in a stable were too much for him—even with extra oats as payment. Cassidy was restless, too. Overeager to finally move on, to avoid his gaze, and maybe put their night in Rose Reach behind them.

He was too much of a distraction otherwise.

"Sure as hell can," she snapped, the wild girl still beneath all the ruffles.

Moone watched, hopelessly amused, as Cassidy kicked at the hem of her gown. She gathered layers of fabric above her knee in one hand and anchored the other on the pommel. Her boot slipped from the stirrup before she could hoist herself from the stone pavers.

She swore, blowing a curl from her forehead as she tried again and again… and again.

As fun as it was, Moone couldn't stand to watch her struggle. Not for long. Not without remembering what she said the last time he boosted her into a saddle.

"Okay, *enough*," James grumbled, clamping his hands on her hips.

He didn't leave her time to argue or scream and shout. His heart had other ideas, thundering away like a stray filly on a summer's day when he held her so easily and hoisted her onto Solo's back.

"Why in the hell did you go and do a thing like that?" She glowered down at him, wiggling against the frame of the saddle, trying in vain to swing a leg over the other side. "I can't ride like this. I don't know how."

"You don't need to know how," Moone smirked, vaulting himself behind her. Every minute of her riding experience probably argued over the mere *idea* of riding sidesaddle. Maybe more so than the idea of them riding together.

He could've sworn she gasped at the contact. James tried not to think about it, the burning tingle in the tips of his ears when his chest pressed against her back.

Cassidy jerked her elbow, likely aiming for his ribs—a reminder of what they were to each other. Who she was beneath the silken ruffles. "James Moone, there's barely enough room for me in this saddle, let alone the two of us."

Moone wound an arm around her waist, tugging her into his lap. His fingers wandered down her thigh, bending her knee to settle over the top of his. Sure, there wasn't enough room in the saddle for both of them, but if *he* were the saddle—

"We'll just have to get nice and cozy," he breathed in her ear, catching an intoxicating whiff of violets. "With any luck, the ride to Beatrice won't be too bad. Just so long as you quit bellyaching."

Cass ignored him, huffing when Solo seemed to agree with a nicker. He pawed at the ground, inching forward the longer they bickered. When she didn't answer after a moment, Moone urged the stallion on with a gentle press of his heels.

He couldn't help shamelessly flirting with her. He knew she didn't want to want him, to think about the idea of *them*. She said so herself. But being so close, avoiding the temptation for long was impossible.

Moone needed some way to prove it was real, what it meant to feel this way about her, to be trusted by her. He wanted to stay a moment longer, to linger in the kiss of her hair against his cheek. The memory would never be enough, not if it was about to end the second they stepped into the den of vipers.

He intended to cut the head from the king snake, but there was no telling what lay on the other side of the act—or if what Cassidy planned would be enough.

After a mile or two of her silence, bathed in the scent

of violets, Moone gave in and brushed his nose along the supple valley between her shoulder and ear.

"I can't stand the quiet. Talk to me, Freckles." He paused, tenderly kissing the stumbling canter of her pulse. "While we still can."

"I can't," she whispered in return as the tiniest hairs on her neck lifted into fine pinpricks.

Gold-hued sunlight bled into inky twilight. Oil lamps along the road stretched the shadows, hiding their most sinister fears in the deepest reaches of the darkness—far enough, they looked all the more terrifying.

Moone felt her apprehension in the tenseness of her shoulders, the stiff lean of her neck. He did what he could, keeping his arms firmly around her as Solo continued at a steady trot.

He'd been surprised the elegant beast listened almost as well as he did for her, giving in at the slightest tug of the reins at a fork in the road.

James hadn't given any indication if the barkeep that afternoon knew where Ransom's fortress sat. He never asked, and merely offered Cassidy the city where it lay. If she wondered why he guided Solo with such ease—as if he seemed to know where he was going—she didn't say a word.

Even if she was suspicious, there was no time to question it, not when a mammoth mansion rose like a colossus on the horizon.

"We're here," she uttered.

"That we are," Moone answered, barely a whisper. Any ounce of playfulness from before evaporated in a second. "Welcome to *Colina de Dragones*."

He gently drew back the reins, bringing Solo to a stop.

"What are you doing?" Cassidy asked, voice brittle when

he carefully unseated and dismounted. "There's no time for delay."

"We're making the time, Cassidy." Moone reached for her, drawing her down by the waist. He started to count the touches. How, despite the tension of Jack Ransom just steps away, Cassidy lingered close. Her hands balanced on his shoulders, fingers spooling between his when he made to step away.

"It looks so inviting," she said softly, face shifting from wonder to bitterness in a breath. "It's a lie. A castle might be beautiful, someplace for a fairytale, but this one…" She trailed off, shaking her head. "This one has a monster hiding inside."

Moone brushed his thumb over the back of her hand. "Care to fill me in on your plan?"

Cassidy worried her lip, peering up at him. "What, you don't want me to turn back and go home?"

"Of course I do," he answered. Moone was prepared to do whatever he needed to keep her safe. Cassidy didn't need to come along if he was going to deliver on what was asked of him. "But I know your mind, Freckles. I can try changing it all I want, but it'll be useless."

The weight of the possibilities, the chance to bury it and forget any of it ever happened, was overwhelming. A stuttering sigh scraped out of her throat, and she choked on the truth; the thought of living the rest of her life knowing Ransom was still out there would be unbearable. Cassidy Kathleen Callaghan was haunted, a vessel for revenge. The ghosts of her past would never rest until the deed was done.

Moone knew well enough that if she ever wanted to be cured of it, if she were to ever be still, she had to see it through.

She summoned an unconvincing smile. "Never say never. I give it a day before you start begging me to go."

"If you're still speaking to me by then."

Cassidy worked her jaw. "Yeah, I suppose there'll have to be some distance between us."

"What's your angle?" he asked, rooted to the spot, even in the middle of the road. Anything to keep from getting caught up in the gale of what was to come.

She shrugged, mouth thinning. "I'm just another girl sent from Madame Dubuisson. She told me where I ought to go, what to expect. I'm pretty enough. The best I can do is hope he'll notice me, or I can weasel my way into his good graces and make him. If things work out how I hope, then this won't take long."

Moone's gut churned. He knew Ransom would home in on her in a second, no matter how much he wished it wasn't true. Cassidy wasn't just anyone; she was beautiful beyond compare, even without all the trappings. *Of course*, he'd notice.

"For how long?"

"However long it takes, Moone." She lifted her chin. "Whatever it takes."

"*Whatever it takes*," he echoed, grinding his teeth in a flash of jealousy. "I am begging you, Cassidy. Don't let it get that far."

Her face softened, eyes shining. "Don't."

"Don't what?"

Moone's heart nearly leaped from his chest when her fingers traversed his jawline and hugged his face. She drew him down, nose nearly brushing his.

"Don't let whatever this is get in the way," she breathed, lifting her chin—an invitation. A goodbye.

His gaze shifted from her lovely, freckled face in the moonlight, eyes closed in anticipation, to the sprawling Spanish Colonial looming on the hill. A million unsaid things lay heavy between them, too heavy for him to consider taking one last taste of her.

Instead, he pressed his lips to her forehead and breathed her in. A torturous, beautiful moment they'd never recreate. She leaned into him, gripping the folds of his jacket. For a moment, he wondered if she might insist they saddle up and ride for Gallow Gorge.

Until he broke the spell with a handful of syllables.

"I'm sorry."

Cass stared at him, sliding a boot back in loose gravel. "For what?"

Moone didn't answer, towing Solo up the long, winding drive. He expected her to shake him, to beat her fists on his chest for an answer—one he wasn't going to give. Not yet. Not with eyes watching them from the gate twenty paces away.

He pushed her behind him with a rushed whisper as they approached. "Be quiet. Say *nothing* unless you have to."

"Moone—" she started, but voices cleaved through the night air.

"Who's there?"

James stood straighter, eyes narrowed, and he slipped the skin of that other man on like a favorite jacket.

Two men stood between towering stone pillars and a wrought iron gate. One rail-thin, suspenders barely hanging onto slight shoulders. He ran a hand over his close-cropped hair and glanced at his companion. The other, an older man still holding onto relics from the war, scrubbed at the Confederate gray cap on his head.

He should've expected this, nary a flicker of recognition. "I'm here to see Lord Ransom," he commanded.

The younger of the two chortled, eyeing Cassidy hidden away behind him. "His Lordship ain't expectin' any visitors at present."

"He'll see me," Moone answered, a nervous shiver clawing down his back, knowing Cassidy heard every word.

Their laughter continued. "Yeah, and who the fuck are you?"

"James Moone."

A part of him preened at how their faces went slack, eyes widening in recognition—how something as simple as a name held so much power.

That *he* held so much power.

The guards let them pass without further argument, Cassidy's grip made of iron on his sleeve.

Colina de Dragones was as imposing and beautiful as he remembered. Bright plaster, red pavers, and jewel-toned tiles made for a house impossible to forget. He knew it as a fortress, but it didn't look like a fort in the traditional sense. No ramparts, no towers. Just a beautiful, sprawling hacienda with untold secrets and power within its walls.

"Come on," he said once they were in the shadow of the house, tying Solo off at a post. "We best not dawdle."

Cassidy stared at his proffered palm. "What's going on?"

"Time's wasting, Freckles." He shook his head, motioning at the towering front doors.

She pulled back, attention darting to the light spilling onto stone pavers at the back of the house. "Madame Dubuisson said to go through the back door. The housekeeper manages the girls once they arrive… *all* of Ransom's girls go through her."

He hooked his fingers through hers, chest heaving. "We don't need to go through the back door."

Questions. Moone was sure her mind was filled to the brim, overflowing as the seconds ticked by.

At the front door, her eyes grew wide when he dropped the weighted knocker, and it swung open as if someone was waiting for them on the other side.

Moone knew it would happen, knew the firmly set scowl of an aging man. His gray eyes took her in, first, then James. It only took half a second, maybe less, for his weathered face to go slack like Scrooge facing Marley's ghost.

"Jimmy?"

Moone cleared his throat, stepped into the light, and left Cassidy alone on the terrace. They shared a quick exchange, but his attention was fixed on her, on the lies that flowed one after the other.

A moment later, Moone slipped her hand in the crook of his elbow when they were led inside. It left her free to gawk at the interior of the sprawling estate.

Pillars lined a red-brick walkway around a vast, domed courtyard wrapping around a grandiose staircase. The veranda above was dotted with arched doorways. Pretty girls leaned on the balcony, whispering behind their fans as Cassidy blindly followed behind him.

They passed by half a dozen men. They went through the same flurry of emotions—a wide-eyed stare quickly followed by the tip of a hat and a curt "Jimmy."

Moone was wordless. Any good feeling, any ounce of power he felt at the first flash of recognition, disappeared into the sea of his guilt. With each face, it grew and grew, knowing Cassidy's questions were insurmountable by now.

He battled it back with square shoulders and a stiff back.

He carried himself like a different person, the opposite of the man who'd lean on anything that stood still long enough. Not the cadence of a deputy, but one of a gentleman.

The butler led them into a plush sitting room. A lavish collection of velvet-covered furniture with a roaring fire. The familiar scent of expensive tobacco clung to everything. It made his head spin, how much Moone felt like he *belonged* there—at home amongst fine paintings and crystal decanters filled with expensive whiskey.

"Wait here, Jimmy." The old man offered a mottled smile, *happy* to see him. "He's been looking forward to this."

When they were alone, Cassidy broke the brittle silence.

"What the hell is going on, Moone?" she bit, pacing between a wing-back chair and a grandfather clock. "They keep looking at you like they saw a ghost… *Jimmy?* Explain that to me right now."

"Do what you're told, Cassidy." Moone's attention snapped to her. "I fucking told you to be *silent.*"

Regret. James was sure the well of it would never run dry. Not with how she blinked at him with hurt or the cold slap of betrayal when a man strode through the door.

The absent Sheriff of Gallow Gorge.

The Scourge of the West.

His mentor and master…the hand that wielded him

[19]

CASSIDY

IT PLAYED OUT IN SLOW MOTION, A SERIES OF NEVER-ENDING seconds unfolding before her very eyes. The groan of the hinges, the spice of tobacco and cinnamon. Slow, heavy footsteps. A shadow that proceeded him.

Moone smiled, extending a hand to the man striding through the doorway. They shared a laugh. Then, wonder of wonders, Jack Ransom *embraced* James Moone like he'd done it a thousand times before.

He was taller than she remembered; handsome, too. Maybe as tall as Moone, though sharper, more angular—high cheekbones and a sloping brow framing a long nose. Truly aristocratic like the heroes in the novels she devoured.

In the lamplight of a posh sitting room rather than between dusty floorboards, he didn't seem at all like the man in her memory. His eyes practically glowed from within, tinged gold in the firelight. They sparkled as he mirthfully took in the sight of her companion, never mind she was there. A shadow in the light of their reunion.

Ransom hugged Moone's face, patting him on the cheek like a small boy. "It's been far too long. Why don't you ever come to visit?" His smile fell, gaze sliding over Moone's shoulder. A flicker of recognition passed over his face. His mouth quirked as if she, too, were a ghost. His lips formed a word, a name. One she hoped haunted him. *Aisling.* "What beautiful creature have you brought with you?"

Moone spun, eyes snapping to her like he'd only just remembered she was there.

Ransom stepped around him, reaching for her hand with a smile. Her heart pounded, mind screaming that sheep ought to run when a wolf comes calling, even if they wore a gentleman's clothes.

But she wasn't a sheep, rather a lioness on the hunt, prowling unseen until it was time to strike. This was better than she could have hoped. There was no other choice but to play along.

All at once, the mystery revolving around Moone and Ransom unraveled. Her head spun, and her heart rattled away. She was sure it might burst through her ribs if it had its way—especially when her parents' killer took her hand and pressed his lips to her knuckles.

Moone said he'd met Ransom before; the result of a debt gone bad by his father. But, evidence suggested that not only had he met him, James Moone knew Jack Ransom. He knew him *well.*

"What is your name, pet?"

"Cassidy." Her stomach flipped when her real name slipped from her lips without thinking. She scrambled for a name. Any name that wouldn't give away a link to Aisling and Ian. "Bennet. Cassidy Bennet, at your service, Mister—"

He smiled. She shivered again. "Ransom. Jonathan Xavier Ransom. His Lord, actually."

She dipped her head. "Pleasure, *my Lord.*"

Cassidy felt like a character in a novel. A parade of pretense to convince him she was worth keeping, more interesting than a warm place to dip his wick for the night.

"Is this fine lady your wife, James?" Ransom crooned, looping her hand through his arm like Bingley would for Jane, bringing the three of them together.

She plastered a broad smile on her face, clinging to it when Moone's head cocked with a look she'd never seen him wear. Something wicked, not at all one belonging to her good deputy.

"I've brought you a gift," he purred, reaching to pry her from Ransom's grip. The warmth of his touch on her jaw burned, his hold commanding. He held her like something he owned, offering an appraisal to his master. Cassidy searched for the man she knew between flecks of cornflower blue, but he was nowhere to be found. She wished they were strangers.

"Oh?" Ransom gleamed with amusement and curiosity, carefully regarding her like she was an artist's canvas, inspecting each and every brushstroke.

Moone nodded. "I recall you having an affinity for redheads."

"Maybe once." Ransom's jaw ticked. "Not in recent memory. Have you known this lady long?"

Cassidy slid a foot back over the Persian rug. Just a breath, enough to withdraw herself from his embrace, to tear away from their assessment.

He told her to follow his lead, to be silent, but she was never *that* good at doing what she was told.

"Certainly not. We've only just met. You see, I've been sent by Madame Dubuisson. My horse threw a shoe, and I only turned up here by his kindness—until he demanded I arrive here *with* him." She dipped her chin as she imagined a lady might. "My deepest apologies. I understand there's a certain way things are done here. It wasn't my intention to go against the grain."

The gentleman's brows rose. "Such manners. I'm surprised at you, James. I thought I raised a gentleman."

"Raised?" Cassidy lent a more feminine lilt to her voice. So unlike her usual self. Another detail for the character she had to play. "Is Mister Moone your son? I don't see the resemblance."

Ransom chuckled, a deep, delectable sound. Like the sickly-sweet poison of oleander, it was beautiful but deadly. She wouldn't trust it, no matter how pleasant it was.

"Mister Moone was my ward for a time. He was certainly a favorite, a son if ever I had the pleasure of having a child of my own. He's made his father proud, that's for certain—an incredible student I was sure would inherit all this someday. Alas, even the river changes course before returning to the sea."

Cassidy's gut twisted. Icy cold sweat prickled on the back of her neck. She huffed through her nose, still wearing her smile, no matter how she worried it might waver. "My, how impressive. I've never met someone's *heir* before. And to think, I'd been alone with him all that time. What an honor."

"I don't know about an *honor*, Miss Bennet," Moone argued, jaw set, eyes looking anywhere but at her as he backpedaled. "The honor was surely mine being in the company of such a lovely lady."

Cassidy stared at him; she hoped it burned. "I'm sure it was."

A flurry of activity in the hall drew everyone's attention to the door. Two men hovered, positively out of place in

attire Cass would've felt at home in—dusty leather britches and jackets that were a little worse for wear.

Ransom's demeanor shifted. He stood taller. His eyes darkened and took the rest of the room with it. "What is it?"

"We need you out back, Boss. Ball's back." The pair exchanged looks; one Cassidy could decode blindfolded: fear.

Her gaze snapped to Moone, whose face was unreadable. They both knew the last known whereabouts of Lawrence Ball was Gallow Gorge… in *her* possession. At least, until he took Ball into custody, and the bastard escaped when she was busy sleeping.

Ransom slipped from her grasp, wearing his smile again—a beast baring his teeth—but the bemused gleam was gone. He turned his back to the door, smoothing a hand over the inky purple ascot pinned to his shirt as if he were gathering every ounce of his rage before it scattered to the wind.

"Now, my darling. I'm intrigued by you. Might I convince you to stay?"

"For dinner?" Cassidy preened, making a show of eyeing a clock on the mantle. "I'm afraid the hour seems a bit late."

He laughed again. An ounce of light returned. *Good.* Maybe that meant she made a decent first impression. "Longer than dinner, I hope. As you said, there's usually a certain order to things, but"—he paused, attention raking over her from stem to stern—"I shall keep you to myself, though perhaps not in the usual way. A private suite—would you like that, pet?"

Cassidy smiled, dipping like she imagined the Bennet sisters would upon receiving a visitor for tea. "Undoubtedly, sir. Thank you."

Ransom hooked a knuckle beneath her chin, lifting her gaze as Moone had done outside. For a moment, Cassidy worried he'd see right through her. As if the Devil himself peered straight into her soul and saw her for what she really was. But he surprised her. He did what she hoped—fondly, curiously inspecting her for the hundredth time in a few minutes.

"You certainly appear to be a rare bloom. Wouldn't you agree, James?" He firmly held her chin, even when her attention shifted to her companion.

Moone rolled his jaw, the rest of his face unreadable as he offered an imperceptible nod. "That she is, sir."

"You look so much like someone I used to know." Ransom tugged her focus back, skimming his fingers along her cheek, creases forming around his eyes. "Such lovely surprises this evening. A welcome one, to be sure." He slipped his touch over the curve of her ear with a nod. "I shall watch your time here with great interest. Now, off to bed, lovely Cassidy. We'll talk tomorrow."

Cassidy was wordless, a captive audience when he bowed over her hand the way she'd imagined a hundred different ways in a thousand daydreams—the ones where she thought herself to be a princess in a story, the one where she convinced herself as a child was Aisling's *real* story. The one where the lady ran from her betrothed and fell in love with the stable boy.

In light of her childhood fantasies, Cassidy felt the impossible—she *liked* it.

Ransom brushed his lips across her knuckles, nodding at Moone as he straightened.

"Welcome home, my boy. You'll find your rooms unaltered since you've gone. We've all been waiting, and here you are—the prodigal son, at long last. This time, I think we'll keep you closer to home."

Moone nodded. "Thank you, though, I'm not sure I'll be staying long—"

Ransom held up a hand. A chill fell through the air.

The monster awakened.

"Nonsense. You're here. Now you'll stay." He smiled again, colder, more calculating than before. "Get settled. We'll speak later. For now, it appears I have some business to attend to."

Cass clasped her hands, dipping her chin as Ransom stepped out the door with a flutter of his coat.

Tomorrow, then. She'd finally see this through and taste what she hungered for.

CASSIDY

A MAID FOLLOWED IN SOON AFTER, YANKING CASSIDY from the charged silence of the parlor before she had a moment to think or *breathe*. She ushered her up the central staircase to a bedroom grander than Cass had ever seen. Far too much for someone like her.

A grandfather clock ticked against bright white plaster. Dark wood beams split the towering ceiling, and a fire blazed in a rounded corner fireplace. Gossamer curtains danced in the caress of the evening wind breezing in from wooden doors open to a balcony. Oil-fed flames flickered in a chandelier above an ornately carved four-poster bed.

She'd never seen anything like it, never thought she belonged in a place like this. Not within the humble cabin her Da built with his own two hands. Though, hidden within those hewed walls laid a sharp juxtaposition, something that argued with the idea that Ian Callaghan was Aisling's first choice: the trunk of treasures, emerald journals filled with a past Cassidy couldn't read at the time, and a diamond ring worth more than the land where their home sat.

The two halves argued and bickered, and Cassidy was

never sure where her boots would land. Maybe somewhere in between, but never this, never here in this finery.

When the maid stripped and scrubbed her clean, once she was smooth as a polished stone and dressed in a heavenly soft chemise, Cass thought maybe Cassidy Bennet could. Just for now.

Once they were finished, the hour was late, and the house quiet. Sure everyone in the house was asleep, Cassidy slipped on her skirt and tied a cinch around her waist.

A chill ran through the air. The breeze carried the sweet spiciness of sagebrush through the heart of the hacienda as she tip-toed out her bedroom door, down wrought iron and stone, and past sleeping guards in the moonlight until she heard the telltale whinny of a *very* moody stallion.

She slid through the carriage house door, relieved to see Ransom had no men posted down the long row of stalls in the sprawling stable. Past one, then another, and another. Cass smiled when she spotted the tips of Solo's ears in the glow of an iron lamp hanging from the barrel-vaulted ceiling. It only grew when they flicked her way.

"Hey, sweet thing," she whispered. Some of the day's tension bled away at the sight of him, though an ache remained deeply rooted in her chest, one that surely had to do with Moone. All this time, every warrant, every crooked smile, everything she started to hope for at the end of all this—poisoned, gone for good, tainted by his betrayal.

Cassidy started to need him—an awful, wonderful thing. She began to believe there might be something to look forward to after all this, no matter how hard she tried to battle it back, to keep it at bay. Perhaps that part of her sensed his deception; maybe it was all a way to protect her from being hurt, to keep her from getting too close.

Solo pushed his muzzle against her the minute she slid the door open, grumbling an affectionate nicker as he nibbled at her shift. The sight of him, the weight of his attention, was a comfort she couldn't describe.

Cass rubbed the star on his forehead, leaning against him. "I promise you won't be stuck here long. Once I'm finished, we'll ride home as fast as you want."

"Better not say, 'I promise.' Everyone knows that things go to shit real fast when you say that."

Cassidy stiffened. The ache in her chest flared, but she refused to look at him, keeping her focus on Solo.

"Figured you'd probably wander this way, eventually. Been waiting," Moone murmured, drawing her gaze over her shoulder with the softness of his voice. "You are two of a kind. One can't exist without the other for long."

"You're right." She nodded, pressing a kiss to Solo's nose.

Cassidy turned, setting her eyes on Moone leaning against the far wall. He'd done away with his coat and tie, sleeves rolled to his elbows. He looked more like himself, the man she knew.

But he wasn't *him* at all. Not anymore.

He rolled his shoulder against the washed stone, working his jaw. "I'm sorry."

"Don't talk," she said, closing the space between them. She slotted her feet between his, gathering her shift with a bend of her fingers until the roughness of Moone's trousers brushed between her thighs. "I'm so tired of talking. Let's do something else instead."

Cassidy walked her hands up his chest, feathering the hair at his temples, searching every detail in his handsome face—looking anywhere but his eyes, where that other man lived. A million different things went through her mind, a hundred different ways she thought things might've gone that evening.

None of them compared to what actually happened.

Moone closed his eyes, brows creased deeper the longer Cassidy's touch lingered. She traversed down his throat, circled the buttons barely holding together his shirt, and slipped her fingers beneath the gun belt around his waist.

"*Cassidy.*" He swallowed a groan, black lashes parting over cornflower blue. "This isn't the time or the place."

"Isn't it?" she cooed, leaning into him with another sickly-sweet smile. "This is what you want, right? You want *me.*"

"Yes." Moone kept his palms against the wall, breath stuttering when she circled her nose against his. "But you don't want me."

"Didn't I? Don't I still?" Her stomach twisted, body and mind arguing over which was which. Cassidy wouldn't give in; not again, not ever. She held onto the charade, brushing her lips along the curve of his ear while her hands wandered.

"No," he growled, firmly pushing her back a few inches with a broad palm against her clavicle. His chest heaved, tawny curls hanging over his brow. "No, you don't, Cassidy. This is a trick."

She cocked her head, stepping back another inch. "How can you tell?"

Moone pursed his lips. The crinkle of his smile from the days before all but faded away. "You're pissed."

Cassidy sucked in a deep breath, glancing down at the pistol she slipped from his hip when he wasn't looking. "You're right."

The pearl-gripped revolver felt heavier than usual in her

palm. Cass held it firmly, chin level as she pulled back the hammer and pressed the barrel against Moone's temple.

He didn't move a muscle; she knew he wouldn't dare. At least he was *that* smart. If only she'd been smarter.

"Tell me why I shouldn't put a fucking bullet in you right now." Her voice was brittle, shaking. Cass hated it. How had she been so foolish to let her guard down, to let him in the slightest inch?

"I can think of a couple," Moone answered, flinching when she pushed harder with the barrel. "For one, you'd draw a little bit of attention with the noise. Isn't the whole point of us coming here to blend in until you get what you want?"

"Or shoot Ransom dead," she snapped. "I'm not picky. And honestly—"

"Like you've ever had a problem sharing your honest opinion with me, Freckles," Moone drawled, shoulders square as he shifted on his boots and took a step closer.

Cass chewed her cheek, eyes narrowed as she held the gun steady, determined not to let him see how twisted up she was on the inside. She was nonchalant. Unattached. That's what she was best at. Cassidy Callaghan didn't care; she had drive, instead. But dammit, Moone made her care, and she hated him for it.

"*Honestly*," she bit with a too-casual shrug. "The less time I have to spend here in a corset and around you seems like the better option. I ought to go upstairs right now and just take care of it."

"You can't." Moone's face was somber. "There's no way in hell you'd be able to get close enough to him. Not with the men he's got around."

"You're certainly the expert, aren't you? Care on filling

me in some more?" Cass feigned a smile, though her voice thinned, trying and failing to hide her hurt.

A shadow settled over his face. "It's complicated."

"I'm sure it is." Her smile remained, trembling at the edge as her heart hammered away. "Here I was thinking you wanted to help me because you cared. You opened up to me, and I thought we were the same. Stupid, *so stupid*. When you said you'd met him, I didn't realize you *worked* for the man. Did he really call you his heir?"

"*Cassidy*," he pleaded, tilting his gaze, taking her in with a single, long glance. She surely looked the fool she felt, twisted up in a borrowed dress that made her feel further from herself than she'd ever been. Maybe she'd been the fool for a while. Lord knew Moone only made it worse, trailing her along like an animal he meant to trap.

"It was a long time ago, Cassidy. I'm… I'm different now. Different since I got to Gallow Gorge. Different since I met you."

She blinked back the threat of tears, stubbornly willing them away, nodding as each poisonous thought and sliver of shame pummeled her from the inside out.

"I knew it. I've known forever." Cass crammed her eyes shut, still holding her pistol to his skull. Tears streamed down her cheeks. Her hands ached to wipe them away before he could see. "*This*. This is exactly why I do everything on my own. Why I didn't want you to come, why I don't want to talk to you. I let you take care of me. *I shared a bed* with you. For what? For you to lure me here and throw me into a den of wolves?"

"No." Moone shook his head, eyes soft, unyielding against her fury and barrel. "I wanted to help you. To protect you. I still want those things."

Cass coughed out a laugh. "You have a funny way of showing it."

"I mean it." His eyes were glued to hers, patient, as always. Steady as a river, he waited for her to lower her gun.

"Tell me something," Cass murmured, finally drawing it away. Her gaze fell to the floor, almost sure the legs hidden behind yards of emerald fabric couldn't be hers.

"Anything." Moone's voice was resolute, sincere enough that Cass almost let herself believe him. Almost.

She rolled the question around in her mind, weighing it on the tip of her tongue, sure she already knew the answer. It soured her stomach and urged the sting of her tears. But she couldn't give in to him, no matter how sorry he looked. She'd toss away her distraction and keep her eye on the prize. Moone wasn't her problem anymore; he was Ransom's. And if he got in her way, so be it. A bullet would belong to him, too.

Cassidy's eyes slid to Moone.

"Lawrence Ball didn't really escape from the Gallow Gorge jail, did he?"

Moone shifted, staring at his silver-tipped boots as he chewed his words. She watched him battle with it—the truth— deciding if the consequence of his actions was worth it. If her easily won mistrust was worth it.

"No." He shook his head, wearing something that might've looked like shame. "No, he didn't."

Cass hated being right. She wished her wariness to trust in Moone could've been unshakable, that she would've kept him at arm's length like everyone else. She wished she hadn't let herself get wrapped up in the sweet things he said or the foolhardy hope he made her feel. She wished there'd never been the taste of more. Then maybe she wouldn't feel sick about it now.

Every ounce of oozing regret she felt was what she deserved for not trusting the more important person in her life—herself.

Silence stretched between them, punctuated by soft blows from the horses lining the stable. His eyes burned into her, willing her to meet them, to forgive him. But with each excruciating second, as she built a suit of armor around herself, Cass couldn't bring herself to look. Not until she was her cold-hearted self again.

Nothing but the job mattered. Moone made that much clear.

"Who let him go, then?" Cass's attention snapped back, a veil of indifference settling over her face—even though the signs of her broken heart were written in tracks down her cheeks.

Moone's shoulders sagged, face haggard when the answer they both knew hung between them.

"I did."

A bitter smile curled across her face. Cass laughed. She couldn't help it.

She stepped closer, slapping the pistol to his chest.

"If you lie to me again, I'll kill you."

Before

H E WASN'T A STRANGER TO THE TASTE OF A MAN'S FIST. Night after night, especially once his Ma died and left his father to the bottle. It'd come without warning, without cause. Over and over until he feared it might change the shape of his bones.

At night, planted on a stool by the piano in a grimy casino or left to listen to someone else's screams in the smokey halls of a whorehouse, he prayed for some kind of retribution—a deliverance from the pain. For him and all the others that man inflicted his rage upon.

The reckoning came in the middle of the night. Men in blue bandanas sought to deliver a message and demand payment of a debt past due. They pushed down the corridor in a dark cloud—six of them at the very least.

James gave him up with no remorse, pointing to the door just across the way.

No, the scrape of knuckles on his cheek wasn't unfamiliar. But the way they beat his father that night was a brutal thing. A woman skittered out beneath the arm of one of the thugs in time for them to rip him from a brass bed.

There was yelling, the thump of bone against bone, and the clatter of furniture. Then the dull impact came over and over, one after the other, until the sickly squelch of blood joined the chorus.

He couldn't look away, even glued to the wall opposite the door. The view was just enough to see the jerk of his Pa's feet with each rhythmic thud of his beating and the growing stain of deep crimson on his clothes. Like staring into a fire, it stirred something in him, a power he'd never tasted. He did this; he brought the men to his door. With his mother gone and his father getting exactly what he deserved, this was all he had now, this feeling. Something he could tame and use to his advantage, a monster to hide in his back pocket for whenever he needed.

Footsteps sounded down the hall. A hushed, killing calm followed him, a man made of shadow and bone. James didn't dare lift his eyes to look beyond the shine of silver tips on his black boots. He didn't need to see him to know the kind of man he was, not when a chill sliced through the air.

The smallest hairs on his neck prickled when those boots stopped before him.

"Thank you for your help, my boy." A hand found his chin. Even then, he didn't dare meet his gaze. Not yet. That'd come later, a time he'd hold it as an equal.

The stranger swiped the thumb of his free hand over a tender spot on his cheek. James didn't need a looking glass to know it ran so deep, it was nearly black. He fought a wince, biting the inside of his lip. He wouldn't show weakness, he'd stay strong. He'd stay in control.

Always. No matter what.

"Shame," the man tutted, sighing. "My father did the same to me once. He met a similar fate, and it was the best thing that ever could've happened to me. Now"—he forced James' gaze upwards to meet glowing embers instead of eyes—"Would you like a new one? A better one, perhaps? I'll teach you things you never even dreamed of."

[18]

Cassidy didn't know what to do with her hands. While she'd played the long game before, that always meant a night spent at a poker table or stalking a man as he moseyed from town to town. Never like this, never *as* this. She didn't know where to start or how to weasel further into Ransom's good graces, though his influence came for her early the first morning.

The housekeeper arrived before the sun and quickly set to work.

Her copper curls sprang into their usual form while she was sleeping, but the other woman coaxed them into shining, perfect coils with an iron before molding them into an elegant twist atop her head.

Clothing came next, but Cass wasn't prepared for how involved the process would be, even after the former afternoon at the hands of Madame Dubuisson. The cotton shift she slept in was peeled away, replaced by a chemise of finer quality with delicate lace along the edges. Next, a pair of silk stockings with intricate crimson embroidery on the ankles, tied with a matching ribbon below her knees.

Layers kept coming; more underwear than Cassidy had worn her entire life—a ruffled pair of pantalettes tied around her waist below the chemise and a gold-hued corset around her waist, covered with another decorative layer to smooth the steel boning.

"Is it always going to be like this?" Cass asked when the housekeeper settled a ruffled petticoat over the padded bustle she'd just tied over her backside.

"Like what, sweets?" she clucked, giving a lavender skirt a snap as she pulled it from a wardrobe.

"So involved," Cassidy mumbled, carefully navigating her way through the opening of the skirt when it was lifted over her head. "The other girls' dresses didn't look this… complicated."

"Goodness, no." She slapped Cass's hand when she itched at a pin in her hair. "His Lordship had this sent up special for you—he sent me, as well. However, a trip to Watkin's will be needed. This trunk isn't near enough for a proper trousseau."

Cassidy's eyes widened. "More?"

"Naturally." The housekeeper buzzed around her, slipping a matching bodice up over her arms. "A lady must be prepared for a myriad of occasions. Morning, visiting, walking, shopping, traveling, and evening, of course. There must be an accessory to suit each one. Some are easier than others." She ran knotted fingers over the glimmering lavender fabric along Cassidy's cinched waist. "There's another bodice which matches this gown to take you to dinner, but sometimes a grander gown is required."

"Why?" The question was heavy on her tongue once the older woman drew the curtains. She didn't mean for it to come out so sharp. "What's so special about me? First the room. Now this. Madame Dubuisson said there was an order to things, that you'd put me with the other girls. I—I was only supposed to stay a night or two."

A week, maybe. Cassidy planned on garnering his attention long enough to get him alone. Untethered, unguarded. Long enough, close enough, she might let her hair down and stick him between the ribs.

The woman's eyes warmed.

"I'm not the housekeeper, little dove," she said, smoothing out a wrinkle on her skirt. "I've known His Lordship a long time—since he was a boy, really. I was a ladies' maid at his ancestral home. I dressed all the young ladies at Windemere Hall. There were… *plans* for me with the family. For him, too, once he arrived in this country. I've stayed close by in Sacramento should he need. Perhaps if a special lady caught his eye. Lo and behold, he called for me last evening. I assume after he met you."

Cassidy shook her head. Wrong. It was all wrong. "I don't understand. He doesn't know a thing about me. How can he trust I'm worth any of this? All this feels—"

"Sudden?" she interjected, blotting rouge on Cassidy's lips. "He mentioned that you reminded him of someone. I knew her well." Her eyes softened, inspecting every curve of Cassidy's face with the softest of smiles. "I see what he means. You *do* resemble her so."

Aisling.

Cassidy's insides churned. This was all to avenge them, to make Ransom answer for what he'd done. Things were getting more complicated by the minute. Were his crimes worse than she understood? Was there more to the story?

There had to be, and she'd use this time, his fascination, to find out.

"So, he trusts me… just like that?"

He shouldn't, and if he did, Cassidy wondered if he was a fool. One she could wrap around her finger and make justice taste that much sweeter.

"Trust, I'm not certain. But His Lordship is a clever man. He's not the sort to make a decision unless he's *sure*. I suppose, if you see it from his point of view, this isn't sudden. Not for Lord Ransom. He's been waiting a long time, a lifetime, really. Maybe he sees you as a second chance of sorts. Give him one, as well?"

Sure, but perhaps not how the lovely old lady hoped Cassidy would.

The woman offered a smile, leaving her alone with little instruction other than Ransom would find her whenever he was ready. She was free to wander the grounds, with no mention of the hour nor the day he would call upon her.

Cassidy thought of making nice with the other girls, but when none awoke until well after lunch, she'd walked the house's perimeter twelve times. It only took an hour before the smell of opium drifted out from beneath the door of their shared suite.

Its sticky sweetness lingered in the sweeping side corridor, sending Cass running for clearer air at the heart of the hacienda. It was quieter than earlier that afternoon when it came alive as a dozen men cycled in and out. There'd been rumblings of a hunting party, though she couldn't be sure what kind of hunting they were apt to do so close to the city—unless they planned to *hunt* soiled doves in a luxury brothel in Sacramento.

Cassidy started to wander the halls, caught up in the quiet, propelled by boredom and curiosity—and there was a lot to see. Fine paintings dotted brightly colored walls. Jewel-toned tiles adorned the corners and pillars, hand-painted treasures she couldn't help but admire.

She was happy to get lost among them, biding her time. It was all fine and good, a mediocre pastime, her attention focused on drawing a map of the estate drawn in her mind. So focused—*too* focused.

Cassidy stopped dead, wobbling in her damned carriage boots as she nearly collided with a mountain of a man who turned the corner. She swore. Weak, weighed down by too beautiful things.

Moone lunged, reaching to catch her. He opened his mouth to speak but quickly thought better of it, clamping it shut when she shirked his touch like a malady.

She couldn't stand the sight of him, wouldn't let the sting of unwanted tears claw to the surface. Not with her anger—his betrayal—still so fresh, wretchedly wreathed with a craving that itched at the back of her mind like an addiction. But she wasn't those girls upstairs; she'd resist. She wouldn't lose her head.

Cassidy stood ramrod straight, chin high, as she attempted her best haughty, detached stare. Not at his eyes, no. She didn't want to see what might lay there, the temptation to let up the slightest inch.

Marching down the corridor, she ignored him, chasing the soothing echo of birds in the central atrium. Moone's gaze bored into her back. She couldn't break free of it until she turned a corner.

She slipped around the bottom of the central staircase to an adjacent hall on the other side—the further from him, the better. Only when she was sure he hadn't followed, Cass resumed her study of *Colina de Dragones.*

As she trailed her fingertips over sunshine-hued plaster,

she came to a breathless stop at a door that stood ajar.

Cassidy eased it open, sighing softly when she was greeted by the last thing she expected to find in the possession of Jack Ransom—a library.

Lingering in the doorway, she marveled at the sight. She'd only been lucky enough to have a single book in her possession at a time. But *this*. There had to be five hundred, a *thousand* different volumes.

The smell overtook her the moment she stepped foot inside. There'd been countless times she'd stuck her nose into the pages of a worn novel, inhaling the sweet, musty aroma of ink and paper. Maybe it was her imagination, but each one smelled different, an individual like the characters lovingly scribed inside.

To her, books were a magical, mystical thing. They spun tales of unattainable and unfathomable things to her—home, family… *love*. A story beyond nightmare and memory waiting behind closed eyes when night fell. An escape.

Gripping the folds of lilac silk, Cass stepped to one of the oak bookcases. Her eyes moved from one leather-bound spine to another, mouth silently forming titles and authors as she made her way down the row.

Shelley. Voltaire. Defoe. Dickens. Austen. Brontë.

Each one stole her breath more than the last, overwhelming her with the adventures waiting on every bound page. The question remained: which would she choose?

Cass hooked a fingertip on the curved spine of *Jane Eyre*, chewing her lip as she slipped her fingers between the pages and opened the cover. It only took minutes to lose herself in the words, right alongside a poor, lonely orphan like her.

She didn't mean to linger so long. A page became two. A

few pages became a chapter, and soon, Cass found herself leaning on a lonely marble pillar by the window, devouring each word of Mister Rochester's arrival at Thornfield.

Absentmindedly chewing her thumb, she was oddly aware of the slow tick of a stately grandfather clock in the corner, too wrapped up in the Master of Thornfield's questioning Jane of her family over tea to notice the stirrings of life in the house around her—or the shadow haunting her from the doorway.

"Well, this is certainly a refreshing surprise."

Cassidy's eyes shot up, stomach twisting when her eyes landed on Jack Ransom.

"I-I'm sorry," she stammered, motioning toward the shelves. "The door was open, and I couldn't resist."

She made to close the book and return it to its home, but he stopped her with a quick word.

"Don't move." His voice was soft, gentler than she imagined it to be. "You're as pretty as a picture. T'would be a crime not to capture the scene, somehow."

Ransom gave her an encouraging nod when she thumbed the pages back open. He offered the smallest smile as he strode to a roll-top desk, pulling out a thin, leather-bound book and a stick of charcoal.

Cass was transfixed, unable to look away, when he crossed the room again and settled into a wing-backed chair by the fireplace. She told herself it was because Ransom couldn't be trusted. The man from her memory needed to be watched. She shouldn't look away from a beast.

This man, though… she couldn't put her finger on it, but there was a gentleness to him she hadn't counted on.

He was handsome; she couldn't deny it, perhaps more so when his amusement hid in the corners of his eyes rather than his mouth. They flickered to and fro, catching her off guard every time they met hers, no matter how she tried to keep her attention on the page.

"How old are you?" she blurted, hopelessly snagged on the same three words over and over. Distracted.

"Forty-five next winter." Ransom kept his focus down, graphite currying over paper in a song of *quick, quick, slow.* "I don't typically bother myself with such details. In my experience, age does not determine if someone is a man or a boy. Time lends itself, naturally, but I was grown long before I was as tall as I am. Still"—he paused, lifting his attention to her—"You've piqued my curiosity about yourself."

"Twenty-four," she said to Brontë. Fifteen years since the birth of another girl, a baptism of blood.

"Hm," he answered, returning to the sketch. "Tell me, does your age determine how *old* you are, pet?"

Cassidy's jaw ached; she clenched it so hard. All of it, the pain, the loneliness, growing up too quickly—it'd all been because of him.

"No," she said, shaking her head. "I've been a grown man as long as I can remember."

Ransom snickered, mouth tilting at the corner.

Cassidy glared at poor Jane, printed in black and white. It wasn't her fault, but Cass couldn't stand being so still. Not then. Not when he laughed in the face of her pain, the pain he caused.

She sucked in a sharp sigh and slapped the cover shut, a decidedly unladylike behavior that caught his eye without effort. She couldn't help herself, always a little too eager to push when she ought to stay still. "Do you dress all the girls here like a doll?"

"Decidedly not, my darling. You fascinate me. It's as I

said, you resemble someone I once knew. Now I've spoken to you, you remind me of her even more." Ransom let out a deep, dark chuckle that set her teeth on edge. "So many questions. Am I being interrogated, dear Cassidy?"

"No, of course not." *Most definitely.*

She chewed the inside of her lip, worrying she'd given too much of herself away. She turned her head to steal a glance, unable to ignore how the afternoon light lit every dusting of silver-hued scruff, each unexpected smile around his eyes, illuminating molten gold within them.

The desert was as deadly as it was beautiful. Ransom was no exception, rotten to his very core.

He was focused on his task, sharp jaw moving when a barely perceptible grin tugged at his mouth. Cass wondered what was on the page, her curiosity insatiable the longer she was forced to stand so still.

She ought to return to Jane and Mister Rochester beneath her fingertips. But dammit, despite everything, she was intrigued by the casual way Ransom's wine-red tie hung a little loose, allowing a glimpse of every bob of his Adam's apple.

Cassidy blamed Moone, the fire he lit. It still smoldered beneath her skin, defying the depths of her anger, of his lies. It flared through the night in her dreams, painting a vivid picture of them in Rose Reach if she hadn't stopped things.

Blurred and beautiful like the fine paintings on Ransom's walls, Cassidy saw herself and Moone, his hands traversing her skin as his mouth—

"I said," Ransom's smokey voice interrupted her fervent daydream, drawing her gaze to his with a shiver, "*don't move.*"

She nodded, lips parting when she turned her eyes back to the book, softly tracing her thumb along her bottom lip while he continued.

"As it turns out, Miss Bennet—"

"Cassidy," she whispered at Brontë, hoping he hadn't caught onto the name she borrowed from Lizzie and her sisters; a volume of *Pride and Prejudice* only steps away.

"*Cassidy*," he echoed, halting his work for a moment, like the action of her offering it to him had been a pleasing thing. "As it turns out—" His voice drew closer with each word; she kept her gaze glued to the page. "I like you. I like your questions. It's… different. Perhaps it's something I've been waiting for. While I've met plenty of women in my life, many of whom vied for my attention, as you can imagine, none of them held a candle to a woman I once loved. She was well-read, too. I realize it may be out of fashion, but I prefer my women to *think*."

"That makes you one in a million when it comes to men," Cassidy drawled, breath catching when she lifted her chin and found him standing beside her. She already knew he wasn't like most *people*, with an unmatched taste for blood. But when her eyes fell to the sketch in his hand, she wondered if Jack Ransom might surprise her yet.

It was impossible. There was no way the woman in the picture was *her*. Cassidy went a long time avoiding being anything remotely close to pretty. She knew she might've been in another life had things been different. But the girl on the page was further than she ever imagined.

Was this how she looked to other people? To him? *To Moone?*

From the soft curve at the tip of her nose to the swell of her lips, the man she hated most captured her in a way Cass had never even seen herself.

While it was just a quick sketch, Ransom had talent.

Cassidy couldn't help but get caught up in how perfectly coiled curls fell across her shoulder or how the back of her neck was kissed by the light.

She was speechless. How could someone so ugly make something so beautiful?

"As first impressions go, Miss Bennet, it appears you may be of the same rarity." He laid his hand atop hers, brushing his thumb against her knuckles. It made her insides squirm. "I'd say we'd make quite the pair, don't you?"

Cass wet her lips, throat bobbing as she swallowed the feeling with a nod. "If you say so."

Her eyes followed the feeling of his touch, eyes widening when she spied a black smudge he inadvertently left behind.

"Curious," Ransom hummed, stepping closer. Part of her wanted to scream out, for the tips of her fingers to twitch for a revolver and end it right here.

"What is?" she asked, lifting her chin when he brushed a loose, copper tendril away from her cheek.

"It seems like I've left my mark on you, Cassidy." Ransom smiled again, but only in his eyes—just the way she noticed before. It was inviting and dangerous—a trap laid by a beautiful spider. He lingered there in his web, holding her gaze another beat. "Now, you're mine."

Cass shivered, mind reeling when she impishly argued, "Am I?"

Her reply amused him. It drew another chuckle when he pulled the copy of *Jane Eyre* from beneath her palms, snapping it shut before tucking it under his arm. "We can argue the semantics of payment in exchange for possession later. Over tea? Perhaps a stroll around the grounds."

"Quarreling in the garden already?" she tutted, coquettishly cocking her head. "At this rate, we'll be an old married couple by dinnertime."

Again and again, she charmed him. This was no different, but more than all the others combined.

His mouth split wide open, revealing his teeth as a *ha* clawed its way out. He caught her hand, bowing low, brushing his lips over her knuckles.

"The garden it is."

Ransom may be a predator, but she was a hunter with traps of her own. Cassidy would snare him, eventually. Even if it made her the bait, too.

[22]

Moone

T HE NIGHT THEY ARRIVED AT *COLINA DE DRAGONES*,
Moone feared he'd never lay eyes on her ever again.

As a maid led Cassidy up the central staircase, he carefully cataloged the curve of her neck and the copper sheen of her hair. Memorizing all of it, all of her.

He should've known better, known she'd demand a final word—one final say-so to show him she was still in control, even though he'd taken so much of it away. Even though she let him.

Trust was a hard-earned thing for Cassidy Callaghan. Moone strove to gain it. Now she knew the depth of his lies; she'd never trust him again.

He could accept that; he deserved it, though he didn't deserve her. Moone would never have her, now. That fever, the fire within him that craved her, burned brighter than ever.

Cassidy was angry. He lived in the feeling, carrying the sensation of her barrel pressed against his temple to bed. There, amongst the phantoms of his past, James shamelessly took himself in hand.

He imagined every libidinous thought he harbored, finishing every scene they left unfulfilled—from the livery after Ball's *escape* and the firelight against a stone bluff to their room at The Palace Hotel in Rose Reach. Every stroke was a beautiful agony, never as fulfilling as he imagined her to be. Still, he persisted, holding onto the thought that she cared enough about him to put a gun to his head and *not* leave him dead and bleeding.

Cass Callaghan never showed an ounce of doubt in a kill—but she did for him.

Moone wanted her but only had his shame when he choked out her name in the moonlight that first night. It burned through him, festering the next day, growing stronger in the light of her indifference when they came face-to-face again.

He didn't mean to track her; their paths crossed over and over. Each time, he'd open his mouth to speak. She scowled and paraded away, catty and aloof—an act, he prayed. One convincing enough, he didn't stop to think why she freely wandered the halls. He supposed she'd been allocated to the ladies' parlor, spending the day doing things she never saw much use for. Things Moone could never see her doing.

Though, later that afternoon, when he heard her bell-like voice from the library, Moone couldn't have imagined what he discovered—her and Jack Ransom cozied up in a corner. Her, wide-eyed, looking as if she beheld a rare jewel for the first time. Him, speaking to her, *touching her* in ways Moone dreamed up for months before she ever let him.

A rustling of activity, the jangle of spurs on stone shook him from his sentry. Moone tore his gaze from the sight of them, insides churning when the pair remained burned into his retinas, his memory.

The group of men who tumbled in was too rowdy and dusty for a place like *Colina de Dragones*. Shoulders bumping, they jostled like a crate of whiskey on the back of a wagon, hatching devious plans to be carried out in the name of their master.

Their smiles shifted at the sight of him, shoulders leveled, backs straightened. The effect of Moone's presence in the house was plain as day on their faces, but they ought not to be afraid of him. He wasn't the monster. Not yet.

One of them, younger than the rest, stepped forward— mostly ears and muddy eyes. Moone guessed he might've been about nineteen, still a kid when he left for Gallow Gorge.

"Hey, Jimmy. Long time. How's things been wherever the hell you disappeared to?"

Moone sniffed. "My name isn't Jimmy."

"We know that, don't we, Higgins? Some of us have known you a long time, is all. I've watched ya grow up and go off with the master all those years. I know I saw you come back a man but can't help but call ya whatcha were when we found you." Another man, Wayne Marion—older than the rest, with a white beard, bulbous nose marked by disease, and bristly eyebrows—slapped the chest of one of the other men. He shook his head, and the other shrank back; a word of warning.

"Where *have* you been, anyway? Been years. Boss said you were leavin' but never said where." A third chimed in, thin as a pole, dark hair hanging in greasy columns over his forehead.

Moone's eyes snapped to the library, door still ajar. Cass's shadow shifted and his stomach twisted. He couldn't give up where he'd been: their home. Not without risking everything they'd built there, everything Moone fruitlessly hoped they might have if they never chased Lawrence Ball across the desert.

"A dusty little shit hole four day's ride from here."

Speak of the devil. Moone's blood simmered. His fists ached, twisted in the memory of Cassidy contorted with the fever he caused. He should've beat him half to hell. He could've killed him; Lord knew he had the chance. But fear of what it'd cost them—what it'd cost Cassidy—was too much to bear.

Killing Ball would've done exactly as he warned her, exactly why he tried to keep her from the truth. Hell would surely come knocking on the door of Gallow Gorge, only bringing pain where Cassidy sought justice.

Moone would take the punishment of killing one of Jack's men if he could—it'd only be the start if he had his way. It'd put an end to a life painted in guilt for what he'd done, the things he'd been taught, what'd been asked of him—the life he loved a little too well until he severed the tie, determined to set fire to the bridge.

Cassidy spoke of distractions, blaming his affection for her as a knot in her path for vengeance. Moone knew all about it—about being distracted. She was his; the reason he never returned to *Colina de Dragones*, to Jack's side how he was supposed to, the motivation to give it all up. Now, she was the reason for his unholy resurrection.

Lawrence Ball's scarred, bruised face sneered up at him in the place he used to call home with the woman he was so desperate to shield just steps away.

Moone's mind swam with what to do next. He hoped the desert would've claimed him, but James wasn't that lucky.

He'd have to make his own luck if he wanted this to

work and for Cassidy to succeed—if he wanted to keep his end of the bargain.

Moone summoned a haughty smile. It might've been unconvincing, but Ball didn't seem to notice. "*Lawrence*. If I recall, it was me who got you out of that shit hole. You oughta thank me."

"I never would've ended up there if it weren't for that little ginger bitch." Ball rolled his tongue along his lip, exposing teeth tilted and stained like cracked headstones in a cemetery. "I suppose it's lucky she just happened to work for you, huh? A happy little accident."

Moone's jaw pulsed. He wanted to hit him again, to flip one of Cassidy's revolvers from his hip and put Ball down right then and there for speaking about her as such. That'd only spell disaster. They were playing the long game now. He needed to find a way to keep Ball away from Cass or else risk her exposure.

Then, everything they'd done, everything she'd been through, would be for nothing.

Wayne stepped between them, clapping a knotted hand on Moone's shoulder. "We were about t'head to town. Boss needs us to take delivery on a shipment, then we thought we might go huntin' for some doves. How about ya come along? Spend some time with yer old bedfellows, make old friends new again. Maybe even dip yer wick and relieve some of this here tension."

Moone met the old man's gaze, pleading, like he knew James played both sides.

"Is Fisher's still the old haunt?" He swallowed his anger with Ball. It'd have to wait.

Wayne nodded, squeezing Moone's shoulder like a fond old friend. "You remembered."

"You took me there when I was barely thirteen." He quirked an eyebrow, hoping it'd disguise how his attention slid back to Cassidy and Ransom in the library. "Kinda hard to forget."

The shadows in the doorway shifted. A flash of red hair behind broad shoulders. The pair was headed their way. No matter how Moone wanted to stay or whisk her away from the den of vipers and ride for home, he knew she'd be safer if he put space between her and Ball.

Ransom would have to wait, too.

[23]

CASSIDY

THE LIGHT IN SACRAMENTO WAS DIFFERENT THAN CASS was used to. Warmer, somehow. Friendlier, too, if that was something sunshine could be.

Ransom guided her down a stone staircase into a stately English garden on the estate, holding her hand a little too long once they reached the bottom.

Cassidy flexed her fingers, gripping the handle of a lace parasol like her life depended on it. She held it aloft to block the sun like she'd seen so many ladies do, chuckling when she thought of the sheet of freckles across her nose and how little an umbrella would help with the matter.

The sound of it drew his attention.

"Cassidy." Ransom savored each syllable, like each letter would wring out an answer about her. "Tell me about yourself."

"There's not much to tell," she answered. *I have a bullet with your name on it, and a pin I could kill you with right here.*

"I can hardly believe that to be true," he mused, unbeknownst to the wishes rattling in her mind. "An educated woman in this world is a rarity. One who can get as lost within the pages of a book as you did surely has an interesting detail or two to tell."

You have no idea.

"You have so many. More than I've seen my whole life." A sliver of truth tumbled out, surprising her. Why here, why now—*why him?* She'd never spoken about it to anyone but Daisy Booker.

"What, books?" He gave her a quizzical smile, leading her through a boxwood archway. When she nodded, he looked at her with something like awe at her wonder of something so simple, pulling her hand more snugly into the crook of his arm. "They're a wonderful thing, aren't they? I brought many of them with me. Years ago, now. Some volumes are well-read enough that they feel like old friends. They've certainly treated me better."

"I understand," Cass murmured, giving the parasol an anxious twist. She didn't understand why she let a conversation with Jack Ransom, of all people, feel so *real.* "I always looked for things I wished for between the pages." She wondered what sort of thing Jack Ransom searched for in the worn volumes of his library, what secrets hid between the pages. "If you brought your books, then might I ask— where is home? Your accent isn't exactly like everyone else's in Sacramento."

"I suppose it doesn't take a keen ear to notice?"

"Not really, sir." Cass kept her eyes down, a demure lady watching every peek of her shoes from beneath lavender silk.

"Jack."

Ransom drew her gaze, leaning to peer beneath the lace-lined edge of her parasol. His expression glimmered; a fervent, unexplainable curiosity surely reflected in her own.

She couldn't help it.

Yes, he was a murderous fiend. What he'd done was deplorable, unforgivable, and built Cassidy's entire life—her whole being. But, he also proved to be a fascinating study. The longer she spent in his company, the more of his attention she garnered—the more Cassidy wanted to learn, to understand what led to that day in Faraday Creek.

Cassidy needed to understand what made her.

"*Jack*," she echoed. It was all going better than she imagined and so much worse. Cassidy visualized the moment of their meeting more times than she could count. It filled her dreams, haunting every choice, every bounty that'd lead her closer. But now, face-to-face with the monster she built in her mind, she questioned if she ought to whip the blade Madame Dubuisson gave her from her chignon and end him here.

It'd be easy enough. Maybe she could strangle him with his tie and ride for home before dinner. That was before she caught his eye. Before she captured his curiosity. Before he ensnared hers, as well.

Cassidy had an itch to discover what other stories might be hidden away. What pieces of her mother he knew, if there were treasures to be found in the form of a memory. Secrets to unearth.

Ransom nodded, encouraging her to continue, as if he wanted to reveal what'd been buried, too.

"How did you end up here? You don't seem like the type who fits in California. Not in the usual way," she asked.

"The same could be said for you, dear Cassidy." He paused, plucked a lavender rose, and held it to her. "You look like you've stepped from the pages of my library, my darling. From my imagination, my deepest wishes and regrets."

I know.

Her heart skipped when she remembered his last feeble offering to Aisling.

"Yes, the woman I remind you of from your home. May I ask where?" Cass asked, lifting her voice to hide the burning anxiousness and twist of guilt when she took the proffered bloom with a smile. She wasn't actually *enjoying* Ransom's company; she wouldn't. He was the Scourge of the West, her parents' killer—evil, through and through.

"England," he answered, dark eyes focused far and away. "I spent much of my time in London, but Devonshire is my ancestral home. Would you believe it if I told you I once lived in a castle?"

Cass glanced up the hill at *Colina de Dragones*. Light shimmered around the edges, shining through arches in the courtyard down the hill. "Don't you already?"

Ransom chuckled. "Too right you are. These, though— they're different. Stone walls and cliffs where the sea rages just outside."

Cassidy thought of the heather-speckled cliffs of Ireland, of Ian and Aisling's home they told her so much about. For a moment, she wished to be back in her daydreams where she stood there, hand-in-hand with her mother. "It sounds like a fairytale."

"Doesn't it just," he tutted, looping her hand tighter in the bend of his arm. He was quiet for a beat, gently skimming his thumb over her knuckles as if he were the one in need of a comforting touch.

Cassidy felt the wrongness of it. She knew they ought not to be alone. Moone would be pissed if he found out. But she didn't care what he thought, if he might think it improper—or worse—be jealous of it.

More than anything, though, beyond etiquette Cass only half-understood and mainly gathered from the novels she read, her crime flashed red every infinitesimal moment she let herself forget *why* she'd come in the first place; every time she let herself enjoy the trappings of maybe eventually being his favorite.

With the memory so far away and her normal life pushed so far to the background, she was tempted to give in, dance the dance, and enjoy the charade for a little while. If she was determined to play pretend while she learned the details of what happened between Ransom and her parents, she ought to play the part to perfection and leave everything else behind.

It would be worth the effort. It had to be. Her Da deserved that much.

There wasn't any room for the same hard-hearted woman she built herself to be. Cassidy Bennet was someone else. Someone softer, sweeter—kinder, even. That's how Ransom saw her. Maybe that's who she could be while a detective hid beneath the surface.

Just for a little while.

Ransom's hand slipped down her arm, fingers tucking into her palm to guide her around a row of colorful petunias to a stone bench hidden in an alcove.

"You know—" He held firmly to her hand, stooping to gather her skirt as she sat before joining her. "I've never spoken of home to anyone... and I've been here a long time."

"Oh?" She kept her voice soft, closing her eyes to revel in the small victory that she got him to open up. Inside, she burned with questions, though wary of pushing too hard and drawing his suspicion instead of curiosity. "I enjoy hearing about your home, about you. You fascinate me, my Lord." The word felt strange coming out of her mouth; even stranger to think she'd been right about Aisling being a *lady*, too.

"Jack," he echoed, more firmly than before. "I insist."

"*Jack.*" Cass nodded, lifting her gaze to his with that same demure smile, a flash of her teeth. "I'm sorry."

His eyes crinkled at the edges, and she was reminded that, unlike the monster she built in her mind, Jack Ransom was handsome. Undeniably, so. A dangerous distraction waiting to happen. In the warm sunshine, she swore they sparkled.

"Don't be, pet." He brought her hand to his lips, leaving a swift kiss against her knuckles. A foreign shiver tumbled down her arms. Affection wasn't something she was used to, something she allowed or accepted; she was leery of letting anyone too close to her black heart.

Cassidy rubbed her fingers over the feeling he left behind, waiting for her next question to take root, but Jack spoke first.

"I could tell you the story if you'd like."

She met him with a smile, though it trembled. Every part of her threatened to break apart with anticipation, fearing what she'd learn. "I'd like that very much."

He stared straight ahead, wearing a familiar, faraway look. "I had a brother once. Not by blood, but something beyond that—a kinship born out of boyhood and a shared thirst for adventure.

"They never thought we'd be friends. We came from two different worlds—as different as could be. But I loved him, I really did."

Cass burned with questions. They came one after the

other, her heart hammering all the faster with each one. She wanted to ask them all, to demand answers about her parents she never got from Aisling, always made to make up stories in her imagination. Instead, she waited with bated breath as the truth began resembling childhood daydreams about a princess and a scoundrel.

"You mentioned a woman." Cassidy might've whispered it. Ransom's eyes fell to hers for a moment, shadowed by their ghosts.

"Yes. Yes, I did." He swallowed, squeezing her hand—not out of affection, more like he held it tightly to keep from drifting away in a tide of memories.

Something in her chest constricted when a flicker of hurt passed over his face. Her mind reeled—the monster in her memory didn't *feel.* He killed without remorse. She'd never forget the look of cold indifference in the moments before putting a bullet between Aisling's eyes.

This man, though. He was haunted by the past, filled with an aching longing Cassidy could see with her eyes closed.

How could they be the same man at all? Maybe he felt everything; perhaps he felt it so profoundly, so wrongly, that's why he killed them.

"She was so beautiful." His brows pleated, faraway smile wavering. "Even as a girl when she first came to live in England. I still remember the moment I laid eyes on her—merely a boy of seventeen. I might've even loved her, then. We were friends, the three of us. But, as we grew older and neared adulthood, things became different. Naturally, when we weren't children anymore, how we looked at her changed, too. I could scarcely believe it when our families decided to join… to join *us.* We were happy."

The ghosts of the past danced over his face; he anchored

himself to her. Cassidy squirmed beneath her skin.

"Our wedding was only weeks away, just after our twenty-first birthdays. I still have the ribbon she was going to wear in her hair. I look upon it often. I think of *her* often—what our life would have looked like. I'd been reluctant to take up my family's title and inherit the estate as my father planned. But she made me feel like I could do anything, be anyone, so long as she was there by my side."

"Your title?"

He smiled. "I didn't grow up in a castle by the sea for no reason, pet. My father was an earl. He was not long for this world when our marriage was arranged. She would've been a countess."

"A countess?" she breathed, stomach fluttering as they came closer and closer to the fiction she wrote in her head. "I couldn't imagine being anything like that."

"Mm, she was divine, a heavenly creature perfectly suited to the role. My family adored her. *I* adored her. But—"

Cassidy's mind raced. Was her mother really the grand lady she imagined her to be as a child? Were she and Ransom so in love as he claimed? What happened? What kind of betrayal occurred for her to run away from a life like that?

"I should have known it wouldn't last… not because of her. She was *beautiful*. Well-read, like you. I would have given her the world. We could have had it all together, she and I, if it weren't for him. He… we started to disagree. It wasn't the same as when we were boys. People change. And he—" Ransom's voice cracked. He paused momentarily before pressing on, dripping with a deep sadness Cass understood. "He stole something precious from me. It was only days before the wedding that they disappeared. My family insisted I move on, telling me there were other matches, better matches. But I wanted *her*, so I gave it up to chase a ghost. I made my own fortune instead. All of it, everything, all of this—I did for her."

"Did… did you ever find her again?" Cassidy's voice trembled, her fingertips absentmindedly tracing a scar on the back of his hand.

"I did." Jack's voice was darker, deeper, threaded with something more than hurt and grief, like he'd gone and dipped it in a quiet, unending rage. "Years went by as I carved my way through this country, building an empire. But, eventually, yes. I found her nine years later—fifteen years ago, now—and it was worse than I feared. I was heartbroken to see she'd been tricked into believing that leaving our home, that leaving *me* was the right choice. I tried to get her to return with me, but he—" His story halted, voice quaking. "They're both gone now."

Cass didn't know what to think, how to move, or even breathe. How could the stories be so different? Not like her parents had much to offer on the subject other than what she witnessed through the floorboards of Callaghan General Goods. If she hadn't known or hadn't seen, she wondered if she might've felt sorry for Jack.

Glancing up at the mansion, Cass sucked in a deep breath, their hands still intertwined. She wanted it to feel wrong, to be repulsed by his touch, by the hands that killed her Da. The longer she lingered in his presence, the less wrong it felt.

She could take advantage of it, of his vulnerability. She could find out the truth of what happened. Somewhere between what he told her and what she witnessed. Perhaps she could discover the heart of the man she thought she understood.

Logic told her there wasn't anything else to know besides what she'd seen. Why not take advantage of his unsuspecting state right now and strangle him with her bare hands? Would anyone be the wiser? Would she doubt her actions with his side of the story so fresh in her mind?

Jack rose to his feet and eased her up beside him, offering her a handsome smile in the shadow of the boxwood walls of the garden. "I'd like to thank you, Miss Bennet."

"Cassidy," she echoed, giving him her best, most ladylike grin in return, hoping it would be enough to keep towing him down the line of her charade.

"*Cassidy.*" He lifted her hand to his lips, lingering too long for how a gentleman ought to behave. Then again, he wasn't the regular sort of gentleman, and she wasn't a lady. They were the Devil in disguise and a wolf lying in wait; beasts veiled with pretty clothes and prettier words. "It's been a pleasure strolling with you this afternoon, but the hour is growing late. I have business to attend to. I'll find you tomorrow, and perhaps we can continue this little rendezvous."

He tucked her hand into his arm's bend, leading her back toward the house. Her stomach twisted at the thought of returning to her room alone or being forced to sit quietly in a corner with the other ladies, waiting until she was called upon. Not when Jack's company was so much better than any mark she'd ever had.

He seemed to think the same of her.

While Cassidy's plan had been to get him alone and kill him without remorse, now she wondered if that was too quick, too easy. She'd already let two of those chances come and go. What if she was meant to do more as Cassidy Bennet? Perhaps Ransom's reckoning might come in the shape of love—love for *her*. One she'd set ablaze, bask in his anguish, blood finally repaid.

Before

J AMES MOONE WASN'T A MAN ANYMORE. HE DIDN'T KNOW when it happened or how he hadn't noticed when that part of him slipped away. The first time he killed a man, his hands shook for days. His stomach soured from even the sweetest food. The usual distractions for his so-called ailment never quite eased the ache from watching life fade from that man's eyes. But somewhere along the line, the burden of having a heart was a thing he no longer carried.

He had to do it. He had to kill the part of him that was soft, the one who thought that blue handkerchief was so heavy. That boy wouldn't have survived, couldn't have carried the burden of being so soft-hearted, of caring too much.

So, Moone tore it out, tossed it in the fire, and didn't even notice when he'd done it.

But they didn't call him Jimmy anymore. Not for years. Not when he stood shoulder-to-shoulder with their master, as charismatic and cruel as he taught him to be—a monster of Ransom's creation.

A weapon to be wielded.

But now the silence where his heart used to be was deafening. All it took was the look in a young girl's eyes, a look of fear James would never be able to unsee.

He used to be good. He used to be what a mother taught him to be. Now, he was so far away from those days that they were all he wanted.

Moone stared at the clock on the mantle, at his reflection in the glass. He was a gentleman, molded and branded with a rich damask waistcoat, a high-collared, high-waisted jacket, and a cravat. He didn't look like the other men; he didn't act like them. His hands were bloodier, too.

Only twenty-one, James Moone killed more men than he could keep track of. He'd graduated to the muscle when he was fifteen and the master's apprentice not long after. Looting a man's house became studying law. He learned other ways to take a life—first with a bullet, then a blade. Even his bare hands.

There was no room for a heart. Now, it was all he could think about, how to wash his hands of it all, to take back what he'd thrown away.

"I missed you at dinner, boy." Ransom's voice jolted him to the present, to the relentless ticking of the clock.

James didn't bother mincing words. He didn't bother saying anything, not when he was still sorting it all out. There wasn't a book to teach him how to beg for his life. Though, that afternoon might've been lesson enough.

Jack's hand found his shoulder, father enough to see something in Moone was broken. "You alright?"

"I can't do this anymore." The words poured from him like a flood. His mentor's fingers gripped harder, spinning him so they were face-to-face.

"You'll have to elaborate, James," Ransom said, posture

looser than usual, like James struck some unseen part of him that actually cared.

Moone chewed the inside of his lip, repeatedly replaying the moment in his mind. Four people. A woman, her children, and the man who'd stolen from Ransom. That's what they'd been told, anyway.

He let it anger him. As if the cost of a case of opium skimmed off the top was something he'd notice missing from their boundless coffers. Still, Moone acted as the monster he'd been molded into, shoulder-to-shoulder with his master, as always. A dog to be beckoned, to bite back at those who'd done the same to the hand that fed them.

James didn't think of it, of the sound of their cries when he put a bullet in the mother. The darkest part of him only wanted to motivate the man to give back what was his. He didn't think of the consequence when he pressed the heat of his barrel at the back of a young girl's head.

All he wanted was the result.

The anguish in her father's face, the pained stare and guttural cry that tore from his lips—that was the catalyst which stirred the cold cockles of Moone's long-dead heart. It roared to life, as loud as a train's whistle, ringing in his ears as he staggered out of the room. He ripped the blue handkerchief from his neck and stormed away.

James didn't plan on looking back, not until a gunshot rang out from the barrel who did the deed instead of him.

No, he'd never forget the dead stare from wide brown eyes, skull blown apart from the end of a Colt .45. It didn't matter that he hadn't been the one to do it. He was ready to.

"Since when has killing a child been an acceptable thing in this house?" James ground out, stepping around Ransom. He paced through the library, unable to sit still, to think of anything except getting out.

"An unfortunate cost but a fruitful one all the same," Ransom answered. "We gained back what was ours to begin with."

Moone stared at his palms, idly wondering what it'd take to wash the blood from them. Would it take years or a lifetime of good deeds to fade the stain?

"It's too much." He shook his head over and over, throat thick when he raised his eyes to meet the man who made him into this monster. "I can't—"

"Oh, my boy," Jack tutted, palming his cheek like a doting father ought to. "I understand. A heart's a heavy burden. It's what makes you human. Though, we aren't just men, are we? To them, we're gods. With time, I'm sure you'll be cured of it."

Moone's stomach churned. "I don't know if I can."

"Might I convince you otherwise?" Ransom stepped back, wearing a grim smile. "Tell me what you need. What can I do, my son?"

James twisted, rubbing circles on his temples as he stared into the fire. "I can't stay here. I need something—I don't know, maybe a change of scenery. A change of pace, of light, to recalibrate myself. To figure out the man I'm supposed to be."

Jack hovered close behind him, determined to anchor him at home at *Colina de Dragones*.

"What if you already are that man? Otherwise, what's all this work, the tutors, the time by my side, been for?" His hand found his shoulder again. "You've served me well, from the very beginning. I knew you were special. Meant to be, even. I remember having aspirations of leaving home. My father never allowed it, and I found my way without him. If he had"—a squeeze— "maybe I never would've left. Maybe, if I do what he wouldn't, you'll find your way home eventually. Like I never did."

Something inside James flared, brighter and more beautiful than he'd felt in ages. Hope. "You'll let me go?"

"Because I know that whatever belonging you are looking for pales in comparison to what I offer. There's nothing out there to tempt you for long. That, and I trust you to come back. To remember us while you're away." Jack wore a gleam in his eye, as if he already knew James wouldn't make it a week without running back like a loyal dog to his master. "Where will you go?"

Moone shook his head. "I don't know."

Ransom lifted a brow but didn't argue. "Not far, I hope. California? Nevada?"

"I don't know that, either," James answered.

"For how long?" He chuckled, long and low. "Let me guess—you don't know."

"Not a clue." His own smile, one of excitement and relief. "I'm grateful to you. For understanding. Can I... should I write?"

"I'd hope so." Ransom's fond grin slipped. "I'm sure there'll be important things to discuss while you're away. What you're up to, who you're seeing. If there's anyone familiar—friend or enemy."

Maybe Jack was hatching a plan for him while he was away, but James didn't care. Just so long as he could leave, wash his hands, and grow back his heart. Even if just for a little while.

He surged forward, wrapping his mentor in a firm hug. A father of sorts—though Ransom was young enough to be a much older brother.

"Thank you," James managed.

Jack gave him a squeeze, pulling away with the same glowing ember in his dark eyes.

"Now, tell me. How shall you bide your time away from home? I can get you any job you want, wherever you want. So long as you still serve your family, perhaps turn things in our favor, even from far away." A cold smile curled across his face. "Deputy Moone has quite the ring to it, doesn't it?"

[24]

CASSIDY

Another dress arrived in Cassidy's room the following day. Another gift from Jack. More beautiful than the last, with pale silver ruffles and artfully precise tucks and folds that made the fair green gown appear like a work of art rather than something she should wear.

Perhaps she was the thing that was on display, a pretty plaything meant to be admired, to be decorated with baubles until she shone—an Aisling doll for Ransom to play with.

The library called to her again and again, through breakfast and even after an hour or two of reading in her room. Cassidy couldn't stay away long, especially when she finished *Jane Eyre* and required more reading material.

Part of her whispered that she ought not to feel so comfortable amongst those shelves. Those pretty things and pretty words made Jack Ransom more dangerous.

Cassidy wasn't stupid. She knew she could keep her eye on the target, stay on task, and remember why she came— romantic hero or no. There was only one man who proved to be a distraction, and she hadn't wanted to see his face from the moment they stepped foot within Ransom's fortress.

That didn't keep him from haunting her dreams, though.

The second night was worse than the first. More vivid. A vision that left her parched upon waking. A thirst she could only satiate herself in the moonlight, hidden behind the gauzy curtains of a bed that was too big without him in it beside her.

Cassidy hated that she knew the difference.

Her fingers danced over gold embossed spines, snared on the thought of how hers pirouetted to the idea of Moone and what might have happened if she hadn't put a stop to things in Rose Reach. If she rolled over when he lay beside her. If her mouth found his again, what awaited on the other side of friendship?

A warmth curled in her belly, lovely and familiar. But the cold bolt of rage, the sour twist of betrayal, battled it back, snuffing it out when a low voice murmured behind her.

"What are you doing, Freckles?"

Her skin prickled, her jaw ached, fighting against how much she enjoyed his warmth on her arm.

She lifted her chin, stepping to the side. "Reading. What's it look like?"

Moone made a strangled sound, frustration plain as day. She couldn't care less. Let him be frustrated. Let him keep asking questions she was determined to leave unanswered.

"You know what I mean," he said.

Cassidy read the names printed on the spines in her head as she made her way down one shelf, then another. Something to keep her occupied, aloof, just as she'd been aiming for the first time they'd come face-to-face.

James Moone didn't know Cassidy Bennet. He bought her for Jack. And damn it all if Cass was going to let him get in the middle of things.

"I'm sure I haven't the faintest idea, Mister Moone," Cassidy said, smooth as silk, moving from title to title—trying her best to ignore him.

—until his fingers clamped around her wrist when she reached for an unmarked book.

"Let me help you, Cassidy," he said, rushed and low.

Cassidy wouldn't look at him, not even with his face so dangerously close, shoulders hunched so he might catch her eye-to-eye.

"Why would I let you help me?" she whispered, staring at the deep green leather, drawn to it more than any of the others. There was something she couldn't put her finger on, a pull that even Moone couldn't distract her from.

"Because we want the same thing," he answered. "Let me finish this. I'll take care of it, and we'll go home."

"No." Cassidy finally met his eye, the desperate valley carved between his brow and the pleading look so earnest, she almost wanted to believe him.

His face shifted. "Why not?"

She pivoted back to the shelf, hooking her finger on the green riddle, determined to find out what lay within its pages. "I need to know more. I'll finish it when I'm good and ready, once I've squeezed him like a sponge—until he's got nothing else for me to take from him."

Footsteps sounded in the atrium. Goosebumps crawled up her arms, every part of her aware of the eyes and ears that might be hiding nearby. He had to go. He had to go *now*. Everything would be ruined if they were caught.

"Cassidy," James implored. Like he knew what she'd do next.

She shoved at his chest. "Get out of here before someone catches you whispering in my ear."

"I can handle myself," he argued.

"I'm sure, but something tells me that no one touches his things." *Look how well it went for Ian.* Her stomach plunged deep at the thought of Moone taking a dagger to the gut. She'd seen enough death at Ransom's hands. Losing James might push her over the edge. Cassidy worried she might never be the same if it happened to him. She shoved again. "Moone, *please—*"

James hurriedly glanced over his shoulder, jaw ticking when the voices grew louder. Cassidy wished she knew what to say, what to think when he looked back at her. Something that looked like *I'm sorry*, or worse—*I love you.*

She wouldn't let herself consider it or the way he pressed a hurried kiss to her palm before slipping through the crack in the door. His booming voice joined the chorus a second later, drawing it away from the quiet confines of the library.

Moone bought her time. Cass was nearly overwhelmed with gratitude, especially when she finally got a good look at the cover of the nameless book she'd drawn from the shelf.

Her thumb brushed over a finely carved knot in the leather. Two ropes intertwined by a sailor's hand, meant to be a way to remember their loved ones during a long voyage or great distance. On and on it went, never ending—a bond that cannot be broken.

Cassidy knew all about them, those earmarks of their homeland. Especially this one.

Her Da told her so.

A vice squeezed her heart when she flipped through the pages, dizzy with anticipation when her eyes roved over the delicate looping swirls of hand-written words. Writing Cassidy recognized but was never able to read—until now.

Aisling Callaghan's words filled every page to the brim.

She wanted to read them all, to devour them, and put together the pieces of her mother she always wished to know.

Her hands trembled as she thumbed through the pages, eyes flittering from phrase to phrase. They'd never moved so quickly, not even at her fastest draw. It still wasn't quick enough to combat the rising thump of her heart with each word.

He understands me.

I've never felt this way about a boy.

What will my father say? I hope he'll approve. This wasn't the plan.

He is a good, honorable man. There's no one like him.

I never want to be parted from him.

I love him.

A breathless smile tugged at her mouth as she took in page upon page of secret rendezvous, first kisses, and the kind of love Cassidy had only read of in books. Now, between her palms, was the most extraordinary love story of all—the one that led to her. The one she imagined and dreamed of when Aisling refused to tell her how she and Ian met, with nary a detail offered before her birth in Chicago.

But *now*, Cassidy had it all, even if it was just a piece. The contents suggested more journals, more secrets to uncover—if only there were others in the library.

She traced a finger over Aisling's words, soaking up the lovely warmth of feeling closer than she ever managed in life, when her touch landed on a name.

Jack.

Cassidy's mouth went dry. She knew there'd been a history. Her memory told her as much. Ransom filled in his own details the afternoon before. But now, it was clear that not only did Jack love Aisling, but she loved him equally, so.

And he killed her for it.

Rage's cold grip slithered around her limbs, around and around, until any bit of light was leached away by her darkness.

Cassidy's plan had always been to end him, to avenge her parents, but now she'd do one better.

She'd make him hurt the way Aisling must have. Cassidy Callaghan would make him fall for her like he tricked her mother into thinking he was a good man.

Sure, it may take longer than she anticipated, but Cassidy was prepared to play him like a game of chess—one move at a time.

It'd be easy to stab him in the heart if she held it in the palm of her hand.

"I hope you're thinking about me, pet."

Cassidy slapped the cover closed, hiding the book in a pocket of her dress. Further investigation would have to wait.

She whipped around, flashing her teeth. "My Lord."

No matter how often she said it, the formality felt odd, jarring beyond the pages of a novel.

"Missus Hughes has outdone herself again. You look beautiful." Ransom appraised her from the doorway. Others may have squirmed under his attention, but Cassidy relished it. Every compliment was a feather in her cap—another move of her pawn.

"Thank you." She dipped her head. "I'm fond of the green."

"Then I shall buy you more of it." Jack stepped into the library, drawing a book from beneath his arm. "I've brought you a gift."

"Oh?" Cassidy met him halfway, sweeping over expensive, imported carpet with a swish of her hips.

He nodded, holding out the copy of *Jane Eyre* she'd been reading the day before. "I'd very much like to give this to you."

"You remembered." She held out her hand, offering a genuine smile, but Ransom held it just out of reach when she went to take it.

Had it been Moone, Cass would've answered with a swift fist to the side, playful or not. But this was different. This required a softer touch—Cassidy Bennet's.

"I *will* give this to you, pet. On one condition," Ransom tutted, closing the space between them again. So close, Cass caught a hint of his expensive aftershave. She hated that she noticed. "How about you and I take our little rendezvous elsewhere?"

It was unexpected. Cassidy from a week ago would find spending time with him a chore. The prim and proper nature of her act, the kind of frivolities she'd sneer at. Cassidy Callaghan didn't need any of those things. Now, it

was a mission. The drape of a curl and the easy smiles were a mask. A tool.

Cassidy's cheeks warmed, thoughts trained on Moone and what she'd done in bed before the sun rose. She hadn't considered needing to take things with Ransom that far. True, the guise that allowed her through the door spoke to a certain kind of activity to be expected of her, but she was determined from the first day to make him see her as something else.

"Elsewhere?" She gulped, wide-eyed. "Upstairs… with you?"

Then, Ransom did something unexpected. He *laughed*. Full out, head back, mirthful chuckles ringing out into the atrium.

"Certainly not, dear girl." He stepped forward and cupped her jaw with the tips of his fingers, drawing her heated gaze to steal her breath with a single glance: the remnants of his laughter and a budding fondness. "You said you found yourself in the company of Madame Dubuisson because of circumstance, but there's something special about you. Something I can't quite put my finger on, but I like it—like you. Color me intrigued—*very intrigued*. So much so, I'd like to take you *out*. Officially."

"Out? But I—" She glanced down at her dress.

"Not to worry, pet. That was only the beginning. You shan't want for anything now if I'm to be your benefactor. Is that"—he took a step closer, skimming his thumb along the bottom edge of her lip—"Is that something that interests you, dear Cassidy?"

Her eyes darted between his, twisted in the ghost of her memories, the tantalizing promise of the truth, and so much more. She ought to say no, insist they skip everything else, and go to bed. There, she could end him as he slept. Easy. If she agreed, it'd spur on the budding trust between them. If he liked her, if he *trusted* her, there was no telling the things she might accomplish—or how sweet her vengeance would taste if she broke his heart as she put a bullet through it.

What would happen if she said no? Be booted back home to Gallow Gorge, no closer to justice than she'd been before? If she said yes, doors would open, opportunities presented—all for the low cost of pleasant conversation and enjoyable company with the man who just so happened to have murdered her parents.

CASSIDY

A WEEK AGO, IF SOMEONE TOLD CASS CALLAGHAN SHE'D be tucked into a luxurious carriage that cost ten times what she earned in a year, she would've called them a liar. A day ago, if someone told her she'd be in the heart of Sacramento, up on a pedestal in an exclusive shop as a seamstress held bolts of fabric against the hue of her eyes, Cass would've thought someone poisoned her whiskey when she wasn't looking.

Sometimes, the truth was stranger than fiction.

She wasn't sure how much time had gone by. Hours, maybe, since she got swept up in the niceties Jack gave her. All it took was a nod.

She tried staying anchored in her task, in what she hoped to achieve at the end of the line. She tried telling herself that enjoying silks, petticoats, and too-beautiful-to-eat petit-fours was *silly*.

Cass Callaghan wasn't silly. No, she wasn't the girl who'd fall for such things. She was the stubborn piece of work who hated being beautiful. It was never any use, only a hindrance until now.

The girl looking back at her from a gleaming mirror was a stranger. Cass recognized who stared back when Madame Dubuisson wrapped her in borrowed green silk. This girl, this *woman*—wide-eyed and flushed pink—was unrecognizable; a stranger who, if Cassidy forged ahead, might find anything she wanted in her grasp.

Even the Devil's end.

Cass Callaghan had no place at *Colina de Dragones*. She wouldn't even get past the front door. As Cassidy, the elegant woman she daydreamed of as a little girl, not only did she get past the front door, she'd get into the deepest, darkest corners. She'd tiptoe along the Devil's backbone, whispering the sweetest lies he wanted to hear until the moment she stuck a dagger between his ribs.

In the back room of the dress shop, they stripped her green afternoon dress away. The seamstress was quiet, buzzing like a bee in the summertime. She twisted Cass up in fresh undergarments lined with supple pink satin. Each layer was more decadent than the last. For once, she wasn't convinced she hated it.

Her wild copper hair was tamed, twisted around a hot iron, and wound into an elegant *something* Cass didn't know what to call. All she knew was that the silken curls falling over her freckled shoulder were too beautiful to touch, made all the more so by the soft pink flowers carefully tucked along the crown of her head.

It was foreign, dazzling, and sublime. Too beautiful to be real. This wasn't her. She was a doll being dressed to the nines as an assistant filled a third trunk with more satins and silks that'd find their way back to *Colina de Dragones* before night's end.

"It's our pleasure to have such a lovely young lady

here at Lord Ransom's behest." The silver-haired woman beamed, thrilled to have an infinitely lucrative customer sweep through their doors. "We've heard all he's done for the Union but never seen a lady on his arm. What a lucky woman you are, Miss Bennet."

The woman lit up when she and Jack arrived, eyeing Cass with a curious, tempered smile as he instructed her on his exact wishes—what he wanted Cassidy to be.

He disappeared with a final, sweeping kiss upon her knuckles, murmuring a promise he'd be back from the haberdashery before she knew it, that she was in *very* capable hands.

"It's by pure luck we had this," the seamstress told her as half a dozen hands lowered rose-colored striped silk over Cass's new hoopskirt and promptly began lacing it closed over her corset. Her fingers were cold as she straightened delicate lace around the curve of Cassidy's shoulders, curling her touch over the top when she met her gaze in the mirror. "This is the height of Parisian fashion. You'll be the talk of Sacramento tomorrow, my dear."

Cass swallowed a nervous laugh. "Is that a good thing?" It certainly wasn't her goal.

"In the company of Jack Ransom, yes." She strode around to Cass's front and plucked a tin jar of rouge from her apron, blotting it over her lips before stepping back with a satisfied smile. "Other girls would *kill* to be in your shoes."

"Why?" Cassidy twisted back and forth, fluttering the skirt around her ankles. "They aren't that comfortable."

"They *are* expensive." An amused smile tugged at the corner of her weathered mouth. "How did you come to be on his arm?"

The lovely woman in the mirror resembled her but was

more like Cassidy stole someone else's skin and slipped it over hers. Though jarring, she wasn't half bad to look at.

"Happenstance." Cassidy traced a finger over the faint rosy hue on her lips, meeting the gaze of the dressmaker. "I don't know much about him. Though, he's kind." To Cassidy Bennet, he was. She knew the truth of his cruelty.

"That he is." She nodded, pulling a pair of long, ivory gloves from a bureau. "There are whispers about his reputation. Idle gossip, methinks. I like to think a gentleman such as Lord Ransom shows himself in his deeds. He's caused no hurt to the people of Sacramento. Of that, I'm sure."

A bell rang, carried on a whisper of dust-tinged evening light streaming through the open door.

Cassidy snapped to attention, whirling to meet the gaze of the handsome man who stepped inside. The Devil in disguise. She couldn't lose sight of that. He was like her, using those pretty things and pretty words to lure the people into thinking he wasn't a monster. Cassidy knew better than to give in like them.

"Well." He stepped forward, wordlessly reaching for the gloves from the seamstress. "You were as pretty as a picture before. Now, you're a *vision*."

"I feel naked." Cass let out a soft breath, wishing her bosom wouldn't rise *so* far with each anxious breath.

Jack chuckled, fond and deep, reaching for her hand before sliding the kidskin glove up her arm. "You're beautiful, pet."

"Thank you." She shivered, meeting his eye for a single, breathless moment when his fingertips trailed along the inside of her elbow. *Wrong.* It was all wrong.

"Are you afraid you might catch the attention of an

unwanted suitor at the opera?" Ransom made quick work of the second, slipping it over her fingers without effort.

Cass wished he wasn't so close. She wished she couldn't smell his aftershave's sweet orange blossom and sandalwood. She wished she hated it as much as she hated him.

She shook her head. "No."

"Good." Ransom's hands gripped her waist, slowly spinning her to look upon her reflection. He skimmed a shiver-inducing knuckle down the back of her neck, meeting her eyes with another, wicked smile. "You're mine now, remember?"

CASSIDY

CASSIDY NEVER SAW ANY PLACE LIKE IT.

She was thankful for Jack's firm hold on her gloved hand, keeping her steady as her eyes wandered over towering granite columns brightly lit by gas lamps. On and on they went, reaching skyward to gilded paradise—carved stone flecked with bits of gold that glimmered in the warm evening light.

She was distracted. Cassidy couldn't help it. Every thought of vengeance flittered away the moment they stepped inside.

Her plan would keep until tomorrow.

Voices murmured, swelling, echoes upon echoes bouncing off the marble floors. People watched her. She must've looked like a child, filled with wonder; a stranger amongst the Sacramento elite.

Cassidy didn't pay them any mind, not at first, too wrapped up in the beautiful sight of full skirts and shining silks every color of the rainbow. She'd lived a colorful life, filled with storied experiences no other woman had. Between the people she met and the challenges she faced, she never

considered herself to be left wanting.

Until that moment, Cassidy never thought of how grey her every day was.

The sharp, curious attention of hundreds followed them as they strode down the grand foyer to a sweeping, wine-red staircase.

Cass hated the thought of being watched riding down the bridleway in Gallow Gorge. This—this was almost too much to take.

Her cheeks heated. "Everyone is staring at you."

Jack stepped up first, beckoning with an outstretched hand as she gathered a delicate fistful of peach and rose silk in one hand, meeting him with the other.

"No, my darling." He smiled, drawing her closer. "They're all looking at you."

Cassidy huffed an overwhelmed laugh. "I can't imagine why."

He pulled her up another stair, looping her gloved hand through his arm. "Two reasons, pet. Would you like me to tell you?"

She stared at a crystal chandelier, letting out a soft sigh when the upstairs corridors of the mezzanine proved to be just as beautiful as the foyer. "Enlighten me."

Jack laughed; a soft rumble, the promise of a hurricane blowing in on the horizon. "I'm known in Sacramento society."

"So I've been told." Cassidy glanced over her shoulder into the grand foyer, where many guests milled around in colorful skirts and crisp tails. Almost all of their eyes followed her and Ransom up the stairs. "So I can *see*."

"I've been a bachelor for a long time." Jack squeezed her hand, pulling it to his lips to kiss her knuckles. A river of whispers fluttered through the crowd. "And I've never brought a woman to a social engagement before. Not until now." He stopped, hooking a knuckle beneath her chin. "Not until you."

A flutter built within her, foreign and divine. She first thought to swallow it, smother it, and never recreate the feeling again. Instead, she reveled in it, caught in the web of his gaze, leaning in where she ought to run away.

Perhaps it was some sort of magic, a potent spell that scrubbed away at the memory of Jack Ransom, polishing it until every tarnished bit of his character she'd simmered in for half her life disappeared. The more she knew him, the less sure Cassidy was that Jack was the same man at all. From the square of his shoulders, the light of his eyes, and the bend of his mouth—all of it, all of him, was different. He wasn't a monster; he was merely a man.

Wrong. All of it was wrong, but so right. The way he looked at her said that the plan was working better than she could've hoped. Cassidy was a second chance that landed in his lap—bait and a trap.

When he pulled away, she wrung a fan in her hands, mouth quirking when a gentleman with swarthy sideburns and a barrel chest heartily shook Jack's hand. He jovially exclaimed about generous campaign donations and a boy's home Ransom had built; the governor, she learned once her companion returned.

The lights on the mezzanine's lobby flashed once, twice. Jack wound her hand tighter in the bend of his arm.

"At last, pet. No more interruptions until intermission." He led her up another short set of stairs and lifted a heavy, velvet curtain. Cassidy dipped beneath his arm, chest heaving, eyes alight when the opera house opened before her.

Red velvet seats stretched to the edges of a gilded ceiling, voices clambered and churned, reverberating off a warm, blue fresco that brought the brilliance of the California sunshine in. Golden-edged balconies were stacked two, four, six—filled to the brim with people she'd brushed petticoats within the marbled hall moments before. Cassidy wondered how they'd be able to see the stage from so far away or how the soprano's voice might reach.

She needn't worry for Ransom and herself, not with their box perched on the edge of the apron. It was close enough, Cassidy might reach out and touch the gold fringe on the curtain.

The corset kept her back straight when she sat. The beauty of the opera house would've done the same, holding her like a tether until the light of the grandiose central chandelier dimmed to nothing and the orchestra played the beginnings of a mournful prelude.

Music swelled, lifting the hair on her arms. Within moments, Cassidy was transfixed, caught up in a story whose words she couldn't understand. The meaning danced through complex melodies artfully performed by sopranos and baritones swathed in colorful costumes.

"Isolde," Ransom murmured a shiver-inducing whisper in Cassidy's ear. "An Irish princess, brought to England to wed a king. His nephew, Tristan, is to escort her."

"But?" Cassidy tore her eyes away from the stage, meeting the quiet glow of Ransom's gaze; so close, she felt the kiss of his breath on her face.

His mouth quirked. "The pair are madly in love. Watch as she begs him to take poison with her so she doesn't have to marry the king, and they can be together in eternity."

By the end of the first act, half the eyes and opera glasses around them were trained on their box, collecting details of her and Ransom's every move to gossip about tomorrow.

She paid them no mind, too wrapped in the story unfolding on stage to think about the one happening in their box or others conjured by feather-wearing, silk-wrapped strangers she'd never met. Not when Tristan and Isolde's secret love affair became known to her husband, the king.

Cassidy loved stories, tales of romance fraught with complications and obstacles. The characters in her mind lived there without cost, happily milling together until she'd draw upon the memory of reading them to hold close as she fell asleep by a fire's glow. Being there, seeing it unfold free from her imagination, right in front of her very eyes, spurred a feeling she couldn't have fathomed before.

Her heart caught, twisting like her real lover was injured when Tristan fell. When she gasped, Ransom squeezed her hand as she gripped the box's edge with the other.

"Will he die?" Cassidy whispered.

Ransom's touch skimmed the inside of her elbow, silver-striped hair nearly brushing her cheek. "Look closely, my darling. Watch as she goes to him… but he's already gone."

Cassidy sat transfixed, doing the unthinkable as Isolde sang her last, mournful lament—laying her touch over Ransom's as the beautiful princess breathed her last to join her lover in the afterlife.

Tears. Cassidy hadn't realized they'd been streaming down her cheeks, freckling the rosy flesh of her aching bosom. Not until Ransom plucked one from its perch on her cupid's bow with the corner of his handkerchief.

It wasn't until they returned to *Colina de Dragones* that she realized it'd been clutched in her palm from the moment he bestowed it upon her.

Still fragrant, though wilted, roses pulled from her hair, Cassidy rubbed her thumb over his embroidered initials. Her reflection was wide-eyed and flushed; the stranger whose skin she borrowed from the moment she shirked her dusty boots and unbound her braid. She buzzed from the miraculous day. Fiction made real; a Mister Rochester for her very own, and she the orphaned Jane.

Had she been wrong about him? Perhaps he had a brother responsible for what she witnessed as a child. At barely nine years old, how could Cassidy be sure the monster from her memory and the man whose company she happily enjoyed all evening were one and the same?

No, *no*. Cassidy shook her head and balled the soft bundle of cotton in her fist until her knuckles ached.

Jack Ransom was a murderer, the Scourge of the West. She wouldn't fall into his web, wouldn't lose sight of why she came, why she obsessed over finding him her entire life—no matter how enticing the web might be.

Still, she was tempted. There was no denying the provoking lure of trailing him along, convincing him of her adoration until she took an empire for her own. Then, she could use it all—the power, the money, the influence. She could do whatever she wished; days spent amassing a force to dole out justice, and nights enjoying an orchestra in the lamplight.

Cassidy met her wild gaze in the looking glass, smiling when she thought of the opera house, the carriage, the foreign flutter in her belly when he whispered in her ear. Maybe playing the role a little while longer wouldn't hurt; the slightest distraction so she might enjoy the delirious daydream a little longer.

None of it changed the thirst for his blood as repayment

for his crimes. Cassidy deserved to take him for everything he had, everything he was. None of it would replace what she lost, but it was a start.

Handkerchief in hand, Cassidy wrapped herself in a fringed shawl and stepped out onto the veranda overlooking the grand central courtyard of the hacienda. She tiptoed over stone still warm from the day's sunshine. Down half a dozen closed rooms and around a corner, tucked into the shadows deep in the belly of the sprawling mansion, Cassidy found a pair of intricately carved double doors.

She stopped short, clutching the wrap to her pounding heart when the door opened, and a young woman spilled out.

Half-disheveled, wild-eyed, and tearful, her face contorted when her dark eyes met Cassidy. She straightened, dusting off her chemise, and shouldered by with a frown.

Cassidy had seen the handful of other women around the house since she arrived, a revolving carousel of the best Sacramento had to offer to keep certain thirsts well-quenched. The number dwindled in the last day, and the scornful look in the woman's eyes told her another was being shown the door—and it was her fault.

Jaw set, Cassidy lifted her chin, unyielding when the other woman went by. She wasn't here to make friends. She didn't have time for attachment—except one.

James Moone was the one thing that hadn't left her mind all night. He was a fixture, permanently rooted there like a mighty oak. The pieces of him were too deeply ingrained to leave her be. Wishes for his whisper in her ear and his handkerchief in her hand.

Stepping up to the door, she closed her eyes and drew a steadying breath, hoping Ransom wouldn't take her showing up at his door as an invitation Cassidy wasn't ready to deliver upon—probably ever.

A quick tap of her knuckles against wood, the shuffling behind closed doors moments before bursting open. When they did, Cassidy didn't know where to look or if she should.

"I apologize for the late hour." She licked her lips, cheeks flushed, heart twisting, body thrumming in uninvited ways.

Jack Ransom leaned against the frame like a much younger man, wearing naught but his trousers, half-buttoned and barely hanging on from carved hips.

Cassidy couldn't help it when her eyes kept climbing back to Adonis notches and taut lines casting shadows over a surprisingly sculpted chest despite the silver-threaded hair hanging over his eyes. She was only human, after all—a woman starved from what she and Moone started but never got to finish.

His mouth quirked, gaze bright as it flickered over her, from her bare feet to naked shoulder kissed by moonlight.

"Cassidy," Jack purred, pawing back his hair. "You surprise me again."

She thrust out his handkerchief. "I forgot to return this to you."

His smile widened, catlike and potent in how it made her stomach churn and hairs stand on end. "You could've kept it, my darling. I have a collection of them. Although—" He grasped her wrist, unfolding every finger against his chest like a long-awaited gift, trailing the soft bundle from her palm as he held her gaze. Ransom twisted it around his knuckles and held it to his nose. His eyes closed as he breathed it in, breathed *her* in. "This one might be my favorite after today."

Cassidy shivered. "I had a good time. Thank you," she murmured, thinking of every splendid moment, every second she adored despite her better judgment. It wasn't a lie; she *was* thankful. For the experience, the music, and the opportunity to draw him further in. "Thank you for your generosity, your kindness… for everything, Jack."

Ransom's bemused grin fell but danced behind his eyes. It wasn't hard to see his name on her lips pleased him.

It shouldn't have, but it pleased her, too.

The sound falling from her lips was involuntary, merely a symptom of the shock running through her when Jack gingerly held the curve of her jaw between his hands, cradling her like a precious piece of porcelain. He tilted her face this way and that, inspecting her every freckle until, as the thousandth shiver fell down her spine, he pressed his lips to the corner of her mouth.

One movement. That's all it would take for Ransom to snap her neck and leave her dead on the floor. A flick of his wrist, and it'd all be over.

She should've been afraid. Should've pulled away instead of leaning in. It took everything in her not to push Jack into the darkened suite and ask him to do it again and again.

No, not him. Not Jack, but Moone, down the hall. She'd take him down to the carriage house if she had to. A whole other side of her was *awake*, whose voice was louder than a locomotive's whistle. The slightest touch would be enough. Just a moment to remember it was him she wanted, not the wolf who stared at her like a meal he'd like to devour.

"It was my pleasure," he growled, trailing his nose from her jaw to her temple. "I thoroughly enjoyed doting on you, pet. But—"

Cassidy's eyes flashed open. A foreign feeling curled through her, snuffing out the fledgling flame of unbidden desire—*disappointment.* "But?"

Another smile, the gleam of curiosity in his eye. "The hour is late." He tucked a spray of copper curls behind her ear. "Rest, now. Everything else will wait for another day."

"Everything else?" Cassidy's cheeks flushed, eyes sliding over his shoulder into the shadows of his suite.

Ransom's shoulders straightened as if he moved to teach or scold her. "Am I wrong in thinking our budding affection is an illusion?"

Yes. Cassidy shivered. *And no.* She shouldn't, but cats often played with their prey before doing them in. Why couldn't she enjoy it right up until the end?

Cassidy shook her head. "It's all so unexpected."

Unexpected, indeed.

"As are you, my darling. You're a gift, like fate sent you straight to my door." Ransom rolled his jaw, as if he tried to contain another smile. "I thought we might embrace it, this chance. And perhaps have a more... *traditional* courtship. So, yes. Everything else will wait."

The voice inside her preened, thrilled to catch his interest so keenly. There was every reason to distrust him; memories growing foggier by the minute, masked by each new encounter, every conversation, and kind gesture. They all scrubbed at her excuse of playing a role—merely an actor in the grand opera of her revenge.

Cassidy wasn't a player. She was the star of her own charade.

[27]

MOONE

T HE DAY BLED AWAY IN THE DARKNESS OF THE OPIUM den's sickly sweet, spicy cloud—one of the dozens tucked across Sacramento. They'd grown in number and luxury since Moone left for Gallow Gorge.

Ransom kept his men busy, blurring the senses of the city's elite, holding them under his thumb behind closed doors. Money spoke volumes, and he worked it to his every advantage, sticking his fingers in every pie from Sacramento to Chicago.

His reach was wide, further than anyone ever thought possible for an aristocrat and foreigner. But, where Ransom was rich, he was also shrewd, unyielding in his iron hold. The city's inhabitants were none the wiser. All they saw was the gentleman who frequented their shops but shipped illegal opium through their neighbor; a generous donor who swayed elections in his favor behind closed doors; the benefactor of orphaned boys who'd call upon them once they were men to do his bidding.

Moone stuck to the last threads of light seeping through velvet curtains, the silver-tipped toe of his boot holding

open the door to let fresh air bleed in. He wasn't interested in partaking; he never was. Ransom taught him well. Moone never let anything distract him; not drugs, drink, or even women—except one.

James thought of her, of Cassidy, and how he left her in the hands of the wolf. He hoped she was able to weasel herself away and conjure space between her and Ransom's fervent fascination. He wished it were a canyon, one that'd keep Jack Ransom far, far away from his wild girl.

Moone swallowed his worry. She was smart, capable, and stronger than an ox. She'd never believe him, even if he said it straight to her face. She'd keep her wits about her. She'd stay true to the plan—unless he found an opening to enact his, first.

A flash of copper caught his eye.

Gone before he had a chance to really look, Moone chased the sight out into the evening air, abandoning the men he told himself to survey. The sidewalk in the upscale neighborhood swarmed with people. Carriages noisily clattered over cobblestone, punctuated by the metallic *plunk* of steel horseshoes; a happy little march to the sprawling opera house a quarter mile away.

Top hats and silks bounced and bobbed, blocking his view to the end of the block. Buzzing voices, effervescent with excitement covered him like a blanket. In the haze, Moone spotted it—spotted *her*—again.

Dreaming, yes. That's what was happening. The woman he saw held the color of her hair, maybe the shape of her jaw. But James Moone *knew* Cassidy Callaghan. She wasn't about silks, petticoats, or flowers in her hair. They certainly wouldn't make her smile like his imagination tricked him into thinking.

Still, he chased the mirage, shouldering his way through the crowd, pushing further, faster, until a hand on his chest blocked his way.

"Ticket, sir."

Moone craned his neck through the doorway. His stomach twisted when the lovely lady smiled, chin tilted down as her companion murmured in her ear—a man who was undoubtedly Jack Ransom.

"*Sir.*" The usher pushed him back. "I'm afraid, if you don't buy a ticket, I cannot allow you inside."

Moone sifted through his pockets, eyes glued to the couple as they were swallowed by a cloud of colorful silks and petticoats. He pulled out a handful of coins, slapping them into the man's hand as he forced his way in.

He lost them, unable to follow through the sprawling, marble-lined lobby to the private boxes—only given the briefest flash of peach and rose-colored silk when she turned out of sight.

Like a school of salmon swimming upriver, Moone fought the current to the fourth floor of the mezzanine, plucking a pair of opera glasses from a breast pocket of a stranger.

In his seat, among the lesser Sacramento members who couldn't afford to sit on the edges of the stage's apron, Moone searched. A blur of faces filled his vision as he peered through the glasses, going box by box until he settled on the one closest to the stage.

His stomach dropped. His vision swam.

Moone *knew* Cassidy. He thought he did.

The woman in the box was her, he didn't bother denying it. Not now that he'd seen her clearly, differently than he ever had. Her hair had been ironed and twisted, something he'd seen executed before, but never so finely as she looked now. A crown of pale roses was carefully pinned and tucked into delicate plaits, and rouge blotted on her lips.

Beautiful.

The thought wouldn't leave him alone, repeating over and over until he thought he'd burst. Moone always considered her to be, even years before when they were both practically still children.

Now, as this *lady*, Cassidy was a vision. Ransom's work, surely.

Moone rubbed his eyes, blinking in the darkness as the lamplight bled away. The music swelled, and the show began—a mournful tale he suddenly found himself in the middle of. He was Tristan, she Isolde. He delivered her to the king, made a bride of her, and lost his heart in the process.

He thought he might be sick, though the ache from his clenched jaw and tight fists might not allow it. Hours ticked by, and hushed whispers shuffled between acts. All of them were about her. All of them asked who the woman was, and why Ransom chose *her* after years of bachelorhood.

Moone barely gave them any consideration, too wrapped in the thought of—*why not me?*

CASSIDY

R ANSOM SENT CASSIDY TO BED WITH THE PROMISE OF TEA the next afternoon.

The morning after the opera, trunks began to arrive one after the other. A magnificent trousseau filled to the brim with colorful silks, shimmering taffetas, and ribbons of every color. The clothier had been busy, catering to Jack's every whim to dress her as she ought to be, especially after her society debut.

Three days passed. Then a week. Then two. Whispers found their way to the estate, ones printed in black and white: Jack Ransom was rumored to have the hand of a lady no one ever heard of. To them, she wasn't a bounty hunter with no use for pretty things. She was elegant, meant to be seen, and the envy of every woman from Sacramento to the furthest reaches of the Nevada desert.

Pretty things were Cassidy's tool, her way to fit seamlessly in a world she never belonged in. The far-off figment of her imagination became real. When she trailed her fingers over a bouquet of feathers and jewels meant for her hair, Cassidy couldn't be completely sorry for getting caught in a web.

Not when it all worked so well in her favor.

Afternoons were spent in the library, or the garden, strolling along the lazy bend in the Sacramento River as Jack regaled her with stories of his past. She learned his mother's name, a dog he'd been fond of, and how he took his tea.

He said nothing else about the Callaghans—her parents. It vexed her, the dam he built around that part of his past. With no other volumes of Aisling's journals in the library, Cassidy had no other way of finding out the rest of the story. It didn't stop her from studying the only one she found, reading and re-reading the pages until her eyes ached.

Between them, she found no answers beyond a young woman's unfortunate first love. Reading it brought a stomachache, knowing how it would all end in blood.

Cassidy avoided Moone. The scorching bolt of anger at his betrayal remained. It was twined to everything else, tangled in their history, and those feelings for him she'd tried so hard to avoid. All of it, the good and the bad, surged when their eyes met across the dinner table or passing each other on the stairs.

To Ransom, they were strangers. Cassidy wanted to keep it that way. It made things easier. He wouldn't pose a distraction if she never saw him.

The sun shone brightly over the pages of *Wuthering Heights*. Cassidy leaned on the lonely pillar by the window, a now-favorite perch. The library, too, grew in her affection; the divine smell of ink and parchment too tempting to avoid for long.

"I thought I might find you here." Ransom's voice set a shiver down her arms. His touch, too, summoned the tiniest hairs to stand on end, reaching for more when his fingers brushed a bundle of carefully ironed curls from her neck. He followed it with a kiss as swift as could be. It was a promise of what was to come if everything went according to his plan—then eventually, hers. "You belong in the sun, my darling. Like this."

"Is that so?" Cassidy smiled, eyes still on the page. The longer they lingered at *Colina de Dragones*, the less she sounded like herself. He started molding her into someone different, someone who slept until the sun was high and who moseyed the day away. There was no work to be done, no one to chase. The leisure *was* the work. Every second spent by Jack's side, studying him, liking him against her better judgment, was another feather in her cap, another step on the ladder to finishing things once and for all.

"Undoubtedly," he purred, winding a knuckle over the curve of her neck, from sunshine to shadow, and every freckle in-between. "Then, more of these might be left behind. They suit you."

"Oh?" Cassidy lifted her chin, meeting his darkened gaze.

Similar moments arose after the heated, instantaneous thrill following the opera. They'd passed like a fleeting shadow, ones Cassidy worried she might get sucked into. During them, she held onto the idea of Moone, the light in his eyes, his crooked half-smile. She let him moor her and keep her from plummeting.

Jack was close, so much closer than other times. Her eyes flickered to the corner of his mouth, shadowed by fine flecks of silver amongst a day or two's scruff.

Cassidy thought of James, of the quiet in the Palace Hotel, where he reverently tended to her, and she thanked him with a kiss.

More.

The word lingered in the back of her mind all day after, until the doors of *Colina de Dragones* swung open and revealed the depth of Moone's lies. It lingered, still, in her dreams. Night after night. Where she expected Jack to eventually appear, Moone stood center-stage, stoking the fire Cassidy was once determined to snuff out.

A distraction. That's what he was, what he'd always been. And she couldn't be more grateful, even if she avoided him. Seeing him was dangerous, but having him close wasn't something she could risk. Not if it meant she'd fail.

Moone held her attention, then. For a moment, her breath, her gaze, and her heart's beat intertwined with Ransom's in the bright early afternoon light. Cassidy blinked and saw *him*, saw Moone. Not over Jack's shoulder, nor standing in the doorway. But in his face, a silent wish to replace one man with the other.

The sun might be deceiving her. Her dreams, too. Eyes of blue, tawny curls, a lopsided smile—all gone in a second. Ransom came into focus, a shadow in his own right, blocking the sun's gaze upon her face. He hovered a hair's breadth away, close enough to kiss, tracing a thumb along the bottom edge of her lip.

Cassidy wondered if he'd make good on the gleam in his eye, the silent wish thrumming between them like the taut string on a violin. Part of her hoped he would; the sooner she could paint the house red in his blood and her betrayal.

"Boss?"

Cassidy's attention swept over Jack's shoulder to a man standing in the doorway. Her mouth went dry, fingers aching with the memory of pulling a warrant from her vest a hundred, two hundred times. She memorized the sketch, his angular face and scarred cheek, the rot of his teeth. Four counts of murder. Six counts of attempted murder. Seven, if she counted herself.

Her cheeks heated, no matter how she tried to keep aloof, indifferent.

"Don't fret, my darling. Business calls, but I shall return shortly." Ransom held her chin between his thumb and forefinger. The same chill from their first meeting cleaved the pleasant mood in two; annoyance plainly illustrated in his gaze. He squared his shoulders, growing a foot taller in the process as he faced the interrupter. "What is it, Lawrence?"

Ball's beady eyes flicked to her for a split second, too afraid of his master to linger on her for long. "It's, uh—"

Ransom blindly reached for Cassidy's hand, pulling her to his side with a kiss upon her knuckles. "Miss Bennet is a fixture here. You ought to consider her the lady of this house. Anything you have to say, you can say in front of her."

Cassidy's stomach twisted while her mouth quivered.

Lady of the house.

While it wasn't what she intended when they arrived, the phrase pleased her to no end. Jack saw her as a fixture, someone important enough to tie himself to—a target on his back for her to shoot at.

Brought front and center, Cassidy couldn't hide from Ball. There wasn't any avoiding her former bounty's gaze. His eyes snapped to her once, twice more, lingering on the third. His brows puckered; a fleeting recognition. She was a long way off from the woman who sat across from him at a poker table in Lonely Bellow, though, far from the polished, corseted lady in front of him. It was the one hope she held onto.

She scrambled for something to say, an excuse that'd

keep her from being face-to-face with Doc Ball for too long, risking her exposure.

"That's alright." Cassidy wound her arm through Jack's, pulling his attention. The blackness of his eyes softened under her touch. "I might take some air in the garden. You attend to what you must, then meet me for a stroll?"

Ransom sucked in a breath, drawing back the glimpse of the monster within. *Good.* She might have influence, as well. He held her face, a habit formed over the weeks spent together; inspecting her like a rare treasure or a delicate bloom, pressing a kiss to her cheek when he was satisfied. "If that's what you wish, my darling. Another time, perhaps."

"If that's what *you* wish, Jack."

His mouth quirked. "Every kingdom ought to have its queen, yes?"

Cassidy looked to Ball waiting in the doorway, hanging on their every word. Her stomach churned the longer he watched her.

"All in due time, my love." She snapped her book shut, stretching on tiptoes to convincingly return Jack's affection, freeing herself from the library without further delay.

Ball tracked her all the while, eyes narrowing as she made her escape. And if Ball was suspicious, then Cassidy and Moone were in trouble.

[62]

MOONE

L AWRENCE BALL KNEW MOONE WATCHED HIM. JAMES haunted him like a shadow. He did what he could to keep Cassidy from being discovered. The first week, Moone went largely unnoticed. After, it all became an easy source of entertainment.

Ball goaded him, poking and prodding the younger man in hopes he'd leap across the parlor and connect a fist to his knotted face. He'd like that. He'd like to draw Ransom's attention to Moone like *he* was the bad apple.

Maybe he was, but Ransom didn't know that—not yet.

On the eighth day, with the crunch of his boots following Ball's every step, the flick of his eyes told Moone he'd started to make him nervous. The task was easy enough, with Lawrence so much slighter where James was tall and broad, but a chore, nonetheless.

Moone wanted Ransom to send Ball away. Part of him was tempted to ask or conjure a false errand for him to run two states over. Then he might be able to watch Cassidy instead and finally have the chance to catch her alone.

They'd barely said a few words to each other in the three

weeks at *Colina de Dragones*. Nothing beyond a *pardon me* or shy *good morning* after the library.

Ransom was *always* by her side—the price of pretty petticoats.

Moone wouldn't have minded as much if she'd stuck to the original plan. If she'd been like the other girls, it'd only be a night. She would've already killed him, and they'd be long gone before the third week went by. The further they went, the worse he worried she'd changed her mind about his master.

To her, Ransom wasn't a shadow. He was everything Moone wanted to be, everything he couldn't give her. Her eyes shone over the pages of a new book, another gift from the man who learned even that precious detail about her.

Moone tried. He tried for ages to know her. He *did* know her. He used to, and it took years to crack her shell.

Ransom did it in days.

It burned Moone from the inside out. Especially on days when Ransom and Cassidy appeared in the morning—hand-in-hand as if they were rulers of a desert palace. Days they'd do everything together: breakfast, reading in the library in the afternoon. Cassidy's touch on his back as he lit a pipe. His hand on her waist as she drew a fresh volume from the shelf. Disappearing in their eveningwear, disappearing again up the stairs to do God knew what.

Moone became grateful for the task of watching Ball. The rest of Ransom's men were pleased with their new mistress. She eased the iron fist of their master and smoothed out his sharp edges. James knew it wouldn't last. The monster would come out, eventually.

On the twenty-first night, as coyotes sang at the river's edge, Moone loitered in the doorway of the smoking room.

His cigar burned down to the end, and so had the second—reduced to ash as a game of Faro carried on an hour too long.

"*Boy*, come with me."

Moone sniffed, shaking away the rise of gooseflesh beneath his collar. He snuffed out the stub and answered Ransom's call, following into the parlor.

Ransom took a chair at the hearth's edge, folding his hands together as Moone sat in the other.

"You've been avoiding me, son." Ransom ran a long finger across the seam of his mouth. Moone wondered how many times he kissed Cassidy with it.

"I haven't." He had, unable to drum up the nerve to catch him alone and drive a knife through his heart.

Ransom's lips quirked. "Lies don't become you, boy."

Moone shrugged. "Preoccupied, then."

"Aren't we all?" Another threat of a smile.

Moone stared down at the chair's arm, digging his fingernail into crushed velvet. "I won't stay. I like it there."

"Better than your home?"

Moone's eyes raked around the room. He saw himself in every corner—heir to the kingdom he never planned to want.

Ransom stood, thumbing the gleaming curve of the dirk at his hip as he stared into the flames. "Time is an odd thing, James. It falls away like leaves in the wind. I hadn't realized how quickly it'd gone until you went with it. Until you never came back."

"I'm sorry."

He wasn't.

Ransom slipped the blade from its sheath. The sound of polished steel on firm leather sliced the quiet crackle from the flames. He held it aloft in the firelight, the gleam reflected in his eyes.

Moone saw it, then—the monster, inside. As if the blade held every ounce of blood Ransom ever spilled, a reflection of his sins pressed into steel.

"There are so many things I wanted to teach, show, and *give* you." Ransom's gaze snapped to Moone. "Given half the chance, boy, those things can still be yours. They *should* be yours. Though, perhaps differently than we might've planned."

Moone sat straighter. "Different, how?"

Ransom hid the blade away in its sheath, making a show of its removal from his belt. His fingers curled around finely stitched leather—the one possession James never knew him to be without. He shook his head, rolling his jaw when another smile fought to break free.

"Life is strange, James." Ransom's eyes lifted. "Second chances are an odd, precious treasure. They spring up when you least expect it."

"I wouldn't know." Moone's fingers curled into a fist on his knee. All he could do was hope for one from Cassidy. "I never knew you to give many."

"None, in fact," Ransom tutted in agreement. His face darkened for a moment. A ghost of something—regret, perhaps—washed over him, gone before taking root. "I've considered it, just once. It was enough to put me off from the idea. I have little patience with betrayers."

Moone's chest tightened. "I know."

"And yet—" Ransom paced before the fire, circling around to his back. James kept his gaze firmly on the flames. "Here we are, with a feast of opportunity."

"I don't understand." Moone tracked his steps as he

settled back in across from him.

Ransom steepled his fingers beneath his chin. "Curious that fate should drop two ghosts on my doorstep the same night. Fortuitous, indeed."

"Stop speaking in riddles." Moone should've shrank in the aftermath of his boldness. Perhaps he could gather that courage, bottle it, and use it to his advantage.

Ransom's eyes flashed, more amusement than anger.

"Cassidy Bennet."

"What about her?" Moone kept his face passive, though his stomach churned at the mention of her name.

"I intend to marry her."

Ransom may as well have stuck Moone in the heart with his dagger, twisting the blade until he was run through. Spots crowded his vision. His jaw ached from locking it into place. He searched for words, the clock on the mantle counting the seconds he loitered.

All he managed was, "Oh? That was fast."

His mentor chuckled. "She reminds me so much of a woman I once loved. I let her slip through my fingers, and I won't do the same with dear, sweet Cassidy."

"What if she refuses?"

Ransom smiled. Cold, calculating, pleased. As if he'd already asked. "She won't."

"Congratulations, I suppose." Moone stood, stuffing a hand in his pocket as he turned away. He scrubbed his jaw with the other, eyes closed to gather his bearings, come to his senses, and see things clearly—without the thought of Lady Cassidy Ransom clouding his vision. "What's it have to do with me?"

Ransom commanded Moone's attention, wordlessly plucking the sheathed dirk from the mantle to hold between them.

"You're important to me, boy. Like a son."

Moone nodded. His chest heaved. He hoped Ransom wouldn't see. "I know."

Ransom stepped closer. "I need something from you."

James knew better than to make promises with the Devil. Still, he held out hope that he might be able to twist whatever it was to his advantage.

"Anything."

"My enemies are many." Ransom circled his fingers around Moone's wrist, drawing it into the firelight. He stepped closer, dark eyes gleaming with his request. "If something should happen to me—" He paused, working his jaw, as if he had emotions and fears to sort out before he uttered them aloud. "I cannot lose her again. If something should happen, I want you to take care of her, all of this. It'll be yours."

"Take *care* of her? The house, your contacts?" Moone's brow knit; he couldn't be asking him to step into his shoes. He didn't know if he could return to the monster he used to be. But, to accomplish what he set out to do, he might have to.

"All of it, boy." Ransom squeezed tighter.

Moone tried to pull away. "Are you sure you don't have some child, a long-lost son who'll inherit all this? Why me?"

He didn't want it the same way Ransom did. He didn't want to be the Scourge of the West or the scourge of anything. He could let it all burn and leave it behind—as long as he took Cassidy with him.

"God-willing, maybe one day. But until then, there is no one else I'd trust with this. Her, perhaps, but she cannot do it alone." Ransom stepped closer. For a split second, Moone saw something soften within him. A fatherly gaze or fear of what he built being left to wither away. "I've prepared you for this your entire life."

"I'm ready." Moone nodded, reaching for the jeweled dagger.

Ransom yanked it away. "You swear it? You'll keep her and all this safe?"

Yes. From you.

Moone mulled it over. As Ransom put it, it may be a second chance, a veiled opportunity. No matter how much he hated it, hated seeing her wrapped around Ransom's finger, Cassidy *belonged* in this life. She fit so well, and Moone couldn't hope to give her anything like it as the Deputy of Gallow Gorge…unless he took every brick and cent with him before the end, bleeding Ransom dry. Payment for his life—and hers.

So, with a voice like gravel, he answered.

"I swear."

[30]

CASSIDY

T HE QUIET RUSH OF THE RIVER SOOTHED HER. WITHOUT pins or skirts weighing her down, Cassidy thought she might float away on the sound. The evening breeze carried the sweetness of sagebrush through her hair, already curling in the damp night air.

The house had been quiet for a few hours. Jack retired to his study, bidding her goodnight at her doorway with a kiss on her cheek.

They were on the edge of something, something terrifying and wonderful, full of possibilities. None of the ones Cassidy ever considered at the beginning.

A separation formed between two men: Jack Ransom, the gentle, kind man she'd grown inescapably fond of against her better judgment, and Ransom, the Devil she'd witnessed command the slaughter of her family and an entire town. One, she was determined to kill, cleansing the world of unimaginable cruelty and evil. The other gave her pause, and she hated herself for how distracted she'd become.

She arrived at *Colina de Dragones* with a preconceived notion of who he was, what to expect, and how she'd handle him like any other bounty. Just like she had a different idea of who Moone was.

People change. Men lie. She'd done both now.

Evening air provided a peaceful clarity, without ribbons, trappings, or Jack's honeyed whisper in her ear. So, with bare feet and a shawl wrapped around her shoulders, Cassidy chased it as the stars rose in the sky. She slipped through the central courtyard and out the back door, winding through the garden as the babble of a lazy river called her name.

A distant whinny tumbled down the stony hillside, sweeping around her in a blanket of guilt. It'd been too long since she'd gone to see Solo, too long since she felt the wind in her hair and his mane on her face, too long since she slept beneath the heavens with only her 'brother' and a book to keep her company.

Cass smiled. Maybe a trip to the stable wouldn't hurt.

She dashed up the hill, gathering her shawl against a sudden chill, winding her way through limestone crags jutting from soft soil. She held her breath when the kitchen door creaked, met with soothing silence inside the house. Not even the bedrooms stirred with activity, especially with most of the girls sent away within days of Cass's arrival.

The thought brought another smile that held firmly while she plucked a handful of sugar cubes from the pantry.

Her heart stirred when the iron hinges groaned again. Cassidy froze, gripping cold terracotta tile with bare feet as she fought the urge to run or engage. Fight or flight. She told herself it was the resident cat, hunting for mice under the guise of moonlight, without heavy boots to step on a tail or scare the prey away.

Cassidy couldn't shake the feeling that *she* was the prey.

The fingers of her free hand twitched, reaching for a

weapon, a pistol that was far, far away from her reach.

Sliding her toes over a seam in the stone, she moved from the pantry into the kitchen. A chitter, a growl—then a hissing scream. Sugar falling from her hand, Cassidy stumbled back into the butcher block, gripping her head when it collided with hanging iron pots.

The cat yowled, flipping its orange tail in distaste.

Cassidy deflated with relief. "Copernicus, I swear. You damned thing scared the ever-living shit out of me," she hissed, bending to gather the broken pieces of cubed sugar from between her feet.

"How about me, yer majesty?"

Cassidy smelled his rotten teeth before anything else. Had he breathed seconds before, she might've had ample time to react, but it was already too late.

Doc Ball yanked her by the hair, smothering a cry with knotted, gnarled fingers over her mouth. His arm twisted around her waist, towing her across the stone floor.

She kicked and flailed, tearing her teeth through leathery skin, but Ball persisted.

He dragged her into the chill of the night air, breathing ragged in her ear; the harder she fought, the more he struggled to keep a hold of her. The house on the hill shrank, but no matter how Cass called out to someone, *anyone*, her muffled screams weren't enough.

"I had a feelin' it was you. You sneaky little bitch. I don't know how you got in here, but *hell*, sure sniffed you out, didn't I?" Ball threw her into the dirt, crashing the toe of his boot into her ribs—payment for what she'd done to him.

Cass groaned, rolling as she wheezed. Pain shot through her; she'd likely broken a rib. "I don't know what you're talking about."

Ball crouched, pressing his weight into her with a knee. Cassidy screamed.

"I didn't recognize you. Not at first." His breath kissed her face, spittle slipping between rotten teeth, spattering well-worn freckles. "But a shined-up penny is still a penny. Still fuckin' worthless."

"You won't get away with this," she spat, blindly combing the ground for a weapon, coming away with a hard chunk of stone. Limestone tucked into her palm, Cassidy swung as hard as she could muster, connecting it to his head.

Ball swore, stumbling back, blood spouting from his temple.

Cass scrambled to her feet. Bramble tugged at her shift, wind whistling through her hair. She gripped the stone until her hand ached, wondering how good of a shot she'd be without a bullet.

"Right." Ball staggered, righting himself with a grunt. His beady eyes focused on her, a sneer twisting across his scarred face, blood coating his teeth. "I thought about killin' you quick 'cause yer a lady and all. But, *now*…" His knotted hands tore at his belt. "Now I've got other, slower plans."

"The fuck you do," a growl cleaved the night air.

Cassidy's heart leaped. She knew it shouldn't have. Part of her was still angrier than a bull, but when James Moone's handsome face slipped from the shadows behind Ball, she felt nothing but relief—any of his transgressions forgotten.

He pressed a shining blade to Ball's throat, drawing blood with the slightest pressure. "You have no idea the shit you just stepped in, Lawrence."

"Jimmy, if you think you'll get in good with the boss after this, you've got another fuckin' thing comin'," Ball spat, face contorting when James pressed harder.

Moone held firmly, a hand fisted in Ball's greasy hair. A wicked grin bloomed on his face, nothing like Cassidy had ever seen him wear. "Oh, you haven't the faintest idea what I've been up to, Ball. I didn't need to let you out to get in Ransom's good graces. I *live there*."

Cassidy's stomach twisted. What on earth could he mean?

Moone's gaze slid to her, eyes wild. They shifted, darting over her body, piecing her together bit by bit. "You alright?"

Cass shivered, thinking he might want to eat her alive with that look, thinking she'd let him. "Yeah. M'fine."

James tugged on Ball's hair, lifting his head past a broad shoulder until the man's feet dangled above the ground. "What should we do with him? Tie him up? Toss him in the river?"

"I should've done this a long time ago." Cassidy charged forward, wound her fingers around a pearl-handled grip in Moone's belt, and jerked the pistol into the night air.

James yelled. Ball's black eyes grew wide. Cassidy squeezed the trigger.

Blood spurted from the gaping hole in Ball's skull, pulsating with the final quiver of his cold heart.

Cassidy buzzed, chest heaving, every part of her thrumming from the thrill of a kill. Ball deserved it, especially after what he'd done to her, what he planned to do. In the light of it, painted in wicked nirvana, all she could think was *more*.

Her eyes snapped to Moone. She fisted a hand in his shirt, pulling him into the kind of embrace she'd thought about a hundred different ways. The kind she'd been on the edge of with him, with Ransom—always left wanting. Cassidy was tired of wanting, so she'd take what she needed.

More.

Cassidy crashed her lips to his. It tasted like hunger, like desperation and blood.

Ball's body fell. James looped his arm around her waist, hoisting her from her feet. Things shifted, climbing, spiraling. He groaned, long and low, like it'd been all he could think about, as well.

Their kiss deepened, darkened, and set fire to every unspoken feeling. Her tongue twisted with his, teeth grazing his lips. She tugged his flesh between them, one thought, one need—

More.

"What's going on? Who's down there?" A voice split through the haze of her desire, panic rooting deep. Had they seen what she did to Ball, or worse—what she and Moone were doing?

James tore himself away, dragging his knuckles against kiss-bruised lips. Ball laid in a heap at his feet, and blood spattered his square jaw. Seeing it sent a shiver down her arms, making her want to steal another taste of his mouth.

"God dammit, Cassidy. There was a quieter way to do that," he hissed, rubbing his ear. "You could've shot me."

"If I wanted to shoot you, you'd be dead already." Cassidy flipped her hair over her shoulder and stared up the hill, grazing blood-soaked curls over white linen. Lamplight from *Colina de Dragones* illuminated half a dozen figures headed their way. "Besides, we've got bigger problems."

Moone drew closer, bending so his whispers couldn't be carried uphill. His mouth brushed the shell of her ear, tempting her to do something miraculously stupid. "Should we make a run for it? Avoid the fallout—"

"Don't be stupid," she snapped, shoving him back. "The

plan is working."

"Fine," he bit, squaring his shoulders as the group drew further down the hill. "Don't say anything. I'll claim this. I can handle him."

"Maybe not half as well as you think, Moone," she argued, skin prickling when they finally came face-to-face with the group whose attention they'd accidentally garnered.

Cassidy recognized them all: shadows of Lawrence Ball. There were two kinds of men in Ransom's house: saboteurs and puppets who looked at Doc as their leader. Ones who whispered in darkened corners about Moone and thought she wouldn't notice. They all thought Ransom's prodigal son was finished, ne'er to return—the fortune and power theirs to claim. The other kind surprised her, men like Wayne Marion, who looked upon James as fondly as Jack did— maybe more so. Cassidy wondered, if they ever needed help, they might be the type to run to.

The group gaining on them was the first.

The man in front—tall, willowy, younger than the rest— stopped short at the sight of Ball's crumpled body. "What in the hell did you do?"

"Nothing he didn't deserve," she replied, standing her ground with a lift of her chin.

"Cassidy," Moone warned. Familiar. Too familiar. So much so, that Ransom's lackeys noticed without effort.

They jumped into action, gripping Cassidy by the wrist. She kicked and hollered, screaming out when a white-hot bolt of pain shot out from her ribs. A second man joined the first as others fought to subdue Moone, a Herculean task as he fought his way down with his fists.

"The boss'll have your head, Jimmy." Opium-stained breath brushed her ear. "And hers, too, if you've been causing trouble."

"The only one who's been causing trouble was *him*," Moone growled, pushing against the three men who finally restrained him. "Ransom would have his head—*literally*—if he caught Ball doing what he was aiming to do. What I stopped him from doing. If anything, I did your pal Lawrence a favor because *no one* touches Ransom's things and gets away with it."

"I guess we'll see what the master says about that."

The group towed them towards the main house. Cass made it as much of a chore as she could, dragging her feet, pulling backward—even shouting Jack's name. Anything to help assuage her obvious guilt painted in the spray of blood on her chemise.

The group grew silent when the crunch of footsteps rounded a corner of the sprawling hacienda. Ransom slipped from the shadows, though more seemed to settle around them like an icy fog as he took in their group. His dark eyes moved from face to face, flaring when they landed on Cassidy—bloodied and bruised, held captive by his thugs. Lady of the house, indeed.

"What is the meaning of this?" The sinister rumble of his voice cleaved the air with a chill.

Cass fought against the hands holding her, ribs aching the harder they squeezed. "*Jack*."

"We found the two of them down on the bank, boss." A brave lackey stepped forward, motioning toward two others who dropped Ball's limp body at his feet. "Ball's dead. My guess is they were plannin' on dumpin' him in the river."

"You think *she* did this?" Ransom stared down at his former lieutenant, jaw working with a slow, simmering rage.

"Or him." Another nodded toward Moone beside her.

"Stinks like a backstabbing, sir. Or somethin' suspicious. 'Else, why'd they be out here, alone?'"

"Maybe he caught 'em doin' somethin' they shouldn't. Somethin' improper."

"I'll show you improper," Cassidy bit, giving another determined lurch to try and shake their grip free.

Ransom's attention slid to the man holding her. "Release her, Landry. *Now*."

The vice around her ribs loosened just enough. Cassidy pivoted, connecting her fist with his jaw. Each man stood straighter when her captor hit the ground, a ripple of looks shared when he remained an unconscious lump.

She shook the burning ache from her knuckles, adrenaline pumping through her veins. Her vision prickled, the sensation growing when her eyes met Jack's. Had she just given herself away? Was she next on his list, her lies found out, a betrayal as bad in his eyes as Aisling and Ian—or worse?

He unhurriedly stepped over Ball's fresh corpse, attention fixed on Cassidy. His expression was undecipherable, thoughts locked behind a fortress until he reached her.

Ransom cradled her jaw, a well-learned habit over three weeks, face crumpling when he gingerly skimmed a thumb over a blossoming bruise on her brow and a cut on her lip.

Her heart thundered—everything she'd been working for lay in that look. *Love*, if that's something a monster could do.

"What have they done to you, my darling?"

His hands slipped down her arm, touch caressing the ache in her knuckles before kissing them to banish the pain. It only made her heart beat faster, with her crime spattered over her shift, clinging to the ends of her hair.

"I'll be alright," she murmured, attention moving to Moone beside them. His brow furrowed, gaze glued to Ransom's hand wrapped around hers. Her mind flashed to moments before, his mouth slanted over hers, desire flaring brighter than ever before. She hoped Jack wouldn't smell his kiss on her, wouldn't pick up on the flush in her cheeks or the heat climbing her throat when she thought of what could've happened if they hadn't been caught.

But Ransom *did* notice, eyes locking onto Moone, silently decoding every minuscule gesture.

"Him too," Jack murmured in a dark, dangerous whisper, nodding to release Moone. "Now." He brushed his touch over her lips before stepping away. "Explain yourselves."

Moone cleared his throat, pawing a hand through his hair. "I've been tracking Ball for weeks. He'd been rambling on about Dusty Fulton when he was brought in. Lucky he was, lucky I trailed him here because he was planning something dirty. Then, I noticed him watching her." He nodded toward Cassidy. "It's like you said. Your enemies are many. Gossip travels a long way, and what better way to hurt you than to take what you love?"

Cassidy's mind reeled. She didn't know what game Moone played, how this would help—or what other kinds of lies he might tell to save his own skin… or hers.

Ransom stared, licking his lips with a haughty, disbelieving chuckle. "Fulton wouldn't dare—"

"They would," Moone argued, stirring the pot of a bitter rivalry Cass didn't understand. "So, I thought it best to follow her, as well. To make sure she was safe. And good thing I did."

Ransom was eating it up, convinced enough—for now. So, she decided to add her own spice, her version of what happened. More reason to trust her and want to make her his queen. Then, she might finally get what she came for.

"I couldn't sleep. I thought a turn around the grounds might soothe my head, but he"—she nodded at Ball's corpse—"He followed me. Dragged me down the hill, beat me. I tried to fight back. I *did*, but it only made him angrier." Her voice broke, trembling in the memory of what might've happened, of the truth. "H-he was going to try to… *take* me. He would've had Mister Moone not intervened when he did."

"Who's responsible for this?" Ransom motioned at the dead body behind him, staring at Moone, at the group of thugs surrounding them.

Cassidy stepped forward. "I am. I did it. I killed him."

"*You*, Pet?" Jack's brows lifted as if he couldn't believe she was capable of such a thing. If only he knew the death toll at her hands. If only he knew she only killed as she paved a bloody path to him. Every bullet had a consequence, and almost all of them had been worth the cost.

Cassidy lifted her chin, twisting it to her advantage. Let him see the truth in a way he'd admire.

"You pluck out the weed, root and stem. So that's what I did." She slipped her fingers into his palm, drawing his gaze with a voice as clear as a bell; every man around them needed to hear that she wasn't to be trifled with. "It's like you said… every kingdom ought to have its queen. I merely dealt with a turncoat like my king would."

Ransom's aura shifted, eyes dancing as he leaned down and brushed his lips against her ear. "You bewitch me, my darling. Who would've thought we'd make such a pair?" His attention shifted to the group of men behind them. "Landry. You're the one who thought my dearest lady was the betrayer here?"

Cassidy peered over her shoulder, wickedness tugging at her smile. Landry's dark eyes grew wide, shifting between his master and her.

"Boss, I didn't mean—"

Ransom held up a palm, tutting. "Decisions come with consequences. Jumping to conclusions doesn't suit anyone." He drew closer, one sure-footed, sinister step at a time, until he reached for Landry like an old friend. The young man bent under the weight of Ransom's stare, features crumpling when the older gentleman's grip upon his shoulder sent him to his knees.

"Now," Jack murmured over his shoulder, softer than a song. "James, my boy. You're to stay with dear Cassidy any moment she leaves her room. Any time I am not able to accompany her, you shall. Is that clear?"

Moone shifted, making to argue. Cassidy, too, needed to protest, to keep the space between them, but Ransom silenced them with a single look.

"If my enemies are hiding within the walls of my house, I need precious things to be protected by someone I trust. I *can* trust you, right James?" His dark eyes flashed.

Moone squared his shoulders. "Yes, sir. You can."

"Good." Ransom's eyes sparkled with a hidden smile. "Now, take my dearest Cassidy upstairs. See she is tended to for her injuries. I must stay and make sure Landry is properly dealt with."

"Jack." Cassidy tried one last time to implore him. She didn't need a guard; she'd proved that much by dealing with Ball, by telling Ransom a half-truth of what happened. She didn't *want* anyone to watch her, least of all Moone. "It really is alright. I'm perfectly—"

"That's enough, Pet," he tutted, gaze sliding to her for the briefest moment. "The hour is late enough already. Time for bed. Now, off you pop."

"Alright," she conceded, dipping her head as Jack's attention returned to Landry. "Goodnight, Jack."

She slid a bare foot through the gravel, taking in the scene one last time as Moone pulled her away—the glimpse of the monster within, proof there was something else, something more sinister beneath. The Devil was a gentleman, one who just showed his teeth.

Back in the house's warmth, Cassidy's skin prickled, though she couldn't decide if it was from the leftover chill or Moone's arm brushing against hers in the stone-lined corridor. His fingers threaded through hers when she moved to climb the central staircase.

"Not yet." His blue eyes moved down her body and back. "Not like this."

He led her into the kitchen, whisper quiet. Not even Copernicus prowled through the shadows. Shadows Moone lengthened with the twist of the knob on an oil lamp.

"Moone," she argued, tracking his movements as he lit a fire in the curved stone hearth and filled a cast iron kettle of water, setting it over the flame. "It's fine. I'm fine."

"Hush," he countered, bending to lift her from her feet, carefully avoiding where Ball bruised her ribs.

Pressed against his chest, in the charged quiet, things felt different; they felt *good*—like before. Moone gingerly sat her upon the butcher block, turning away to pour the now-warm water into a porcelain basin.

Nestled between her knees, so close she felt the heat of him *everywhere* through her chemise, Moone set to work. He gently drew a wet cloth along the edge of her jaw, carrying away every drop of Lawrence Ball left behind. Every anxious thought of being found out by Ransom. Every heated notion, from the kill to their kiss, all but washed away.

Cassidy watched his eyes, how they traversed over her freckles, hand cradling her head to keep her steady as he worked. The lamplight illuminated the cornflower blue, crinkles around the edges, and how his brow bent when he painted a layer of medical salve over a cut in her lip.

Her mind ran away, leaps and bounds, taking her back to their room in Rose Reach. Back when she was broken, when he put her back together again. When she'd thanked him with a kiss and wanted so much more. Back when he hadn't been a liar.

They were tempting again. James's taste remained. So potent, Cassidy wished she'd never sampled the flavor. Then she might not want to have it again so badly.

Moone leaned closer, brushing his nose against hers. "Let's just go. Let's go home."

Cass sat back. "Go home?"

He nodded, holding her face, eyes so bright, so hopeful. "Yes. Let's just hop on a train and *go*. It doesn't have to be Gallow Gorge. We can go wherever you want. Where do you want to go, huh, Cassidy? Want to see Chicago? Let's do it."

"Moone—"

"Ireland, maybe?" His face split into a smile. "We can find the rest of your family. There have to be other Callaghans. We can learn about your Da, your mother. Find those lost journals of hers."

"The journals?" Cassidy pursed her lips, mind buzzing. She never recalled telling him about them or the volume she'd discovered in the library. "I don't want to go home. You go on ahead, travel to your heart's content, Moone. But

I'm not going anywhere anytime soon. I'm not finished."

Moone blinked, the same hopeful smile melting away. "Cassidy… *please*."

He was too close, too kind, too kissable. She regretted doing it, that it ended so soon, that they hadn't done it a year ago. That they'd done it at all. He was a distraction, and Cassidy couldn't decide who she spoke to—the man she knew or Ransom's protégé who betrayed her.

"I can't," she murmured. "I don't want to."

Moone's shoulders squared. Frustration fell over his face. Hurt, too. He liked what they'd done just as much as she did. He saw her bluff the moment she thought it. "You act like you don't want me here."

She shrugged. "Maybe I don't. I certainly don't *need* your help. So go on ahead—*leave*." Lies. So many of them, one after the other.

He rolled his jaw, biting back a bitter laugh. They both knew Cassidy couldn't resist a fight. A fight was the best way to keep space between them. Space they needed. "Like you *didn't* need me a few minutes ago? I've been watching Ball since we got here. I've been keeping him from you. Tell me, who will protect you from yourself if I go?" Moone drew closer, blue eyes pleading. "I miss you, Cassidy. Maybe we won't leave tonight or tomorrow. Just… please stop pretending I don't exist. I can't stand it."

Cassidy grimaced, breathing through the beginnings of an indignant smile. "I don't *want* to talk." She wanted so much more. That was the problem.

"Just to him?"

Her cheeks heated. She hopped from the butcher block and crossed her arms. "Don't act like me spending time with Jack is anything like what you've done."

"Oh, *Jack*, is it?" Moone worked his jaw, staring someplace over her shoulder. "Maybe it's too late to make a run for home. You're already here."

"Stop," she bit, laughing him off. "I have everything under control. I have a plan."

"Yes, because Ball catching you unaware in the middle of the night is exactly what I'd call *under control*. Was Ball violating you part of your so-called plan?" Moone paused, closing his eyes as he took a steadying breath, like he feared what might have happened. When he looked upon her again, his gaze was softer than before. "Let me help you."

Cassidy stepped back, sliding around the corner of the butcher block to the other side. She needed the space and breathing room—an obstacle preventing her from doing anything stupid. "You've helped enough. Believe me, I'm grateful for what you've done, for what you prevented, but that doesn't change everything else."

Moone's shoulders slumped. "You're still mad."

"Of course I am!" A fresh bolt of anger snapped her synapses to attention. How could he be so stupid, so naive? She braced her palms on the block, silently counting every mark gouged into the wood. They reminded her of the scars on her heart, some *he* put there. Ones she never wanted in the first place. "I want—I want you to leave me alone. I *need* you to leave me alone. Things are too muddy, otherwise."

Moone shook his head. "I can't do that."

"Can't or won't?"

"Both. He'll be suspicious if I don't do what he says."

"I don't know what to tell you." Cassidy skimmed her tongue along her teeth. This was too much, too much of a distraction. Too much risk of it all falling apart. She couldn't let that happen, not when she was so close to the end. "Figure it out. Go read a book. I don't care. I'm going to bed."

[31]

MOONE

MOONE WANTED TO TRUST HER. HE *DID* TRUST HER, EVEN though she'd probably never trust *him* again after what he'd done. No matter how badly he wished she would.

He tried to warn her. He'd seen things. He'd *done* things. His regrets from being at Ransom's side were too numerous to count; perhaps the worst sin of all was letting Cassidy step foot at *Colina de Dragones*.

What started as a fool's errand, an end to a life-long crusade, morphed into something else, transforming Cassidy into someone he didn't recognize. Any man would've told him he ought to delight in a woman embracing her true beauty, that Cass being dressed like a lady would bring him some sense of joy.

All he saw was a little girl playing dress-up. An actor playing a role.

A lie.

Yes, that's what he told himself. He had to because the truth unfolding over the last three weeks was almost too much. His wild girl was gone; someone else took her place. A girl who smiled, who behaved. One who used her manners

and didn't swear.

One Jack Ransom wanted to marry.

Cassidy embraced the character of her borrowed name, flourishing as the kind of lady he never thought she wanted to be. The longer they stayed, the further into the abyss she fell.

Moone worried if too much time went by, the flame of his wild girl would be snuffed out forever, dampened by the man she supposedly hunted.

He hated the thought of Ransom putting his hands anywhere near her, seething at the sight any moment the two were together—which was almost always. No matter how Moone tried to honor his promise to stay with her when she was alone, Cassidy found ways to wiggle out of his grip and flounce back to Jack with a smile.

James knew he was a stoic fellow, saving his smiles and laughter for one particular pain-in-the-ass bounty hunter. But, as the days melted away, he became more gargoyle than man.

He wished he didn't worry and long for her in ways he shouldn't. That watching her slip further away didn't burn him up inside.

Still, he remained vigilant, keeping a watchful eye on things, on her; something he would've done, regardless of whether Ransom commanded him to. A bench in the central courtyard, tucked between broad-leafed plants and palms quivering in a warm wind breezing over painted tile, provided a picture-perfect view of Cassidy's door.

Hushed voices on the balcony's edge drew his attention from the pages of his book. Cassidy was there, a soft smile playing on her lips when she emerged from her suite—Jack waiting with an open hand.

She was beautiful, even wrapped up in the image of some other girl. Ransom outdid himself in fitting her in a ladylike mold, sparing no expense regarding her trousseau. Wrapped in yards of sapphire silk, she kept her gaze turned down as they descended the stairs. Never mind James was waiting steps away—a captive audience for their affectionate display.

Moone's feet moved before the rest of him realized, casually jogging around the corner to the base of the staircase. Just in time for Jack to curl his fingers beneath her chin, their eyes to close, and—

"Mister Moone?" Her eyes locked with his over Ransom's shoulder.

Mister Moone. Right. They were acquaintances. That's what they meant for everyone to believe until he saved her from Ball and forced Ransom's hand. Moone became her bodyguard, protection from an enemy hiding in plain sight. If only he knew the enemy was the one he wanted to wed.

"Ah, James, my boy." Ransom twisted, offering him a smile—warmer than he'd ever seen him wear. Maybe she was positively influencing him. The same kind she had on Moone that made him want to leave this life behind for good. "You're just in time."

James stiffened when Jack clapped him on the shoulder. "Is the Missus headed out?"

"Indeed." Ransom preened, lifting her gloved hand to his lips. "With the Governor's birthday around the corner, I've arranged for dear Cassidy to wear something special. Alas, I have some business to attend. If you'd accompany her, I'd be eternally grateful."

Moone wore a tight-lipped smile. "As you wish."

"What's that you've got?" Cassidy's lilted alto split his

heart to the core; those green eyes trained on the book in his hand.

He lifted it, twisting it back and forth. "Oh, nothing. Waiting around for the lady. Just thought I'd use the time to do some reading, is all."

With a rustle of silk, Cassidy plucked it from his grip. Moone tried not to let it show on his face how his heart stuttered when her fingers brushed his. He wished he didn't care so much that he could leave well enough alone. If only she hadn't ridden into Gallow Gorge. He'd never know her, never been wrapped up in her crusade. He wouldn't be reminded of what he left behind or be tempted by what Ransom offered.

Cassidy's gaze slipped to him as her touch danced down the spine over the title. In a single look, she told him something secret, something special.

He knew she kept the novels she dragged with her a secret. He knew little Daisy Booker stole books from her Ma to sneak into Cass's hat when they thought no one was looking. But someone always was—*him*.

Moone was always looking where Cassidy Callaghan was concerned.

Liking her was never part of the plan. She was a pain in the ass who skirted around the law as often as she could, just to test his patience. God, she pushed hard, but Moone never gave up easily in a fight. The more she pestered him, the more they *fought*, the more he looked forward to his wild girl galloping into town. The more he wanted to play.

James never partook in things like opium. Never had any interest in being addicted to something the way the wealthy of Sacramento depended on their fix.

Cassidy, though. Moone was addicted to her, dependent

on the buzz in his chest at a flash of copper curls beneath a black hat, desperate for a glimpse of a smile. Even her fists. Now he'd tasted her lips; he'd be addicted to her kiss, too.

"How are you enjoying Austen, Mister Moone?" Her voice yanked him back to the present, the smallest of imperceptible smiles tugging at the corner of her lovely mouth. "She's one of my favorites."

I know.

He shrugged. "I like it just fine. A girl back home in Gallow Gorge loves this damn book— loves books. For her, I thought I'd give it a try."

Moone realized his crime once it left his mouth. He'd meant to make her happy by taking her advice and trying something she loved. He aimed to garner a smile, like when he and Solo made friends, but there was a shadow of horror in her eyes instead.

To her, he was the fool who told Ransom where home was.

Ransom looked at Moone with a fatherly smile; he was *happy* for him. "Ah, it seems my boy has a special lady whom he admires?"

"It's nothing. No one of consequence," James argued, unable to tear his eyes from Cassidy's burning into him. "She doesn't see me that way."

"Surely she'll realize her error in time." Jack's grin only grew. "She must mean a great deal to you if you ventured to that corner of the library. Lord knows I tried often enough when you were a boy but never quite succeeded." He turned to Cassidy, curling his fingers under her chin. "How lucky are we to have found such well-read women? They're a rarity in this world, a treasure to behold. Though, I'm surprised at you. Why leave such a pleasant-sounding creature behind?

We ought to fetch her and bring her home."

"She had something important to do, I suppose. More important than waiting around for me." Moone forced a smile, tight-lipped when Ransom's touch forced Cassidy's gaze away.

He hummed, skimming his thumb along her jaw before pressing a lingering kiss to her cheek. How far had it gone? Based on how her eyes slipped closed and how she leaned into his touch, Cass gave a convincing impression that she was as infatuated with him as he was with her.

Every part of him simmered with a quiet rage, spurred by every moment they lingered. With every labored breath, every second his chest constricted at the sight of it, Moone started to feel like the odd man out. He was witnessing something private. It made his stomach turn.

Was this her plan? Did she expect to come along and take up the title of the unfortunate wife, Cassidy Ransom, all sins of the past forgotten so long as she was swathed in shining silks and crisp taffetas? If not, what in the hell were her intentions once the deed was done?

If she wasn't sure, Moone could understand. He understood her falling in love with the idea of a big house and pretty dresses. Never hungry, never hurt, never left without.

Cassidy grew up on her own, half-raised by a whore and the desert (and a horse). He understood her want for a family. He understood how, when showered with the kind of attention she told herself she never wanted, she might come to depend on it.

It was his story, too.

Could Moone give that to her? As Deputy of Gallow Gorge, no. As Ransom's protégé, he might. Hell, he'd do the deed for her, take up the reins, and give her the life she'd gotten used to, where she fit so naturally. Sure, he'd miss the wild girl, but then, at least she'd be his.

Cassidy spilled enough blood because of Ransom. What good would another kill be? Would she hang up her pistols for good? What would her existence be without vengeance as the tether that led her?

"You ought to get a move on, pet. Mustn't keep Mrs. Watkins waiting. It's bad form." Ransom held her face, bending to press a swift kiss to the corner of her mouth. When he pulled away, Cassidy's eyes flitted to Moone, only for a moment. Her ladylike grin remained, but the lamplight within them dimmed.

Wordless, she surveyed Ransom's every movement when he turned to Moone.

"You take good care of her. Keep a watchful eye." He turned, brushing his lips over her knuckles again. "Until later, my darling."

Ransom disappeared down the hall, maybe to fraternize with politicians or threaten someone at knifepoint. Moone didn't care, too caught in the charged silence stretching between him and Cassidy.

Tension buzzed. Every hair stood on end, reaching for her, for something to say, something to point him in the right direction. Who should he listen to—his former master or the wishes of the woman he burned for?

Cassidy answered for him, spinning with a swish of sapphire silk before charging out the front door.

James would be one hell of an idiot if he didn't chase her.

[38]

MOONE

B Y THE TIME HE FOLLOWED, THE CARRIAGE WAS MOST of the way down the gravel drive. Even at his fastest, Moone couldn't catch up on foot. However, the thought of throwing himself inside a carriage alone with Cassidy made him smile. She'd probably hit him; he'd want to kiss her for it.

He dashed across the grounds, searching out the next best option—the carriage house. It'd been emptied for cleaning that morning, its inhabitants roaming free in a white-fenced pasture.

Solo let out a loud whinny when he spotted Moone jogging along the fence line.

"She's fine, I swear." He boosted himself on a wooden slat, brushing his fingertips against his muzzle. "Whaddaya say you and me take a ride and go see her, huh? It's been a while since she's been out to see you."

Moone should've felt foolish talking to the black-eyed beast. Still, as he got to know Cass's so-called *brother*, the more Moone realized the sable stallion was unlike any filly or gelding he'd likely ever meet.

Solo pawed at the ground, shifting back and forth as they shared a look Moone wanted to believe was some sort of quiet understanding.

"Here goes." Fingers hooked in his inky mane, Moone heaved a leg over Solo's back. The carriage's dust swam on the breeze, providing a trail for them to follow. Hooves beat the ground in a wild frenzy. So fast, Moone worried he might slip off his back end when the mustang leaped over the fence like it was nothing.

With a determined squeeze of James's thighs and a nudge of his heels, Solo surged forward like a locomotive fed a fresh round of coal.

Every time he thought they were close enough to catch her, spurred on by the exhilarating glimpse of a black carriage, they'd turn a corner, and Cassidy would be nowhere to be seen—lost around another bend in the road.

Ransom said Watkins. Moone's mind reeled. He'd heard the name before and swore he'd walked past it a hundred times. While Sacramento was vast, the places Ransom frequented were few. James shifted through every faded memory, drawing up a time when he'd accompanied a girl to a dress shop as a teenager.

With a kick of his heels and a sharp *heyaw*, the pair skirted around a corner, sending a group of colorfully skirted ladies skittering in all directions like a freshly flushed flock of birds.

Too much time had gone by since he had lost sight of her. Every painted sign blended in with the last, and the further into the city they wandered, the less hope he'd get to speak to her, to ask her what was on her mind and voice all his worries: that he was sorry, that he loved her.

Moone gripped Solo's mane, steadying the frantic rhythm of his heart when the thought crossed his mind. He

tried not to, sure she wouldn't let him even if he did. Still, the idea of her face at the forefront of his mind—wearing a scowl or the rarest of fleeting smiles—brought him a special kind of joy and a unique kind of hurt.

Did he really love her? *Fuck*. Yeah, he might.

After ages of zigzagging through the heart of Sacramento, Moone spotted a sign shining over a shop with expansive windows and a well-dressed lady breezing out the front door.

His heart flipped. It had to be the one.

Moone slipped from Solo's back, searching the sidewalk for something to tie him to.

"What do we do?" He frowned at the beast, staring into his soulful, black eyes—they'd taken off at a canter without a bridle or saddle. Moone thought quickly, loosening his pale blue tie. He looped it around Solo's neck, hoping someone wouldn't mistake him as lost. Still, James was sure Solo wouldn't wander off with just anyone without a bit of a tussle.

He shifted and blew a huff of hot air into Moone's hair.

James laughed, patting his neck, still unsure how they got on such good terms. "You stay here. I don't want to get in more trouble with Cassidy than I already am. Can't have you getting lost."

The sable stallion answered with a—dare he let himself think it—fond nicker and a gentle push at Moone's back. It was as if he encouraged him to venture inside and see that his human sister was doing alright.

The delicate chime of a brass bell rang out when he pushed open the door, immediately met with a scornful look from a woman behind the counter.

Moone cleared his throat, rubbing the back of his neck,

wishing he left his tie on. With the top two buttons of his shirt undone, he never felt so naked in his life.

His eyes danced around the shop, searching between every bolt of fabric for a thatch of copper.

"I'm looking for a girl. Red hair. Prettiest blue dress you ever saw. One I'm assuming you fine ladies stitched together." Moone gave them his charmingest smile. Could flattery work?

The older of the women bristled, standing straighter. "We have many patrons coming in and out throughout the day, sir. If you have any clothing business to attend to, I suggest you visit the men's clothier down the street."

"Here's the thing, ma'am." Moone couldn't keep his eyes in one place, too busy flashing from end to end of the shop, past dress forms, to the black-eyed gaze of Solo in the window. "Jack Ransom sent me. She's his charge, and I've been told to give her an urgent message from him."

"From Lord Ransom?" Her tough exterior softened. Moone prayed the lie would stick. Hope flared in his chest when her eyes flickered toward the back of the store. "I'm afraid Miss Bennet isn't in a position to receive visitors, but you're more than welcome to wait, Mister—"

Moone didn't give her a chance to finish, bolting down a short hallway to the back room. He waved away her clucks of protest, brushing his fingers along a wide-open door to a private room, then another, before stopping at a third with voices behind it.

He gave the knob a twist, holding a finger to his lips to silence a woman sitting inside the door. It was small, split in two by a crimson curtain. Moone was sure Cassidy was on the other side.

The attendant opened her mouth to speak. When

Cassidy's voice rang out, Moone grabbed the poor thing by the wrist before she could answer, mouthing *I'm sorry* as he flung her out into the hall.

"Anna, I need some help with my laces. Could you be a dear?"

His heart thundered, too loud for its own fucking good, as he slipped a shaking hand between the seams of crisp velvet. He shouldn't. She'd be furious at him for even entertaining the idea. But he'd already seen her in as little as her skin—what would be the harm?

He should've known better. He *did* know better. Not even the memory of Cassidy Callaghan asleep in the bed of The Copper Queen or fresh from a bath after the massacre at Cody could've prepared him for what he found.

Back turned with her hair pinned as artfully as before, perfectly coiled curls cascaded over a slender, freckled shoulder. An iridescent, pale green gown laid over a chair in the corner, speckled with glittering beads he was sure would make her more breathtaking than she already was.

His delay cost too much time; her dress fitting was already done and over with.

He could've stood there for years, inspecting her every curve. The fabric of her shift was impossibly thin, offering a glimpse of the shape of her beneath. With a lick of his lips and a hard swallow, Moone tried to banish every lewd thing, every wish and thought he harbored of how he wanted things to go.

Tried.

Maybe she'd turn around, whispering his name as sweet as a song. She'd brush her fingers against his cheek and let him hold her all the ways he ever wanted to. The memory of her body against his, tucked together in the safety of a shared bed in a darkened room; a chaste kiss over the edge of a copper basin; her hands in his hair two nights before. All of it was etched into his mind, haunting every waking moment.

Now, Moone couldn't help but let his imagination run away like a herd of mustangs on a wide-open plain, painting an image of them twisted together in various ways. One where he loved her, and she let him.

More than any one part of her, though, Moone couldn't tear his eyes from the angry red imprints crisscrossing the fair skin on her back. Cassidy wasn't meant to be contained in any way—especially by a grand house or a corset.

He stepped through the curtain, spurred by some odd sense of bravery or stupidity. Moone wasn't sure which. Probably both.

Even while doing the unthinkable, James always had a steady hand. He was unshakable when making a keen-eyed shot or pouring a finger of whiskey after one too many. None of it helped ease the trembling of his hands as he wound her corset strings around his knuckles.

Moone tugged the cords, closing the space over the valley of her hips. He wondered how long he could prolong the action and stay close to her a while longer.

When his knuckles brushed against the still-pink lines creased into her back, Cassidy let out a sigh so soft it sent every part of him tingling with the need to hear her do it again.

Little by little, with a gentle tug here and a sharp pull there—one that nearly sent her colliding with his chest—Moone tied up every last inch until the grommets strained from the pressure of being cinched so tightly.

A moment passed, then another. Tucked in the

spellbinding quiet with the racket of carriages in the street so far away, Moone imagined them to be in a world all their own. One where they weren't sad, lonely orphans following the wrong path because they thought it was what they needed to do.

No. Together, all alone, anything was possible. Just a chance, a single moment. One he couldn't resist, even if someone paid him to. Even if it meant risking everything they were fighting for.

Moone gently swept the curls from her shoulder, giving into the tug of a smile when she leaned into his touch. He pressed his nose against the freckles he found there, breathing her in like it was all he'd ever be allowed.

"I knew it."

Her voice ripped him away, leaving him little time to think when she spun around. He thought she'd surely strike him for being so sneaky, for looking upon her in such a state, but the look in her eye said something else.

"M'sorry." His ears burned, telling him to run. When Cassidy didn't pull away, he couldn't bring himself to either.

"For being a fuckin' liar or sneaking into my dressing room?" Her voice was low, gaze trained on him like he was the target at the end of her barrel.

"For lying." Moone skimmed his touch against her hip. He couldn't let go. "Can't say I'm too regretful about the other."

Cassidy didn't budge, eyes shining as she whispered. "You told me you didn't read; you only studied. Now you're reading Austen. I don't understand—why now?"

"I was taking a lady's advice." He shrugged, hooking his fingers under her corset to bring her closer. "You seem real fond of those books."

"But you—" She wet her lips, parting when his attention slid to them. "You said *no one of consequence*."

Moone lazily drew his palms over her shoulders, taking her lovely face. "I lied."

"I said"—Cassidy's breath stumbled—"I said if you ever lied to me again, I'd kill you."

This was it. A moment he thought of a hundred different ways. One they'd gotten close to more times than he could count, toeing the line between friends and *more*, longer than she'd ever been a fine lady. They stumbled over it in ways that haunted him. With her so close and finally willing, Moone wouldn't let the chance go to waste.

Just once more, just a taste.

"So be it. *Kill me*. I think, after today, it'll be worth it. I can die a happy man as long as I do this one last time." Moone tilted her chin, eyes taking in every freckle as he bent and pressed his lips to hers.

In a single moment, they rode the wave of the instantaneous thrill. Moone coiled his arms around her waist, relishing the feeling of her body pressed into his. Pulling her flush against his chest, he held firmly to the curve of her jaw, only encouraged by her song of quiet whimpers.

Their history presented itself in how they moved, so well-attuned, effortlessly intertwined with each slow exploration of their hands and fluid dance of their mouths.

Cassidy surprised him. Instead of pushing him away, she deepened the kiss, skimming her palms up his chest with a brush of her tongue over the seam of his mouth.

Moone answered with a low groan, regretting it when she tore herself away at the sound.

Eyes wild, cheeks flushed pink; the sight of her only made him want to kiss her more. Harder, longer. Forever, even. Even though kissing Cassidy Callaghan was the best and worst thing that ever happened to him.

What started so slowly and wonderfully soft ignited a fire within them both for more. Cassidy twisted her arms around his shoulders; he pushed her back against the wall— every inch too far, each kiss too chaste.

"*Cassidy.*" Her name fell from his lips. She responded with fresh fervor, lending it to the rhythm as they lost themselves to the feeling again and again.

He wasn't sure where her body ended, and he began, not for lack of exploration of their hands. Cassidy's touch slipped between the buttons of his shirt, popping another free to skim her fingers through his chest hair.

Moone parted her lips with a tug of his teeth, bending to hoist her by her ass. Her back hit the opposite wall with a *thud*. She hooked her legs around his waist, rolling her hips, bringing them closer to the unspoken thing they craved.

There was something about her weight in his arms, the way she lingered in every salacious second like she memorized his taste, like it was their final chance. The moment they stepped outside, everything would return to the way it was.

"*James.*" Cass tore her mouth away, voice stained with regret between every fevered breath.

The way she said it broke his heart. All he wanted was to kiss her again and keep her from saying anything that'd keep them from doing it some more.

She slipped her feet to the floor, silently smoothing out every wrinkle as Moone waited for her to say something—to give a good reason why they ought to stop.

"We can't," she breathed, pressing her knuckles to her lips. Hair mussed, face flushed, she was so much more like his wild girl in the span of a single, heated moment than she was in the time since they arrived in Sacramento.

"Why not?"

"You know why not," she answered.

Moone reached for her, tugging her forward with a quick snap of still-loose corset strings. "Wasn't all bad, was it, Freckles? I might even think you don't hate me as much as you say you do."

He moved to kiss her again, eager to pick up where they left off, to make every second of their tryst count. He could finally convince her to give up the whole thing, saddle up Solo, and ride home.

"I've never hated you, James." Cassidy's gaze slid to his, deflating the fleeting hope as quickly as he'd thought it. "I have too much to do. As tempting as it is, as much as I care for you, I-I can't let this get in the way of what's important."

"What's important?" He barked out a laugh. "*Revenge?*"

"*Justice*," she hissed, stepping back.

Moone shook his head. This was so like her, like them. Another fight, another hurdle she built to keep them apart. "Justice is a point of view, Cassidy."

"I'm doing my job." She spun and jerked on the deep blue skirt she'd been wearing. "My duty."

"This isn't another bounty, Cass." Moone frowned, crossing his arms.

"You're right," she snapped, blindly tying the skirt around her waist. "This is so much more."

He should've known they'd end up here.

She couldn't resist a fight like it bit her in the ass. How was he dumb enough to think he'd get more than a few blissful moments when Cass couldn't let anything go and let herself linger in something good?

"*More.* You mean playing dress-up. Fraternizing with

the enemy. Stalling." Moone's jaw clenched between every word. He wished he could keep them from spewing out. He couldn't help himself, too eager to get her in any way he could have her, to hang onto their contentious, momentary solitude before Ransom claimed his wild girl again.

Cass gasped out a bitter titter of laughter, slipping the sleeves of her bodice over her arms. "You mean the man who raised you? *That* enemy?"

"You two are getting awfully cozy, Callaghan." Moone chewed his words, sure each one forced a wedge further between them. So much for taking advantage of the moment. "Tell me, how long did you wait before he had you wound so tightly 'round his little finger before you followed him into bed and let him fuck you? Lord knows I've been trying to get you to let me in, to let me know you, for years. You spend an afternoon with the monster who murdered your parents; you let him whisper sugary sweet poison in your ear and let yourself fall for this life. Is that what you want—is that what I need to do for you to finally see me the way I see you? To want me that way?"

Cassidy remained fixed on her frock's buttons, taking her time with each one. She ruminated on her emotions; he finally struck a nerve. Only it was the wrong one.

"So, you came here to tell me that you're jealous. Is that it, James Moone?" She plucked a parasol from the corner and poked him in the chest. "If you thought picking up a book would be enough to make me forgive you, then you're dumber than I thought."

Moone laughed. It deepened her frown.

Cassidy wrinkled her nose and ignored him, bending to peer into a looking glass to tie her blue, feathered cap below her chin. When she straightened again, her shoulders were square, every perfectly imperfect wrinkle of his wild girl ironed out as she brought the veil of Lady Ransom over her lovely face.

"Orders from Jack or not—don't get in my way again."

Moone bent his face into a cocky smile, stepping closer. "Or what? You'll hit me? *Kill me?*"

Cassidy's chin lifted the closer he came. "Yeah. Maybe I will."

"What if I told you I liked you better the other way? What if I told you you're wrong?" James closed the space between them. It was different than before. He thought for sure she'd make good on her promise, but when he brushed his fingertips along the inside of her wrist, she didn't move to pull away.

Moone could scarcely believe it. He was being given another chance—maybe his last one—and to hell if he didn't take it. Even if she hit him after.

"This doesn't change anything, James," she sighed, green eyes darting every which way when he bent and gathered her face between his palms.

"It changes everything, Freckles. You'll see." Moone smiled, skimming his thumbs over a blanket of kisses left by the sun before bringing his mouth to hers. He couldn't be sure how long she'd let him, but the longer he breathed her in and tasted her sweetness, the more lost he felt.

Lost—not in a sense of himself, but of what he wanted, what she wanted, and what he needed to be.

Before he could delve in, delivering on the promise of twisting themselves up how they'd been moments before, Cassidy's hands fisted in his shirt and shoved him away.

"*Stop,*" she gasped. "I meant what I said. We can't be doing this; it's too much of a temptation—he'll find out, and I can't bear what he did to them happening to you." She rested her head on his chest, melting into him for a heart-stopping moment. "I don't think I'd survive it, James."

He should've wrapped his arms around her right then, should've told her that he'd take care of her if she gave up her quest. He'd take up the reins and do it for her if she wanted. He'd protect her—he'd love her. That he'd love her so much, everything else would be forgotten. Nothing else mattered but the two of them. Not Ransom. Not revenge or justice. *Them.*

Instead, he waited too long. Her shoulders squared, stubborn pride quickly settling over their fleeting, libidinous moment.

When she lifted her eyes again, every ounce of softness and affection he'd been lucky to witness was gone.

"This is dangerous. You keep getting in the middle, and I cannot have it anymore. For both our sakes, leave me alone."

"No," he argued, taking her hand. "Like it or not, you need me, Cassidy."

"Yes," she breathed, blinking slowly as he traced the lines in her palm. "You're everywhere I look, stuck in my head like a song. Sometimes, you're all I can think about—a distraction. You said I'm not myself. You say you like me better the other way, but this is a necessity, whether you like it or not. I haven't fallen for anything; I've chosen this. It's who I am now—the petticoats and the pretty things. Whatever it takes for as long as it takes. I need you to accept that or leave."

Moone smeared a palm over his mouth, hoping he could keep the sweetness of her kiss and ward away the bitterness of her words. He was afraid she was lost in the charade, too caught up in the act she was putting on to see things for what they really were.

"You ought to take up the stage, you know that? You're a real swell actress, Callaghan. You convinced him and me… and you sure as hell convinced yourself."

Cassidy didn't argue or even give him a balled-up fist against his jaw. Moone wished she had. At least, he'd be sure his wild girl was still somewhere beneath all the silks and ribbons.

With a turn of her heel and a sapphire rustle, she wrenched open the door and stormed into the shop. Moone followed swiftly—her shadow, as always.

A trio of women, rosy faced with low whispers of how scandalous a thing they'd done, scattered like leaves on the wind as he chased after her.

He laughed, though it was dipped in disappointment when she slid to a halt and looked upon the sable stallion peering into the shop's window.

"Solo?" she whispered, turning toward Moone with a glimmer in her eyes. "He let you ride him?"

Moone shrugged, scrubbing the back of his neck. "You ran so quick. I couldn't exactly hitch a ride on the back of your carriage. I needed to see you."

"*Stupid*," she muttered, blinking back tears. "You shouldn't have."

Cassidy's eyes were *everywhere*, filled to the brim with a flurry of emotion as Moone and Solo looked on.

He knew her. She might argue differently, but Moone wouldn't let her lie to herself.

But she didn't want to listen. She didn't care, illustrating it plainly when she marched out into the sunshine, too caught up in the act, too twisted in her lies to spare her 'brother' a second glance.

Moone bolted out the door to follow her without a second thought or a single breath. She was faster than he gave her credit for, shifting this way and that through the afternoon crowd.

"Cassidy Kathleen Callaghan, are you going to talk to me or not?" he bellowed at her retreating back, pushing past finely clothed ladies and haughty gentlemen with intricate mustaches and bowler hats. She was close enough to touch, and he was close enough to take a parasol to the head when she blindly flung the contraption open over her shoulder.

Moone swore, drawing the scrutinizing gaze of an older woman passing by. Back and forth he went, chasing Cassidy's every step. Down the street and around the corner. All the way through a doorway that, upon glancing around, had Moone feeling alarmingly underdressed, hair mussed and shirt buttons undone halfway down his chest.

Towering palms scattered shadows over sun-filled corners, and pearly tables dotted black and white marble floors, all accompanied by the delicate tinkle and chime of silver against china.

He'd never been able to picture Cassidy in a place like it. Now, he took in the beautiful picture, and what he had to do was finally clear.

Cassidy spun, green eyes wild with a rushed whisper, "I told you to stay out of my way, but you're making a mess instead. What on earth is so important, you couldn't let things fucking be?"

"I might love you, Cassidy." The words poured out of him. He worked his jaw, sorting them into an order that felt right and *true*. "No, I *know* I love you. I can't sit idly by any longer."

Her lovely, freckled face went slack, lips parting with

a sigh. For the briefest moment, Moone was sure she was about to say something—until her attention snapped over his shoulder.

"Cassidy, my darling."

A cold shiver ricocheted down Moone's spine when Ransom's voice split the din. He turned, meeting the man's dark gaze with a feigned smile he was sure didn't quite reach his eyes.

"Jack." Cassidy gleamed under Ransom's careful study, beaming as she stretched out the letters of his name. She leaned into his touch when he draped an arm around her waist and pressed a kiss on her cheek.

Moone hated every second, wishing nothing more than to finish the job right then and there, snatch up his girl, and ride away home. Instead, he went along with the act the same way they'd been dancing the last three weeks.

"Will you join us for tea?" Ransom stared at her, an appraisal of a doll he longed to place upon a shelf, in a glass case, only for him to admire. It infuriated James; every touch, every look. Moone knew her longer, knew her better, and loved her more. How was he able to get everything he ever wanted so easily?

James's attention lingered on Cassidy, wishing he could interpret the look in her eye. He wanted to decline if only to avoid a front-row seat to the beautiful, torturous nightmare unfolding before him.

Besides, he had an errand to run, a plan of his own to enact. One that might make Cassidy want to be on his arm instead.

"Can't." His voice sounded like he swallowed a mouthful of gravel. Part of him wished he had. It'd be preferable to the taste of her kiss as he watched her bloom with happiness for a monster after pushing him away for the hundredth time. Enough was enough. "Miss Bennet is finished with me. I ought to get going."

Ransom barely heard, too busy trailing a thumb along her bottom lip—still flushed and kiss-bruised from before. From *his* kiss. "Are you sure we can't convince you to linger?"

Moone shook his head. "No. I've got things to do this afternoon. Apologies."

Cassidy tucked her lip between her teeth, hiding it away, gaze turned to the marble floor.

"If you're sure. Though you're always welcome, James." Ransom nodded, looping his arm around blue silk to lead them into the tearoom.

Jack smiled. Cassidy laughed. Moone seethed, rooted to the spot as the ghost of his wild girl strode away.

[33]

Moone

CASSIDY WAS IN OVER HER HEAD. MOONE WANTED TO give her a chance to finish things; he didn't want to take it from her. His sins were many, marks carved into his soul, but if he took what she dreamt of her entire life, no penance would ever be enough. And she'd never forget, either.

He didn't want to carry the burden of the task, not at first. Even when Katie Mays and Madame Dubuisson asked him to take the brunt of Cassidy's fury to save her soul from the devil. But it'd gone too far, taken too long. Moone's errand was proof.

None of it was fair. It was too much for one person to carry. He wanted them to do it together so badly, but they'd passed the point of no return in so many ways. It was his fault, his own cowardice that kept him from killing Ransom that first night and every night after.

Loving her made him stupid. Reckless.

James stared at the limestone building, gilded doors shining in the late afternoon light. The grandest, biggest, oldest bank in Sacramento. Like so many other things, Ransom owned it, too.

Keys he gave him, *trusted* him with, burned into his palm. The reason his master sent him tore him up inside. He'd taken Cassidy bit by bit, chipped away at Moone's soul until he shaped him into a weapon to use at his bidding.

But he made a mistake. Jack raised James to be cunning, clever, and ruthless. He wasn't the same as the others who blindly took orders, following the strongest male in the pride. No, he'd take it for his own, bleed Ransom dry as payment for what he'd done to them both.

Inside, the lobby stretched on forever. Towering green marble pillars held a frescoed ceiling. Tall enough, they made James feel small.

Tellers perched behind open counters. There was no need for bars at their windows like banks in other, more unsavory towns. No, this place was an institution, a partner to the powerful and elite. No bandit would dream of holding it up.

That didn't mean no thievery would happen today.

James strode over the intricately patterned tile under crystal chandeliers to the back of the building. A gentleman, wearing a fine suit and gray ascot, waited at the head of a corridor. The president of the establishment, he presumed.

"Mister Moone," he said, nodding, "We're pleased to have you here at Lord Ransom's behest."

"I'll need a bag."

"Yes, sir, of course." The man nodded vigorously, patting his pockets before pivoting to find one.

James flipped open his pocket watch, putting on his best haughty, arrogant air. He counted the quiver of the second hand. One. Two. Three. As if every second cost him dearly. Time was money, after all. After today, Moone would begin to have plenty of it.

"This way, Mister Moone." Bag in hand, he motioned around another corner.

Most rich men held a deposit box. Ransom had many to keep what he didn't trust to stay within the walls of *Colina de Dragones*. It may be a fortress, but Jack was clever—he knew the sort of men he had at his beck and call. There was no reason to leave such temptations for the wicked.

Moone stood in a square room lined with them, impatiently staring down the banker until he excused himself.

Finally. He burst into action, unlocking the first of many. Stacks of cash and coin lined his borrowed bag. James took a little from each one, enough that Ransom might not notice as his fortune slowly leaked away. He'd come back again tomorrow, and the day after, and the day after that.

Two gold bricks, money by the dollar, pound, and franc. The deed to his London house. Those weren't the treasures Ransom sent him to retrieve.

Moone stared at the box's brass number, thumbing the key. This box was unique, different from the others. The thought of what waited inside, of what he helped put there, and what it meant for both his and Cassidy's future—and their past—held him in a chokehold.

He hadn't realized the part he played in Cassidy's history. Not until Jack asked him to bring back a ring. Until then, James hardly thought of that day. So many things came after, and that was just the start.

Moone was barely thirteen when he'd been sent to find it. The other men—Lawrence Ball included—were too lazy to get off their horses to comb the house for what their master sought. Jimmy was their errand boy and their punching bag. He didn't have any choice but to venture inside.

Beautiful things were hidden there: a perfume bottle,

silver hair combs, and a dress made of the prettiest fabric he'd ever seen. The diamond ring tied to a green ribbon, though, spoke of an opportunity to turn things to his advantage. A way to break free from beneath the boot of Ransom's cronies.

So, James pocketed it and lied to Ball and the others. Instead, he delivered it straight to the hands of his master. The credit was all his. He proved cunning and clever enough to become Ransom's protégé not long after.

But that wasn't the only treasure Moone found there, and he'd only just realized.

He spent years without connecting the dots, without seeing the little girl whose hiding place he discovered in the woman he knew. Those glass green eyes, stark against black eyelashes. Plaited red hair and freckles painted in dried blood.

At the time, he didn't think about what would happen should she be discovered by the men waiting just outside. Perhaps she would've been a cure for his unfathomable loneliness; maybe he would've done the same for her.

Moone liked to think that was precisely what happened, where their paths led—just a few years later.

Still, his instinct ensured she stayed hidden. Who knew the kind of deplorable things Ransom's men would've done if they'd discovered her instead.

From time to time, the girl he found passed through his mind. The utter terror when he found her hiding place or the soft breath of relief when he warned her to hush and bought her some time. Now, Moone wondered if he'd been the one who condemned her to live alone all those years.

If Ransom had known she was hiding there, the daughter of his old friends and enemies, maybe she would have shared in the life he gave her now. Perhaps he could have corrupted her, making her a weapon unlike any of them imagined.

Maybe she was already on her way, and the diamond ring he'd stolen—the one that belonged to her mother—was what would seal her fate.

Lady Cassidy Ransom. Hell hath no fury like the Devil's bride.

Jealousy bloomed, hot and heavy, in the pit of his stomach. James couldn't fathom it, couldn't stand the thought of her tying her to himself that way. Was that what she wanted—Ransom's power for her own? To take everything he had, the same as Moone hungered for it, too?

Is that who James needed to become, the prodigal son, no more? Perhaps he'd finish their quest and fulfill Ransom's wishes simultaneously. With Moone in his place, he wouldn't be the Scourge of the West but something else.

Maybe, with the fortune he was owed, Moone could become something different—something finally worthy of Cassidy.

So, he'd hide what he pilfered, maybe in the cellar. Perhaps he'd break it into pieces and scatter it throughout the house, tucking it all into dark places where no one would look. Moone would conceal his inheritance, blood money repaid. Like always, his sins lay there for anyone to see if only they looked.

James and Cassidy were alike, shapeshifters lying in wait. Only, where she was all that was good and right in the world, he was the monster. One who ought to be added to her list, hands bloodier than half the men she lined up for a well-deserved hanging.

He wondered if she'd wish the gallows for him if she knew the part he played or if she'd ever understand. Maybe she'd be the one to rope him and bring him in, just like she promised. Perhaps he'd prove to be as challenging as he vowed. For all he knew, they'd rise above it all and make a different kind of vow together—despite everything and everyone.

Only time would tell. One thing was certain: Moone's blade would taste Ransom's blood before the fortnight was out.

[34]

L AYERS UPON LAYERS OF FABRIC. SO MANY, CASSIDY couldn't be sure where the skirt of her gown ended and she began. Trimmed with thousands of tiny, shimmering beads, green silk floated over a hundred yards of petticoats in an elegant cloud. Every movement, every twist of her hips, sent delicate pieces of glass sparkling like a crystal chandelier.

The seamstresses at Watkins outdid themselves. Cassidy looked in the mirror and saw the princess she conjured in her dreams, every bit of the lady she imagined Aisling to be.

Once, Cassidy snuck a pink gown from her mother's wardrobe. One too fancy for life on their homestead. She'd never seen Aisling wear it, only look upon it often when she thought no one was watching.

Cassidy wrapped it around herself. She'd prance about, mimicking the chime of her mother's accent, wishing she, too, once lived in a castle.

She never knew if Aisling ever did. But the memory of precious treasures told pieces of a story Cassidy dreamed about her entire life: silver hair combs, satin ribbons, a pair

of blue silk shoes, and a diamond ring hidden in the bottom of a drawer. She filled in the rest with what Jack told her of his life in England and the precious volume of Aisling's journal she'd discovered in his library.

Is that what'd cost Aisling in the end? Would things be different if she'd stayed with him and remained in love? Could she still be alive?

Cassidy took in her reflection, from the white roses tucked into a thick, braided crown, copper ribbons cascading down her back, to the wash of freckles over bare shoulders, framed by pale lace and delicately stitched appliqués. Her bosom heaved the longer she stared, spilling from the tightly sewn edge. The entire thing might unravel with a wrong breath, gasp, or a laugh.

She lifted her chin, tracing her fingers around an ivory cameo hanging from a black ribbon. All of it was too much, but wonderfully so. She looked like a princess; she felt like a *queen*, entirely too at home in Jack's castle. Not his ancestral home, no, but the one he built. She didn't care how, not anymore. All Cassidy had was how she felt, caught up somewhere between a dream and a nightmare.

She was unprepared. She could never have been ready, not for what she'd been swept into at *Colina de Dragones*, the role Moone insisted she was playing.

Moone. His touch, kiss, and words burned through her, even days later. She wished she could make him understand that, as beautiful as the trappings were, they weren't something she wanted but something she needed. A tool. A path of *yes*, every gift irrefutable. Every piece of it was another in the puzzle of making Jack love her. The more he did, the more he wanted her and needed her, the sweeter it'd be to rip it from him.

However, the more time ticked away, the less sure she became that the woman in the mirror was as much of a mask as Cassidy initially thought. She *liked* it. She was fond of Jack, the version of him who courted her so sweetly. With every day that passed, the further away he became from the monster she built in her mind. And if she lingered too long, Cass wondered if she'd eventually lose sight of the story's true villain.

Still, her Da's face haunted her dreams; a sorrowful ghost, wordless and bleeding, just as vivid as the day it happened. It was the one thing that kept her from slipping beneath the surface, the one shred of herself Cassidy grasped onto.

Ransom said he wanted to make her his queen, and she'd played along. As beautiful as what he gave her, she didn't care about the riches or titles. She would use all his gifts to smoke him out and burn it all down.

Cassidy needed a distraction, a fixation to drive her through the rest of the evening. Something to hone her focus on the task at hand and take her mind far, far away from what transpired between James and herself in the dressing room.

Maybe a dance lesson. So what if Cassidy pretended Moone was her invisible partner?

Gloved hands held aloft, she summoned a smile at no one, sliding her feet across the polished floor, skirt flouncing with every step. A week's practice with a ladies' maid hadn't been enough to make her much of a dancer. She'd have to tell him she was sorry for stepping on his toes ahead of time.

"Don't tire yourself, darling." Jack smiled from the doorway, elegant in his black dinner jacket and white bowtie.

Cassidy stopped short, skirts twisted mid-spin around her ankles, cheeks flushed. "I won't."

He hummed, striding over polished walnut to take her hand. He turned her, palm resting over the firm boning of her bodice. She shivered when he pulled her flush against his chest, resting his chin upon her shoulder.

Their gaze met in the mirror: Ransom's dark, tempting, flavored with forbidden fruit; Cassidy's, flushed and ready to be devoured. She didn't mean for it to be so convincing.

"Are you ready, my darling?" Jack shifted, trailing his nose along the curve of her ear, breathing her in one painstakingly long second at a time. "We mustn't be late."

Cassidy chewed her lip, a smile threatening to break free. They'd grown closer and closer, according to plan. Ransom honored his wish to court her more traditionally, never inviting her into the darkness of his bedroom. And yet, it was the only thing on her mind. She was a woman with needs, tastes, and thirsts to quench—none of them belonged to him.

Jack was hungry, too, skirting along the line he'd drawn, further and further every day. The touches were more flirtatious, intentions known without a second look.

His wasn't the kiss Cassidy kept thinking of, though. She hadn't even tasted Jack's to wish for it. Every touch, every breath, every desire circled around one man.

Ransom fanned the flames without ever knowing.

"How does one get invited to a party like this?" Cassidy sighed, leaning into him when he trailed his touch down the curve of her bare shoulder, leaving a lingering kiss at the base of her throat.

"You mean the governor's birthday?" Jack lifted his eyes to hers in the mirror, grasping the tip of her glove. He pulled it free, bringing an avalanche of goosebumps in his wake.

She hummed. "Yes. *Him*."

Ransom laughed, a quiet crackle of thunder, the promise of a storm. "Who do you think put him there, pet? I am the great orchestrator of all of this—the *King*. And you"— he kissed her shoulder again, twisting her fingers with his—"You'll be the Queen. I'll show you all the power we'll possess… together."

Cassidy huffed, lips parting when he held her hand aloft—a glittering diamond now perched on her left hand. "*Jack*."

"Would that interest you, dear Cassidy? Would you join me? Will you let me take you home and make you a *real* Lady?"

She moved her hand in the lamplight, eyes wide, heart thundering away like hooves in the desert. It wasn't what she wanted, but could it be? Was there a way to turn it to her advantage? He might be the head of the empire, but what if she was the neck, twisting and turning things whichever way she wanted? Could she take up the life her mother left behind and use the time to find the answers she sought? Could she forget the past and look forward to a future with power?

"This isn't why I came here," she whispered the truth, the clearest thing in how muddy her life had become. Especially once a cold bolt of recognition speared through her. It wasn't any diamond, but the one she slung around her finger as a child—*Aisling's*.

"The best gifts are the unexpected ones." Another kiss, a different sheet of shivers. "Never shy away when destiny is knocking. You'll see. *I'll show you*."

"And then?" Cassidy drew his attention away from her bespeckled skin.

"Anything you want, my darling. You could ask for the

world, anything you dream of—I'd lay it at your feet."

Cassidy remembered her mother and Ransom's promise as Cassidy hid beneath the floorboards. Then, all at once, the mud cleared, and for a moment—the monster looked back at her.

But she was a monster, too. One of Ransom's creation, no matter which way the mirror pointed—the lady he molded out of silks and ribbons and the creature born from her Da's blood, hellbent on revenge.

She fiddled with the ring, thinking of cold desert nights and the relentless, brutal chase she gave daily, a threat lingering around every corner—from the coyotes to the men she hunted. Sure, Jack might be the Devil, but what was there to be afraid of if his will was hers to bend? If he loved her, anything might be possible—except her loving him back.

Anything you dream of, I'd lay it at your feet.

If she were the underworld's queen, if she could control him, would it really be so bad?

She turned from their shared reflection, heart racing, sliding her palms up his chest. Jack's fingers found her waist, leaning into her touch. Cassidy shuddered, bending on tiptoe to bring her lips to his.

Behind her eyes, she saw a gaze of blue, tawny curls, and a lopsided smile—Moone, haunting her, taunting her, *loving her*. As if she were worthy of such a thing. As if she were capable.

"Yes," she whispered, kissing him again, hoping she could drown the feeling with the image of another man in her mind. "Yes, I'll marry you."

Ransom curled his fingers around her neck, drawing her closer when she pulled away. He kissed her again, deep and wanting, speaking of every unfulfilled hunger.

She'd broken the seal. There'd be no turning back.

"Come," he growled, rolling his forehead against hers. Jack slipped her glove back on, dawdling at the buttons at her wrist, as if he wished they could stay and he might undo her instead. One by one, he closed them, pressing one last heated kiss against her lips before stepping away. "We'll be late if we linger too long."

Down the stairs and to the carriage, even as they traveled to the city, Cassidy couldn't shake the oddest feeling. She couldn't quite put her finger on it. Grief, maybe. She stared at the diamond on her left hand and couldn't help but consider what would have been.

[35]

I T MESMERIZED HER, THE SWIRLING SKIRTS OF EVERY COLOR, all moving in time; the clap of five hundred hands in unison; the sound of the music between the timed *rat-a-tat* of fine shoes on a polished floor.

It'd been an hour, maybe two. Cassidy's feet ached already. Ransom had been called away. The third time they were interrupted mid-waltz, he kissed her in front of everyone—etiquette be damned—and disappeared into a back room.

Cassidy wound her way through the crush, smiling here, nodding there, hoping visiting dignitaries and senators wouldn't see through the mask that only fit half the time. She searched for someone, a familiar face, hoping Jack would return and distract her from the discerning eyes judging her every move. Ones that whispered behind decorative fans as they danced around her.

"Fancy a dance, Freckles?"

Her cheeks warmed, spreading down her throat, blooming in her chest the longer she waited to turn and face him. The sight of him, though, polished like a freshly minted coin, only served to flare a different kind of heat.

Moone's shoulders, broad like a mountain's face, were only accentuated by the crisp cut of his jacket, clean-shaven jaw all the sharper with a white bowtie, and eyes the bluest she'd ever seen with his hair combed back.

Cassidy dipped her chin, skin prickling when the images of him she'd imagined earlier flashed through her mind. "I suppose."

Moone swept in, snaking his arm around her waist. The press of his fingers in the small of her back set a flutter tumbling down her spine, illuminating every memory, every moment, every unspoken want they ever harbored.

The music swelled, Moone moved, and gravity fell away.

"You're better at this than I expected," he murmured, pulling her more firmly against his chest.

"So are you," she answered, avoiding his gaze. Why did the energy between them feel so brittle?

"An unfortunate talent I inherited in another life." Moone's jaw set, and his once-rapt attention drifted over her head. "Did Ransom abandon you already?"

She lifted her chin, gripping his shoulder until her knuckles were white. "He had important people to see, I suppose."

A squeeze. A flash of his eyes. They drew her in, his chest heaving against hers. "More important than his fiancée?" He lifted her hand, brushing his thumb over the raised edge of the diamond beneath her glove. "Don't think I didn't notice this. Notice the two of you."

Cass bristled, cheeks heating again. Of course, he'd been watching. "That's not any of your business, is it?"

Moone laughed, a warning if Cassidy ever heard one. "Wrong, again, Freckles."

He sent her into a spin, pulling her back in like a yo-

yo. Round and round they went, blurring the edges of the ballroom as the music swelled.

"*James*," Cassidy whispered when he leaned, stretching her out like a steeple's shadow until she was only inches from the floor. A curl slipped from his hairline, hanging in his eyes, reminding Cassidy of all the times before when it was less complicated. Times that left her wishing they'd stayed home in Gallow Gorge, she'd never taken that warrant, and that Jack Ransom never existed.

But he did. She had.

Moone's face softened. "How can you keep ignoring it, Cassidy? This thing between us."

"We need to forget." Cassidy shook her head. He sent her into another spin. "You have to forget."

"What if I can't?" Moone tugged her closer, brushing his lips against her ear. "What if I don't want to?"

Could *she*? Would she even want to, herself?

Cassidy clung to her excuses, all the reasons why she kept him at arm's length. First, it'd been because she hadn't thought herself worthy, with heart enough to love and be loved in return. Then, it was her want for revenge and her need to see Ransom's blood spattered over the floor. Now, it was the weight of the diamond on her hand, the softness of silk against her skin, and the power within her grasp.

Moone rolled his jaw. "That's what I thought."

"You know I can't."

"That's horse shit."

Cassidy ground her teeth. "It isn't. You only say that because you're jealous."

His mouth thinned. "Maybe I am, Cassidy."

"Why are you here?" Cassidy slipped from his grasp, holding his hand with the tips of her fingers as he led her in a wide circle. From the outside, their dance might've been beautiful, lovers quarrel unbeknownst to them all. It was fraught with tension up close, more like Darcy and Elizabeth at Netherfield—a battle of wills instead of a waltz. "I asked you to leave me alone."

"A reminder."

"Of what?"

Moone brought her back to his chest. "Of who you are beneath all this."

"I don't have a choice."

"You keep saying that." Another spin, another turn, another moment from his arms. "But I'm not convinced. So, tell me something, Cassidy."

Moone's feet stilled. His thumb brushed her cheek, eyes soft. "What happens when it's all said and done? Who are you without revenge as the flag you carry? Would it be so bad if it didn't go according to our plans? *Let's go.* Let's go home and forget everything else. It isn't too late, but eventually, it will be." He paused, expression going cold—a quiet realization. "Unless you plan on riding off into the sunset with the man who murdered your parents."

She shook her head. "I'll be alright. I can control him."

"No, Cassidy, you can't. You haven't seen it yet, but you will. He'll show himself, eventually. He always does." Moone released her, scrubbing a palm along the edge of his jaw. "You're a lost, scared little girl, Cassidy. Without this, what's left? Be honest and say you've never thought about what comes after once this is finished."

"I have," Cassidy rasped, withdrawing sharply, colliding with another couple. Moone pulled her back, drawing her away from their stares.

His brows shot up. He didn't believe her. She didn't

believe herself, either.

"What'll you live for if you kill him? What could you live for if you don't?" Moone drew closer, nose brushing hers. Her breath caught, and for a moment, Cassidy thought he might kiss her right then and there, regardless of who might be watching. "Why not me? Why not Gallow Gorge? Can't you see how the people of that town love you? How *I* love you? There isn't anything for you here but blood and guilt. You don't see it now, but you will. You'll realize it, and by the time you do, you'll be nothing but a pretty bird in a gilded cage."

"It might," she whispered, uncaring of how the ballroom turned around them. "It might be too late."

Moone held her face; so kissable and close, her heart stumbled.

"When I first met you, Cassidy, you demanded I treat you like everyone else. Now, you *are* everyone else, and I hate it. That's all fine and good, but here's the thing. This"—he ran a finger along the beaded fringe of her heaving bosom, making every row tremble and catch the lamplight—"this isn't you. This isn't the girl I know. You aren't just anyone, Cassidy Kathleen. You're fire and rain. You bring the fucking thunder and shed such a light on me, you made me *believe* in the man I thought I wanted to be."

Moone skirted his palms up her shoulders until his fingers were in her hair. Never mind the attention on them, the music or Ransom hidden away in some back room, bound to return at a moment's notice.

"You breathed life into me." Moone's eyes fell to her mouth, thumb tracing the long line of her bottom lip.

"And now?" Cassidy murmured, fingers wound in his lapels.

"And now"—Moone bent, kissing her so softly, Cass thought she might've imagined it once it was over—"Now I'm not sure I know you anymore. I'm not sure I know *me* anymore."

The music ended, the attendees applauded, and Moone strode away—more dark cloud than man.

Cassidy stood at the center as the silk and taffeta cyclone began again, watching him disappear into the colorful cloud. A moment passed, maybe two. Maybe another after that. She forced her way through the throng, throwing dancers off-kilter, gathering frowns and unkind words the harder she pushed, the more determined the chase after a pair of square shoulders and tawny curls.

She crashed through a wall of meddling mothers and down a darkened corridor, sure she'd seen him disappear around that particular corner, hopeful she'd find him.

"I-I'll have it for you next week, I swear it." A voice behind an unlatched door stopped her. Finely beaded silk rustled around her ankles.

Cassidy held her breath, too afraid to draw any unwanted attention.

"I'm afraid your promises hold no value here, Mister Smith."

Jack's voice joined the first, carrying the same chill as the first night she'd met him.

Cassidy stepped into a band of light streaming through a crack in the doorway, pressing fingers to her lips to stifle a sob when her eyes found a body on a polished floor. It shone like the surface of a lake, still from a windless sky. But the longer she stared, the more she heard their whispers, Cass realized it wasn't polished anything—it was blood.

Ransom shirked his dinner jacket; sleeves rolled past his

elbows. He stood over a man held by two blue-bandana-wearing thugs. He took a proffered knife from beside him, holding it aloft in the lamplight.

Ears ringing, Cassidy grew roots, unable to look away as he twisted the blade this way and that, dark eyes aglow like a lone fire on a desert plain. In the depth of them and the twitch of his jaw, Cass recognized something; the monster she'd convinced herself had been a figment of a young girl's imagination, slithering to the surface of the gentleman's skin he wore.

Just like in her memory, Ransom prattled on. The man shook his head, and in the blink of an eye, he sunk the knife into the man's chest, lingering close enough to drink the soul from his lips as the light faded from his eyes.

Cassidy thought she might vomit, tempted to tear the fine clothes away, eager to climb on Solo's back and ride with the wind in her hair like she used to. Everything she thought to leave behind, every warning about him she shirked, every detail she convinced herself she could control, came flooding in.

Her eyes opened, her heart blacker than it'd been before. Cassidy swam in the realization as her conscience was weighed down by the trap she let herself get lured into.

She'd lingered long enough. She'd played with her prey. There wasn't any more time to wait, to waste. Now, it was time for Ransom to die.

CASSIDY

COLINA DE DRAGONES WAS ABUZZ FROM THE EVENING'S festivities, filled to the brim with jovial sounds and camaraderie well past midnight. It might've been a welcome sight if Cassidy hadn't known better.

But she *did* know better. The wool was finally pulled from her eyes.

Her anger was palpable, mostly at herself for getting drawn to the taste of honey, for letting it take so long. Ransom and his sickly-sweet poison convinced her. She almost gave up her fight, almost fell for the man who ruined her life.

No, what she felt for Ransom wasn't anything more than a little girl's morbid fascination. What he offered wasn't a happy ending. It was a beautiful nightmare that'd cost her in the end, like it did Aisling.

Ransom's touch drew her back to center.

Cassidy summoned a feigned smile as they reached the hacienda's courtyard.

"Did you enjoy yourself, my darling?" He guided her in a slow circle, letting her balance her palm in his as she

gathered her skirt and stepped onto the bottom stair.

"I did." She nodded. "More than I expected."

"Oh?" Jack answered, rolling his grip to expose her glove's buttons. He undid each one, flicking them open with a twist of his thumb. His gaze slid to hers, fingers grasping the end, drawing it away with an achingly slow tug. Hours before, caught in the beautiful trappings and his tantalizing web, Cassidy might've welcomed the shiver of delight.

Now, the spell was lifted; she *hated* it more than ever.

"Oh yes," she sighed, holding to the charade, to the character of Cassidy Bennet a little longer. He was within her grasp. There was no letting up now. "It made me—"

She hesitated, gaze turned down. She wished she could summon a rosy flush to make it more convincing.

"It made you what, my darling? You can tell me anything," Ransom answered, thumbing the edge of the diamond ring he'd shackled her with hours before.

Cassidy shook her head. "I shouldn't say. It's *very* unladylike."

Jack's smile grew as he brushed his lips against the inside of her wrist, drawing an involuntary prickle up her arm.

"All the more reason for you to say it, dear Cassidy," he purred, stepping closer.

She answered in kind, dancing her palms up his lapels, leaning in with a low whisper. "I want to be alone with you in the dark." She painted her touch along the edge of his jaw, trailing a fingernail down his throat. "I want to see what you look like sprawled out in the moonlight beneath me."

Ransom's gaze darkened, darting over her every freckle when she pulled away. He skimmed a finger along the pale lace over the slope of her breast, coiling a shining copper curl around it.

Cassidy held her breath, clinging to the ladylike guise when he lifted it to his nose.

Eyes closed, he growled as he breathed her in, opening them again with a lick of his lips.

Jack let the curl fall, but the fire in his gaze remained, one that stirred a flicker of fear in her gut when he wrapped his fingers around her throat.

"I confess, that is my wish, as well," he answered in a silken murmur. "Perhaps we'll celebrate our engagement tonight?" He didn't wait for an answer, pulling her closer, skimming his thumb against her cheek before pressing his lips to hers.

Cassidy's anger flared, but she played along, following his lead. She wanted to encourage his belief that she was an object which belonged to him. That, as he claimed her with his tongue, he was sealing the contract to say she would be his forever.

Hours before, she had nearly believed it herself, convinced she wanted to throw her plan away, that she could control him. Her stomach twisted at the thought, stirred by her mother's face in the back of her mind.

Run.

No. Cassidy was done running. She was finished chasing him, chasing this dream. The hunt was almost over. With the kill in sight, she couldn't help but be reminded of Moone's words when he held her fast amongst colorful, swirling silks and petticoats.

What would come after once it was all said and done?

She shoved the thought away, shifting her focus to Ransom's lips pressed to hers. Cassidy leaned into him, twisting her arms around his shoulders with a quiet whimper. She hoped it would be enough to mask the bitter taste in her mouth.

Cassidy broke away first, feathering the threads of silver at his temples, offering a convincing smile—a promise for what's to come.

"I have some business to attend to in the smoking room. Would you like to join me, my darling?" Jack traced his nose down her cheek with a groan. "This will soon all be ours. It'd only be right for my queen to be by my side."

Even the beatings and the executions? Cass bit back the sting of her mother's final moments at the end of his barrel.

She shook her head with another prize-winning grin. "You go, dearest. I'll rest my eyes for a while. It's been such an eventful evening, and I wish to have all my energy for what's to come."

He bent, kissing the back of her hand. "If you're sure."

"Surer than anything I've done in my entire life." Cassidy let the truth spill out.

Ransom smiled—genuine and effortlessly handsome. Seductive enough, she was almost tempted to forget all the rest and stride away on his arm. "I look forward to it, pet. Midnight, then?"

"Midnight it is." Cassidy held onto her feigned tenderness as he walked away, waiting until he disappeared down a corridor on the other side of the house. Once she heard the distant click of a door, she gathered up green silk and bounded up the stairs.

There was no time to waste. She had to pack, saddle Solo, and ensure they were ready to ride like the wind once Ransom breathed his last. Most pins were pulled from her hair before she reached her suite's door.

Her room was whisper quiet, a welcome comfort for her racing mind. She leaned against the door with a sigh, rolling her head against polished walnut as she counted the drumming of her heart to the gentle ticking clock on the mantle.

A fire crackled softly in the rounded hearth, low enough to stretch the shadows and set her teeth on edge.

"What in the hell are you doing, Cassidy?"

Moone's voice rumbled from the darkness. She shivered, blood heating from the sheer sound of it, of him waiting to corner her and tell her she was wrong.

She squinted, peering past gathering, glimmering shadows and the fevered flicker of firelight. The cherry of a lit cigar flared, illuminating the blue of his eyes with a rosy, eerie glow where he haunted her balcony.

"I know I asked you to leave me alone, but I didn't think you'd finally listen. I'm not sure I like it much. When you left… I—" Cassidy worried her lip. "Why?"

"Don't change the subject," he growled, flicking the ember over the balcony's edge. "Answer the question."

Another quaking quiver tumbled down her spine when he emerged from the shadows, more wolf than man—so unlike the James Moone she knew. The one who was warm and smiled at her without trying, even when she pushed him to his patience's edge.

She liked it.

Cassidy found him unacceptably handsome in his tails at the ball that evening. He was still dressed in his formalwear, but his tie was undone, jacket discarded, and sleeves rolled to his elbows. It only made her want him more.

Cass wondered if she could take him up on another invitation to dance. One less complicated, with fewer eyes. One where he could tell her he loved her without Ransom waiting in a room down the hall.

Still, no matter how handsome he was or how she wished she could wash away the bitterness from Jack's kiss with the memory of Moone's, to drown in the feeling he stirred in her—it didn't change that she'd set the plan in motion. Cassidy refused to get him mixed up in it.

It was time to say goodbye and good luck; she was sorry they didn't have more of it. It didn't change how fifteen years' worth of anger bubbled to the surface, boiling away at every happy feeling she allowed herself the last three weeks. It didn't change how she threw away their future.

Cassidy lifted her chin. "None of your damn business, that's what."

Moone squared his shoulders, somehow more handsome the deeper his frown became. "Everything you do became my business from the minute you took that warrant for Doc Ball out of my hands, Cassidy. From the second you set foot in Gallow Gorge. I know you. I see your mind working. What's your plan?"

She inched back, bare skin of her shoulders colliding with the door. "You won't answer my question, so I'm not telling you a fucking thing." She twisted the knob and wrenched it open, pouring a river of light over him. "Fair's fair. If you don't like it, you can walk away again."

Moone crossed the sprawling bedroom in a step or two and pushed the door shut, crowding her with a palm on the wood over her shoulder.

"Are you trying to kill me, Freckles?" Moone growled, bending to brush his nose along the shell of her ear. His free hand traversed over the bend of her shoulder and down her arm, fingers looping through hers.

"I dunno. Depends on the day." Cassidy was breathless, boneless—*distracted*. Too distracted to notice that he pulled away Ransom's engagement ring until he held it between them. "Give that back."

She reached for it, but he yanked it out of the way, diving to brush his lips against hers. Cass didn't think. She *shoved*, pushing her fists against his chest.

He cocked his head, smirk tugging at his perfect mouth. "You pissed about something, sweetheart? Your life is looking pretty good about now."

"How could you tell?" Cass glared up at him with a wrinkle of her nose.

Moone wasn't stupid. He saw through her bullshit in a second, and he was right—she *was* angry. She was angry with him for always being around, that he had the gall to call her out and demand an answer for what came next. She was angry he suggested she wasted her life chasing a twisted dream. That the feeling of another man's blood on her hands wouldn't be a balm to wash away the cold, abominable feeling of her Da's on her face.

She was infuriated James Moone had the nerve to tell her he loved her. *Her*—a bitter, cantankerous pain in the ass with little to offer but a bad temper and a pretty face.

More than anything, Cassidy was angriest with herself. She didn't mean to let things get so far. Without a doubt, the girl from Gallow Gorge wouldn't recognize the woman who let herself get so caught up in a beautiful web—too distracted by pretty words, prettier things, and the prettiest face on the darkest soul to see him for what he truly was.

"Tell me." Moone held the glimmering diamond into a red-hued shard of light. "Lady Cassidy Ransom, hm? Is this what you want?"

"No," she bit, shaking her head. "I'm doing it. Tonight. I'll make him choke on it if I have to. Then I'm going home."

Moone stood straighter; a shadow fell over his face. "No."

"What do you mean, *no?*"

He scrubbed his fingers against a five-o'clock shadow, shifting on his polished boots. "You can't. You shouldn't."

"Why? Hasn't this always been the goal—the *reason* we came to this damn house in the first place?"

"I told you to *go home* and forget this. It's suicide. They'll catch you and—"

"And what? Hang me?"

"*Flay* you." His steely gaze snapped to hers. "You haven't the faintest idea the shit he's capable of. What they'll do to avenge him if you succeed."

Cass balked, eyes flashing with a silent warning.

"I know *exactly* what he's capable of," she spat. "I saw it with my own eyes. I'm… I'm finally seeing things clearly. *So fucking clearly.* So what if I get caught by his thugs? He'll be dead. Nothing else matters. I don't care what happens to me so long as I do right by my Da."

Moone clenched his jaw, staring at his boots a beat before returning to her. "Do you think *this* is what he wanted for you?"

Ian Callaghan's face flashed through her mind, smiling proudly as she remembered, wrapped in golden-hued sunshine as a breeze tugged at her pinafore. Something inside her flared when she wondered where he was now, what kind of eternity the good-hearted, loving Callaghans earned. Maybe they were waiting on rolling emerald moors with white cliffs. Maybe she could join them.

"I'm not afraid to die."

Moone shifted, chewing his words. Cass thought he might pace a hole in the Persian rug, buzzing with impatience to find out what was so hard for him to say.

His blue eyes blazed when they met hers again, so earnest, Cassidy shivered when he placed a shaking palm over his heart.

"*I'm* afraid, Cassidy. I'm afraid of what'll happen to me if you die," Moone whispered, closing the space between them as he pressed on. "You say you want this; you want to kill this man, and this is the only thing you can do to make things right. But there has to be another way. *I need there to be another way.*"

"There isn't," she bit. "You've been following me, begging me to go home. You've been holding me back from every part of this plan. I would've been happy to do this a much easier way, but you tugged on the reins, and I fucking *let* you. Why, *why* is it so important to you that I let it go when you know full well this was always how it would be?"

"God dammit, can't you set aside your fucking pride for a minute and look around you? Can't you see that maybe you're worth the things you've always pushed away? Maybe it isn't my history that has me trying to stop you, but our future that does? Why can't you just let me love you? Or are we both kidding ourselves? Maybe all this is *your* inheritance; all it took was you selling your soul to the Devil."

Cass's breath caught. "You say that like you know what I want, that you have the faintest idea what I've been through. Why this is so important to me." She tried to keep her voice down, to keep it steady. But now it all started to pour out, she found it impossible to stuff the cork back in the bottle. "You weren't there. You didn't see what they did, what *he* did. You come tell me you understand when you've watched the light fade from your Da's eyes as you wipe his blood from your face. Don't judge me for taking advantage of being here when you did the exact same thing. You *grew up* here. Three weeks is nothing compared to a lifetime. He owed me that much, and I'd take more than a ring and the pretty dresses as payment if I could. I owe it to my family to *finally* finish this. This is the only way, and there isn't a damn thing you can do to stop me."

In a rustle of green silk, Cassidy lunged for the ring. Moone caught her around the wrist. Without a second thought, she swung around, leaving a stinging slap on his face.

Moone's face shifted, practically unbothered. His mouth carved into an amused grin.

"What are you smiling at?" Cassidy spat.

"You're a pain in the ass, you know that?" he growled, twisting his fingers in her hair, crashing his mouth to hers.

[37]

CASSIDY

HER FINGERS GRIPPED BLACK SILK, MEANING TO SHOVE him away. But her traitorous body pulled him closer, melting into the heat of his chest pressed against her aching bosom. She didn't know who she was, where they were, or what they were doing. All that existed was the feeling of his touch tangled in copper curls, the smell of sweet tobacco on his collar, and the taste of whiskey on his tongue when he twisted it with hers.

His kiss was demanding, unwavering, and everything Cass imagined when she was with Ransom. Heat pooled in her belly, hairs standing on end, reaching out with the need for more.

A log noisily crackled and popped in the fireplace, painting the shadows with glimmers of red gold. Cassidy returned to her senses, shoving him away with a shallow pant.

Moone's smile still lingered while he traced the tip of his tongue along his bottom lip, like he was collecting her taste to store away in his memory.

In a single, hungry flicker of his eyes to hers, Cass forgot

the blazing heat in her core and found her anger all over again—like she put a dagger in the back of Cassidy Bennet and returned fully to herself.

With his kiss still fresh on her lips, she reached back, sent her weight forward behind a balled-up fist, and connected it to his jaw to beat the smug smile off his face.

He rolled his body with the hit, stumbling back a few paces as he shifted his jaw side to side. What Cass wished was blinding pain melted into something closer to self-satisfaction when he let out a deep laugh.

"You've been in this house too long, Freckles. Three weeks ago, you woulda knocked me on my ass, but your form is suffering a bit."

"I'll show you good form." Cass's hand flew to her hip in a flash of muscle memory, but Moone was faster, fingers snapping around her wrist, twisting to pin it to her back.

Her cheek met the wall, his breath kissing her face when their hips sealed together. Cassidy groaned, heart stumbling when he rolled into her. Moone wasn't a small man, tall and broad enough to take up all the space in the room. She figured that, between the length of his fingers and the size of his boot, *other things* would be equally thick.

Proof her suspicions were right sent a white-hot bolt of heat straight to her sex. Even through the layers of fabric, she felt him—evidence of his growing lust pouring kerosene on the embers of their shared desire.

"There's my wild girl," he growled, lips brushing her ear. He wove their fingers together, sliding one of her palms up, then the other, grip unyielding as he kept them fastened to the wall. His mouth found the crook of her neck, sweeping down her shoulder as the fingers of his free hand wandered down the curve of her corseted waist to palm her sex through her skirt.

Too much. Too close. Too sweet. Too much temptation to take him up on the thousandth plea to leave it all behind, but not before she begged him to fuck her first.

A lost, scared little girl. That's what he called her, demanding to know what she'd live for once it was all said and done. And she… she hadn't really given consideration to anything but this. Every twisted thought and tear-fueled nightmare only led to one place—Jack Ransom at the end of her barrel.

Moone, though. He knew her. He *loved* her.

Love wasn't something she ever considered, either.

"Wait—" she panted, whirling to face him. It was a bad idea of the worst kind. The sight of his lips so kissable and close, the hard press of him against her skirts. He was worse for her than whiskey. How was she supposed to keep a clear head when she wanted to drink down every morsel of him? She pressed a palm on the heat of his chest, holding him at arm's length. "Why are you here?"

He blinked, working his jaw until Cassidy's ached from watching him. "I realized I can tell you all the reasons not to do this until I breathe my last. A million of 'em, why you shouldn't do this, why I shouldn't let you. But I can only think of one that matters more than the rest."

Silence stretched between them. The air buzzed with everything that'd gone unsaid in the years they'd known each other. There was one thing in particular. One reason. A singular thing so wonderfully unbelievable in the grand scheme of things, it made her want to run. Something Cass saw so clearly, she couldn't keep pretending she couldn't.

"Did you mean it?" she whispered, chest heaving with every anxious breath. "Did you mean it when you said you loved me?"

Moone dipped his head, tawny waves hanging so close. Cassidy was tempted to sink her fingers into them and plunder his mouth again, but not before he gave her an answer.

"Yes."

"Why?" Cass spied the hint of a smile he always wore when she argued. "I'm a cold pain in the ass bitch, so why me? When? Why would you, when we both know I've never been particularly kind to you."

Moone stood a little straighter, reaching around her to lock the door. Quiet crackled between them as he stared at his boots another second, maybe ten, maybe one hundred, before his gaze snapped to hers so sharply, it stole her breath.

"I look you in the eye, Cassidy, and I know you're not cold." He stepped closer, thumbing the curve of her cheek. "I know everything about you. How you feel, how you smell—how you *taste*. I could find you in the dark. So yes, Cassidy Kathleen Callaghan, I love you. Lord fucking knows I shouldn't, and it'll probably be the death of me, but—" The purest smile tugged at the corner of his perfect mouth. Such a beautiful sight, Cass thought her heart might leap onto the floor; years of fondness and love wrapped up in the simplest gesture. "I watched you gallop into town on that devil horse of yours in a flurry of freckles and hair. You swore at me like a sailor and threatened me to boot, and that was it for me. I was a goner. There was no other choice, no other road but this. You and me."

Cass slipped her hand up the growing scruff on his jaw, tucking an escaped curl back into place. Her eyes took in every line worn into his handsome face, body lit like a fuse, with only inches to spare until detonation.

"Then you're dumber than I thought."

Before she could say anything else, his mouth was on hers. This time, she didn't move to strike or push him away. Her fingers twisted in his shirt, and Cass yanked him closer, tongue dancing with his. It was more insistent than before; lips slanted over hers, hands everywhere, none of it enough.

They'd tiptoed along the blade's edge for too long, kept the open flame of their desire burning next to an open powder keg. Moone's face, mouth, and body often invaded her thoughts and dreams. Cassidy's fingers spread that warmth over herself in the solitude of her room; it was only a matter of time before things finally combusted.

It was so hopelessly *them*—half fight, half game.

Cass couldn't help it. Couldn't help how his fingers pressing into her so firmly had her wishing she could wear his touch as a brand. Couldn't help pulling his bottom lip between her teeth or sucking on his tongue. It was what she needed, what *they* needed; years of their game come to a head in a final battle—one where they'd both get a prize.

Moone broke away, wearing the infuriating smile he only put on for her.

"You've been thinking about this just as long as I have," he stated as if he were reading from a page, and she the book he plucked from the shelf. The flame burning in his eyes told her he wanted to split her open and devour her, reading every cursive line with an unbreakable focus until the deed was done.

"Don't give yourself so much credit." Cass wished her voice wasn't so soft, wished she played their game as well as she used to—something to convince him his wild girl was still here.

One look. The tug of a cocky smile said Moone saw it,

and he might devour her whole because of it.

"Oh, I will." He nodded, grinning from ear to ear. "You love me, don't you?"

"Shut up," she snapped, drinking down his chuckle. She tore at the buttons on his shirt, swearing when they wouldn't give way, half tempted to rip it open and expose his skin to the firelight so she might finally be able to look upon him.

Moone's arms shifted, grip vanishing from her waist, her hair, her everywhere. Cass mourned the brief loss of his heat, but only briefly before he shrugged off his shirt and blindly tossed it to the floor.

Cassidy's eyes slipped to the pile of white cotton for a split second. It was all the time he needed to come for her again, only—it wasn't for her mouth.

Moone dipped to the floor, wrenching up green silk, fingers easing between her thighs. He gripped the tenderest spot, holding firmly to hoist her feet from the floor until her back met the bedpost.

She anchored her palms on his shoulders, dragging her mouth over his skin to muffle her moan when he swept his fingers through her folds. He pressed his thumb against her throbbing peak. Another cry, back arching, hips rolling to bring herself closer, to ease the building ache inside her. Her mind raced, flooded with one word the minute he rolled his shoulder and was knuckle-deep, crying out as he filled her and turned her molten with desire.

"*More*," she gasped.

Moone swore, teeth grazing, nipping at the tender flesh at her throat.

Cassidy whimpered when he pulled his hand free, eyes wide when he slipped a finger between his lips and sucked it clean with a gravelly moan of his own.

"Fuck, you taste good, Freckles. Better than I ever thought you would," he groaned, palm grazing over her bosom to hold her by the throat, stealing another breathless kiss. His tongue invaded her mouth, twisting with hers, painting her senses with the salty sweetness of *her*.

For a moment, she agreed with him.

His words stoked the heat from all the times they'd fought. All the times his body melted into hers when he pushed her up against a wall. The times he proved to know her, her mind and soul, better than she ever planned to let him.

She wanted to slap him again, wanted to beat him, kill him, *fuck him*.

Cass swore Moone saw the instant the thought passed through her mind. He smiled again, more wolf than man. She hated and loved him all the more for it.

His smug, self-satisfied grin returned, curling at the edges of his delectable mouth when he pressed two fingers into her, pumping, fucking her as he kept the other hand anchored along her jaw.

Moone dragged the tip of his thumb along her bottom lip. She rolled it between her teeth, pressing her tongue against it, imagining it might be *him* in her mouth—something she'd take for herself if they ever had the chance again.

"Say it, Cassidy."

Sharp gasps fell from her, twined with the rhythm of his fingers. A knot built within her, twisting tighter, pleasure stacked upon pleasure seeping through her senses, different than anything she'd ever experienced before.

There'd been others. Women, mostly, and one other regrettable time with a boy in a stable before she left Sacramento for good. None of them, not even the sweetness of Katie Mays, compared to the heat coursing through her.

All he'd done was *touch*.

"Say what?" she whimpered, barely able to string a syllable together.

Moone nipped at her lip, plundering her mouth again until she could barely breathe. Her pleasure charged forward as his fingers plunged in and out of her, too fast, too slow, too much, and simultaneously not enough.

She wasn't used to needing anything the way she did James Moone. No matter how she pushed back against the building pressure, her body screamed to let go and bathe in the feeling, to pack up and leave so she might stay like this with him for all eternity.

"Tell me you love me," he growled, kissing her again and again. "Go on. Say it."

"I'm—" Cass rolled her head against the wooden post, closing her eyes. She trapped her bottom lip between her teeth, practically tearing at the tender flesh to silence the cries threatening to come free and wake the entire house. "I'm not telling you anything."

The dam inside her broke open, shattering her composure. Her body bucked and shuddered.

Moone held her, kissed her, lips drinking down the sounds she made as he guided her feet back to the floor.

"I'm going to take that as a yes."

Moone's smirk infuriated her, one she'd seen a thousand times before. Cassidy decided she let him get away with it one too many times.

She raised her hand to strike him, but he was a quick learner, fingers snapping around her wrist a breath away from his cheek.

He held her fast, yanking her forward to catch her mouth

in another bruising kiss.

Cass tore herself away, but not before whining, body pleading for more.

"If you keep putting words in my mouth, I *will* hit you, Moone," she bit, glaring up at him.

"Shh." He pressed his thumb to her lips. "Lies don't become you, Cassidy. Besides, I can think of something else I could do with that pretty mouth besides arguing about something I know is true."

She shivered, caught up in whatever new and bewitching game they were playing. Part of her wondered, if she ran, would he chase her like he used to? Heat surged through her at the thought. Her eyes flashed. She might as well try.

She shoved him in the chest and *bolted* across the room.

Moone, ever the quick thinker, caught her by a handful of beaded silk. The force of their cat-and-mouse chase snapped the threads piecing it all together, and Cass wasn't sure who to blame when a sea of glittering crystal beads skittered across the floor.

He answered with a forceful push of his own, palming her breast when her back collided with the wall. His fingers slipped between the satin bodice. The roughness of his knuckles against her skin had her throbbing, trembling with need to have him.

Moone dipped his chin, eyelids heavy with lust, when he tore the fabric wide open.

Her breath caught. Part of her wanted to mourn the loss of such a beautiful gown, but the thought flittered away like a wisp of smoke when he bent and slipped a knife from his boot.

His blue eyes bored into hers as he delicately traced the tip of the shining steel over the supple curve of her breast, settling it in the shallow valley between them.

Her heart thundered away, so precariously close to the point of his knife. Cass wasn't sure if fear or desire made it beat as such. It wasn't until he caught the taut fabric of her corset with the blade that she realized which.

Moone bared his teeth, jerking the knife forward, tearing the damned contraption to shreds in a single slice. His eyes glowed, blown wide as he raked his gaze over her, not wasting a moment to tug down her chemise, leaving her exposed in the lamplight.

He groaned in appreciation, dipping to take her breast in his hot mouth. He laved his tongue over it, sucking, nipping, fanning the throbbing heat within her. "I need all of you, Cassidy."

Her skirt was the next victim of his blade, ripped wide open as he slipped the gleaming dagger from stem to stern— determined to shred every inch of Cassidy Bennet and the mask she donned for Jack Ransom.

He leaned away for a moment, proudly examining his handiwork, hungrily skimming his tongue between his teeth.

"*My* wild girl," he hummed, thumbing the soft curve of her breast. "Are you ready to talk?"

"I told you already." Cassidy slipped beneath his arm, backing toward the door with a coy smile. "I'm not telling you anything."

She was fast, darting across the room, but James was quicker.

He coiled his thick arms around her waist, knife still in hand. The blade's bite pricked her ribs through her shift when she kicked her legs out with a yell. Her pulse thundered away like a runaway train when he lifted her from the floor and hauled her toward the bed.

"Would you shut up?" he hissed, hot breath on her ear summoning a thousandth shiver.

Cass twisted, climbing him, hooking her legs around his middle until the heat of him pressed against her sex. She languidly brushed her mouth against his, tugging his bottom lip between her teeth.

"First, you want me to talk, now you want me to be quiet? Someone needs to make up their mind," she tutted, sucking on his lip until he groaned, words mumbled when she refused to release him. "What, you don't want me waking the house?"

"Not from screaming like that, no," he growled, crushing his mouth to hers for another, quick-as-lightning kiss, breaking away with a low whisper. "But I got some ideas."

Moone tossed her onto the bed, pinning her with his weight.

She moaned when his mouth found the nape of her neck, his fingers clamped around her wrists. He rolled into her, the hard bulge on the back of her thighs a promise of what he was bound to deliver within a moment or two.

Her body was alight, trembling in his wake as he dragged his teeth, his tongue, his hands over her skin, painting her freckles in pleasure.

Cass moved to push against him, to be a handful, and frustrate him to the point of *fun*—just like old times. No matter how she writhed and wiggled, she wasn't a match for his strength.

He slipped his palms up her thighs, accordioning the fabric of her shift around her middle until he wrapped his fingers around her waist. She knew his hands were big, fingers long enough, strong enough to tear a log in two, but her breath caught when he gripped her around the middle and spanned her ribcage with only a few inches to spare.

Moone flipped Cass to her back, pinning her hands back above her head. She cried out when he parted her thighs with his knee. The same haughty smile bloomed when her body responded without thought, the need to press into him merely an instinct for more.

"See? Your body knows, Cassidy." He dipped his head and took her breast in his mouth, flicking her nipple with his tongue.

Cass canted, back arching from the bed with a honeyed whine when he did it again, and again. "It's—*ah*—just… just lust. Nothing personal." Lies. All lies. They both knew it.

Moone didn't answer, not with words, shoulders shaking with laughter.

He lifted his head and sighed, a curtain of waves shadowing his eyes.

For the briefest moment, Cassidy saw a different sort of man than the one who'd been toying with her the last few heated moments.

Kind, gentle, and understanding. The man who wanted to keep her safe, who begged her not to come. The one who saved her life, who told her she was radiant.

The one who *loved her.*

A gasp fell from her lips when his face grew soft, trusting, even. Cass found herself entranced by him, not for the first time, led by the way each cursive line of rugged, corded muscle bent and moved in the lamplight.

"You love me, Cassidy," Moone stated, sliding back on the bed. His eyes burned with a desire so wild, Cass both feared and craved it, unblinking when his hands sank to the waistband of his trousers. He pulled his belt free, stalking forward with a beguiling gleam. "Say it."

"No," she argued, breasts heaving with each labored breath, eyes darting over every newly exposed inch of him. He held her rapt attention, from the bullet-shaped scar in his shoulder and the dark trail of hair below his belly button to the size of him, swollen and angry with need—ready and weeping *for her*. Nothing held her gaze more than the dagger still tucked snugly in his palm. "I only want you to fuck me. Nothing else. Don't get any ideas this means anything other than that."

More lies.

Moone crawled over her, coiling the fingers of his free hand around her jaw. "Stop denying it. I *know* you. You have a bigger heart than you're willing to admit, and I can see it looking back at me in your eyes. You *love me*."

Cassidy shook her head.

"I mean it, James," she breathed, offering a trembling smile when she caught him off guard with his name. Careful, she needed to be so careful not to let the word touch her tongue. "Someone like me isn't made for that sort of thing. I—*he*. I might be broken."

He was quiet, chewing on his words before sending a bolt straight through her heart.

"Then I'll love you enough for the both of us."

She huffed. "Don't be an idiot."

Cassidy tried to turn her face away, but Moone's grip was unyielding, yanking her back to crush his lips to hers. She couldn't think. His taste made her dizzy, and her mind reeled far, far away from any thoughts of love.

His kiss was so deep, drowning her in the depths of her pleasure, Cass barely had a chance to register the feeling of him easing between her thighs.

Any other thought washed away in a tidal wave of

pleasure, their voices in harmony as he sheathed himself one torturous inch at a time. For a moment, both of them were frozen in it, basking in the sudden rush of heat that followed.

Moone dragged his mouth along her jaw, lazily twining his tongue with hers as his chest heaved against her breasts.

Too much. It was too close to the feeling she was trying to avoid. She needed to move, to feel him, to have him pound into her, crying out until she was hoarse or split in two—whichever came first. None of this achingly romantic, molded-together nonsense. Not when it'd only feed the idea he built in his mind.

No, they needed something more *them*.

A breathless smile curled through her kiss. She had a wonderful, *wicked* idea.

She didn't think twice, reaching for the knife, catching him off-guard as she hooked her ankles around his back and flipped him with a twist of her hips.

Her time in the desert made her stronger than she looked.

Cass smirked, wrenching the blade from his grasp, and placed it to his throat. Her head swam from the feeling of him seated inside her, overwhelmed by the new position. Full, *so full*. The slightest movement sent lightning crackling through her limbs straight to her core.

She lifted her chin, steeling herself, placing herself in control.

"What did I tell you, Moone?" she purred. "I'm not the loving kind, and you're a damned fool if you think you can love the likes of me."

He didn't fight her, eyes alight with something *new*, something hungrier than before when she dragged cold metal against the day-old scruff on his jaw—like he preferred the fire within her to the courtly lady.

"You're wrong." He lifted his back from the bed, fearlessly pressing his flesh against the dagger until a bead of crimson fell from lustrous steel.

"No," Cassidy repeated, voice catching when his fingers gripped her ass and buried every glorious inch of him deeper. She wasn't sure if the word was for his benefit or her own.

Relentlessly daring, or just as dumb as she suspected, Moone twisted an arm around her waist and began to move, guiding each roll of her hips with the other hand.

Her determination dwindled, breath coming in sing-song gasps. She succumbed to the way her body sang with them finally bound together in such a way.

Still, part of her loathed herself for closing her eyes; she despised her body for giving in to his soft touches so easily. She hated how her heart beat with unfathomable emotion. The kind she tried to avoid. But she held the most contempt—the most love—for the man who held her bare breasts against the heat of his chest.

The one who convinced her so thoroughly she was capable of more than she ever thought she'd be.

James held her close. Cassidy wrapped her arms around his shoulders in return, humming when his mouth found hers again, whispering her name so quietly, she might be able to taste it on her tongue.

She explored the feeling, slanting her lips over his, blade still pressed to his throat. Cass swept her tongue over the seam, along the roof of his mouth, and *moved*.

The feeling was electric, and a fresh jolt of pleasure surged through her with every bend, every breath, every movement. Cassidy decided that, if this was it, if she'd die at Ransom's hands tonight, it would've all been worth it because she had this—just once.

Moone's eyes danced over her face, nearly feverish as they settled into a steady rhythm as they had with dancing, riding, fighting. Now this.

"This doesn't mean what you think it means," Cass whimpered, head falling back, losing herself completely to the feeling of being so utterly *full*, wrapped so perfectly around him. Her body throbbed and wept. She nearly felt like weeping herself. Not from falling into his arms, not for how he made her feel, but for the life he insisted she could have if she gave up her plan.

She wished she would've been stronger, fought harder against the way he stirred and lit a flame in her cold heart. She wished she would've known better than to let herself get caught up in the feeling—ravenous for another taste, another moment, another reason to prolong him being so deliciously inside her, body and soul.

The heat of her pleasure coiled deep in her belly, the warmth of her desire growing brighter like a blacksmith's forge fed by the bellows. What would happen if—*when*—she finally lost control?

Cassidy's body shuddered, her breath trembling when she started to buck and jerk from her inevitable orgasm. The dagger slipped from her grip, falling out of sight.

James cradled her, flipping her to her back. His hand caressed the creamy flesh of her thigh, hitching her knee against his chest as he snapped his hips against her with quick, measured, *deep* thrusts.

"No, Cassidy," he growled, laying another lazy kiss upon her lips, collecting her moans and mewls. "This means *everything*. I can see it." He pounded into her, grunting between each one, barely gasping out every word. "I can feel it." Another kiss, one that stole her breath, flaring the white-hot coil within her. "Why can't you?"

He anchored his forehead against hers, breath rattling as their pleasure crested.

Cassidy twisted her fingers through his hair, forcing his eyes to meet hers as they came apart together. She wanted to hold onto that glimmer and keep it tucked away in the deepest part of her heart where her most secret thoughts lived.

Her orgasm rocked through her. She cried out, tears streaming down her face from the sheer force of it.

Moone devoured the sound, drinking down her moans with a final few punishing snaps of his hips.

She felt it, then, clearer than she ever had.

He loved her.

James peppered her face with the softest kisses, pulling her to his chest as he rolled to the side.

The clock on the mantle ticked away, an ever-constant reminder of the task at hand.

Cass sighed, trailing a path through his downy chest hair, almost sure he'd drifted off to sleep. A yawn forced its way from her mouth, practically begging her to join him.

Her mind won, sharper than the blade's tip on the blanket beside her. There was so much to do; no matter how badly she wanted to linger, she had a job to finish. She'd never let a bounty go unchecked. Not to mention what would happen if they were caught.

Cassidy lifted Moone's dagger into a shard of pale lamplight with a twist of her wrist.

The memory of a younger man holding it aloft in the Callaghan General Store was overwhelming, stamping out the burning ember within her.

No, not Moone's dagger—*Ransom's*.

The jeweled handle was unmistakable, the star of her darkest nightmares, ones vividly painted in her Da's blood.

She looked from the gleaming steel to Moone's soundly sleeping face, mind racing with questions of how he came to have it.

He said what happened between them meant everything. But something shifted when she held the weight of Ransom's blade. It spoke her soul's truth. Her heart flipped when she briefly entertained the thought of waking Moone and bolting into the night without a trace.

His words, what they'd done, battled with the vow she made; vengeance so close, she could taste it.

Still, tucked in James's arms, she wondered if *he* was what should come after.

Cassidy balanced on an elbow, a spill of copper curls falling over her shoulder. She traced a fingertip along the seam of his mouth and allowed herself—for one fleeting, beautiful moment—to forget about bounties and revenge.

She pressed a featherlight kiss to his lips, smiling softly with a whisper.

"You're right, and I'm sure I'll regret it, but—I *do* love you."

[38]

CASSIDY

M IDNIGHT DREW CLOSER. CASSIDY SPENT TOO LONG already, waiting in the wings when she should've taken center stage, should've done the deed before she sank too deep.

She sighed, tracing a fingertip through Moone's chest hair, staring up at the canopy as the clock ticked away the hour. She was running out of time, and there'd be consequences to pay if another man was discovered in her bed when she promised herself to Ransom.

Cassidy leaned over him—her love. She trailed her touch over his nose, his mouth, through his hair. There, in the quiet afterglow, uncomplicated joy warming her chest, she understood his point, his want to leave everything else behind.

Still, it didn't compare to the smoldering need to finally see her task finished. To have Ransom bleeding on the floor. She couldn't give up, not now. Not after what she'd done.

"I love you," she whispered, brushing a featherlight kiss on his lips. She slipped a foot from the bed, then the other, throat thick when James shifted, groaning as he curled his

arms around a pillow. Frozen, Cassidy counted every rapid drum of her heart as his breathing evened out until she was sure he'd fallen back to sleep.

Standing in front of the open wardrobe, Cassidy stared at the rows of delicate gowns and colorful ribbons—what was she supposed to wear to kill her life's obsession? With the whispered promises made by her body, she figured there was only one way to get his guard down low enough for her to strike.

As little as possible.

Cassidy pulled on her finest chemise and plaited her hair down to her waist. The motion summoned a smile. Even with a gold-lined corset and a fringed robe hanging from her shoulders, the braid served as a potent reminder of who she was, what she fought for, and why it was finally time to deliver.

She soundlessly slipped from the suite, taking one last glimpse of a beautiful James Moone sprawled over the sheets. Her heart twisted; his voice rang in her ears.

Stay. We'll go home in the morning.

Cassidy shook her head. Too late. It was too late. *She* was too late.

The house was quiet, save for the skittering of a hunting cat and the mouse who evaded him. After a brief stop in the pantry, Cassidy made her way to the carriage house in record time, sneaking past dozing guards without notice.

Solo stomped and pranced upon the sight of her and her heavy saddlebags. Weighted with food and supplies for their long ride ahead, the mustang reared his head, swished his tail, and jolted forward like a coiled spring ready to break loose.

She saddled him and slipped on his bridle, taking one

last look inside the saddlebags. A loaded gun belt and a stolen pistol laid on top. It was stupid to venture into the desert without protection. She thought of tiptoeing back upstairs to collect the pearl-gripped twins from Moone's possession. They'd make a poetic end to her journey with Ransom, but a pistol was too bulky to hide beneath her shift and far too noisy. One shot would wake the whole house, sending Ransom's men into a frenzy. Cassidy would be lucky to escape with her head.

No. She'd have to be more creative than that and use something more straightforward. Something more Ransom's style.

Solo sidestepped, pushing against her with his impatience. He swung his head back, letting out a low nicker, telling her to hurry so they could get a move on and finally feel the wind.

"Hush, sweet thing." Cassidy rubbed the star on his forehead, hugging his muzzle to her chest in an unhurried embrace. "I think there's been enough of this fancy house for the both of us. No more sugar cubes and bubble baths every day. We're leaving real soon, or else we'll go soft."

His black eyes warily followed as she disappeared through the barn door.

Cassidy shivered when her bare feet slipped through damp grass kissed by a nighttime dew. The warmth of the house, holding onto the heat of the day's sun, was welcome, drawing her hair on end.

"What are you doing down here, pet?"

Her shoulders curled inward, fingers pressing to her stomach, searching for purchase when Ransom's voice summoned a different sort of tremor. She searched for Cassidy Bennet, dragging her to the surface for a little longer,

then it'd be over. She'd be dead and buried, and Ransom alongside her.

Cassidy turned, meeting his darkened gaze with a smile. She hated how handsome he was, despised how she noticed the way he leaned in a doorway, silver-flecked hair hanging in his eyes. A red robe hung from his shoulders, giving her the slightest glimpse of finely carved muscle beneath.

It was similar to the first time she'd seen him this way, back when she was hungry, curious, and confused about who he was—about who she was.

Cassidy wasn't confused anymore.

"After everything that's been on my mind, I needed some fresh air to cool my head," she murmured, closing the space between them. Her fingers wandered, gliding across his bare chest.

Before, he might've stopped her, but now the diamond, his diamond, *Aisling's* diamond, glimmered on her left hand. Cassidy had permission to do what she liked. This was her house, her library, her everything.

Even Jack belonged to her.

"Oh?" His fingers covered hers, knuckles speckled with fresh bruises. She didn't have to wonder how he got them.

Cassidy swallowed her anger, pressing on to drown it in a different feeling.

"Yes." Cassidy continued, pushing him into the soft, inviting firelight and the sweet smell of the library. "I thought I might find you down here. Maybe we—" She lifted her chin, brushing her mouth against his. "Maybe we could have a drink?"

Ransom groaned, twisting his fingers in her hair when his back met the wall. "What's your poison, my darling?"

She brushed her nose against his. "You."

Cass brought her lips to his. Eager, firm enough to make her dizzy. Enough to conjure the image of James Moone behind her eyes.

Her stomach twisted, the burning hot coil Moone lit reignited, body thrumming and ready to find the same divine release again. It spurred her on, telling her to push harder, kiss more fiercely until he couldn't breathe. Maybe she could drown in it and take him with her. Then, at least the bitter taste in her mouth would be worth it.

Ransom's hand found her jaw. He pushed back, coiling the other arm around her waist. He tore his mouth away, breathing ragged. "Not here," he growled, eyes alight with the same terrifying gleam as when he killed.

Cassidy shivered in the shadow of it, danger so close and tantalizing, she was half-tempted to say yes and satiate the darkest part of herself that craved him.

His touch slipped down her shoulder, over her waist, down the curve of her thigh. His rapt attention scorched her. Unwavering, even as he lifted her to his chest like a bride. One eager to be bedded by her betrothed—ripe, virginal fruit to be plucked for the first time.

Up the stairs they went, the picture of the king and queen in their blood-drenched kingdom, just as Ransom imagined them to be.

He kicked open the door to his bedroom, carrying her into the darkness, a place she hadn't been allowed until now.

Hushed, save for the quiet cluck of a clock on the mantle. Ransom set Cassidy to her feet, kissing her again in his own time, his own rhythm, drawing a moan from the deepest part of her—one not meant for him. He peeled himself away a torturous inch at a time until only his lips remained.

Cassidy opened her eyes as lamplight bloomed and cast

shadows over his suite.

Blood was everywhere. Not in pools on the floor or staining fine fabric, but in the shade of the velvet drapes, the hue of a wooden bed frame, and the crush of burgundy woven into the blankets upon it.

Fingers clutched the edges of her robe; she took in every detail, finding a way out, an escape route should she need one. She buzzed with a quiet calm, teetering on the edge of breathless anxiety, a thrilling sense of finality.

Was this the end? Could she finally move on and live the life Moone said she could have? One where she was happy and he was by her side. Where he loved her, and she let him love her in return?

"A drink, my darling?" Ransom's stormy timbre stirred Cass from her thoughts.

She drummed up another smile, stepping into a pool of light, fingers brushed against his on a proffered crystal tumbler. Whiskey whispered to her, another in a long list of temptations. She hadn't had a drop in weeks, not since she'd replaced it with finely bubbled champagne.

Cassidy eyed the amber liquid, reminding herself that she didn't drink on the job, that here, of all places, was where she ought to keep her wits about her.

Ransom shouldered by, pressing another swift kiss to her lips before venturing into the heart of the suite.

Cassidy clutched the glass to her chest, staring at the ripples for a moment, maybe two, maybe a hundred.

No more waiting.

Lifting it to her lips, she drained the liquid and abandoned the empty vessel on a credenza.

Chin held high, chest heaving. Cassidy turned the lamp's knob, snuffing out the light until only the moonlight and

Ransom's eyes remained.

One more act. One more performance. Then Cassidy would burn it all down and build something new.

"*Jack*," she murmured, stepping forward to palm the curve of his chest. She let him press into her, curling his fingers around the nape of her neck. "I've been waiting for this day for a long time."

"Have you?" he growled, dipping his head, plundering her mouth again and again as she blindly pushed him across the room. She'd let him do what he liked as long as it helped lure him into her trap—a web of her own making.

"Yes," she preened, wearing a catlike smile when he stumbled back upon the bed. She slipped her fingers beneath his robe, over his shoulders, drawing it away inch by inch until it came free.

Ransom was clay, she the artist, bending to her every whim the further Cassidy tested the limits of the power he allowed her. Down he went, splayed across the bed as she peppered his face, his neck, his chest in kisses. Each of them another nail in his coffin.

Cassidy stood back, pulling her braid over her shoulder. "I want to tell you a story, dearest."

A flicker of curiosity flashed across his face. "Now?"

"Yes," she purred, pulling her copper curls loose, one plait at a time.

He nodded. "Alright. But hurry."

Cassidy hummed, drawing the velvet robe from her slender shoulders. She inched forward, stepping from the fabric on the floor. One knee on the bed, then the other, framing him between her thighs. She shivered. *Wrong*, so wrong. The sliver of want swelled from her still-buzzing body, leftover from her tumble with Moone an hour before.

"Once upon a time," she said, a curtain of hair hanging over her shoulder as she pressed her chest to his. "There was a man."

A kiss to his temple.

"A woman."

Another on the other.

"And a daughter."

"And they lived happily ever after, I suppose?" Ransom leaned on his elbows, rising to twist his arms around her waist and regain control. Cassidy was faster, planting his wrists on the blanket.

"No. Not at all." Her fingers traced his chest, lingering in the places where she bore scars.

Cassidy's skin was marked by a hard life well-fought, a life Ransom condemned her to. The worst of them weren't visible to the eye. Even Moone carried dozens of his own, but Ransom had none.

Tonight, he'd gain his first and last.

Ransom's face darkened. He was growing impatient with Cassidy toying with him.

She needed to focus.

"Enough of this." He moved to rise. Cassidy acted quickly, devouring his mouth with another distracting kiss. Harder, insistent, more demanding than the rest. She rolled her hips, drawing a groan from his lips as she did it again and again.

Cassidy reached for her laces. "The woman was haunted by a darkness she could never shake. Even though she was happy with her family, it chased her. Eventually… the Devil found them."

Ransom's brow lifted. "And then?"

Cassidy sobered. Flashes of her Da's face flickered

through her mind. Her mother's cries. The drumbeat of the lovely ladies and their cowboys condemned to die in a burning church.

"He killed them in cold blood."

He tutted, "Not much of a story. Better if you stick to the likes of Brontë and Austen, my love." A vein in his jaw twitched. Fingers pressed into her waist, Jack flipped her to her back with a grunt. His mouth found hers, knee pressed to her center, kissing her so fiercely Cassidy nearly lost all sense of where she was and what she came for.

No. She anchored herself in her rage, in that mission. Her vow. *No more distractions.*

"Did you mean what you said?" She gasped for breath, brushing the hair from his eyes. "Anything I want? Truly *anything?*"

Ransom's face warmed; misplaced affection for a ghost. "Anything, my darling."

Cassidy smiled, slow, catlike, and wicked, lifting her hand. Fingers gripped around the blade of the jeweled dagger she took from her and Moone's bed—Ransom's, soaked with the blood of a hundred men, even her Da.

Ransom's smile faded. His jaw rolled, the rest of him deathly still when Cassidy pressed shining steel against his throat.

"I want you to die like he did," she spat. "Only *slower.*"

He didn't budge an inch, but his eyes roved over every inch of her face below him. And, for the first time, Cassidy thought Jack *saw* her. Not Cassidy Bennet or someone who reminded him of another life, but herself—pieces of people he knew, people he claimed to love and killed instead.

"*Aisling,*" Ransom breathed, a flurry of emotions passing over his face.

"No." Cassidy pressed harder. He winced; she smiled. "Not Aisling. Not Ian. *Cassidy.* I saw everything, Jack. I remember it all, from the moment you killed my Da, to the second you shot her in cold blood when she refused you, and when you burned an entire town to the ground because you didn't get your way. You punished them all, and for what?"

"It all led me here, my darling." Ransom leaned into the blade, twisting a copper curl around his finger. His brows pressed in, eyes darkening until the monster finally looked back at her. "Now I have you."

"Not for long," Cassidy bit, tightening her hold on the dagger.

He smiled, boldly closing the space between them. Her lips tingled with the memory of his poisonous kiss. "You're right."

Blood slid down gleaming steel as Ransom bravely bowed down, tracing his fingertips down the edge of her jaw. He kissed her again, as if the threat of his death only roused him. As the kill did. As the kill did for her, too.

"You're mine," he growled. Eyes glowing, his hands found her throat. He leaned into her, drawing a sigh from her lips when the pressure banished every thought. All she had was the feeling, the memory of Moone feasting on her, filling her.

Wrong. All of it was going so wrong.

Cassidy's vision fuzzed. The dagger slipped from her grip as Ransom's tightened. She gasped for air, slapping at his shoulders, his face. Clawed at him until she drew blood; blindly searched for the jeweled hilt of the blade so she might cut herself free and end it once and for all—even if he took her life in the process.

Her chest burned. Tears streamed down her face. The

whisper of a name hovered on her lips as the blackness seeped in.

"Moone."

Cassidy wished she'd done things differently. Wished they had more time.

"*Moone*," she gasped out, smiling sleepily when his face appeared through the inky night; a last sliver of light before the end.

A crash rang out. Then the weight, a weight so heavy, Cassidy wondered if it was death closing in. But her vision cleared. The burning in her lungs ebbed. The blood-tinged lamplight of Ransom's suite came into focus.

Moone stood over her, chest heaving, shattered decanter in hand.

Cassidy blinked, rolling away Ransom's limp body. She sucked in another stuttering breath, palming the ache in her throat, stomach twisting when they came away covered in blood.

She lurched, tearing at Jack's limp body sprawled out on the bed. Blood poured from a crack in his temple, staining the flecks of silver in his hair.

Breath rattled in his chest, and part of her sagged in relief.

Alive. Ransom was alive.

Eyes wild, Cassidy whirled. "What have you done?"

Moone threw away the crystal bottle, flicking whiskey from the ends of his fingers. "I just saved your life."

[39]

CASSIDY

LIFE STIRRED IN THE HOUSE. MUFFLED VOICES. THE SLAM of the kitchen door.

Moone grabbed her by the wrist. "We need to get out of here before anyone else wakes up."

Cassidy ripped from his grip, eyes wild, heart pounding. "I'm not finished."

She dove for the blade, knees slipping on the edge of the mattress.

Ransom's body tumbled to the floor. Cassidy chased it, lifting his dagger to end him once and for all.

Moone's arms clamped around her waist, hoisting her from the floor. "Cassidy, we can't stay here. You're going to get yourself killed."

"I don't care!" She flailed, kicking out, twisting in his grasp the further he pulled her. "No! I'm not finished. It… *isn't… finished!*"

"I care!" he bellowed. Moone threw his weight, anchoring her against the wall. His breath tore through him, chest heaving, blue eyes shadowed. Tawny waves still wild from their tryst hours before, his jaw was set, brow creased as a sob tore from his lips. "*I* care if you die, Cassidy. How many times do I have to tell you that? How often do I tell you I love you before you believe me?"

His lips found hers, plundering her mouth in a kiss so quick, so fierce, Cassidy worried the darkness would cloud her vision again.

She tore away, gasping for breath.

"I know you do. I believe you." Her gaze slid to Ransom's body a few steps away. It'd be so easy to kill him now. Too easy—but would she be satisfied? Bitter, angry tears slipped over her freckles. "I want to, but I'm so close. If I leave now, then I failed him."

Moone's attention darted to more muffled voices below. He pawed a hand through his hair. "Failed who?"

"My Da," she whispered.

James deflated, gaze soft as he collected her face and kissed her tender and slow. "You didn't fail him, Cassidy. Not by choosing to live and be done with it. It's time to let go."

He kissed her again, more demanding, more insistent than before. Like it'd seal in his words and make her believe.

Cassidy sniffed, nodding. "Let's go home."

Moone took her hand, reaching for the door handle. A shard of light cut his face, illuminating the depths of blue as he peered into the hall. "If we're careful, I think we still have a chance at sneaking out of here unnoticed."

Lead sang, splintering polished wood.

Moone swore.

Cassidy snatched a pistol from his belt, ducking beneath his arm to fire a shot across the hall.

A man sank to the carpet in reply, a clean shot between the eyes.

Cassidy tiptoed from the doorway, peering to the head of the hall. "Someone's bound to have heard that."

"You can't ever do anything the quiet way, can you?" Moone groused, poking at the body with the toe of his boot, stripping away the man's gun belt. "So much for that plan."

"Now what?" Cass caught the bundle of leather and bullets, diving to the floor when another crack of gunfire rang out. She twisted the belt around her waist, flipping one of her pearl-gripped revolvers into the holster.

Moone grinned, fiendish and fiery. "Now, you show me how good you are with those pistols, Freckles."

As if in answer, one of Ransom's men appeared from around the corner. Then another.

Cass darted to her feet, putting him down, the other before his shadow fully cast upon the floor.

She blew a red curl from her forehead. "We're sitting ducks. Let's move."

"Were you planning on walking out the front door?" Moone pushed on, picking off another as he and Cassidy rounded the corner.

In view of the atrium, Cassidy knew they didn't stand a chance for long unless they played their cards perfectly.

Shielded by a stone railing, she peeked, taking stock of every trace of shadow behind a pillar and the quiet clink of a spur hidden behind closed doors.

They were outnumbered, outgunned. They'd be lucky to escape without a scratch.

"Solo's saddlebags are all packed. We just have to make it to the stable."

Moone nodded, barely flinching when a *zing* rained bits of stone over their heads. He shot up, firing off a trio of bullets. Enough to buy them a few seconds to bolt to the top of the stairs.

Cassidy buzzed, body alight as they fought their way down. Toppling a man from the balustrade, leaving another bleeding in the doorway of the library.

They were close, so close.

Once they reached the first floor, Cass and Moone quickly cleared the long corridor leading to the kitchen. It was all so easy. *Too* easy.

Moone gave her a victorious smile, beaming as he beckoned her into the night's shadows with a stretch of his hand—

Until a voice called her name.

James's blue eyes were wild. He shook his head when it called for her again—when *he* called for her. "Don't."

Cassidy's heart shattered when he looked at her with such pain, with such hope she'd want him more. But when Ransom's voice sang her name like a lover, her mind had been made up before he polished off the last syllable. Fate stirred the depths of her heart, tugging on the thread of her desires.

It was giving her one last chance.

Her voice cracked. "I have to try. I *have to*."

Moone played his part to perfection, falling into the role he abandoned, the darkness that raised him, and the twisted games he didn't want her to stain herself with. She'd learned that James Moone was better than all that. He was better than the trappings and the death deals. He was *good*. Her good deputy, *the* best of all of them. She had to try, even if just to save him.

"I'm sorry," Cassidy whispered, shivering when Ransom purred her name again and again. Her eyes went to Moone, fingers gripping his shirt. Her lips found his, a quiet reminder of what they were, what they could've been. "I wish we had more time. I'm sorry I wasted it with all this."

"We *will* have more time. Plenty of time, Cassidy. I'll meet you out front." Moone rolled his jaw, a flurry of emotions etched into his handsome face. He didn't want to let her go; he wanted her to run. But more than anything, he *understood*. "Don't miss."

She grinned and kissed him again before shoving him into the brisk night air. "I won't."

Stomach leaden the moment he vanished, Cassidy emerged from the shadows of the kitchen corridor, hand hovering over the pistols on her hips. Every muscle coiled at the ready, eager to practice her quickest draw yet.

The eyes.

Cassidy felt them first. They glowed like bats in a cavern, hovering on the edges of the balustrade, appearing one after the other. Her first thought was to cover herself, to shield the sheet of freckles on her chest and the swell of her breasts perked against the night's chill beneath her shift.

But they watched her for another reason. She was the one who got close enough to best their master. Cassidy smirked at the thought.

"Such a pretty, murderous little thing. You've made quite a mess of things, haven't you?"

Cassidy's eyes slid to Ransom on the second floor— chest bare, head bleeding, dark eyes filled with fire.

She shivered.

He looked like he could eat her alive.

She gave him a simpering smile, gaze unyielding as she side-stepped toward the front door. "Not murderous enough if you're still standing."

One step at a time. She might have a chance to escape if

she could keep him talking.

Ransom chuckled, a dark, dangerous rumble. It set her teeth on edge. "You've certainly got spirit, Cassidy. Spirit in *spades*. I had hoped bedding you proved exciting, but this"— he brushed the crimson line on his throat—"was more than I bargained for."

"Sorry to disappoint," Cassidy spat, sliding another foot toward the door.

Ransom threw back his head and *laughed*. It set a chill to the air, as if a dragon delighted in the moments before roasting his prey alive. "Disappointed? My darling, I am *overjoyed*. More tantalizing than Aisling ever was. I very much look forward to our wedding night."

"Wedding night?" Cassidy barked out a laugh. "After all this, after everything I told you, you really think there's *marriage* on the horizon?"

"But of course. I *love* you." Ransom cocked his head, cold smile frozen upon his face. "You're mine, pet."

Mine.

The word echoed through her, the ring on her finger like lead. Every inch of her skin prickled.

"I'm not." Cassidy stood straighter, squaring her shoulders, planting her feet the way her Da taught her. "I don't belong to *anyone*. And you wouldn't know love if it spat in your face."

"What an odd thing to say." Ransom lifted a brow. "I loved her, too. Him as well."

Too long. All of it was taking too long.

Cassidy chuffed. "Look where that got them."

"Yes." He leaned over the railing. "But we're different, Cassidy, you and I. So different from them. Think of what we could do together. Think of what we could conquer."

She shook her head. "I don't want that."

His smile wavered. "And me?"

Cassidy's fingers ached, twisting toward her pistol as more faces appeared on the mezzanine around their master. They could be hers if she wanted, if she was willing to live in this gilded cage.

Anything you wanted, I'd lay at your feet.

"I've never wanted you in any way but *dead*." Cassidy's hand flew to her holster, firing off a shot before any of them could blink—

And sent a rainfall of glass down upon them when her bullet blew a hole in the glass atrium.

Ransom didn't flinch, hadn't balked. As if he knew her bullet wouldn't find its target.

"You wound me, pet," he tutted, nodding to no one.

The world around her exploded with gunfire, tenfold what it'd been before.

She dove behind a plant, terracotta blistering, flying, and flinging.

A shot. Two. Another.

Bodies fell.

Her ears rang. Someone shouted her name. Lead ripped through the flesh in her thigh. Fire erupted in her veins. Glass bit her cheeks. But she couldn't give in to the pain. Not yet. Not ever.

Cassidy's eyes darted to the door.

Steps. Only steps away.

She flung herself from behind her hiding place, unloading each chamber, squinting against debris as she wrenched open the oak door and flew into the night air.

A fearsome squeal split the darkness. Hooves beat the ground. Moone bellowed her name, cantering on Solo's back with an outstretched hand.

His fingers gripped around her wrist as she leaped, wounded leg be damned, vaulting herself into the saddle behind him.

Moone's drumming heartbeat beneath her fingers was a welcome comfort, warding away the brittle chill from her bare shoulders.

The relief lasted only a moment when Cassidy took a nauseating look back.

The manor on the hill shrunk into the distance, a gilded halo on the horizon. But, at their backs, pinpricks of shadow against the electric glow of Ransom's house, were a dozen riders.

"Faster!" Cassidy shouted over the thunder of hooves beating the earth.

Solo surged forward, flying over sagebrush and stone—a beautiful beast whose tether had been cut free.

A bullet zinged past, ricocheting against a boulder.

Cassidy glanced back and swore. "They're gaining on us."

Another echo of gunfire. One after the other, until Cassidy thought a storm rolled in from the Pacific.

She flipped open the cylinder of her pistol, shakily pressing six rounds in their chambers as she held to Solo's back with a squeeze of her thighs.

Cassidy flipped it shut with a twist of her wrist, pressing a free hand to Moone's chest as she turned to fire.

One rider hit the ground. Then another. And another.

Lightning ripped through her shoulder, shredding through her flesh like wildfire down to her fingers. Her grasp on the pistol loosened. She groaned, crying out when the gleaming pearl grip slipped from her fingers and fell to

the ground.

"I'm shot," Cassidy gasped, pressing her cheek to Moone's shoulder.

The warmth of his hand covered hers, voice buzzing beneath her fingertips. "Come on, pal. She needs us. They won't chase us after a mile."

Untethered, Solo *flew*, leaping over stone and bone-dry creeks like they were nothing. The air split with sharp staccato blows of his breathing and the rhythm of his hooves. Cassidy swore she heard his heart beating as loud as a song as he rode as hard and fast as he could—for her sake.

Another half dozen shots rang out, pealing through the blackness one after the other.

Solo veered, loosing a fearsome squeal and surging forward faster than before. He'd become the night itself—limitless darkness curled with the wind as it carved through desert bluffs and star-hewn sky.

Cassidy's head swam, her thoughts fuzzy. Time slipped away, giving way to blackness of another kind.

"*CASSIDY!*" Moone's voice stirred her. The wild blaze of panic that followed sent a flood of energy through her.

The sable stallion ran faster than ever, but his breathing was ragged; heavy and wet with her worst nightmare.

"He's wounded." Moone's voice cracked. "I noticed a half-mile back. We've lost them, but he won't quit... he won't let up."

Cassidy's heart shattered. It roared in her ears, screaming for a way to fix it, to fix him.

"Solo, *steady* now." She kept her voice level, soft as a whisper. His black ears flicked back, but he wouldn't give in.

Moone peered over his shoulder, blue eyes alight with pain. "I don't know what to do. I dug in my heels, pulled on the reins—*nothing.*"

"I know," she murmured, chin quivering as the wind whipped through her curls. Cassidy slipped a hand around Moone, reaching as far as the wound in her shoulder would allow. Her fingers brushed against Solo's silken coat. "Hey, sweet thing. It's time to rest. We can't run all day, no"—her voice crumpled—"no matter how much you want to."

Solo wheezed, letting up on his speed. But now she'd pulled the pin, the stallion lost his momentum, staggering once, twice—

"Hold on!" Moone twisted, clamped his arms around her, and *leaped.*

Down they tumbled across sharp crags of stone and biting sand. Cassidy cried out as she slid, blindly searching for purchase, for Moone, for Solo—for anything.

"James?" Cassidy bleated, wheezing, rolling to her back.

"Here," he answered, boots scuffling through soil as he crouched. His eyes darted over her, hands hovering over the wounds in her shoulder and leg. "You're hurt."

"M'fine." Cassidy moaned when he gently hoisted her to her feet. "Are you—"

His gaze softened, thumb caressing the curve of her cheek. "I'm okay." He cast a look over her shoulder, brows pleating. "I'm sorry."

Cassidy whirled, chasing the sound of Solo's rasps. She clenched her stomach, batting away Moone's hovering hands. Her toes dragged through the soil, legs like lead when she spied the inky bulge on the earth.

His ribcage shuddered. Glossy sheets of blood coated his side, pulsing from the base of his neck with every breath.

"Hey, sweet thing." Cassidy sank to her knees, laying a palm on his velvety cheek. His soulful eyes blinked at her, nose flaring as he gave a half-hearted attempt at a nicker. It rattled and stalled, shattering her heart to smithereens. Her shoulders shook, vision blurred. Hot tears streamed down her cheeks.

This was *her* fault. She good as signed his death warrant the moment she put him in that stable, as if too few sugar cubes would be payment enough for what he'd done for her.

Solo had been there for her longer than *anyone*, steadier than the Mississippi, more loyal than the bravest of knights. They'd grown up together, and now—

Now Solo gave *everything* for her.

Cassidy pressed her forehead against his cheek with a whisper. "You did good."

She surged to her feet, stumbling into Moone's arms with a pained keen. It echoed through the night. Loud and long enough, the coyotes answered her call.

He held her until her cries ebbed, stroking her hair with quiet, loving whispers.

"Cassidy…" Moone held her face and pressed his nose against her cheek. Comfort reverberated through him, through *her*, but nothing took away the sting of what came next. "We need to help him."

Cassidy lurched back, bile rising at the thought.

James stepped closer, his voice as soft as a father to a child. "I can do it. I'll put him down. It's what's best, Cass."

"I know it's what's best," she hissed, closing her eyes with a lift of her chin. She reveled in the silence, in the chance to think, to breathe. But the reminder of Solo's pain split the quiet with another squelching wheeze.

Cassidy opened her eyes, gasping out another sob when Moone hovered a breath away.

"He's my brother." Every syllable trembled. "I have to

do it."

Moone nodded. "I know."

She stared down at her hands, throat thick. "I've never loved anything or anyone except him." Silver-lined green met blue. "Not until you. And I didn't deserve it. I *don't* deserve it. I—I abandoned him. I *left* him instead of loving him. How do I make up for that?"

"Because you love him, Cassidy." James slipped the handle of a revolver into her hand. "That's how you show him your love. End his pain."

[40]

Moone

Moone ached in places he didn't think possible. From his shoulders to the very marrow of his bones, there wasn't an inch of him that didn't complain.

His pain was nothing compared to Cassidy's.

Her wails rang in his ears long after the revolver's echo ebbed to nothing, cutting through the night sky like a shooting star. In the shadow of it—of her sorrow—even the midnight chatter of the desert went still.

Moone's mind ran as he held her. He hoped to stave off the chill while she shivered through her sobs. Every time he tried to release her, Cassidy's fingers dug into his sleeve. Her silence spoke volumes.

Please don't go.

He whispered in her ear, cradling her to his chest as the moon sank toward the horizon and coyotes yipped and yowled on the wind. "Cassidy, we can't stay here. You'll freeze, and they aren't going to stay away from the body for long."

Moone stripped Solo of his saddlebags and blanket. He hesitated when it came to his bridle. It wouldn't be of any use to them on the road, but he took it anyway, gingerly pulling it free from over the stallion's ears. Cassidy might want it—a keepsake of the brother she'd been forced to leave behind.

They made it a quarter mile before the coyotes closed in and commenced their desert burial of the sable stallion. The mutts sang of him until dawn stretched her fingers into the depths of inky blue.

Cassidy was silent.

When morning came, they set off toward Rose Reach. They'd nearly made it the night before. If it hadn't been for a bit of lead, or Moone stopping her from finishing it; if he'd had the courage to do it himself weeks ago—if it hadn't been for Ransom at all—stepping back into The Palace Hotel might've felt different.

Moone allowed himself to whip up a fantasy in the darkest recesses of his mind before they stepped foot in Ransom's house. One where Cassidy turned back from Madame Dubuisson's, and they ventured straight back to Rose Reach and discovered each other in ways he'd dreamed about.

Gear slung over his shoulder, Cassidy in naught but her bare feet and Solo's saddle blanket over her shift, the concierge's face went pale like he'd seen a ghost. Maybe that's what they were. Maybe their time in Beatrice made them slivers of the people they were the last time they'd rode into town.

Neither of them were the same. Maybe they'd never be the same again.

Moone slapped down a stack of money, more than enough to secure them a suite for a month or more—no questions asked. It was all he had. He'd have to find a way to go back for the rest and finish the job.

Cassidy was worse than before, battered and bloodied. Eyes half-closed and unfocused. Shoulders slumped. Broken. It was hauntingly different from the shadows that haunted her after the massacre at Cody. So different, Moone wished it was the former all over again. At least, then, he knew how to put her back together.

In the safety of their suite, Moone bathed her again, trailing a damp cloth over her curves, bandaging her feet, and kissing the bruises until only the bullet wounds remained. Those would require a different touch.

"Drink." Moone curled her fingers around a bottle of whiskey.

He half expected her to argue, to push when he ordered her around. But she brought it to her lips, drinking it down in fat gulps as she stared at nothing on the wall from the edge of the bed.

Cassidy's eyes cut to the waiting needle and thread; scrounged up by the concierge from the in-house seamstress. Another swig, then a nod.

Moone knelt, thumbing the hot flesh where a bullet tore through her shoulder.

"Through and through," he murmured, motioning for the bottle. She wordlessly passed it, brow barely wrinkling when he poured it through the wound. "You're lucky you're not dead, Freckles."

Cassidy's chest quivered, closing her eyes when the hooked needle pierced her flesh. Her fingers found his shoulder, pressing deep into the muscle while he knit the pieces of her back together. He'd let her squeeze him until he fell apart like aged stone; he could take it. It showed him she was still there.

Moone was content in the silence, with only the whisper of the fire and her breathing as the metronome he worked to. He never expected her to speak.

"I'm ready to talk." Each syllable shuddered, laced with pain and grief.

Moone slipped a bloodied thread around his finger and tied off the end, severing taut cotton with the tip of Ransom's jeweled dagger. "You don't have to."

"I want to," she bit out when he moved to the other side. "I need the distraction."

"Alright," Moone answered, twining a fresh strand of thread through the needle.

As long as he'd known her, he'd wanted Cassidy Callaghan to open up to him. He wished for it more times than he could count. Demanded it.

It was the longest fought battle in their history.

All the times he'd imagined it happening—all the times it finally did—she'd only ever give a glimpse, the barest taste of her. Other times, the truth spilled out, sometimes more than he ever gave her about his own past. Still, all her truths, every word—merely footnotes of who she was.

Never did he think it'd be like *this*, her story spelled out in blood as he stitched her back together. Another battle lost, a victory out of reach, and Cassidy broken in ways Moone wasn't sure he'd be able to heal; in ways he wasn't worthy to fix for her.

"As long as I can remember—" Cassidy paused, running a tongue over dry lips. "I've thought of my mother as a princess. I knew she and Da came from far away. He always sang about Ireland and told me stories of emerald hills and white cliffs. All of it, all their songs and tales only cemented the idea.

"Sometimes, I wandered through her things." Cassidy's expression shifted, pivoting from staring at nothing, to exploring something Moone couldn't see: a place in her mind, in her memories. "I buried my face in dresses I was too scared to pull from the trunk. I'd dance my fingers over words I couldn't read in her journals—dozens of them. I even put her silver combs in my hair. I was sure to be in a heap of trouble if she caught me."

Moone tied off another thread, gathering a ribbon of linen bandages from the bed. The hairs on his arms lifted as he leaned in, cheek brushing over the curve of her breast as he bound the wound to protect his work. He didn't dare say a word, unwilling to break the spell, to stop her in the middle of the story.

Her eyes darkened, without a single ounce of pain as he settled on the bed beside her and began stitching the gash in her thigh.

"I asked her, once. I asked her to tell me the story of where she was from, of how she and Da met—but she refused. I saw something, then. A shadow, like she was haunted by what happened. I didn't know what it meant, then. I didn't know *who*. She brushed me off and sang me a song, instead. Again and again, no matter what. And, since she wouldn't tell me, I took those pretty dresses, those combs, those beautiful words I couldn't understand, and I made one up."

"In my head, I'd imagine those white cliffs, I'd see her in those dresses—that princess. One betrothed to a prince, handsome and sublime. And no matter how wonderful he seemed in my imagination, he wasn't who she loved."

"Your father?" Moone asked.

She smiled again, lighting up her entire face despite the

pain. "The stable boy. I never knew if that's what they were, not really. She hid the journals in a better place before I had the chance to look at them once I could read. But still—imagining them at the bow of a ship, the wind in their hair, escaping a dark fate to live free—it nearly gave me wings as a little girl."

"No wonder you like those books so much."

Cassidy took another drink, hissing through her teeth when he gave the thread in her thigh one final tug. "We were happy. *They* were happy. At least, I think they were. As little as she told me, I knew she loved him in her way. They loved *me*. I never doubted that."

Moone drew himself up, lingering by the mantle after laying another log on the fire as she continued.

"There was always *something*, though—a shadow—this *thing* that haunted them. I'd hear them whisper and argue about it. He'd tell her not to worry. He'd tell her they were so far away, that it'd been so long, there was no way he'd find them. That we were *safe*. But, when I was barely old enough to read, a telegram came. I'd never seen her so scared. Through fires and storms, droughts… nothing scared her like that little piece of parchment."

She stopped with a shudder, a quaking breath that set a chill cutting through the fire's warmth. Moone shivered when he looked at her, shoulders slumped, curled into herself as if she were still a child, and her words hurled her back to the center of the story.

"They came before the school bell rang. I didn't understand then, not for years, that my Da always knew he'd come. He taught me *everything*. He wove a code into my blood. He taught me to be good, like he didn't want me to be like *him*—like Ransom.

"He blew in like a storm and left just as quickly." She shook her head, brows puckered as a tear slipped down her cheek. "If it hadn't been for our shop or the church, you'd think that all of Faraday Creek got up one morning and walked away. That's… that's why I saw red in Cody. *So much* of it was the same, except they left their dead scattered."

"Where were you?" Moone's voice was like gravel.

"He hid me in the cellar." A sob tore through her. She drowned the sound with another swill of whiskey. Maybe then, the ache inside her might be soothed. "I saw all of it, and it was over before I could blink.

"With fifteen years to think about it, I built him up in my mind. I—I conjured the image of this monster, of the Devil, who swept in and took everything I loved in one fell swoop. But, when I met him… when I finally came face-to-face with this *idea*, I realized he's just a man. I thought I could trick him. I thought I could make him believe I was like her. That I was his memory come to life, a fantasy of what he wanted, what he asked of her before he killed her. I thought I could make a fool out of him, but the fool was *me*."

"You're not a fool, Cassidy." Moone swept to her side, kneeling as he took her hand in his. He couldn't let her swim in the darkness any longer. Not alone. Not when what she was thinking was the furthest thing from the truth. "You're smarter than all the rest of us."

She shook her head, wearing a wistful smile. "It's alright. I know I was. I had a plan. I've hidden in plain sight more times than I can count, but we got there, I met him, and I… I got swept up in it. In the life he offered and the sweet things he said. I drank the poison, and"—she closed her eyes, licking her lips—"it was sweet. I won't lie. I tried not to, but I *liked* it. I liked being doted on. I loved reading the day away. I loved it so much, I nearly forgot why I was there. Until he reminded me of who he was. The Devil showed his face, and I'm the fool who nearly convinced herself all of it had been a figment of my imagination. Another story."

She idly traced a scar on the back of his hand, chewing the inside of her lip with a tremble of her chin. "Did I ever tell you they burned the church with all of Faraday Creek locked inside?"

Moone swallowed the rising bile in his throat. She never told him, but he knew. He saw it happen. Still a boy, still green, with a fresh blue handkerchief that branded him as Ransom's.

Faraday Creek was his baptism.

He'd hovered on the edges, too young, too weak to tear the townspeople from their shops as the other men did. Still, Jimmy Moone did what he was told, firmly holding the reins of Ransom's horse while his master disappeared into the General Store.

He never realized there was a little girl hiding just steps away. He never knew it was *her*.

Moone heard the screams. The thunder of fists on shiplap haunted him the same way it did Cassidy, but he'd never tell her how he'd watched Ransom drag Aisling into the street by a handful of copper hair. He'd never utter that he'd emptied his stomach when the shot sliced through the air—or how Ransom's men beat him for it when they found out.

Cassidy wilted, shoulders sinking beneath the weight of her memories. "I waited until the church stopped burning before I made a run for it. I didn't—I didn't want to risk running into anyone who lingered."

"How far did you make it?"

She shook her head. "Not far. Not the first night. I made it home to our ranch. I thought it'd be safe… but they came back the next morning."

Moone couldn't look her in the eye. He *knew* Ransom's men came back as she said. The recollection soured in his stomach. He could still smell the smoke on the wind, the faint scent of fine, flowery perfume clinging to gingham curtains, and the sight of a scared, green-eyed little girl hiding beneath the bed frame.

He never told anyone about it, and he never forgot the taste of his lie when he told the others the house was empty; nothing of value in sight. Least of all the diamond ring he'd stolen—least of all *her.*

It only proved that sometimes, to lie was the best choice—the only choice.

He cleared his throat, squeezing her hand. "How'd you meet Solo?"

Cassidy laughed. It shattered his black heart to smithereens, to see the joy and pain the memory of him brought. "I don't know if I believe in a higher power. My life's been shit half the time. But I swear, God sent that horse to me as a guardian angel. I ran from the ranch until my feet bled. I built a fire, managed to trap something for dinner. When I woke up—there he was. He was so young, so scared. Probably left behind by his herd."

"Like you," Moone said.

"Just like me." She smiled, a haunted echo to what she'd gifted him with in the past. "There wasn't any rhyme or reason to it. It didn't make sense that this wild thing would want to befriend or help me. But, from that first moment, he was my shadow, my protector—*my brother.* And I abandoned him." Her voice cracked. "I left him to rot in that barn while Ransom dressed me up and took me to parties."

Moone hooked a knuckle beneath her chin, lifting her gaze to meet his, if only for a moment. "I'd hardly call what he was doing in that livery rotting, Cass. I snuck him sugar cubes every chance I got."

"Maybe not, but he hated being cooped up. He wanted to *run*. And the last time he got to… the last time I *let* him—"

A sob tore through her; a brief surrender to the grief she'd barely let herself feel. It revealed the truth of her love—the love Cassidy rarely gave to any living soul. Her shoulders shook, breathing ragged.

Moone didn't know where to begin. He'd pieced her together the best way he knew how, but the wounds that mattered most weren't the kind he could bandage.

He gathered her in his arms, sweeping her into his lap without another thought. Hands in her hair, Moone carried away her tears with his lips, replacing the hurt the only way he could think of.

"It should've been me. I should've stayed. I wasn't afraid to die. I meant that. I could've killed Ransom and gone with him. It wouldn't have been the worst thing." Cassidy lifted her gaze, green eyes lined with silver as her body melted against his chest. "But I let myself *want* something beyond revenge. For the first time, I wanted something for myself. I imagined a life—the one you talked about. I imagined *you*. I pictured you every moment I was with him, and it *stirred* something in me. I know I'm all talk so much of the time, but I—" She shifted, eyes blazing, like the fire within her had been lit once more. Moone knew it couldn't last. She needed something he couldn't give her, the kind of rest to quiet her grief.

But when she slotted his hips between her knees, fingers twisted in his hair, every other thought fell away. It was clear, then, Cassidy didn't want to rest. His mind argued, but his body answered the call, springing to attention when her mouth found his.

"Cassidy," he growled, swiping the whiskey-stained taste of her from his lips. The woolen blanket covering her fell to a puddle on the floor. "We shouldn't. You're hurt. I ought to go to an apothecary and get you some proper medicine."

"I'm fine," she breathed, rolling her hips against him. "You have all the medicine I need right here."

Moone would give her anything. He'd crack open his chest and offer up his heart if she asked. Who was he to deny her if it'd help ease her pain?

"You're *not* fine." Fingers pressed into her hips, he flipped her to her back. He couldn't resist touching her for long, palming the supple skin of her stomach. She'd grown curves in their time at Ransom's estate, soft in places she'd been bony before. Not like he was an expert in the shape of her body until the night before, but James Moone studied it long before she donned silks and petticoats.

"I am," she argued, lifting her shoulders from the bed.

"No," Moone said sternly, hand splayed out over her breasts as he pushed her back down. "This isn't going to go the way you think."

"James," Cassidy whispered, eyes blazing, cheeks flushed. Her body spoke to his, the bellow to the flame of his desire, burning hotter when she uttered a single word, *"Please."*

Moone pulled away his vest and shirt, tearing away the layers while she fiddled with the latch of his belt. "I want to give you what you want, Cassidy, but there will be *rules.*"

Her brows shot up. "Rules?"

He nodded, sinking to his knees with a grin. "I know that might be a difficult concept for you, Freckles." He trailed his tongue around the curve of her breast, then the other, smiling to himself when her body canted as he rolled the peak between his teeth.

"W-what are the rules, Moone?" Cass ground out, fingers tangled in his hair.

If she wanted a distraction, if she needed *him* to fill the ache within her, Moone was happy to oblige. But *his* way.

"The last time we did this, it went too quickly." He wound his way down her torso, mapping a path of molten kisses along the way. "This time will require a *gentle* touch. No moving." He nipped at her stomach, lifting his gaze to find her raptly watching him. "If you tear your stitches, I'll be *very* upset."

Moone surveyed her spread out before him, curls fanned out over the bed like a fiery halo. Brushing his fingers down her legs, he met her eye again, silently making it known what he planned. How he vowed to take her again, and again, *and again*—a feast to be devoured—as long as she did what she was told.

Cassidy writhed, choking out another strangled, "*Please*," when his calloused hands held the curve of her thighs.

He smiled, splitting her open, wasting no time in pressing his mouth to the heart of her. He told her it'd require a gentler touch, but he'd only made promises for his cock—not his mouth.

Moone thought about the taste of her a hundred different ways, taking himself in-hand, pumping himself dry with the memory of spreading her feet with the toe of his boot, chest pressed against her back as he slapped a pair of shackles on her wrists.

He'd pictured them against the wall, on the desk, or rattling the iron bars of the cell.

No one else would ever be enough to fulfill him. No one but her.

He tried over the years, but it wasn't as easy as it was for Cassidy, who'd disappear into Ridley's for the night, and come back wearing the smile of a cat who'd eaten the canary. But no matter the girl, none of them satiated him the way he wanted with her—the way he *had* with her.

Moone swore when he traced a finger against her center—amazed at how ready, how perfect she was, how much she wanted him, too.

He sucked at the peak, rolling it between his teeth, trailing his tongue over her, through her, 'round and 'round as she moaned. All the while, he kept a palm pressed to her abdomen, holding her still as he curled his tongue into her core.

"*Moone—*"

"Say my name, Cassidy," he growled against her, giving another unhurried lave of his tongue. "I love the way it sounds on your lips."

She whimpered; boneless, *wordless*. All for him.

"Say it," Moone coaxed, tracing the tip of his finger against her peak. "Tell me what you want, Cassidy."

"James," she keened, head lolling, chest heaving.

His cock strained against his trousers at the sound, begging to be freed, to feel her, to hear his name on her tongue, to steal it away with a kiss so he might carry it with him.

"Again." Moone eased in a finger, grinning like a wolf against her sex when she cried out, rolling her hips to take him deeper, begging for more. "You didn't tell me what you wanted."

"Y-you, James." Cassidy let out a sob when he slid in another with the first, curling them in as he laved his tongue against her, around her, feasting on her like a man starved. "I want you."

Again, she ground against him, singing the song of him—of them—so loudly, Moone was sure they might hear it on the streets below. He pushed harder, keeping the same, achingly unhurried pace, determined to savor the taste of her, of what he did to her.

Cassidy went rigid, crying out as he pumped into her, sucking, licking, and *devouring* until she went limp, tugging on his hair to draw his lips to hers.

Moone groaned, shuddering as she plundered his mouth, stealing away the taste of her on his tongue. Her hands wandered, blindly ripping at his trousers, pushing at them until he sprang free.

"Greedy little thing, aren't you?" he drawled, gathering her wrists between long, calloused fingers. Moone trailed his mouth along her arms, following her freckles as he lifted them above her head. He kissed her, again, anchoring himself between her thighs. "Don't move."

"No promises, Deputy." Cassidy smirked, tilting her chin to press her mouth to his, nipping at his lip.

Moone blinked, caught up in the look in her eyes—his wild girl, the same way she'd looked at him for years. Always a challenge, a game of cat and mouse; one where she'd push his buttons to see what she could get away with, and he'd flip her over his shoulder before the day was through.

Over and over they danced, flirting with the idea of what they should be.

Moone wished it hadn't cost so much to realize it—what

he needed to be in order to have her.

"If you want to play that way, Freckles—I'll play."

Morning came too soon.

Moone granted Cassidy's wish, but his way, fulfilling his promise of something unhurried. The healing kind of comfort she required.

A distraction, just as she always accused him of being.

This time, he was happy to fulfill it until she sang in his ear.

After, copper hair wild and body flushed, Cassidy finally slept.

Moone curled up with her, holding her against his chest in the whisper of firelight. Eventually, though, the faint buzz in the back of his mind won out, summoning him to keep a watchful eye out the window to the street below. Just in case.

He thought for sure they'd leave for Gallow Gorge at first light, likely at Cassidy's insistence. But she never woke him up to tell him so.

The sun stretched above the brick buildings of Rose Reach, wasted daylight for their journey ahead.

Moone counted the minutes, his eye on her instead of the street, carefully observing every steady rise and fall of her chest. Her body curled into the blankets like she was still a child. The hours turned into a day, and when night fell, even the promise of a hearty dinner couldn't rouse her.

So, Moone watched. He waited.

He'd done it plenty of times before, keeping a weather eye on the horizon for her to return with a bounty. He'd do it again.

This was no different.

H E NEVER THOUGHT A HANDKERCHIEF COULD BE SO heavy. That doing something as simple as holding a man's horse could pose such a challenge, or that having a heart was an even bigger one.

The bruises were bone-deep, ones meant to be a lesson for his weakness—deserved for disobeying orders. It should've been simple, they said. One day, he'd be the muscle, but not today. Today, all he had to do was stay put and watch. Watch and learn.

But the screams prickled the finest hairs on the back of his neck. The fire ripping through the church turned his stomach. He couldn't help but dive out of sight to hide how sick he got when his mentor blew a hole in her head.

Not even a hasty burying of it with his boot hid it from his lackeys or the punishment that came swiftly after.

Not like he meant it, that weakness. He'd seen many things in his young life, too many things. It wasn't so bad when his mother was still alive, not when she was strong enough to defend him against his Pa once he fell to the bottom of a bottle. Jolene Moone took the brunt of it, carrying a load heavier than any woman should once it started.

But all bets were off once cholera claimed her.

He used to pray, sure no one was listening. He prayed over her in those final hours, tearfully gathering spearmint and chamomile from her garden to make her tea, wet her lips, and bring the glow back to her cheeks. James wanted to fix her, to save her.

If he did good, if he was good, then the punishment would never come.

Maybe he could be like him. Maybe he could scare those men the way their master did.

Maybe they'd never call him Jimmy again.

[41]

Cassidy's ears rang. She slept for days. Her wounds healed, but the sound remained. Even as the steady *click-clack, click-clack, click-clack* of the train draped over the car, it persisted.

She leaned against Moone's shoulder as the California desert flew by, eyes fixed on a bubble in the glass. Mile by mile disappeared, carrying them closer to home, further away from the nightmare.

After three days, they left Rose Reach. Moone scrounged up clothes for them both—she didn't bother to ask from where or how.

Cassidy eyed his brown wool vest, trousers, and overcoat—gun belt slung over his hips. Her own were tucked away in their luggage. There was no place for a holster on what he'd found for her. She wanted to be sore Moone hadn't brought trousers for them both, but the soft indigo dress was too pleasing for the thought to linger long. She didn't have any use for trousers, anyway. Not when they tried to blend in as they put miles between them and Sacramento.

Civilization fell away, and the finely clothed ladies and

gentlemen departed their car by the fourth stop. Cassidy fell asleep again not long after, lulled by the sway of the train and Moone's warmth against her cheek.

In her dreams, the ringing in her ears grew to a roar, shining a bright, bloody beam of light on Ransom's face leering over her, hands on her throat as she kissed Death hello.

You're mine.

A gasp tore through her, eyes wild, hands trembling. Her breath came in sharp waves, stilled only by Moone's fingers twisted with hers and the low, quiet thrum of his voice against her cheek.

"You're safe, Cassidy. It's over."

But it wasn't over. It never would be so long as Jack's face haunted her dreams, not now that she'd started the story back at the beginning. Over and over, she cycled through it. She was so tired, more tired than she'd ever been. Her eyes would droop, she'd slump against Moone's shoulder, and be ripped back to consciousness a moment later.

Hours went by in a blur, stacked atop the other. The train was faster than any horse—even Solo. The afternoon sun blazed high when the train slowed once more, and Moone rose to his feet.

The station at Gallow Gorge was nothing to speak of. Barely held together boards made up a ticket booth manned once a week with a map of the line. It was the quietest place in the whole town. Quieter, still, once the train pulled away, leaving Cass and Moone alone on the platform.

He puffed his chest out, smile playing on his lips. "You ready to go home, Freckles?"

Cassidy shielded her eyes from the glare, squinting toward the silhouette of Gallow Gorge a quarter mile away.

Her skin prickled, as if an oncoming storm sent a charge through the air.

"Something's wrong."

Moone twisted, grin falling away as he followed her gaze and back. "You can't know that." He stepped closer, thumbing the curve of her cheek. "You're being paranoid."

She rolled her shoulders. The hair on her arms climbed, shifting like prairie grasses in a windstorm. Her eyes flitted back and forth over the horizon, over the meager station, collecting every detail of the town she knew by heart—her home.

"Look." Cassidy stepped to the ticket counter, hand shaking as she plucked a frayed shred of fabric from a loose nail—a piece of a faded blue handkerchief.

She held it between them. Moone's eyes widened, but they could barely consider what it meant when the bright clang of the church's bell split the eerie silence.

Cassidy took off at a run, barreling towards town with Moone hot on her heels. Her feet, her shoulder, her thigh—every inch of her protested, repaired just days before.

The dusty streets of Gallow Gorge were quiet. Every bustling corner silenced. Gone was the tinny twang of the player piano from the saloon on the corner. The *ting ting ting* of the farrier's hammer—vanished. No voices, no laughter. Not even boisterous hollering from the balconies of Ridley's.

A ghost town.

"*No*," Cassidy gasped, fingers gripping her stomach, searching for something to hang onto as she sought a friendly face—something to ease the panic that Ransom had come and taken everything from her all over again.

One appeared, ashen and haunted. Cassidy thought it might've been a ghost, but another materialized in a window in the dressmaker's shop next door. Then another, and another, and three more after that.

One by one, the residents of Gallow Gorge emerged from their hiding places. All of them stared at her, *through her*, carrying her eyes down the bend in the road where a plume of black smoke curled skyward.

"Cassidy, wait!" Moone pleaded, fingers brushing her sleeve when she tore down the street, stumbling in the soft soil as she ran.

Another grating chime of the church bell tolled. The sound towed her, pulling her by an invisible rope around her middle. Her chest burned, and feet ached, but none so much as the shattering of her heart when the evidence of what'd been done rose up before her.

The church, bright white shiplap shining in the desert sunshine, was scarred. Black stripes licked up the sides of smashed-in windows. Parts of it still stood, pieces of charred wood barely holding together as the exposed skeleton in the steeple shuddered beneath the weight of a brass bell—and a bundle of chains around the door handle.

There, weaving from the rafters like a reed in the wind, swung a body. Blackened by the flames, Cassidy knew the shape of a child without thinking.

She lurched, tearing at the chains, kicking, swearing, ripping away. Voices called out to her, murmuring it was no use; they tried, that she was already dead.

"Cassidy, quit." Moone's hands pulled at her. "It isn't safe."

She shoved him away. "No, I have to help her!"

Her ears rang. Her fingers screamed the longer she tore at hot metal and charred wood. None of it mattered. Not the pain, the voices shouting for her to stop, only the shape of her swinging from the rafters.

"*CASSIDY, STOP!*"

Moone's arms were around her, and before she could blink, her lungs burned as they crashed to the ground. The metallic concussion reverberated through her, down to the marrow of her bones. Soil flew, an explosion of it clouding her vision, her lungs.

Cass coughed, palms pressed against James's chest as the dust cleared.

His hands searched her face, wiping away every speck of dirt as he looked for signs of injury. Moone stood, carrying her with him. "Are you alright?"

"I'm fine." She spun, stomach sinking when she took stock of a brass bell the size of a horse half-buried in the ground where she'd been standing a moment before. Clouds of dust curled, settling onto the charred remains of the Gallow Gorge chapel, now half a skeleton of what was.

A crowd had gathered, shadows of the residents that filled their grimy old town with life.

"What happened? Who did this?" Cassidy's gaze slid from face to face. Each one was silent, a somber reminder of the cost, the price for what she'd done. Her stomach sank to her feet. She might as well bury it with the bell when she found the mustachioed face of the general store owner, Mister Booker, and his wife.

"Where's Daisy?" Cassidy's knees wavered.

Booker was bruised, bloodied at the temple. Purple coated his knuckles. Her dress had been torn. They'd fought. They'd fought and lost.

"*Where's Daisy?*" Her voice trembled. This was her fault. *She* did this.

Daisy's mother met her gaze, tear-strewn and grief-stricken. Wordless.

"They came a few hours ago." A voice split the crowd. Cassidy recognized his rounded cheeks and red-tinged beard—the mayor—face as somber as the rest. He slipped a hand into his breast pocket, pulling out a wax-sealed envelope.

"*Who?*" she snapped, even though she already knew the answer. A thread of anger frayed the edges of her vision. "Why didn't you do anything? Why didn't you stop them?"

"Them and their blue bandanas." Another voice pulled her gaze in a different direction. Lucas, the barrel-chested, drunken deputy, was stone-faced.

"Ransom," Moone murmured, gaze dark. His eyes slid to Cassidy when she stumbled back. "You couldn't have known."

"I should have." Her head swam. She threaded her fingernails against her temple, another bolt of white-hot anger splitting her to the core. "This is my fault. They came for me."

Moone gripped her shoulders, blue eyes wide when he bent to her level. "You don't know that."

"She's right." The mayor spoke again. "They told us so."

"Ransom?" Cassidy's gaze snapped to him, a shiver clawing down her spine. "Was he here?"

He nodded.

Her chest constricted. Every breath fought its way out. "Did he say why?"

Daisy's mother choked out a sob.

The mayor worked his jaw. "He… he said he wanted to remind you what happens when you disobey. That the Bookers… that *Daisy* was a reminder."

"What happened to the church?" Moone ground out.

"It's a message." Cassidy closed her eyes, breath stuttering and catching. "It's what he did in Faraday Creek. This time, *he* put me in the church instead of the whole town."

"—which he threatened to do if we cut her down. That he was watching, and if we did anything before this letter was delivered to you, they'd come back and kill us all." The mayor's bright tenor broke. "I wanted to, I wanted to give them that." He nodded at the Bookers. "But—"

"You couldn't sacrifice the safety of everyone. I get it." Moone stepped between them, taking the letter from his grasp. He gathered Cassidy's hand with his, laying the parchment in her palm with a whisper. "I'm right here. I'm not going anywhere."

She nodded, turning her back to the gathering crowd, blinking away her tears when she saw brave souls step through the smoldering skeleton of the chapel to gather Daisy Booker's singed corpse.

The crack of the wax seal sent a shiver up her neck. Ransom's elegant script was as recognizable as her face in the mirror.

It isn't too late.

Fix what's been broken, fulfill your promise, and all will be forgiven.

I'll return in three days to fetch you.

Don't do anything you'll regret.

—Jack

"What's it say?" Moone ground out, chest pressed against her back as he read over her shoulder. His face darkened with every word until he reached the bottom.

"He wants me to go back and marry him."

"So I see," he snapped, jaw tight.

Cass lifted her chin. "I should go."

Moone seemed to grow two inches taller. "The fuck you will. You can't go back there, not after what it took for you to get out."

"It's the easiest choice," she argued, pushing him away from the townspeople's whispers behind them. "If I go back, what happened to Solo wouldn't have been for nothing. Then I'll have done something to repay him—to repay Daisy."

He shook his head. "You don't belong there."

A thatch of tawny curls fell and begged Cassidy to push them back into place. She knew he was right, but part of her whispered that not only did she belong in the finery Ransom offered, but it was a part of her. Part of herself she still didn't understand.

She smiled softly, answering the ache in her fingers to brush them through his hair. "I fit there."

James sighed, leaning into her touch with a roll of his jaw. "You fit *here*. With me, Cassidy."

"I'll be okay." She drew her fingers against his sleeve, walking them up his chest until she held his face. "You know what it's like. We both know it won't be so bad."

"It will. He'll destroy you, Cassidy. It'll happen again. He'll ply you with pretty petticoats and books and the opera. If you go with him and give in, it's the end. It's already over unless we finish this—finish him. He knows where we live; he's been here already. Nothing in our lives will ever be the same until he's dead." Moone's baritone shuddered. He closed his eyes and sucked in a trembling breath before revealing silver-lined blue—*tears*. Tears for her. For *them*. "I can't let you do this. He's going to stamp out every wild thing I love about you. I'd rather we both be dead than see it happen."

"James," she whispered, gaze soft. "I don't have a choice."

"You have *every* choice but that. Kill him or run away."

"I don't. This is my *home*. Our home. The lives of the people here aren't worth less than mine. Daisy's was worth so much more. I owe them that. I owe *her* that."

"You don't owe this town a thing. You've done enough. What about what you're worth to me? I'd do anything to keep you, Cassidy. Anything. If that means this town burns, and we ride off to Chicago tomorrow, I'll light it myself. Do you want to go to Ireland and see those white cliffs? We can do that too. As long as we're together. Nothing else matters."

Her eyes stung. She wanted all those things so badly, she wanted *him*, but—

"It isn't enough."

Moone's face darkened. "No."

"Why won't you fight for us, Ms. Callaghan?"

The voice of Daisy's mother split the silence like a death knell. Eyes wide, she stepped from her husband's grip.

Cassidy's chest grew tight in the face of the woman whose books Daisy stole for her, the woman who raised a little girl so much like herself, Cassidy couldn't help but befriend. She shook her head. "Doing what he wants is the safest bet for everyone."

"Funny, you never struck me as a coward," Mrs. Booker bit, eyes sunken with the weight of her grief, her *rage*. "This is your mess; clean it up. Stop the flood before it happens to someone else's daughter."

They had every right to be angry, but as Cassidy regarded her, she wondered if they all understood the hunger with which she sought Ransom's end.

Mrs. Booker looked from face to face in the crowd. One by one, their shoulders straightened, chins lifted, and eyes brightened. Maybe they all understood; perhaps they hungered for it, too.

"I made a mistake," Cassidy said, voice wavering when she found Katie's face in the crowd. "I've been doing this all wrong—thinking I was all alone, that doing it myself was the answer. I thought I was alone."

"But you're not alone," Katie said, smiling softly. A chorus of agreement fluttered through them like water through a pebbled stream.

"You'll get us justice, payment for what's been done. You've done that for so many of us; you chased it for yourself. Don't give up when it matters the most. You aren't alone, and now we all have a reason to want this man dead. We'll fight for you—for Daisy. It's what she'd want us to do. We can't give you up to that monster. Give us justice. Give yourself that, too."

Cassidy searched their faces, steely and sure. Her gaze slid to Moone. "What about you?"

"I don't know what I would've done if you returned to him. Nothing good… nothin' smart." He stepped closer, hands finding her waist. His eyes darted over her freckles, brows puckered as he bent and pressed a kiss to her lips. "It's like I said, before. I'd do anything to keep you. Even if that means going to war."

[48]

MOONE

"THEY'RE READY FOR YOU."

"Nearly there." Cassidy met his gaze in the looking glass, tongue trapped between her teeth in concentration as she tied off the end of her braid.

He'd watched her from the doorway without her realizing, maybe two minutes or more. James couldn't help but notice how her hands trembled, how her eyes turned glassy every few seconds as she struggled to plait it as quickly as she used to.

Moone knew what haunted her; they were all shadowed by it. Maybe no one more than him. If only he'd done something more, if only he'd lived up to his promises. Then Ransom would be dead, and Daisy Booker might still be alive.

It wasn't only that, but the plan of what came after which plagued her. Moone tried his best to soothe her worries. They'd canvassed the town half a dozen times, reviewing every eventuality. She flitted through the details of what might happen, inspecting every nook and cranny in Gallow Gorge to devise a plan.

They had to make it work, but the odds—the odds were stacked so high against them, Moone wasn't sure they could make the climb. Still, they called a town meeting to scrounge up a plan.

"You know him," Cassidy asked, so hopeful, his heart twisted. "Do you really think we can pull this off, or are we sentencing this town to die?"

Moone shut the door behind him, sealing out the quiet bustle downstairs. They'd taken a room at The Copper Queen, the same he'd put her in after the incident with Doc Ball. The innkeeper refused their money, insisting it was the least they could do.

The whole town came together to help her, even Katie Mays, who scrounged up a fresh set of clothes for Cassidy. In cotton, denim, and leather, she looked at home. She finally looked like herself again.

He hooked a hand on the dirk in his belt, playing it far too fucking casual. "It won't be easy, but it isn't impossible." His gut disagreed, churning and rolling with each minute that ticked by. Many of them would die, and if Moone were lucky, he would finally find Ransom in his sights.

He'd make good on those promises.

Cassidy's attention slid to his hand. He squirmed under her spotlight for far too many reasons. He never thought when Ransom gave it to him that he'd ever use it on her as he did in the darkness of her bedroom.

Moone couldn't help but smile at the memory of gleaming steel shredding through her bodice or the fire in her eyes when she held it to his throat.

"Where'd you get that?" She nodded toward it. "I thought for sure it'd been left behind when we made a run for it."

"Stole it." It was half-true; he never planned to honor what Ransom asked of him, not entirely. To him, it was just a knife, but Moone understood it held a different importance to his master. When he saw it lying on the floor when he discovered Ransom and Cassidy—inches from death—he couldn't leave it behind.

She blinked, her brow raised like she tasted his lie. "You *stole* it?"

"It's just a knife." James brushed her off, closing the space between them. Maybe he could distract her just enough to veer her onto a different path. "The rest of it isn't important. We've got a meeting to go to."

His fingers crawled along her waist, tugging her to his chest. The deepest part of him preened when she shivered. Hopefully, he'd chase all her wayward thoughts away with a touch.

Suspicion. Cassidy lived her life second-guessing every person who came her way—even him. She didn't trust the people of Gallow Gorge. No one saw beneath her armor except Katie, and on a good day, maybe him. But even then, her trust was fraught, brittle, begging to be broken.

She was being paranoid, for good reason. Life built her that way, and Moone understood how she believed for a long time that it was for the best. He watched her battle with it; every hour they spent together begged for her armor to come down, and it did—little by little, layer by layer.

Selfishly, he was glad for it. Cassidy trusted him despite what he'd done. What she was aware of, at least. He never thought it'd happen again, and he wasn't sure he deserved it.

As far as she knew, Moone had no reason to lie. Not after he'd done everything to get her away, after he'd done everything to get himself away, too.

Everything, truly.

A trove was hidden within the walls of *Colina de Dragones*, and James was determined to fish it out and claim his inheritance. Only then could they finally be at peace, all the blood repaid, and he repentant enough—*good enough*—to deserve her.

"I want you to know how beautiful you were in all those pretty things, Cassidy." He circled her ear with his nose, humming long and low when he hooked his thumbs beneath her gun belts.

"But?" she mewled, leaning into him, head tilting when his mouth found her neck.

"Seeing you like this is better than I remembered," he answered, nipping at her deliciously rapid pulse. "Like you're you again."

"I feel like me," she whispered, twisting until her mouth met his. There was something about it, her hands in his hair, the taste of her on his tongue that sent him spinning. It was almost enough to convince him to run and gather all the gold he could find so he could build her a home in every port if she asked him to. He'd do whatever she desired, take her wherever she wanted.

Moone pulled her closer. He nipped her bottom lip, pushing harder, kissing her more fiercely—like he never thought he'd kiss her again. With everything that waited for them, everything he wanted to give her and everything he wanted to be, James couldn't be sure it wasn't untrue.

Cassidy pulled away, wearing a breathless grin. She traced his bottom lip with the tip of her finger, pressing in with another quick-as-lightning kiss. "You're kissing me like your life depends on it, Moone."

His stomach churned, twisted with guilt. He buried the

feeling, bending to collect another, then another longer, deeper kiss after that. "Maybe it does."

She shook her head, sliding a step back. "Our lives depend on this meeting, idiot. Stop distracting me."

A distraction. That's what James was, what she was always telling him he was bound to be. Moone wondered if she ever stopped to consider the thought that maybe she needed distraction. Perhaps he needed it, too.

A part of him argued against it, hemming and hawing every year he lingered in Gallow Gorge. Because the truth of the matter was, of all the distractions, Cassidy Callaghan was the biggest one.

She had him veering from the path he'd been set upon, pushing and pulling when all he wanted to do was be still. She made him indecisive where he used to be steady, lost when he had the kind of conviction a man could use as a compass to guide him through the dark.

Knowing her convinced him of what kind of man he wanted to be, the man Jolene Moone prayed he'd become. Life left him fewer choices than being good or bad; James made himself strong instead. He stared into the open flames his Pa built within him and couldn't tear his eyes away from what waited in the shadows—the thing that'd rule him.

He thought he put it all away, fire doused for good, and the path of ashes he left behind blown away in the wind.

Until he returned to the forge and learned that he hadn't tamed his demons; they'd only ever been kept on a leash. But, maybe, he'd finally have to let them loose to finish what Ransom started.

Moone forced his warmest smile, clinging to the good deputy she believed him to be. In his heart, James knew he was long gone—left behind when he let Lawrence Ball loose from the Gallow Gorge jail.

He stood by the door, hand extended. "Apologies for distracting you, Missus Moone."

Cassidy punched him in the chest. "That was *one* time."

He caught her by the wrist, tugging her to his chest for another bruising kiss. It shifted, an ebb and flow like the bend in a river, leveling out into something steady and sure.

"I had a good reason," he said against her lips, squeezing her around the middle. "I always have a good reason."

Cassidy twisted, reaching for the handle with his breath at her back.

She snatched her hand away at the last second, fist curled to her chest as she peered at him. "What if no one came? What if we're on our own?"

James smiled, softer and more earnest than he felt in weeks. "You've always been a stubborn ass loner, Cassidy. But you've never, *ever* been alone." He reached around her and opened the door, filled with pride for their town—the town he came to love against his better judgment, the people he learned to love. "They came. They *all* came."

Even with all the tables of The Copper Queen pushed together, there wasn't enough room for every soul who gathered that evening. Faces of every shape and color filled every square inch of the dining room. Miners, blacksmiths, and tanners, too. Doctor Murray, the town surgeon. The mayor. Even the Bookers.

Moone twisted his fingers with hers, leading her down the stairs. Eyes watched their every step, the din dying away as Cassidy strode to the head of their makeshift town hall.

He couldn't help but notice the rapid rise and fall of her chest, the flush of her cheeks, and the shine in her eyes as they met tentative smiles. The evidence was all around her.

James prayed she finally believed what he'd been telling her all along.

She wasn't alone. She had a people. She had a *family*.

"It's high time we came up with a plan, Ms. Callaghan," the mayor boomed from the opposite end.

Moone settled into the chair beside her, giving her a confident nod to speak her mind. She was as clever as a fox and more than capable of leading them.

"We can't keep him out." Her voice was too soft, wavering when she pushed the reach of it, syllables jumbling. "If we draw him in and find a way to keep him on Main Street, we might be able to turn it into a shooting gallery. Trap him and tag him. We'll pick them off one by one. If we do that, we might stand a chance."

"How do you know he'll come?" Lucas Smith grumbled, sober and clear-eyed.

Moone's jaw ached, tense from the memory of crystal colliding with bone. He wished he would've hit him harder because now nothing would stop Ransom from delivering upon a well-earned vendetta.

"He'll come." His voice was dark, threaded with rage. "He won't leave this up to chance. He'll come to ensure Cassidy honors her bargain—or pays for it."

Like hell if he'd even let Ransom get close to her. Enough had been paid by the two of them, their town, and the Bookers. Part of him worried Cassidy thought differently, that her guilt over Daisy, over Solo, would lead her to make a spectacularly dumb decision.

"How do we draw him in?" The mayor stroked his russet beard. "There's an awful lot of open space."

Cassidy stubbornly lifted her chin; Moone hated it. He knew exactly what it meant.

"Use me as bait. Ransom wants me. I'm the reason for all this, so dangle me like a carrot. Then keep him in your sights."

Moone jolted to his feet, chair clattering to the floor. "Absolutely fucking not."

Her eyes blazed defiantly. "Do *not* make this about protecting me."

"It always has been, Cassidy."

She shook her head. "It's about protecting the town. The people in it. The ones you're duty-bound to help."

"So you won't have to go with him." Moone pawed a hand through his hair. This was getting out of hand, and they'd barely begun. "I refuse to let you be a sitting duck. What if you get shot?"

"Then you better avenge me, or I'll haunt you, James Moone. Besides"—Cassidy's mouth quirked up—"vengeance would look good on you."

His stomach soured, and he ground his teeth. "Bad time for jokes, Freckles."

"Are you two about done?" The mayor's bright tenor split the tension. Their eyes snapped to the far end of the clustered tables.

"Apologies," he grumbled. Moone righted his chair and slumped into it. Cassidy rolled her eyes like he looked like a boy who'd been told to finish his chores before he could play, but could she blame him? It was a good idea, one Ransom would fall for, and James *hated it.*

The mayor shook his head, a thread of amusement in his voice. "Now, the flirting is finished; let's get back to business."

Cassidy stood a little straighter, and as unhappy as he was, Moone couldn't help but admire how she took in every face around the saloon. Around the tables, along the walls, and down the upstairs balcony—nearly the entire town.

He followed her attention to a brown-eyed little boy and the mother clutching his shoulder.

"We need to hide the women and children," she declared. "As far away as we can, just in case Ransom decides to set fire to the town. I won't let them go through what she did."

"But where?" a voice called from above them.

Moone's mind ran, searching for an answer. It wasn't as simple as putting them beneath the floorboards of the general store. If things went badly, which they'd more than likely do, James knew she couldn't bear Gallow Gorge's children being forced to watch their fathers die like she had to.

Choices, places that might work, all the wrong ones, came one after the other. Cassidy came up with a possible failure for each one until—

"The mine." Her gaze shot to the foreman, hope flaring in her eyes.

Moone felt it, too. Hope flared so brightly in his chest that he thought it might crack open and blind them all. It had to work. They had to make it work... for their sake.

The foreman tapped his chin. "It wouldn't be the safest option."

"You've never had a collapse, and it's safer than keeping them in town," she argued, sliding her palms along the table. "But it'd work, wouldn't it?"

The foreman gave it a moment's thought before giving her a whiskered smile. "It just might."

"What about supplies?" he asked.

They both looked at the Bookers—they had as much at stake in this fight as Cassidy. His heart twisted when he saw the pain in their eyes, but the mother—she burned with the same kind of fire his lover did; the need to see vengeance done.

She stared at her husband, who stood slightly taller, with a stiff nod. "Whatever you need."

Cassidy twisted, beaming at him in a way he wished he could bottle.

A smile tugged at his mouth, just a promise of the joy waiting for them when everything went according to plan. *If* it went according to plan. "This just might work, Freckles."

He had his own plans, just in case it didn't.

[43]

THREE DAYS WASN'T ENOUGH, BUT THEY MADE THE best of it. By the end of the first, they'd concocted a plan. By breakfast the next, a mountain of supplies had been gathered. Wagons laden with water barrels, blankets, oil lamps, and enough food for a week to send uphill to the mine. Sandbags and lumber to fortify their Main Street battleground. Nails, hammers, and every spare ounce of lead to arm their small army.

With every piece that fell into place, Cassidy felt lighter and heavier all at once. Every hour brought them closer to the eventuality that Ransom would come; it'd all end, and some faces who helped her wouldn't be there a week from now.

Still, they made quick work of it all, ensuring they were prepared to put up a good fight. On the third day, most of the windows were boarded up. Sandbags stacked along the edges of balconies. On the outskirts of town, young men and women alike shot tin cans off the edges of a fence post—just like Cassidy used to do with her Da.

Cassidy wandered up the stairs at Ridley's, trailing her

fingers along wine-red wallpaper until she reached a familiar doorway. The press of her hand sent a shimmer of golden afternoon light spilling into the hall.

Katie Mays stood with her back to the door, illuminated by sunshine from the window. Her flaxen hair gleamed, the movement of her hands as she wound bandages into tight coils more like a dance than a chore.

"Are you gonna lurk all afternoon, or do you plan on comin' in?" Katie dipped her chin over her shoulder with a grin.

They hadn't had a chance to talk since before Cassidy ran off after Doc Ball. It felt like years went by instead of weeks.

At the beginning, when Cassidy settled in Gallow Gorge, she'd warm Katie's bed like a bad habit, drawn in by golden hair and a sweet smile. Over time, she grew into a secret oasis, a safe place to rest her head and wash away her worries with the taste of Katie's kiss and her hands upon her skin.

They'd stay awake until the lamplight guttered, talking like Lizzie and Jane Bennet under the covers, and doing *other* things that weren't sisterly in the slightest.

Cassidy's cheeks heated at the thought, painted in the guilt that, now things between her and Moone had changed, things with Katie would change, too.

"Can I help?" Cass pushed off from the frame. She didn't wait for an answer, reaching into a wicker basket filled with strips of fabric. The task was wonderfully monotonous, just enough to keep her thoughts from running away. For a little while, at least.

"Do you want to talk about it?" The blonde kept her eyes on their chore, stacking another finished bandage in a crate beneath the window.

Cassidy sighed. "It's complicated."

"I've known you a long time," Katie laughed, soft as a song. "Like you've been anything *but* complicated, sugar."

She wrung her hands, too fidgety to wrap another bandage. "We're friends, aren't we?"

"Yeah, Cass." Katie lifted her brown eyes, wearing a soft smile that grew the longer Cassidy looked. "I wouldn't call it somethin' conventional, but… we're friends. You could talk to me about anything. It's no different now than it was back then, you know."

"I do." Cass nodded, worrying her lip as she stepped up to the glass. The street below bustled, every resident a busy cog, everyone doing their part to prepare for the coming storm. She sorted through everything that happened and led up to that day—an eventuality Cassidy couldn't run away from, no matter how Moone insisted she should.

Every thought wore heavy on her shoulders. Maybe if she let them out to Katie like she did her story with Moone, she'd feel a little lighter.

"Moone kept the warrant for Doc Ball from me. He told me that if I brought him in, if I took the risk and angered Ransom, it'd make things more dangerous for me than I understood. That retribution would come ten-fold if I put my nose where it didn't belong. I should've listened. I should've left well enough alone. But—" Cassidy blew out a breath, closing her eyes as the familiar curl of her anger that day tugged at the back of her mind. Only this time, she was angry with herself. "When I got that warrant in my hands, I couldn't think about anything besides getting to Ransom. After years of hoping for an answer, I'd never been so close. So, I *ran.*"

"And then you were hurt," Katie murmured, hands still

and brown eyes haunted. "I was scared. Then you left again, and you didn't say goodbye."

It twisted Cassidy up to see Katie's fear and hurt reflected back at her. "I'm sorry."

She offered her a weary smile and a shrug. "You always were a little wild, Cass. I should've known better than to think you'd wanna stay put in one place. You and that horse—you were meant to run. Goodbyes aren't really your style."

Cassidy gave a half-hearted chuckle. "I guess not. I started to forget. I got *distracted*, and running was the only thing that saved me from myself." She nodded out the window, recognizing Moone's broad shoulders and curl of his hair without a second glance. "He's the only reason I made it out of there. If it weren't for him, I'd be dead or worse."

"What's worse than dead?"

"Trapped," Cassidy whispered, shuddering when she realized how close she risked losing herself completely, all for pretty dresses, books, and a complicated feeling.

"That man loves you, Cass," Katie said behind her. "He has for ages. All of us could see it. All of us, but the two of you."

Cassidy's stomach flipped and twisted. Katie was right. Moone tried to tell her, wanted to show her a hundred different ways, tried to learn her, help her—love her. But Cassidy never gave him an inch until it was too late.

"I never thought I could."

Katie frowned. "What, be loved?"

Cass shrugged, thumbing the edge of her sleeve. "There was never any room for it. I'd always been focused on one thing. I never stopped to think about what came after, about what kind of life I'd want to have. But, now—"

Katie's shoulder brushed against Cass's, following her gaze out the window to where Moone boarded up a shop window. "You love him, too."

Something inside her chest swelled, ballooning until she thought she'd burst. "I do."

"Does he know?"

Moone's face broke into a smile, clapping his hand on the shoulder of a passerby who'd stopped to talk. The sight stirred the feeling again, the same dull ache. "Not in so many words."

"You better fix that," Katie said, breathing out a sigh. Cassidy's fingers grazed against hers, a learned habit, a comfort. The blonde spun, flinging her arms around her as she whispered into her hair. "I'm happy for you, Cassidy. Truly."

Katie's brown eyes shone when she pulled away, fingertip connecting the spaces between Cassidy's freckles. A smile tugged at the corner of her lovely mouth as she leaned in to kiss her.

They'd done it before. A hundred times, maybe more. Cassidy never tired of the taste of her, of the feeling of their bodies pressed together, but this was different.

Katie lingered, hands twisted in copper curls, lips tinged with regret, hopefulness, and the saltiness of her tears.

Cassidy's throat was thick, voice cracking. "What was that for?"

"It's like I said—I've known you a long time, Cassidy Callaghan. I am grateful you *let* me know you. I know how hard that is for you." Katie smiled again, collecting a briny drop from the corner of her mouth with the tip of her tongue. "You're a lot of things. Stubborn, strong… *beautiful.* But, there are a lot of things you're not."

Cassidy huffed a laugh. "Oh yeah?"

Katie nodded. "Yeah."

"Care to share?"

"Forgiving. Patient, not when it counts, at least." The blonde stole another kiss, lingering longer than the first time, a little breathless when she pulled away. Her eyes darted over Cassidy's face, fingers drawing a curl between them with a faraway smile. "But of all the things you aren't, Cassidy Kathleen, of all the things you *are*, unlovable isn't a word I'd use."

The flame burning in Cassidy's chest guttered, eyes shifting back to Moone on the street below. How could she ever hope to be enough? Could she learn to love him how he wanted—how he deserved?

"How do you know?"

Katie's lips parted, and her smile lingered, but the warmth in her eyes slipped. "I've loved you a long time, Cassidy." Hands on Cass's hips, she twisted her, pushing her toward the door. "Now *go*. Don't wait like I did. Tell him as much as possible before there isn't a tomorrow."

[44]

CASSIDY COULDN'T REMEMBER A TIME SHE'D SMELLED something so delicious. Her life on the road meant dried meat and beans, maybe a jackrabbit if she felt lucky. But the aroma drifting from the hearth of The Copper Queen flew her back to days as a little girl, bending on tiptoe to peer into a cast iron pot.

She remembered potatoes turned from their garden's soil, ears of corn as yellow as sunshine, and thick crusts of soda bread when there was extra flour. Firelight-colored memories of their family gathered around a table, the sight of Aisling Callaghan's smile and Ian's laugh—her family.

Cass lingered with an elbow on the bar, chewing the side of her thumb as Mrs. Booker and Madame Ridley bickered over how much pepper ought to go in the stew, and *yes*, it needed just a touch of salt. A pair of mother hens, with others hovering on the edge, wiping flour from their hands on aprons that belonged to *their* mothers and the recipes to their mothers before them.

Food piled up from one end of the bar to the other, every piece of it a contribution from someone's brother, someone's sister—all of Gallow Gorge gathered for a last supper.

The air buzzed. Boisterous laughter echoed from every corner, seeping in from the street as everyone meandered inside, bearing bottles of booze, sweet cakes baked with a swirl of molasses, and merriment abound.

If Cassidy didn't know better, she thought it might've been Christmas; such simple, quiet joy filled the air. But, beneath it all, hiding beneath the smiles, was a reminder of what was to come and what the grandness of the meal meant.

Not all of them would make it out alive.

"Who died, Freckles?" Moone shouldered up beside her, handing over a tin plate stacked high with food.

Cassidy offered a half-hearted smile, tearing off a bite of sweet bread. "No one, yet."

He regarded her carefully as they settled in at the cluster of tables. His eyes danced over her face, like he aimed to decode her, untangle her thoughts, and assure her that everything would be okay. She knew it'd be a lie.

"It's going to be fine." Moone squeezed her hand. "Stop worrying. We're ready."

She gave him a look, shaking her head when he offered her a splash of whiskey. "None of this is fine. Look at all these people."

"I am, Cassidy." He leaned closer, a piece of roasted chicken between his fingers. No sense in keeping them for laying when there'd be no one to eat the eggs tomorrow. "What, do you think someone twisted their arm to help?"

"No," she sighed, grinning softly when a brown-eyed little boy tucked a candy-colored piece of licorice in her palm. "Maybe you're right. I just can't shake the feeling like

I'm breaking up this community, this *family*."

"Cassidy." Moone's voice was stern, hand covering her knuckles, breath tickling her face like a kiss. "You've built yourself to be suspicious. Hell, I'm pretty sure you were born wearing a suit of armor. But, if you ever let up an inch, maybe you'd see what I do."

"What's that?" Cassidy leaned into his touch when his hand found her cheek.

"You've stopped being a sad little orphan the moment you stepped foot in this town." Moone leaned closer, pointing to a makeshift table made from a barrel and a board. "Madame Ridley gave you a place to stay. I gave you a job. The Bookers gave you a sister."

Something in Cassidy's chest swelled. She sat back, taking stock of their merry band of rebels. A bad feeling twisted in her gut, writhing like noxious ropes dragging her to the bottom of the well. She watched as the people gathered, trading stories and singing songs.

All at once, it dawned on her.

She'd spent years keeping herself at a distance, insisting she hadn't needed any of them. They all viewed her as a thorn in their sides, a girl who'd been prickly like a cactus from the first moment she'd stepped foot in town.

If she thought hard enough about it, Cassidy remembered the day. Mostly a thatch of copper curls drenched in freckles, barely seventeen. She'd spent three years under the thumb of the Madame in Sacramento who mothered her the best she could, the little Cassidy allowed her. But the moment she'd outgrown a pinafore and spotted a yellowed warrant pasted to the side of a building, she knew she would be different.

Cass sought help from anyone who'd give it to her,

already given a leg up from lessons taught by her Da. She'd impressed teenaged stable boys with the terrifying efficiency she'd display when they dared her to spend a precious nickel at a passing carnival.

Afterward, they took the money she brought to gather the supplies she'd need—things required for a life on the road. The shopkeepers always shooed her away, but with the boys' help and a few months' pay, Cassidy had everything she needed.

She dragged in her first bounty when she was fourteen.

By seventeen, she'd followed them across state lines, picking up the breadcrumbs that might, one day, lead her to a whisper of Ransom and the monster she'd built in her mind.

The months alone gave her an unshakable focus and a sour disposition. One built on how men treated her and how women looked at her. By the time she flew into Gallow Gorge, a bony little thing on the back of a black mustang, her armor was unbreakable.

"When did you know?" Cassidy asked, pushing away her plate. She couldn't eat another bite when every taste went ashen in her mouth and churned in her stomach.

Moone, who'd carefully watched her drift away on her thoughts, reached for her hand. "Know what?"

She let him lead her from her chair, lifting her into his lap, never mind that the entire town was gathered around them. Cassidy didn't care if they saw. Moone was right. They hadn't made her soft. Needing their help didn't take away her armor; it *fortified* it. All this time, she'd had a family. And because of that, she started to doubt if they'd made the right choice in letting them fight.

The easiest, safest way out for them all was for her to

leave.

Then, no one would have to die. Not for her.

"How'd you know we were friends?" Cassidy leaned against Moone's broad chest, twisting his arm around her waist so his thumb hooked in her belt and fingers settled on the swell of her hip.

Moone chuckled. The sound of it warmed her from the inside out until it melted into a groan. He leaned, shoving a free hand between them, carefully extracting her pistol with a grimace.

"I knew the first time you smiled at me."

"That's horse shit," she bit back a laugh, forcing a frown. "Why?"

"I never smiled at you. Probably ever."

"You sure fucking did. The first time I arrested you for hollering your way down Main Street in the middle of the night. You always were the *best* at disturbing the peace." He laughed again, wearing a smug smile. "I knew I *loved* you the first time you threatened to shoot me with one of these."

Moone waved the pearl-gripped revolver, laying it on the table with a clatter.

"How romantic," she muttered in his ear, letting out a whispered sigh when his mouth found a sliver of skin in the bend where her shoulder met her neck.

"Don't shoot me, now," he growled, nipping at freckle-kissed skin.

"I wasn't planning on it." Cass let herself get swept up in the feeling and the thought of what he'd do to her upstairs. "Not yet, anyway. Not unless—"

"—I lied. I know. The truth is, I didn't know I loved you then. Not yet, not for a while." Moone's nose traced up her jawline, setting her hair on end. "I knew I loved you the moment you weren't *you* anymore. Seeing you like a desert rose transplanted into a greenhouse. You were *wild*. I'd convinced myself you wouldn't fit anywhere else but here. I didn't expect you to flourish. But there you were, right in the middle of the world I tried to get away from, looking like you always belonged."

"I don't understand." Cassidy pulled away, brows drawn in. "The point was to blend in. I… I know I let myself get swept up, but I—"

"No." Moone pulled her back in, holding her face.

Cassidy knew people, how to read their bodies and faces. She knew the shape of a tell. She knew *him*, the lines of his body and the taste of his kiss. But there was no decoding all the things he wasn't saying.

"It's not that I didn't like how you looked. I think—" He sucked in a trembling breath, rolling his jaw. "It told me something I already knew, deep down. I loved you before you were ever *her*. Seeing you that way told me I should've said something before you weren't mine to want. Seeing you that way told me you were *his*. You might as well have been wearing one of those blue hankies. You never second-guessed it. You looked so at home on his arm. With you as that lady… I wanted to be him."

Cassidy opened her mouth to argue, but Moone silenced the thought with a searing kiss. Her cheeks burned when his fingers hooked in her hair, drawing out a dulcet whimper from her lips with a swipe of his tongue.

"Are you trying to distract me?" she panted, feathering the tawny waves at his temples.

"Always." The corner of his mouth quirked. He kissed her again. "There was never a time I wasn't tryin' to distract you, Cassidy."

"I knew it." Cass laughed, kissing him again, lingering longer than the first.

Moone's fingers dug into her hair, mouth slanting over hers until every worry, every wayward thought of the next day vanished into thin air.

Words—Cassidy was out of them, out of her body and practically molten when he opened her throat and left a delicious whisker burn behind. Nothing, none of it mattered, not when he tugged on the thread of her desire in such a way.

The sharp clatter of glass against wood shook them free, flushed and panting, wide-eyed like a pair of teenagers who'd been caught in the barn. The entire room's attention was pinned on them, now covered in a rainfall of whiskey thrown their way.

"Get the fuck out of here, you two. Find a bed," Madame Ridley groused from the other end of the dining hall, smile hovering beneath a weathered scowl.

Cassidy met his eye with a laugh, cheeks burning. "You heard the lady."

The chair they'd been sitting in went skittering along the floor, practically sent skyward when Moone swooped her up in his arms. He barreled up the stairs, taking them two at a time, hoots and hollers chasing them the entire way.

With the door shut behind them, the hushed quiet buzzed differently than before. Back when they stood on the edge of a precipice, the point of no return. The quiet led them into a beautiful oblivion.

Now, with death whispering down their necks, murmuring baneful promises for tomorrow, a different sort of thread spooled.

It turned tighter and tighter, hung with every idea, every

worry, and every second thought Cassidy harbored. Not about them. She'd been sure of what Moone gave her once she finally let herself see him.

She hovered in the center of the room, face lit by the faint crackle and pop from the fireplace. Palm to her chest, Cassidy lifted her eyes to Moone.

"I can't let them go through with it."

"Cassidy—" he warned, stepping toward her. He stood, poised like a coiled viper, holding onto every ounce of control. Moone knew when to move and push, when to listen and let her say her piece; his patience with her was never-ending. This was sure to drive him to the edge. "Don't."

"I won't let anyone else die for me." Cassidy *knew* what she needed to do. There'd been enough death already. She'd seen too much of it, and she'd be damned if she was responsible for more.

"*Cassidy*," Moone repeated, lifting a drop of whiskey-flavored rain from her cheek. "Stop it. I don't want to talk about this right now or ever. I don't want to *talk* at all." His hands tugged at her gun belt. There was a whisper of leather and lead, then a clatter when it dropped to the floor.

"I have something to say." She whimpered when his tongue swept away another bead of the whiskey. His hands wandered, blindly flipping open the buttons on her shirt one by one.

"All this time," he growled between demanding kisses, voice dripping with frustration and lust, stained with something else she couldn't put her finger on. "I've been trying to get you to talk to me. You pick *now* to be a chatterbox?"

Cassidy pushed on his chest, gasping for an ounce of breathing room, an inch to think.

"Would you listen to me?" She cupped his cheeks, drawing him in for another kiss, softer, slower, sweeter than she'd let anyone taste. Part of her never held back with him; now, none of her would ever again. With death at their door and no promise of tomorrow, Cassidy saw no reason to keep any more secrets.

"I love you, James Moone." Cassidy kissed him again, slanting her mouth against his, drawing deeper, lingering longer.

She didn't mean for it to taste like goodbye.

But, if the plan went her way, if she could spare his life and all the others, there'd be no turning back. There'd be no more of this. No more them. No more of the wild girl and her good deputy.

To help them, she'd have to become something else.

Moone stared down at her. Something within him shifted, as if he'd unraveled Morse Code from her lips. He chewed on his words, eyes everywhere but aligned with hers. Blue shone with silver when he met her gaze again, like he saw it for what it was—what it had to be.

Cassidy expected him to argue, push back, and fight like they always did. Instead, he wore the quiet acceptance on his sleeve, bending to kiss her again, and again, and again.

"I love you too, Cassidy," Moone murmured against her ear. He rolled the tender lobe between his teeth. His hands tugged open her shirt, gingerly tearing away the layers, peppering every inch of newly exposed skin in tender kisses. "Let's make this count."

Moone slipped the leather tie from the end of her hair, unraveling the plait until loose curls cascaded past her waist.

Cassidy fell into the rhythm of it, the loveliest dance. She peeled away his clothes, pulling at his belt as he nuzzled the bend of her neck. She quietly marveled at the shape of him, taut muscle, carved like a river on a mountain's face. Every inch of him was beautiful, and she wished she'd taken the time to appreciate it, appreciate him. The cursive line of his chest, the map of him laid out in sharp lines beneath a trail of hair below his belly button, and the thickness of his cock.

He didn't let her linger long, sweeping her up in another searing kiss. One led to another, fanning the flames of their desire, of her wanting him, taking as much as he'd give her before time ran out.

Moone nudged her toward the bed, tongue saying everything words wouldn't—*couldn't*— say, not now she'd made her choice. He cradled her as he laid her out, body rolling against hers in the quiet firelight.

It wasn't anything like the times before. No wild flash of fire, none of the desperation or the impatience to get to the core of things, to feed the forge until the world burned. Nothing else than the need to feel him inside her. To be more than just *them*. To paint themselves in everything they were and everything they could have been until dawn—and Jack Ransom—called her name.

A delectable agony, that's what it was. What she felt when Moone aligned the end of him with the beginning of her. The achingly slow, deliberate thrust as he sheathed himself, his choked groan caressing her ear.

"Say it again," he whispered against her skin. "Tell me you love me."

Cassidy gripped his back, rolling her hips to take more of him in. "I love you."

"Again," Moone demanded, driving deeper. His fingers brushed her hair, eyes glimmering, molten when he rocked into her again and again.

"I love you," she repeated, taking Katie's advice. With no tomorrow, she'd tell him everything. "No matter what happens tomorrow, I'm yours—*forever*. And you're mine. *I love you*."

Until that moment, gazes twined together in the firelight, she never felt so beautiful, never felt so seen by him until her words lit him up from the inside out.

"Cassidy." Moone murmured her name like a prayer, like the taste on his tongue was a balm, the only medicine he'd ever need—the kind that could cure a black soul.

His teeth found her shoulder, his fingers her waist. Up he pulled her, shifting his weight until they sat chest to chest, as close as they could come unless he swallowed her whole.

They fell into a faster rhythm, more and more like a dance—a waltz of their bodies timed to the beat of their hearts. Their eyes found each other, blazing bright, molten in the muted light. There was no tomorrow, no past. They weren't orphans, nor a false deputy or a girl bent on vengeance. There, in the charged quiet, Cassidy and James were merely themselves—a man and a woman who loved each other, with never enough time to do it in.

Moone's lips parted, tears brimming on his eyelashes. "I love you," he choked, fingers gripping her so firmly, Cassidy wondered if part of him might be left behind, the very essence of him worn on her like a brand. "I'm sorry."

It was all Cassidy needed. Her climax rocketed through her, obliterating every worry, every thought of tomorrow, drawing a cry from her lips surely everyone in The Copper Queen heard.

She didn't care. Let them hear. Let all of Nevada hear the song she sang for James Moone. Let the wind carry it to Ransom's window so he might know that, while she might be his in body—Moone owned her soul.

He followed soon after, his gruff baritone its own sweet melody in her ear. Cassidy committed it to memory, all of it: the sound of her name on his lips and the feeling of her body wrapped so tightly around him. The electric thrum between them, buzzing like the new bright lights illuminating a city on the horizon.

I'm yours, and you're mine. Mine.

The words, her words, lingered in the back of her mind as Moone carried them to the mattress, unwilling to un-rope the lasso of his arms. His mouth found her hair, pressing kiss after kiss to her temple while his fingers traced feather-soft lines over the freckles on her back.

Cassidy tilted her chin and kissed him. Like all their kisses before, it led to another and another, one never enough to satiate them.

Moone moved his mouth lazily over hers, kissing her so thoroughly, for so long, it wasn't long before their bodies stirred all over again, and they found themselves swept up in each other once more.

It wasn't until the first threads of dawn stretched from the horizon that they finally fell asleep.

It wasn't until daylight shone through the windows that Cassidy woke, and Moone was gone.

[45]

CASSIDY

A NGER.
The anger that'd quieted over the last few weeks. The seething rage she'd built over a lifetime. The bitterness Cass silenced, letting herself fall into the feelings she tried to avoid for good reason. All of it, every ounce, came rushing back at once.

Cassidy shook her head, closing her eyes to shutter every wayward thought. She was jumping to conclusions. She built herself that way. Naturally suspicious of everyone, of everything, Moone taught her to think a different way.

She leaped from their empty bed, covers mussed in a beautiful, tragic way. Cass let herself remember that, remember him. What they had *was* beautiful. It still would be. There was an answer, one she was bound and determined to figure out.

Cassidy pulled on her clothes quick as lightning, sparing a glance at herself in the mirror. Her hair was wild, disheveled to high heaven. It sent an image, a feeling, rushing through her mind of Moone's fingers twisted in it, of a spill of copper curls spread over his back as he held her to his chest, and they made love again and again.

He wasn't gone. He couldn't be gone. He wouldn't have left, not without saying goodbye.

That's something she would've done before he went and put a crack in her armor and slipped right in against her heart.

Cassidy wrenched open the door, taking the stairs of The Copper Queen two at a time. Eyes were on her when she stepped foot in the dining hall—solemn gazes that told her something she didn't want to accept.

Madame Ridley leaned against the bar, swirling around a whiskey breakfast as a cigarillo smoldered between her fingers.

"He's not here, honey."

Cassidy shifted, blinking back at her. "What do you mean?"

She dipped her chin, wetting her lips as she tapped the end of the cigar, sending a snowfall of ash to the floor. "Moone isn't here. He rode out in a hurry about an hour ago."

Cassidy's breath hitched. Everything wavered. Her stomach churned, and no matter how she clawed at it, it wouldn't settle.

"He left this for you." The innkeeper held out a scrap of parchment, eyes soft, like he felt sorry for her.

Cass hated it.

She took the paper with a trembling hand, refusing to let her stony expression waver as her eyes darted over Moone's scrawl.

There was no other way. I had to try.

I hope you'll understand someday, though I'm not sure you'll ever forgive me.

I'm sorry anyway.

I love you.
J.

Cassidy bit back the threat of tears. They burned through her, lifting the veil of her anger. She crumpled the letter, hurling it across the room with a yell.

"GOD DAMMIT!"

Her cry rattled the windows, halting the steps of Gallow Gorge's residents outside.

It didn't take an idiot to know he went straight to Ransom. By now, he and his army were close—too close—enough for Moone to run to the man who raised him—a loyal dog to his master.

She should've known better. She *did* know better. Cassidy lost count of how many times she told herself she didn't need anyone. Didn't need him. That he was only a distraction. But she fought against it, against her better judgment, against all the wrongs she'd witnessed—evidence of why she did everything on her own.

But, no. Moone weaseled his way in. Maybe it'd been his plan all along. To make her need him, to open herself up the way she vowed never to do, to make her love him the way she never thought she could.

Maybe he did it to prove he could. Maybe it was just another game to him, like the one they always played.

Cassidy paced, pressing her knuckles to her lips like it'd keep the tears at bay and stoke the fire of her anger. Fury was of more use to her than hurt, anyway.

Still, she searched for answers, sorting through every moment they spent together. She shivered when she remembered his lie. In the light of a campfire and a shared bottle of moonshine, Moone told her how he knew Ransom. It was only a sliver of the truth.

James Moone was Ransom's *heir*—the son every man wished for. A girl was no use, and even if Ransom had a daughter, she'd never hold a candle to the blue-eyed bastard who'd run out on her, leaving her behind like everyone else.

The details fell into place one by one. Cassidy's thoughts became blindingly clear.

Ransom's blade. Moone's insistence she stay and fight. Him running away. All of it was a ploy to get what he was owed. An inheritance couldn't be given if she gave herself over, and Ransom gave it to her instead.

None of it, the reasons coiling through her and the rage she felt, none of it compared to the shame. She told Moone she loved him. She meant it with every fiber of her being, never believing she could, not with how black her heart was.

Now, it'd stay that way forever.

"Cassidy, there's a saddled-up mare in the tack waiting for you," a tentative voice called from behind her, like sneaking up on a bear with a handful of honey. "We haven't got much time until—"

"I know." She closed her eyes and blew out a trembling breath.

Time was wasting. Ransom didn't specify when he'd arrive to claim her, but they couldn't risk loitering for long. There was still too much left to do.

Cassidy gathered her gun belt and straightened her jacket, ensuring every piece of her metaphorical armor was in place before settling a black hat over her braid and stepping outside.

The streets were busy but hushed. The air was thick with an unseen heaviness, a quiet despondence of what waited for them by the end of the day. By then, the street would be red with blood. All they could do was pray they'd done enough and that there'd still be a Gallow Gorge in the morning.

Cassidy lifted her eyes to the hill overlooking the town, and the puffs of soil lifted from the road as the wagons lumbered their way to the mine's entrance. With the windows in town boarded up and sandbags stacked, the mine was where they needed her. That's where she could help until time was up and the battle would begin.

The barn seemed smaller and quieter without a sable stallion complaining in the stall at the end. Cassidy hadn't dared go inside since they returned from Sacramento, the ringing in her ears still haunting her too loudly to let her lock eyes with another gelding or filly.

Her heart thundered as she neared the soft, throaty nicker from a stall in the center. The sight of a chestnut mare brought a feeling she didn't expect. Meeting her eyes—one brown, one blue—spurred something within her, a warmth blooming in her chest.

Cassidy reached out with a trembling hand, brushing her fingers against the softness of her muzzle. "Hey, sweet thing."

The mare shifted lazily on her hooves, pushing into her with another low nicker.

She looked at a brass plate on the bridle—*Clover*.

"Clover, is it?" Cassidy mused, stepping closer to rub an

achingly familiar star on her forehead. "Are you a lucky one? Lord knows we could use a little extra."

Then, something happened she didn't expect. The mare stepped closer, laid her head over Cassidy's shoulder, and *pulled.*

With their chests pressed together, Cass deflated. Every aching thought, every ounce of fear came pouring out.

She let out a sob, gripping the mare's wither when her shoulders began to shake.

Cassidy never let herself cry, not if she could help it. There were times when a briny tear or two would slip free. She couldn't help it when the music from the opera summoned something inside her she didn't know existed. Tears for something beautiful. That time, it was worth it.

Others came when her soul overflowed. Ones Moone kissed away as he pieced together her broken heart after Solo. Now, she'd been shattered, pieces strewn across the stratosphere. So far, Cassidy wasn't sure she'd ever be able to gather them all. She wasn't sure if she'd want to.

The mare held her like an old friend, a trusting embrace usually built on friendship and time, patiently staying close as long as Cassidy needed her.

Smearing a hand across her nose, she pulled away with a sniffle. The mare pushed at her, blowing a hot huff of air at her cheeks.

"Thank you," Cassidy murmured, rubbing a palm against Clover's silky soft muzzle. "How about we go for a run?

Though only momentary, the wind in her hair proved to be a welcome reprieve.

Cassidy rode out of town like a bolt of lightning. Clover was up to the task, hooves beating the earth as if she were cut from the same cloth as Solo.

They zigged and zagged up tight switchbacks cut into the hillside, leaping over dried creek beds and prickly sagebrush, following wagon tracks creased in the soil. Up, up, up they went until the air was a little cooler and heavier.

Cassidy peered up at the sky when she dismounted, skin prickling when graying clouds rolled and roiled overhead.

"Storm's coming in," she murmured, smiling softly when Clover seemed to answer with a low neigh.

She patted the horse on the cheek and slid her attention to the mouth of the mine.

They'd been busy that morning, painstakingly lowering fresh supplies one load at a time. Water, food, lanterns, and more. Cassidy hoped it would be enough, safe this far from the fray. Perhaps the violence wouldn't find its way all the way up here.

"We're making good time," a woman's voice said.

Cassidy's gaze found her in a moment, her heart lurching when she spied Mrs. Booker, Daisy's mother.

She'd never spoken to her, not more than a few words in passing. Cassidy was good at that, avoiding the people of Gallow Gorge, like their affection and attention were like a cold she'd catch. She avoided the sickness of knowing someone, of building a family. Imagining their indifference was enough for her then.

Cassidy thought of Daisy, of all the ways she wished they could rewind time, go back, and avoid the loss of the little girl—her only friend, a sister of sorts. A loss that was her fault, through and through.

She blinked away the memory of the meager funeral they held. One where the entire town gathered in the cemetery on a hill. She still hadn't had the heart to talk to her then.

Cassidy wrung her hands. "Things are going well? How much longer?"

Mrs. Booker nodded like she knew every wayward thought rattling around in her head. She looked so much like Daisy: cow-brown eyes, dark hair. One braid instead of two. "Not long. You did well making sure we were ready, Ms. Callaghan."

Cass wondered how old she was. There were lines around her eyes, but no threads of grey in her hair. Perhaps, she wasn't much older than Cass, herself.

"Cassidy," she blurted, cheeks heating. "My friends call me Cassidy. Well, they would if I had any."

Mrs. Booker waved along another family, children wide-eyed, clutching handmade lovies to their chest. She bent down and offered a comforting whisper, a mother's assurance that everything would be alright.

Once safely tucked into a wooden trolley, the hoistman rang a bell, sending them down the shaft's ramp and into the darkness.

"You have many friends here, Cassidy," Mrs. Booker answered. "More than you probably realize."

"Do I?"

She nodded. "I hope so. Or else, what's all this for?"

Cassidy's stomach twisted. The words rose up; a thousand of them she wanted to say. All of them would never be enough. "I'm sorry. So sorry about Daisy. I didn't mean—"

"I know." She reached out for her, stilling her fidgeting fingers. "She fought against them, you know. Tooth and nail. It wasn't enough in the end, but she tried. And, for a moment, she looked a little like you."

Cassidy's breath caught. Her eyes stung. "I loved her. I really did."

"I know that, too." Mrs. Booker's face lifted, the most heartbreaking of smiles. "And I knew she gave you those books."

Cassidy's heart guttered, pitching straight to her feet. "You did?"

Mrs. Booker's smile widened, just a touch. "Eight-year-olds aren't known for their stealth. Besides, seeing someone as tough as you foster such a love for reading made finishing her lessons much easier. Makes me want to build a library."

Cass took her hand, squeezing. "Maybe we will. After all this, we'll build that library—for Daisy."

"I'd like that." She nodded.

The two women lingered, ushering families into the belly of the mine. Small groups at a time, the hoistman would send them down after the ring of a bell. Over and over, until only a few remained.

Cassidy wondered as they worked, if she'd opened herself up to the people of Gallow Gorge, if she and Daisy's mother might've been friends. She let herself picture the town, someday, some year after what they were bound for today, and saw the library. A humble little offering with a bookshelf or two in the corner of the Booker's general store. Small, but enough.

She didn't think about it long, not when the haunting toll of a bell rode a rush of wind from the town below.

Her skin prickled, boots grinding against stone as her eyes snapped to the horizon. A black-speckled cloud painted the line between brown and cloud-dotted blue. A hundred riders, maybe more.

Cass thought she might be sick, but there wasn't any time for that. There wasn't any time for anything.

"Time's up." Her attention snapped to Mrs. Booker. "I have to go."

"I know," she answered, gathering Cassidy in her arms for the swiftest of embraces. "Good luck. You bring those bastards down. Make them pay for what they've done."

"Be safe. Take care of them." Cass squeezed her, not daring to linger any longer. She twisted, taking off at a run, vaulting herself into the saddle.

They flew at the swiftest canter, hurtling down the hill back into town.

The streets bustled.

Guns brought to attention, crates of ammunition stacked at every station.

Cassidy shared a handshake with the mayor.

"Godspeed, Ms. Callaghan," he said, giving her a solemn nod.

Her fingers brushed against Katie Mays, heart flipping in the light of her sunny smile and golden hair.

They didn't need any words. Cassidy already knew.

Heart hammering, chin high, Cassidy mounted the stairs through the heart of The Copper Queen. She stepped out onto the balcony, keeping an eye on the dark clouds coming on the horizon.

They were ready.

[4 6]

MOONE

MOONE NEVER WENT TO WAR, NOT THE WAY OTHER men did. He never aspired to be a man like Grant or Sherman. There was never a part of him that wished he witnessed men mowed down by cannon fire or strolled through a tent city, a camp preparing for battle.

But that's what he found in the early morning light. Clusters of them between the sagebrush. Smoke from freshly lit fires curling skyward, carrying the scent of coffee and too-crispy bacon.

It wasn't like the last supper of Gallow Gorge the night before. Theirs was a celebration, a last hurrah to share one last sliver of joy and togetherness with the day's event so unsure. It was beautiful and wonderful—a sight to behold.

These men ate to prepare for battle.

James always loved that town more than he meant to. He understood why Cassidy was ready to sell her soul to the Devil to protect them.

But Moone loved her more. That's why he had to sell his instead.

James recognized the moment she made up her mind to

give herself up. Part of him wondered if he should've come up with a plan. But he needed no plan other than to be a strong, unmovable, and unbreakable barrier. Something to stand between her and Ransom. To end the battle before it began.

Still, the minute he and his stolen horse entered Ransom's camp, he wished he had ironed out the details before bolting out of Gallow Gorge like a bat out of hell.

There were fifty tents, at the very least. Eyes followed him, solemn and wordless behind tin cups of bitter coffee. Face after familiar face, those who used to call him Jimmy. There were others, too; hired guns, debts, and favors owed finally called in.

Ransom built himself an army to win her back— Agamemnon come to claim Helen.

Even without a sound plan beyond putting a bullet between Ransom's eyes and preventing the entire war, Moone never expected to stride right in.

It was a straight shot through the rows upon rows of tattered tents. Their master's stood like a beacon at the center, the beating heart of shadow and depravity. Black fabric fluttered in the barest desert breeze, bringing a chill that could only be caused by memory.

James had only seen it one other time—in the days leading up to the massacre at Faraday Creek. He'd never spent more than a minute or two inside. The jitters that gripped him as he split the folds and freely ventured inside hadn't eased now that he was a man.

Beyond the flaps, James found a war tent fit for a general. A sprawling table lay at the center between wooden posts. Trunks lined one side, and a bed too big for one person covered the opposite wall.

It was made up with the same blood-red velvets and satins he knew Ransom to favor, bedecked with handsome throw pillows, a fringed dressing gown, and a measure of rope. A stack of books sat prettily on a makeshift table. James recognized the names *Brontë*, *Austen*, and others.

It was a bed for a queen. For *her*—and something to bind her with in case she didn't come willingly.

It was too much for one man, far too much. Too her. It didn't take an idiot to see what Ransom planned once he fetched Cassidy from Gallow Gorge. Thinking about it, seeing it, the stage he set to vanquish her, turned Moone's stomach and sent a white-hot bolt of jealousy and anger spearing through him.

He would tear him to shreds with his bare hands if Ransom even thought—

No. James shook his head. There wasn't any time for that. Not when he had a moment to take whatever wasn't tied down.

His eyes landed on stacks of papers on the table. He'd start there.

Fingers wandered over text, property deeds, banking numbers with more money than any man ever dreamed, and the *pièce de résistance*—a living will. It'd been left open, in progress, with an inkwell and pen beside it. Moone couldn't help reading over it, eyes landing on Ransom's familiar, looping handwriting.

Upon my untimely death, my worldly goods and property, I leave to my wife, Cassidy Callaghan, in the care of a dutiful son, James Thaddeus Moone.

They'd spoken about it, but Moone hadn't thought his father of sorts would make the change so soon, so officially. Ransom wasn't a man who worried about death. There'd always be some way he could skirt out from beneath her cold grip. A way to live forever.

James thought about what Cassidy said—Ransom was just a man. If men could bleed, men could die. He hated the thought of leaving her behind—alone, again—but Moone was determined to find a way to finally see it through, even if he met his end as well. It'd be worth it; the pain of being tied to Ransom finally finished.

Without thinking, he folded it up, along with a handful of deeds and a bundle of money, stuffing it in the inner pocket of his vest. Maybe, if everything went as he hoped, it'd come in handy—the first payment of many.

There was no telling how much time was left before James was discovered. He still hadn't devised a plan other than to kill him in any way he could. But, until then, at least he could search for something Cassidy could hold onto after this was all over.

Even with Ransom dead and gone as she hoped and planned, there was still the remaining mystery of her family—how it all began. A mystery he was prepared to help her solve, even if it meant crossing an ocean.

If Jack had been so arrogant to bring something as important as the paperwork in his pocket, Moone knew there *had* to be something else hidden in the tent, something of value, some other clue.

James dove for the first trunk, flinging open the lid, tearing through the contents with little remorse as to what he disturbed. He'd seen them before, those journals. He'd watch Ransom pore over them in his study, reliving the past one volume at a time. It was an obsession, one threaded deeply in his fascination with Cassidy—why all of them were here now.

What's worse, Moone understood it. He lived it. He was living it now.

In a fever, he overturned pale blue satins, green taffetas, and other fabrics he couldn't name if he tried. He dug to the bottom of one, then the other, but came up empty—save for the notion this was all for her. More pretty things meant to tempt her, to silence her.

Moone froze when the light shifted.

"What are you doing here, boy?"

Ransom's voice at his back summoned a chill. It clawed down his neck, battling with the anger-inducing image he last held in his mind. One with the light fading from Cassidy's eyes, and Ransom's hands around her throat.

James squeezed his fists until his bones ached. He turned, lifting his chin. "I came to deliver on a promise."

Ransom let the flap shut behind him. "Which was? Killing your brothers in arms or absconding with my bride halfway across the desert?"

He lifted his shoulder. "I was protecting her like you asked me to."

His mentor huffed, wearing a wry smile as he traced the still-crimson line on his throat. "Something tells me she does well enough on her own."

"No thanks to you."

Jack cocked his head. "It has everything to do with me," he said, prowling closer, wearing the same chilling grin. "Such spirit. So much like her mother. All of this. Her, them... *you*. None of this would exist without me. You ought to thank me."

The thing was, Moone believed it. He didn't know if he believed in any sort of god, but fate—fate seemed to tap at the back of his mind the more pieces of the past he connected. Was he always meant to serve as her shield from that first moment in the Callaghan's cabin until now? Doomed to remain trapped in Ransom's shadow until whatever curse he'd been saddled with was lifted.

No, Moone's belief centered around Cassidy Callaghan. It was at her altar he worshiped. It was she who he sacrificed for, even if it meant more blood was meant to be spilled. Even if it was his own.

"I won't bother lying," James ground out, the words bitter. "I'd probably be dead if it weren't for you. And I won't deny that, with you, I had a better life than I could've dreamed of."

Ransom lifted a brow, circling around the other side of the table. "But?"

"It came with a cost."

The elder huffed out a laugh. "A cost, *really?*"

James nodded. "You ripped out all the good in me. What I already had. Like—" He swallowed the growing lump in his throat. He never allowed himself to think of her, his mother. Nothing of what came before all this. "I had this light inside that even he couldn't beat out of me. A light she put there. It wasn't obvious. It was *never* obvious. I didn't notice until it already happened. Like you slowly bled it out of me year after year. You made me into something I never wanted to be. And Cassidy… she reminded me of who that was. When I left, I never actually planned on coming back. Not after I met her."

Ransom's gaze fell to the table between them, head tilting with a crack of his neck. "I never thought of you as

the ungrateful type."

"I'm not ungrateful. Really, I'm not." Moone shook his head. This was taking too long, too much was at risk, and the shadow of boots gathered just outside. "It's brought me all here. It brought me to her. So"—he circled his fingers around the dirk hidden in his belt—"I suppose you're right. I should thank you for that, but not much else."

Jack's eyes slid to the jeweled blade in James's hand—*his* blade. "Have you come to kill me, then? Your father?"

"I wanted you to be that. I needed that from you more than anything. But no, not my father. A commander, a puppet master, but nothing more." Moone drew in a trembling breath. "So yes, I'm going to try."

His brows bent. "For what reason, boy?"

"I told you." James tightened his grip on the hilt. "I'm here to honor a promise. You made me swear to protect her. I plan to, no matter what. No matter who. I can't let you have her. You'll break everything she is."

Ransom's mouth went slack—a quiet realization. "You love her."

"I'd die for her," Moone bit, bending into a crouch—a rattlesnake coiled, ready to strike. "And you will."

James lunged, slashing with the shining blade. A hundred men's souls were pressed into the steel. It was high time to add Ransom's to the count. Some kind of poetic justice, the kind Cassidy sought, to end him with his favorite killing tool.

Ransom sidestepped it, ducking beneath it, laughing mirthfully. "You'll have to try harder than that, boy."

"I'm only getting started, you bastard." Moone swung, wider, faster, putting his weight behind it. True, his mentor was taller than most men, but James had muscle. The kind earned from running bloody errands, being the comeuppance of those who came up short. He was faster than he looked, and it'd only be a matter of time before he caught the older man off guard.

His knuckles sang when they collided with Ransom's jaw.

Jack wavered, working through the pain with a swipe of his fingers. "After all your training, is that all you can do?

On and on they danced, scattering papers, nearly turning over the table as James pursued him around the tent. Books were dumped to the floor, a wooden pole split down the middle, canvas wilting when they crashed into one of the tent's supports.

Moone's arms finally caught Jack around the middle—a sweet relief coursed through him when he threw him to the ground. He planted a knee in his chest, grinning when Ransom groaned.

It was like Cassidy said. He wasn't a monster, not the Devil to be feared. He was just a man.

And if men could bleed, then men could die.

"There's no stopping this, boy," Ransom breathed, blood coating his teeth. "You're noble to a fault. How heavy that heart must be. That's what will always hold you back. You'll never have this. You'll never be able to make her happy if you let it get the best of you."

Moone flipped the blade around, pressing the tip to Jack's chest. "You don't know that."

A laugh broke free from his mentor. The kind that sent a shiver slithering down his spine, a bad feeling James couldn't shake. "I know a liar, James. Cassidy Callaghan isn't one. She may have thought she was playing pretend, but you forget—I know that world. Those great ladies, like the lovely Aisling Byrne I saw in her. I looked into her eyes and knew she wasn't playing pretend. She fit so naturally, so happily.

You both came to fool me, but she fooled herself instead. As I've fooled you, now."

Something in him twisted, but he wouldn't give in. He couldn't show that weakness. Never again, he vowed. Certainly not now, not when he had their enemy in his grasp.

"I've got you, old man." Moone pushed in with the dagger. "There's no getting out of this."

"Old?" Ransom's eyes flashed. "I'm barely forty-five, boy. I may have acted like your father, but we may as well have been brothers. I had one of those once. One by title, but not by blood. Like you." Long fingers curled around his wrist, grip firm. His eyes narrowed, but that eerie glow remained. The thirst for blood Moone came to recognize. At that moment, he couldn't help but wonder—and fear—if it was his blood he was after now. "I've never forgotten him, what he did… or what he taught me."

"Look what happened to him," Moone spat. "Look where you are. That's some lesson."

Jack's smile grew. "Would you like to know what it was?"

"Only if they're your last words."

"I may have taught you to fence." Ransom squeezed around his wrist even firmer, voice low. "But it was that Irishman who taught *me* to fight another way. Ever heard of *bataireacht?*"

His gut lurched. "*What?*"

"Neither had I," he spat.

Moone should've seen it coming, should have noticed how his free hand reached blindly for the piece of wood. It wasn't a shillelagh, but it worked well enough. Especially when it connected with his temple and sent him sprawling to his back.

He scrambled to his knees, head pounding. A blink,

fuzzy and wet, told him Ransom drew blood.

"Come on, boy. Get up," he taunted him, glaring down with the blunt weapon in his hand. "If you want her so badly, then fight for her. *Kill me*."

James wavered, bending to scoop the blade up from where it'd gone askew. He needed to finish this. He couldn't afford any more mistakes, not with so much on the line. Not with Gallow Gorge's fate, or Cassidy's soul, dangling so precariously.

With a roar, he lunged, swiping with the blade. That was his first mistake, leaving himself so wide open for the sharp edge of the wood rod to send a shock through his ribs. He tried to dodge it, to pivot away, but was met with it on the opposite shoulder, then the knee.

He staggered.

Ransom laughed.

"What a champion you've made. Such spirit, like her. What a pretty, murderous creature she is." Another pelting wallop to the side. Moone saw stars, toppling to his knees. "All the more fun it'll be to break her of it, to breed the Irish out of her. My father would be so proud."

A scorching wave of fury crashed over him, but his limbs were too heavy to rise. Time charged forward, no matter how Moone wished he could turn it back and end it right then and there. But there was no going back, no revisiting the past to fix his mistakes, no helping Cassidy now.

He failed.

Ransom's dark gaze snapped over his shoulder.

James was gripped with a cold surge of panic, heart pounding, skin prickling when he remembered the shadow of men just outside. All of them lying in wait for their master to finish skewering their brother.

Voices surrounded him, a raucous cacophony as his vision fuzzed at the edges, and they bound his wrists.

"What should we do with him, boss?" a voice crooned in his ear. "String 'im up? Leave him for the coyotes?"

Ransom stood straighter, shoulders squaring. He smoothed back his hair and wiped the blood from his chin with a proffered handkerchief. He eyed his protégé, brows bent thoughtfully as he considered him, thinking of the proper punishment for his actions.

"No," he purred, sauntering forward, leaning to pluck his precious dagger from the ground. He turned it to and fro.

Moone's senses snapped to attention, fraught with guilt, with shame, that he'd done her wrong. Now, she'd never know. She'd never understand that it was only ever for her. But when James expected death, when he thought he'd taste the blade's sting, Ransom surprised him.

The men around them flinched when their master slammed the tip of the blade into the table, just out of Moone's reach.

"Keep him right where he is," Jack said as he bent, fingers tenderly caressing his cheek. "He needs to be here. I want him to see what happens to her once I've won what's mine. He needs to watch."

"*Jack*—" Moone bleated, chest heaving as he stared down at him. Maybe some part of Ransom loved him. Perhaps the father he wanted was deep down beneath the monster. Someone who'd see his plight and understand. "Please. Give it up. I am begging you. I'll do anything you want. Just leave them all out of it."

Ransom stood straighter, mouth bending just the slightest inch. "No."

Then the sharp sting in his temple and nothing else but blackness.

[47]

THE SKY WAS PREGNANT WITH RAIN. ROILING CLOUDS crackled with thunder, but the hoofbeats of Ransom's army beat the earth so fiercely it echoed louder than any rumble from the sky.

Cassidy kept a wary eye on the horizon, heart thumping so wildly, she worried it might give her away the second Ransom stepped foot in Gallow Gorge.

Everyone was in position. Each child tucked away in the safety of the mine, out of sight from the oncoming and inevitable danger. Every soul that clutched a rifle to their chest sent a prayer to any god that'd listen for them to make it through the day.

Cassidy didn't see the use. Not for herself. But, when she spied Daisy Booker's father mouthing the Our Father, she closed her eyes, leaned against a stack of sandbags, and whispered a plea to the heavens.

A storm was coming. Though a single drop of rain hadn't yet speckled her skin, Cassidy knew it was only a matter of time. It whispered on the wind, the tangy warmth clinging to the air of water on scorched earth.

A sudden silence swept over them, a chill raising the tiniest hairs on her arm. Then came the voice, calling for her with a lover's sweetness.

Ransom's words tolled like a bell, setting a tension in the air so sharp, one wrong move would send the house of cards tumbling down.

"Cassidy… Kathleen… *Callaghan*. Don't be coy, my darling. Come out and say hello."

Cassidy clutched the brim of her black hat, boots scuffling against wood as she made to stand, pulled to him like a sailor to a siren's song. She wanted to give in. She wanted to surrender, to give herself up and save them all the trouble.

A hand slapped over hers, stopping her before she could get any ideas. Her companion on the rooftop of The Copper Queen was a boy not much younger than her, maybe seventeen, but a good shot.

Cassidy silently pleaded with him, heart twisting the more Ransom taunted her from below.

His dark eyes were wide with fear. "Don't. Stick to the plan, or all of this is for nothing."

Her gaze slid through a seam to the street, breath held as she spied the mayor's shadow stride fearlessly to the center.

"Ms. Callaghan isn't here." He held his chin high, barrel chest out. "She left sometime in the night. As far as we're concerned, your business here involves only her and none of our townspeople. You made your point with the Booker girl. Now, please—*go*."

Cassidy winced at the lie. The mayor tried his best, but the waver in his voice gave him away.

He had every right to be afraid. They should all be scared-stiff, terrified after what'd been done to them—to

Faraday Creek, too.

"I don't take kindly to being lied to, especially after the generous offer I provided you before." Ransom wore a smile in the sound of his voice. The kind that cut straight through the gut of anyone he bestowed it upon. "She's here. And you'll give her to me, or the cost will be much higher than just a little girl."

"I told you." The mayor stood a little straighter. "She isn't here. Left."

Ransom tutted, lip curling. "Mister Mayor, I told you not to *lie* to me. I know she's around here, somewhere. I've had a man planted in this town for five years. He came to me this morning and told me so himself."

The shot sliced through the air before any of them could blink.

Cassidy jumped to her feet, revolver in hand. "I'm here, you bastard."

"Cassidy, *no!*" The boy clawed at her gun belt, but she shook him free.

Ransom's eyes slid to her, shoulders bouncing. "That wasn't so hard, was it?"

She bit back the threat of tears, fury twisting in her gut. "You didn't have to kill him."

"You gave me no choice, pet." His face was cold, unfeeling like the monster she always believed him to be; the mask, at last, removed—obliterated in the light of her betrayal. "You're really going to let all these people die for you? All for what... a decades-old grudge you couldn't possibly understand? They don't have any part in this story. They're nothing. There's no sense in any of them getting involved. Now, be a good lass and come down. Then this will *all* be over, and I can give you everything you ever wanted."

Cassidy's stomach filled with lead. He was right. The people of Gallow Gorge had little idea of the story between her and Ransom, let alone what happened between him and her parents. Hell, even *she* didn't have the full scope, no matter how badly she wanted to know. Aisling's full story died with her, journals lost once she was gone—except for one.

She didn't want to let them all die. She couldn't.

Cassidy, barrel still leveled at Ransom perched on his gelding, looked across the rooftops of Gallow Gorge and felt a hundred eyes upon her. All of them filled to the brim with a quiet determination—they wouldn't let her leave. Not without a fight.

She was their family. Their vengeance personified. Now, they were going to help her get hers.

Cassidy found Katie Mays tucked in a cracked window of Ridley's brothel. The brown-eyed blonde nodded, offering an encouraging smile.

They'd fight. There was no turning back now.

Cassidy took the shot.

Ransom's horse reared. Her bullet nicked his shoulder, barely drawing blood.

The sound sent the street into a tizzy. Shots zinged, wood splintered, and Ransom took off at a gallop.

Cassidy fired again and again, squeezing the trigger until nothing was left in the barrel.

Her ears roared. She took cover, flinching when a piece of lead sent a shower of sand over the brim of her hat.

Cassidy counted, hands trembling as the battle erupted, and the sky split open at last—bringing the long-threatened promise of rain.

One. Two. Three. Four. Five. Six.

She whipped the cylinder shut, blinking sheets of water away as she took aim.

Every shot ricocheted down the length of her arm. Her fingertips buzzed. Her mind did, too, when she sent a rider flying off the back of his horse, spouting blood from a fresh wound in his cheek.

The flash of red spurred her on, urging her to take another, then another. Payment with a pound of flesh, though she'd take a hundred or more for what they'd done to Daisy Booker.

Images of her frail, charred body flashed through Cassidy's mind. They threatened to turn her stomach, to draw tears from her eyes. It was too easy to get caught up in the sight burned into her: the smell, the sway, the way her mother cradled the charred remains to her chest and cried once they cut her down.

No, Cassidy let it *fuel* her. Let the last look at Solo's black eyes propel her forward. Let the ringing in her ears grow to a dull roar, fury boiling through her veins as she picked off one blue bandana at a time.

"Cassidy!" A voice called her name.

She was blind to anything but red.

Ransom's men came in a flood, hooves splattering soaked earth while the rain poured.

A click. Cassidy squeezed the trigger again. Nothing.

"Cassidy!" the voice roared again. A hand yanked on her sleeve as a blast of air went past her ear.

Cassidy fell to her knees, taking cover only for a moment.

Her companion's black hair hung in his eyes, dripping in tiny rivulets over his tanned face. "There's a sharpshooter on the roof across from us."

Her gaze slid across the jagged line of rooftops, stomach

dropping when the wooden railing above their heads splintered into smithereens.

"Shit," she ground out.

He nodded. "Yeah. *Shit.*"

"That sounds wrong coming out of your mouth." Cassidy laughed, flinching when another round pierced the wall of sandbags at their backs.

His mouth quirked up. "I heard you talk like that since you were barely older than me. Thought now was a good enough time to give it a try."

"You're incorrigible." Cassidy flipped open the cylinder, filling the chambers with fresh rounds.

"You're a bad influence, Ms. Callaghan," he joked back.

Cassidy fired off a shot, then another, taking two men with them. Her attention flew back to the boy as he picked off another floozy with his rifle. "My friends call me Cassidy."

"*Cassidy.*" He beamed, sticking out a hand. "Henry."

She heartily shook it. "Nice to meet you, Henry."

They ducked when the bright zing of lead flew between them. The sharpshooter was getting closer.

She nodded toward the Winchester in his hand. "Mind if I give that a try?"

Victory. Cassidy could taste it, sharper with every man they put down. Gunfire ripped through the air, clashing with the flashes of lightning and crackles of thunder echoing close behind.

Her heart twisted when she spied a familiar face in the shadow of the arcade, wide-eyed in death. Casualties were inevitable. Cassidy knew it in her gut. But, as shot after shot peppered Main Street, ringing out from the windows and rooftops, they still had a chance.

Henry tossed her the rifle, pulling a pistol from the back

of his pants.

Leaning against the sandbags, Cassidy closed her eyes for a split second.

Time surrendered, blurring the edges of reality, dulling the sound as she pulled in her focus and set her sights on the gunman trained on them—on her.

Cassidy pulled back the bolt, ejecting an empty round. She sucked in a deep breath, keeping a solid weld of her cheek against the butt, and squeezed the trigger.

It jolted against her shoulder. Sound came rushing back in. The sharp staccato of rain pelting her clothes. An echo of thunder. The splinter of wood and the dull *thunk* of a body collapsing.

Something warm sprayed her face.

Cassidy smeared the wetness away. Her sleeve came away stained red.

Her skin prickled. Her stomach turned, boots slipping on slick wood as she lunged for Henry beside her. His shoulders slumped at an awkward angle, pistol looped around a single finger with his face to the ground.

Hands trembling, Cassidy bit back a sob as she turned him over, falling backward when she saw his handsome, young—so young, *too young*—face shattered through the cheek.

Cassidy rocked on her heels, head spinning, flinching when the ting of fractured glass split the air from across the street.

She staggered to her feet, vaulting the Winchester into the air with the tip of her boot. It lingered momentarily, snatched up with a flick of her wrist as she barreled inside The Copper Queen.

Taking the stairs two, three at a time, Cassidy *flew*. She

flipped the Colt from her hip when she saw a man in the doorway, faltering when Lucas Smith held up bloody palms from his gut as he slid down the wall.

She paused for a moment, kneeling to take stock of his injuries. He was a mess, belly split open like carrion. Too far gone for the surgeon to fix.

"That bad, huh?" He forced a red-stained smile. "I can see it all over your face, Freckles."

Her heart lurched, and she bristled with anger. "Don't call me that."

"M'sorry." Lucas let out a wet cough. His eyes met hers, speaking to her in a way she never thought possible.

"It isn't going to work, is it?" she whispered.

"We're giving it a fair shot, but there's a lot of us down." He winced, groaning as blood pulsed between his fingers like a creek in springtime. "For what it's worth, m'sorry for how I treated you. Y-you're different than anyone else I ever met. I"— his face paled, breaths coming further apart—"I should've been better to you."

"I forgive you." It was the least she could do for a dying man. He might've been a drunk, but at least he wasn't Ransom's mole. Cassidy forced a playful grin. "Though I'm not sorry for slapping you upside the head with a bottle of whiskey."

"I deserved it." Lucas smiled again, squeezing her hand. "Now, take this and go."

Cassidy gathered the short-barreled shotgun from the floor beside him. Messy but efficient. She offered him a grim smirk. "This'll take the head off someone."

"Make it two someones," he wheezed, sucking in one last rattled breath as she stepped out onto the arcade.

On the street, things were worse than she thought.

Worse than she feared.

Bodies freckled the earth. Blood mixed with rainwater, painting Gallow Gorge in crimson ribbons as the body count grew.

A blue bandana thug lunged out from behind a pillar. Cassidy swiftly answered with the thunderous call of buckshot. It ripped through him at the close angle, spraying pale shiplap with red chunks.

Yesterday, the sight might've turned her stomach. She was still too full of hope things would work. That there wouldn't be so much death. That they stood a chance. Now, she was pissed, determined to claw victory from Ransom's cold fingers at the point of a barrel, even if she had to die to do it.

Cassidy obliterated another of Ransom's men, one she recognized from *Colina de Dragones*. He was kind to her then. Now, he'd be kind to no one. Pity he chose the wrong side.

Her heart roared in her ears. A vein pulsed in her temple. The rain should have cut her to the bone, but Cass didn't feel cold. All she had was her rage.

—until a river of blonde hair hanging from the upstairs balcony of Ridley's tore it to shreds.

Cassidy halted, knees wavering. She held a wooden post with a white-knuckle grip, grinding her teeth as they started to drop one by one. The cold seeped in, but not from the rain.

As if the sky took pity on her, the drops began to slow.

Her ears rang. Vision swam. Her feet moved of their own accord. The toes of her boots dragged through the mud, but she held her chin high. One foot in front of the other, leading her straight into oblivion.

No one else would die for her.

It played out as if she watched from beneath the floorboards of the general store. Her mind hovered a mile away, looking on as the end unfolded in a series of never-ending seconds.

The first bullet struck her in the arm. Cassidy fought through the sting, lifting her hands in the air—surrendering, giving up before anyone else bled on her behalf.

She was the one bleeding now. It seeped through her sleeve, dripping from her elbow as she lifted her eyes to the sanguine sky. The storm washed it crimson. As if their fight lifted to the heavens, painting it a deeper shade with every soul lost.

Cassidy saw him, Ransom, a figure standing out against the bright bloom of light. His eyes carefully regarded her every movement, growing wider when another shot rang out.

She'd been shot before. Scars dotted her body like her freckles—almost too many to count. But when the second bullet ripped through her abdomen, Cassidy's world shook.

"ENOUGH!" a voice bellowed, carried by the wind.

Open. She had to keep her eyes open. Long enough to make a deal with the devil.

[48]

C ASSIDY'S WORLD TILTED. THE EDGES OF HER VISION fuzzed, wavering when she blinked.

Hands jostled her. Her boots listlessly moved across the ground. She went through the motions of walking, but an unseen force towed her forward until the cold bite of wood met her cheek.

"What in the hell have you done to her?" a familiar voice snapped.

"None of yer goddamned business," someone answered, followed by a flutter of fabric. "Put her in this."

"Says who?"

"Says the man who'll burn your brothel down with the girls inside if you don't listen." He paused to give a dark, twisted chuckle. "But not until after we all get a taste."

"She'll die before I can do it if you don't fetch me the doctor."

"Doctor's dead."

"Bandages, then. Else, she'll bleed until there's no red left in her hair."

A beat. "Fine. *Bandages.* But make it quick. He's not real

patient."

Cassidy's heart drummed the whole while. There was a pulsating in her side. Her fingers reached, reflexively shrinking back when her touch sent a bolt of pain through her entire body.

Shot. She'd been shot. Worse than ever before.

"Cassidy! *Oh God.*" Another voice joined the chorus, stained with panic and pain. "What do we do?"

"You can't help her in your state. You need a doctor, yourself."

"The hell I can't. I've had worse. Nothin' a needle and thread won't fix. But *that*"—a jagged gasp—"We can't just sew her up. She's bleeding too badly."

Madame Ridley's plump visage hovered above her, weathered face filled with concern. She smelled of sweet tobacco, stained with the iron tang of blood. Her own dried and clinging to the hair around her face.

"I'm sorry about this, sweetheart."

The madam pulled at Cass's layers, gingerly peeling them away as she cradled her weary limbs. She shivered more with each one, teeth chattering as she mouthed the words she wanted to say.

"*Moone.*" She groaned, blinking past Madame Ridley's shoulder. A face hovered there, blue-eyed and handsome. Her fingers stretched, fighting against the pain as she reached for him.

A hand shot out, wrapping around hers in a comforting embrace. Not his, not his face. Not blue eyes, but golden brown.

"He's not here, sugar," Katie murmured, brushing the hair from her face as she pressed a fevered kiss to her knuckles. She twisted toward her mistress, lovely face so horridly pale. Cassidy wondered if she was a ghost, if they all were, if she were already dead.

Madame Ridley's ruddy cheeks blanched, eyes lifting across the room. "Fetch me an iron. *Hot.*"

Footsteps sounded moments later. Rushed voices whispered back and forth. Madame Ridley barked, "Hold her down."

Cassidy's body canted, back bowing from the floor, when the blazing end of an iron rod pierced her skin, buttoning together the hole in her side. Where things had been hazy at the edges before, now she was *awake*, fighting against the burning, piercing pain.

"I'm so sorry, Cassidy," Katie whispered against her cheek, stroking her hair. "It'll be over in a second."

"Yeah, but she'll wish she was dead once she realizes what's about to happen."

"W-what is it?" Cassidy wheezed, head lolling on the floor once the fire ebbed.

"Come on, up you come." Madame Ridley spoke as softly as a mother hen. She lifted her from the floor, setting her in a chair. Their hands worked quickly, unplaiting Cassidy's hair and slipping a bundled fabric over her head. A corset was tied at her back, the pressure a welcome feeling. It kept the pain away.

Madame Ridley's eyes found Cass's again, never able to stay in one place for long. "Think you can stand?"

Cassidy nodded, gripping the table's edge and gritting her teeth as she pushed herself up. Silky, soft, pale silk fluttered down around her ankles. She blinked, vision clearing in time to see a pair of thugs stride her way.

"What is this? What's happening?" Cassidy's stomach leaped into her throat. "I want to talk to Jack."

"Oh, you'll talk to him, alright." One sneered, gripping her arm. Katie shouted in protest, but it was no match for the pistol to her cheek.

Cassidy moved to strike him, to fight back, but her body wouldn't listen. It was useless, too heavy, too slow.

"You've got a date to keep, Missus," the other laughed in her ear.

They dragged her into the street so quickly Cassidy's bare feet couldn't keep up. Her eyes couldn't either, not as they slid from corpse to corpse lying in the dirt—a massacre as bloody as she'd ever seen.

She felt a surge of smug pride at the number of blue bandanas stained red with blood, but not enough to assuage the guilt when she met every dead-eyed gaze from the shadow of the arcade.

Her stomach sank, twisting with horror when she lifted her eyes and met Ransom's sinister smile, hands clasped behind his back, chest puffed out—a groom waiting for her in the charred skeleton of the chapel he burned with Daisy Booker inside.

"Cassidy, my darling," he crooned, lifting a hand toward her.

Cassidy spat at it.

Ransom remained chillingly unruffled, smearing his palm on the chest of the man beside him.

Cass's eyes searched him. She knew his face. Tall, waif-like in his black suit and white collar—the preacher. The preacher whose clergy burned before his eyes and lay dead in the street. His eyes were wide, hands bound, flinching when Ransom touched him.

Ransom stepped over the charred rubble. Cassidy was dragged behind him, an unwilling pawn in his game, a

reluctant bride—white dress and all.

"What is this?" she demanded, jerking a calloused hand from her bare shoulder. "What are you doing?"

Ransom blinked down at her, still wearing his cold, unfeeling smirk. He glanced at the altar, to the preacher, and back to her. "You made a promise. We're getting married, Cassidy, before you can change your mind or run off again."

He reached for her, falling into a familiar cadence; the dance they'd done together in the month Cassidy thought he was under her thumb—but really, she was under his.

Cassidy leaned away, voice soft, hoping that a reminder of what they shared would somehow reach the man inside the monster.

"Jack," she murmured. "You don't want to marry me. You want to marry Aisling. I'm *not* her. I could never be her."

"I have no interest in repeating the past." His dark eyes softened. He brushed a thumb against her cheek—she let him. "I know you're not her, pet."

Ransom bent, grazing his lips against hers.

Cassidy couldn't shake the bitter taste, the reminder of what he'd done, of what he'd do to her if she let him have his way.

"I don't want to marry you," she whispered.

His sneer widened, lingering a breath away. "I wasn't asking." Ransom pulled her by the elbow, standing them side by side. "Preacher, you may start. The quick version, please."

Cassidy's head swam. She wasn't in any shape to fight. A quick glance told her what she felt—Madame Ridley's attempt to cauterize the wound in her side failed. She was bleeding again, staining pale silk with a river of red.

"I can't," the preacher argued, holding a bible to his chest with trembling, bound hands. "Not under these circumstances. Wouldn't be right."

The monster inside Ransom shattered the mask of eerie calm. He struck the clergyman in the face, sending him to his knees before Cassidy could blink.

Her breath came in quiet bursts, heart roaring in her ears as the man shakily rose to his feet and began to speak.

"Dearly beloved, we are gathered here today to witness the joining of these two souls in holy matrimony."

"You left this behind, my love." Ransom took her hand as the preacher prattled on, eyes aglow as he slipped the weighted diamond onto her hand. "With this ring, I thee wed. With my body, I thee worship. With all my worldly goods, I thee endow."

Cassidy blinked, staring over his shoulder, at the preacher, everywhere all at once as they started speaking to her—expecting her to *answer*.

"Do you, Cassidy Kathleen Callaghan, take His Lord, Johnathan Xavier Ransom, to be your husband, to love and obey, so long as you both shall live?"

Cassidy shook her head, over and over and over until she was dizzy. She flinched at a loud whinny out on the street. Her chest ached. The answer sat heavily on her tongue as the weight of her mother's diamond on her finger. She tried to gulp it down, knowing it spelled certain death.

Up it came, anyway, souring in her mouth like bile.

"No."

Ransom's eyes flashed. "What do you mean, *no?*"

Cassidy squared her shoulders, steeling her gaze. The image of Aisling flashed through her mind: an iron will, unwilling to give in, no matter what. "I mean, *no*. I don't take you to be my husband, my anything. I've given you too much of me already. My parents. My life. Even part of my soul. You don't get any more."

"I wasn't asking," Jack repeated. His catlike smile shifted, and his gaze's smoldering warmth grew so cold she felt it prickle on her skin. "You're going to marry me, Cassidy."

"No," she repeated. "I refuse."

Pain speared through her. Ransom's fist slammed into her cheek, sending her to the floor in a heap of blood-stained white silk.

Cassidy coughed, spitting a glob of crimson onto the floor, barely afforded a moment before he had a fistful of her hair, drawing her to her knees while she screamed and clawed at his hand.

Memories flashed through her mind, bittersweet, an irony that she'd end up in the same position as her mother.

Ransom slipped a pistol from his belt, pulling back the hammer with a curl of his lip.

"I'm willing to forgive your little misjudgment, my darling. Just say the word, and we'll leave all this behind."

Cassidy sucked in a trembling breath, eyes darting past the skeleton of the chapel to the bridleway. Bodies scattered the ground. A fire blazed at the end of the street. Thunder grumbled, the passing storm from earlier a distant memory. Her body ached, hurting in places she never thought it could. None of it compared to the pain of being trapped in a gilded cage—a pretty bird with no real use, not even a name. So, she'd be like Aisling: firm, unyielding in her final moments.

In her next life, she'd never be so weak to entertain the thought of him again.

A slow smile bloomed, her decision resolute and unwavering. She hoped he'd burn in the heat of her gaze.

"Never."

Ransom's face quivered, a flicker of disappointment he covered with a sneer. He raised the barrel between her eyes. "So be it."

Cassidy closed her eyes, centering herself on the final precious few beats of her heart, counting each one as she waited for the end. She saw them there, on those emerald moors with the wind in their hair. Her mother's smile, and her father's love just within reach. *Home.*

The gunshot split the air. Cassidy fell to the floor, gasping for breath when she opened her eyes and came face to face with Ransom's wide-eyed death mask—skull shattered to smithereens.

Bloody bits of brain spattered her arms and hands. They shook when she sat up and turned them over, lifting her eyes to find James Moone standing over them—smoking pistol in hand.

[49]

CASSIDY

"WHAT HAVE YOU DONE?" SHE GROUND OUT, SHOULDERS heaving with every labored breath.

Ransom was dead. *Jack Ransom was dead.* And she hadn't been the one to do it.

Moone glared down at the body, wearing an eerily quiet calm, when his eyes slid to her.

"I just saved your life," he declared, as if it were that simple. As if he hadn't just taken everything she ever wanted. First, her trust. Then, the fleeting fool's hope for a future—now this.

It was too familiar, too much like when Moone took matters into his own hands and set things ablaze at *Colina de Dragones.* She should've killed him, then. It would've saved her the trouble of everything that came after.

Cassidy gripped the edge of a pew, feet smearing on the floor as she pushed herself to stand. She stared at Ransom's open-mouthed gape, fury curling past the pain fuzzing the edges of her vision. "I've waited my entire life to do that."

"I saved your life," Moone repeated, lowering his chin. "You'd be dead if it weren't for me."

She met his gaze, lips parting with yesterday's lovelorn worries when she spied the gash in his temple and a bruised jaw. "What happened to you? Where did you go?"

A vein twitched in his jaw. "I don't expect you to understand."

"Just to listen when you tell me you're sorry."

"Cassidy." Moone's voice softened. He reached for her, pistol still tucked firmly in his grip. "I did it for you... for *us.*"

She shook her head. "*Us?* Since when was there an us to do anything for?"

He squared his shoulders, shifting on his feet to stand taller. "Since always. Since you told me you loved me."

"A mistake," she snapped.

"No." The corners of his mouth lifted. "The only mistake was letting him get so close to you. For delivering you into his hands. *My* mistake. I should've taken care of this right away."

The ghost of his smile, the memory of the night they'd spent together only hours before, and the love Cassidy was utterly convinced she felt for him. It all tore through her veins like molten lead. "That doesn't explain why you left."

Moone bristled, his face distant. The opposite of the man she knew, the one who bent to her level, who anchored himself so deeply in those moments with her, she may as well have always been in his arms.

"I suppose not."

A wave of pain passed over her in a cloud, a hurricane of it. Her knuckles ached, fingers quivering with the force she gripped the wooden pew as she tried to focus on her anger instead. Did a wound have to bleed so much?

"Care to share?" Cassidy muttered in a jagged wheeze.

He licked his lips, dusting a palm over his chest. "I was going to kill him for you, for myself… for us. Weeks ago."

"I never asked you to do that," she spat. "I never asked for your help."

"No, you didn't," he answered wearily. "You never did, not ever. But selfishly, I wanted it more for myself. I wanted *more*. Payment. An insurance policy of sorts to make sure he honored his side of the bargain. Ransom named me his heir—it's all mine, now." Moone blinked at the body; then his gaze slid back to her. "And, according to him… so are you."

Lead. Cassidy's stomach was filled to the brim, sinking so far below the floorboards she'd need a shovel to dig it back up. "So, this is about money? Is that all you care about?"

"Not before. I never believed in it, in what he did. Then I met you. I saw the depth of your conviction, how determined you were to get what you wanted, the determination to so unapologetically be yourself, to be good… and I wanted that, too. For once in my life, I believed in something. I believed in *you*, that I could be what you saw in me. But, after everything in Sacramento and at *Colina de Dragones*, things changed. You didn't seem to mind the things you got to do. You liked the things he gave you, who he made you into. You told me so yourself." Moone gave her an indifferent shrug. "I thought you'd be happy about it."

The bitter truth of it was he was right. Those petit-fours and petticoats. Lazy afternoons spent reading in the library, and fabrics so sinfully soft—unlike everything she'd come to associate with herself. She was meant to be different than the bounty hunter; her destiny, a legacy left by her mother.

Still, Cassidy was wilder than that, no matter how well she played pretend.

His wild girl. But not anymore.

"Not if this was the cost," she fumed. They could've had everything. Anything. All the things James promised.

He shook his head. "That wasn't the only thing I was after, Cass. There was something else. Something you—"

"Stop." Cassidy worked her jaw, fighting past the turning of her stomach when she studied Ransom's corpse again. Moone's master—the absent Sheriff of Gallow Gorge. This was just a sliver of the fallacy. Piece by piece, she'd put it together. She'd figure out why. "How long?"

Moone glanced at the body. He knew what she was asking and hesitated before the truth spilled out. "Five years."

She nodded toward Ransom. "On his payroll." A statement, not a question.

"In a manner of speaking." Moone traced his tongue along the inside of his bottom lip, blue eyes vacant.

"To do what, exactly?"

He offered a half-hearted lob of his shoulders. "To steer things in a way that favored him. The bounties I gave you were for the competition or nobodies."

Cassidy's teeth ached, and head fuzzed. Her side pulsed, blood oozing through the skirt to paint thick stripes on the floor. So, *so* much of it. She couldn't think about that now. Not with so many answers within reach.

"What about Ball?"

Moone gave her the faintest smile. "You were too good at your job, Cassidy. The stack got shorter and shorter. I tried to keep it from you, but I knew you'd smell the lie if I told you there weren't any others."

"You didn't want to lie." She laughed, stained with bitterness. "First time for everything, I suppose."

"I didn't lie about what it'd bring you, did I?" He

motioned around the half-scorched chapel. "You crossed him. Now look."

Cassidy lifted her chin. "Maybe not, but you lied about everything else."

Moone stepped closer. "Not everything, Cassidy."

He had that look in his eye, the kind that set fire to her soul the night before. One she was prepared to die for, to keep him safe with everything else she held dear. Cassidy couldn't stand it, the reminder of what was, what could have been.

"Don't," she pleaded, heart stuttering when his fingers tentatively brushed her hand.

"Don't what?"

"Don't tell me that you love me and pretend that it means shit," she hissed, biting back the sting of tears. Cassidy let herself want everything with him. He let her believe they could. And then he ran away and said it was for the greater good. She was so angry she could cry, but angrier still that she hated herself for wanting to believe him, for craving him so badly it made her weak.

Moone sagged, gazing at the body between them with a roll of his jaw. He lifted her pearl-gripped pistol, twisting it to and fro with a tic in his jaw, face shifting like he'd come to a resolution in his mind.

"It's time to let go, Cassidy," he rumbled softly, sucking in a trembling breath before lifting his stare so intensely it drew her hair on end. "Let old things die and think about what's to come after. What *should* come after."

"James," she whispered, shaking her head as an unbidden tear slipped down her cheek. The fire in his eyes was unlike anything she'd seen him wear. Only one man ever looked at her that way, and he was lying dead on the floor at her feet.

"Don't—"

Moone surged forward, capturing her mouth in a bruising kiss. She melted into him, hating herself for how much he affected her, how much she needed him, how much they needed each other. His fingers twisted in her hair. He slanted his mouth against hers, groaning when she met him with her tongue. She couldn't help it. He tasted like memory, like heaven and hell painted in regret, hope, and shame.

It ended as quickly as it began, and for good reason. The blazing lust in James's eyes, the feeling of his body pressed against hers, was almost enough to let the world burn for—almost. But Cassidy couldn't forget his lie. None of them. Ever.

"You lied. You lied about so much. But I didn't." Her lips brushed against his. A sob shook her shoulders. The decision was clear. She knew what she had to do.

Cassidy shoved him back, never mind the pain in her side or in her soul, pulling the pistol loose from his hand as he stumbled over Ransom's body.

Moone landed hard on the floor. He winced, drawing to his knees, palms raised. "I didn't have any choice." His plush mouth was ripe and kissed-bruised. It took everything in her, everything she was, everything she built herself to be, to keep from diving to the floor and doing it again.

"You had *every* choice!" Cassidy cried out, more tears coming when she tasted familiar words on her lips. No, *no*. She wouldn't give in; she wouldn't give away any more of her heart. Anyone else would have to pry it from her cold, dead fingers.

She lifted her pistol and pulled a stony mask of indifference over her face. "I told you that if you lied to me again, I'd kill you."

Moone's eyes widened, grim realization carved in the tic of his jaw. *Good*. He remembered.

"Don't do this," he pleaded, broad chest heaving. He chewed on his words, surely coming up with some more poisonous lies that'd convince her to be something else, to believe him in the glaring light of his betrayals. "I love you, Cassidy."

"If you really loved me, you wouldn't have done it," Cassidy spat, pulling back the hammer. Her stomach churned. If she said any more, she might be sick.

She sucked in a deep breath. Moone closed his eyes, resigning himself to the fate she gave him. Her truth blinding in the shadow of his deceit.

Every bullet had a consequence, good or bad. That's what she had to decide. That's what her Da taught her. What she told him she'd never forget.

So, Cassidy steadied the muzzle, took a breath, and squeezed the trigger.

Moone cried out when the bullet pierced his shoulder, splintering a wooden beam three paces behind him.

Tears streamed down her face. She threw the pistol away, lip curling. "*Run*. Get out of here, and never come back. If you do… if I catch you, I won't miss. I *will* put a bullet in your head."

"Cassidy, please." Moone staggered to his feet, gripping the weeping wound. "I don't want to leave you."

"You already did." She gave him a bitter smile. A sob rattled through her chest. "Now go before I give you a less generous offer."

His boots slid against scorched wood, body slumped as he turned away toward the gathering of Ransom's men at his back.

They all regarded her carefully, the man in front of her and their master dead at her feet. Their fight would be finished another day. Each and every one of them a fresh name on her list.

A stalemate was silently declared with a solemn nod from an older man who held a beckoning palm out to James as he staggered down the street.

"Moone?" Cassidy called after him, drawing his gaze so quickly she worried he might fall. She called upon every ounce of strength, on the cold-hearted bitch she always believed herself to be; James, the fool convinced she wasn't. "Once we've cleaned up this mess, you're on my bounty list. Justice will be served."

"I'm starting to think you can't live without some kind of vendetta, Freckles. So, I have no doubt that I'm at the top of that list." The corners of his mouth lifted the slightest hint. "But like I said before… you've never had a bounty like me. So, good luck. It's going to be one hell of a chase."

Cassidy knew, deep down in her bones, he was right.

EPILOGUE

The Deputy and the Devil

Six Months Later

PIECE BY PIECE, THEY PUT THEMSELVES BACK TOGETHER. Blood was washed from the wood of the arcade. Windows replaced. Bodies buried. The dead mourned but never forgotten, not by her or anyone.

Cassidy, herself, healed over time. A surgeon came a day's ride to piece her back together. The ache still lingered.

Like a forest razed by fire, things grew back greener than before. A fresh coat of paint covered the barest shiplap. Madame Ridley hung new velvet curtains in the balcony windows. Mrs. Booker built Daisy's library.

Cassidy emerged from the sheriff's station, straightening the hem of her jacket and the brim of her hat. She strode to a familiar perch that used to belong to someone else and leaned a shoulder against a wooden beam.

Striking a match on the railing, Cassidy lit the end of her cigar, sending a stream of smoke curling through the air as Katie strode by with a smile.

"Afternoon, Deputy."

Cass dipped her hat, proudly rubbing her sleeve over the silver star pinned to her chest. "A beautiful one, at that."

After everything, all the death and heartache too heavy to carry alone, there was no greater miracle than Katie coming back from the dead. Figuratively, of course, but Cassidy had been wholly convinced, world shattered, when she saw her hanging from the window. Broken enough to stride into the middle of the street to surrender.

Luck was on Katie's side; the bullet grazed her with just enough force to knock her unconscious for a moment or two. Cassidy might finally believe in prayer because of it.

The blonde stepped into the shadow, pulling a parcel from a pocket hidden within her skirt. "These came for you."

"Thank you." Cassidy smiled, smothering her cigar with her heel as she gathered the stack from her hands.

"There's a telegram in there from New York I thought might interest you," she said, motioning toward the small package. "Those, I'm not sure. They're postmarked from someplace I never thought we'd get mail from. All the way from *England*, isn't that odd?"

Cassidy's stomach flipped. She eyed it, rolling it over in her hand. The weight and shape felt familiar, like the smell of home or the feeling of a mother's embrace. Katie hovered over her shoulder, watching as she tore open the telegram.

Dear Ms. Callaghan - STOP
No Aisling Callaghan in our records - STOP
Try additional name - STOP
Ellis Island Records - STOP

"Cassidy, I'm so sorry," Katie breathed, fingers brushing her back. "I know you've been looking like your life depends on it. But it's not the end. We'll find something about them. Don't give up yet."

"I won't," Cass whispered, smiling fondly when her former lover bid her farewell and trounced across the street at the beckon of her mistress—even as her heart sank with disappointment.

She'd searched for a sliver of history about her parents from the moment she was well enough to try. She even traveled to Sacramento to explore the library's deepest catacombs. Perhaps she'd have to travel further to find out more.

While in California's golden capitol, Cassidy couldn't bear to return to Ransom's house. She asked Madame Dubuisson about *Colina de Dragones* and heard it burned down. She didn't bother asking how. Not yet.

The search for Moone went cold from the beginning, losing track of him outside Chicago three months prior.

That didn't stop her from thinking about him, wondering what their life would look like if either of them chose differently—if she took his hand and ruled over Sacramento by his side in Ransom's stead—or if she never chased Doc Ball in the first place.

Her mouth wavered with the beginnings of a wistful smile, one that wished for something that looked like what her parents had—a quiet homestead a mile outside of town. A place where she could teach their children to shoot tin cans off a fencepost just like she and her Da. Or, perhaps, a home overlooking the cliffs in Ireland—a brand new adventure far away from the past and all the hurts the West gave them.

It didn't matter. They didn't choose the right path. It was over. All of it was over.

Cassidy hooked her thumb beneath the brown paper, tearing it open to reveal the most luxurious book she'd ever seen. Rich red leather, gleaming leaves pressed in soft ridges, and a delicate script reading—*Jane Eyre: An Autobiography by Charlotte Brontë*. She sighed, flipping through the pages until she came to the front cover.

Her heart leaped, recognizing James Moone's scrawl in a second, her heart roaring louder as her gaze darted over each word.

Cassidy,

I'm not much for reading, but if you were a book, you'd be a well-worn, well-loved volume. One whose pages I'd thumb through every chance I got, even if the ending was bound to break my heart. I'll never stop wishing we could've done things differently. My life isn't the same without you.

Things have changed, I know, and I don't know if you'll ever be able to forgive me. I'm hoping that one day, you might find it in your heart to try. Even if it's for old times' sake.

You seemed pretty fond of this book. Sometimes, I wonder if you might've thought of him as Rochester, but I don't think that's right. Rochester is me—the liar that broke your heart. I hope one day you'll understand. But now, the manor's been burned down. And I'm still here. He and Jane found each other again. I hope we will, too.

As for the other, there are more if you know where to look.

I love you more than I can say. I don't know how to say anything else. By the time you get this, I'll be back home. Maybe I'll see you soon. Maybe I can help you find the rest. Maybe I'll finally be worthy of your good heart. A man can hope, can't he? This time, it'll be you arresting me instead of the other way around.

Like I always said: if you catch me, I'll come willingly.

James x

Cassidy let out a shuddering sob, smearing the tears from her cheeks with the back of her hand before anyone could see their deputy shed a tear over a letter from her lover.

But he said he'd be home, wherever that was.

She didn't know, but she'd find out—and find him.

Her hands trembled when she slipped the heartbreakingly beautiful book to the bottom, heart twisting when her fingers brushed against worn, battered leather. It was the darkest green, and the cover bore a looping knot with no beginning and no end. The kind twined by a sailor's hand—a way to remember loved ones over a great distance. Like she was remembering him now. Like her Da remembered Erin's Isle.

Cassidy couldn't help the tears, then, not when she thumbed through the pages and found each one filled with a delicate, looping scroll. The very same she'd been searching for in Ransom's library months ago.

February 17, 1845, Belfast

Missus Callaghan is already sick, and we haven't even got on board. I'd rather get back in the carriage and ride home. I would ride a horse through the rain if I had to—anything to keep me here. I don't want to go, but Father says all of Ireland is starving, that it'll only get worse before it gets better. He says I'm lucky to get away.

This is a fortuitous match, and I ought to make the Bryne family proud. But I cannot stand to think about anything else right now but the cold and how badly I want a cup of tea. Still, it will be pleasant to have a familiar face once we arrive in Devonshire. She's more like a stuffy old aunt than a governess, though I don't understand why Mother insists I keep one now that I'm nineteen. Or why her son must come along. I find it unnerving, sometimes, how he watches me. Though he does have kind eyes.

Mother gave me a handful of these books. She says I may want to remember this journey one day. I think she wants me to hold my tongue. Maybe it'll be easier to write my thoughts down instead of saying them out loud.

Blast. I shan't be able to write much longer before my hands tremble from the cold. Missus Callaghan says we're boarding on the hour. My heart might burst from the nerves and the ache of leaving home behind, but maybe there's an adventure, a new beginning, waiting for me in England. Maybe someone. Only time will tell.

Aisling

She could scarcely believe her eyes, heart drumming so loudly, she worried it'd draw the gaze of Madame Ridley across the way.

Her mother's words, the first of her journals, were in

her hand. Cassidy's mind buzzed with questions about how Moone found it and where the rest might be. Had he ventured all the way to England to dig up the past for her?

Where Cassidy burned with a need for vengeance, now she was hungry for answers; answers James Moone held. He tied her to the end of his rope, hoping she'd forgive him for what he'd done. All she had to do was find him first.

She lifted her eyes to the horizon with a laugh, wearing her widest smile in months.

A new game was afoot. Cassidy couldn't help but play.

SADDLE UP,
THE STORY CONTINUES...

THE DEPUTY AND THE DEVIL

Coming Soon

ACKNOWLEDGMENTS

Once upon a time, in a galaxy far, far away (somewhere in Los Angeles, probably), Carrie Fisher said, "Stay afraid but do it anyway. What's important is the action. You don't have to wait to be confident. Just do it, and eventually, the confidence will follow." It's stuck with me from the first time I read it. Since then, I've tried to follow it—especially regarding this book.

I've been a writer since I knew how to hold a pencil and accidentally took a break for about a decade. Writing Star Wars fanfiction helped me find my way back to my keyboard. I was content making space wizards kiss for a long time… but then I got this idea. An idea so good my loved ones encouraged me to finally do the scariest thing possible—write an honest-to-goodness book.

I started drafting in 2018, got braver, wrote more fanfic (are you surprised?), took a We'd Know By Then detour (afraid, but doing it anyway), and wrote a couple other books you haven't seen yet. I didn't finish drafting The Devil's Backbone until January 2022.

Now, you're holding it (how cool is that?!), which would've been impossible without a few incredible people.

To the beating heart of Lake Country Press, Brittany Weisrock. You gave me a chance from the very start. By some miracle, you wanted more of me after I broke your heart (fictionally) and have been making my dreams come true since 2021. My life would not be the same without your generous spirit and boundless enthusiasm.

To my beta-readers, critique partners extraordinaire—

Kat, Hannah, Joy, and Jalen. Your commentary was simultaneously insightful and hilarious. There are a few comments I might frame. Thank you for your expert advice and for putting up with me as I trudged through revisions. This book wouldn't be what it is without you.

To Tara Sexton. You get me, and I am so lucky to have such a brilliant editor. With your help, I found the heart of this story. Your guidance propelled it from good to great, and I cannot wait to see the books we work on together in the future.

To the incredible artists I've had the chance to work with, especially Lilith, Evelyn and Selina. I am utterly obsessed with your talent, continuously blown away by your magical ability to extract an image from my brain and bring it to life. Witches, the lot of you.

Lisa Roumain, my narrator, Lilith, my cover artist, and Andrea Quigley, my interior designer. I am so lucky to have such talented women as partners in this adventure. There's nothing I love more than collaborating with you to make beautiful things. I cannot wait to see where our adventures take us next, and I'm honored to call you all friends.

Speaking of friendship, here's to my favorite people, both literary, fandom, and real-life—Andi Quigley, Alicia McCoy, Thea Guanzon, Sarah Hawley, Beka Westrup, Ali Hazelwood, Erin Mainord, Camri Kohler, Karla Daniels, Han, Mel Wirthlin, Shana Karnes, eKayla Moreau, Kat Davids, Mary Kate Adduce, and Natalie Buys. I am so lucky to be surrounded by such extraordinary people. Thank you for your conversation, enthusiasm, expert music recs, patience as I made this book my entire personality, and flexibility for last-minute Happy Hour. I adore you all to no end.

To my family, but especially to my husband, Trever, and

Mom, Karen Garcia. The two of you encouraged this from the beginning. Thank you for believing in me when I didn't quite believe in myself, for rooting me on to keep going through 4 am wake-up calls and the occasional late nights. Mom, thank you for your excitement when I handed you my phone on a random Thursday and demanded you read the prologue hot off the presses. It was right then that I knew I was onto something. Jorge, my Papá, thank you for that effervescent sparkle in your eye. Making you proud is my favorite thing (second to making you laugh). Dad, thank you for showing me the way of John Wayne and the rest of the greats. This is partially your fault. Trever, thank you for keeping me anchored and balanced. I love you more than words can say. You're my favorite adventure. Our kids: Richard, Lorelai, and Wyatt—I love you most.

To you, dear reader. Thank you for coming on this journey with me. Oh, all the places we'll go.

Lastly, to the rats—none of this would've been possible without you.

xo kb

When Kirsten isn't spinning stories and jumping genres, she can be found playfully heckling batters at Mariners games, making mediocre crochet, brewing beer with her best friend (that guy she married) and knocking things over with her lightsaber. She lives in Seattle with her husband, three smallish humans, and a corgi named Asuna. Her debut novel, *We'd Know By Then*, is available now.

We'd Know By Then

In a monochrome world, Brighton Evans is a splash of brilliant color.

She can see the world in its true, kaleidoscopic form—a privilege reserved for soulmates only after they've found their other halves.

Knowing your soulmate when they come along should be easy, but Brighton can't remember a time when she hasn't seen in color. The past has her convinced that life is safer this way; she doesn't need a soulmate.

When Brighton meets a handsome, delightfully cheeky stranger, her carefully cultivated 'happy enough' crumbles as their meet-cute blossoms into true friendship. Cain Whitaker has soulmate written all over him.

With Cain by her side, Brighton sees the world as she never has before... until circumstance smothers her color and leaves her wondering: if timing is everything... is she too late?